Inside the Cold War

by

Norman L. Miller

ISBN: 979-8-89175-014-2 (sc)
ISBN: 979-8-89175-015-9 (hc)
ISBN: 979-8-89175-016-6 (ebk)

Contents

Chapter 1

New York City, NY

LESTER FETOR CLOSED HIS EYES AND TOOK a long, slow drag on his cigarette then blew the smoke outside the window. He watched it slowly dissipate in the cold night air. It was a bad habit that he believed helped him to calm down. After looking around carefully for several minutes, he eased the van out of the hotel parking lot onto Grand Central Parkway in Queens and quickly blended into traffic.

Rock music blared out of the speakers while his hands vibrated, but not to the melody of the song. Uncontrollable nervous tension made his hands shake as his eyes flicked back and forth searching the highway for any sight of Tony Robelotto's thugs. He should be confident that they wouldn't suspect he was in the area, but past experience made him apprehensive.

After paying the toll at the Triborough Bridge he drove his rust-ravaged ten-year-old Dodge van across the Long Island Sound then turned north onto I-278 leading through the Bronx. In the distance he could see the brightly lit Manhattan Psychiatric Center from the expressway. Looking out the side window at the psychiatric center, he yelled, "That's probably where I really belong, in some freaking nuthouse."

Perspiration chilled his body despite the warm temperature inside the van. Reaching into his shirt pocket he took out another cigarette and lit it. Looking down, he glanced nervously at the package on the seat next to him. Inside the tightly wrapped box was a car bomb he obtained from a militia group operating secretly near Pittsburgh.

Smoking a cigarette with the bomb next to him was crazy, he thought. He flicked the ashes out the window, feeling a bit more relaxed as he thought about his plans. Lester knew two men who were former military explosives experts and arranged for them to do work for the Mafia. Over the years they made a lot of money doing jobs for the Mob and once told him that if he ever needed their services they would help him.

The package contained enough explosives to level a one family house and could be detonated with a remote device from up to a quarter mile away. Wrapped in plastic the explosives could be held in place with duct tape, making it easier to attach quickly under a vehicle. New car alarms made it difficult to wire explosives to starters inside engine compartments. The remote would work just as well, he thought. Plus, he would enjoy watching, the Mafia's highly-paid CPA, John Chapadeau, get exterminated.

It was 2:12 a.m., a frigid winter night. The area was bright from the abundance of streetlights, making it easy to see. The highway went north, the opposite direction from New York City, and eventually he took I-95 to Greenwich, Connecticut. Chapadeau lived in an extremely wealthy community in the suburbs of Greenwich. Lester estimated that the house must have been worth more than a million. Something Chapadeau could never afford as a CPA. Mafia clients must pay him extremely well, he thought.

Just south of Greenwich, he turned off I-95 and 15 minutes later parked on the street a short distance from Chapadeau's home. The house was dark, but he could see John's new white Lincoln Continental parked in the driveway. It was 3:50 a.m. Lester eased his car out onto the street and drove around the immediate area to be assured that none of the neighbors' lights were on.

At the intersection, unsure of where he was going, he decided to turn right and circle the block. Every house in the neighborhood was dark. Moments later he returned to where he could see John's house. He parked near the corner and got out of the van, cautiously carrying the bomb inside a small plastic bag. Thoughts of the bomb exploding while he was walking really disturbed him. His two friends warned him to be extremely gentle with the box. While he walked, his legs quivered from trembling nerves and not the cold air he thought.

Suddenly, a car turned from the corner in his direction. Standing still unsure of what to do, he gawked motionless at the lights. His breath rose slowly in the icy night air and his heart pounded faster as the car moved toward him. He told himself, don't panic and just keep walking with his head down. Carefully, he tucked the bag under his coat to avoid the driver from seeing it; petrified it might slip out and fall to the ground.

Out of the corner of his eye he could see that it was a limousine coming in his direction. His eyes began to tear from the bitter cold air, making it more difficult to see clearly. As the limo passed him he turned his head away to prevent the driver from seeing his face.

The neighborhood was a popular location for many wealthy people who worked in Manhattan, but who didn't want to live in the city. The early morning limousine was probably picking somebody up for work in the city or taking them to the airport, he thought.

The vehicle passed and turned in the opposite direction from where he had parked. He walked slowly until the lights from the limousine vanished, and then he turned around and hurried back to the driveway. Within seconds he had reached John's Continental. The space between the car's underside and the driveway surface was barely large enough for him to slide his massive stomach under the frame.

Finally, he managed to slowly squeeze under the chassis and began searching with his hand for a location to secure the bomb. It was difficult to feel with his gloves on. He was forced to take them off, painfully aware that he had to be quick.

The package with the bomb fit perfectly on top of the metal plate used to protect the engine from road debris. He glided it around making sure the bomb wouldn't drop out if John moved the car before he could detonate the explosives. Satisfied that it was secure, he removed a small roll of duct tape from his jacket pocket and attempted to fasten the package to the ice-cold metal plate. Dust on the metal prevented the tape from sticking. Cursing to himself, he removed the bomb as his finger tips began to throb from the cold.

After he cleared the dirt off the metal with his bare hand, he put the package back on the plate. This time the duct tape's adhesive coating held it to the cold metal. The temperature was nearly zero and his fingers had grown numb. He tried to move the package with the back of his hand to be certain it was fastened. Confident that it was tightly secured, he slid out from under the Continental and walked briskly to his van. As soon as he started the motor he put the heater on high and held his hands near the blower for several minutes. Once he got some feeling in his fingers he drove away.

It was 4:18 a.m. He decided to find a diner near the Interstate and get some breakfast. John would leave between six and six-thirty, giving him time to relax. Lester bought a morning paper and went inside the diner. Glancing at the mirror behind the counter, he noticed the front of his jacket was covered with dust. He went to the rest room to clean the dust off then returned to a stool at the counter to get something to eat.

The excitement of killing John made it arduous for him to concentrate on the news. The next day's paper would have the story - but not the complete story. It wouldn't matter because he wouldn't be around to read it, he thought.

After breakfast he drove back to the upscale neighborhood and parked his car around the corner from Chapadeau's driveway, waiting for John to get into the car. The enormous house had five bedrooms, a formal dining room, and an extra room used to entertain guests. The outside was made of imported stone and was surrounded by lush shrubbery.

The sky over the house began to emit a faint glow announcing the first signs of daylight. Suddenly, a light came on in an upstairs bedroom. Lester looked at the clock on the dash. It was 5:52 a.m. Only a few more minutes until John would walk out the front door and get into the car.

Ecstasy filled his body and he cautioned himself to be patient and wait until John sat inside before pushing the button, ending the bastard's life and giving him incredible satisfaction. The excitement increased his heartbeat and he forgot about the cold as he thought about the impending explosion.

The bedroom light went off and moments later the front door opened. Lester assumed that John didn't eat at home and planned to drive to the City early to avoid the morning rush. He probably goes for breakfast with some of his cronies after arriving at his office in Manhattan, he thought. Unfortunately, John wasn't going to eat this morning.

Lester's heart pounded, and he began to fret as he watched John open his car door and slide onto the driver's seat. For a moment, John left the door open and appeared to reach over to the side near the glove compartment. Lester wondered if perhaps John might have some sort of device that could detect a bomb in his car, but then he thought that was impossible. Moments later, John moved back squarely behind the wheel, looked in his rear-view mirror and closed the door.

This is it he thought. He instantly pressed down slowly and firmly on the remote's button. An unbelievable blast ripped through the neighborhood. Even with his van windows up, the intense sound hurt his ears. The explosion shattered the glass in the front rooms of John's house and ripped away the siding from the frame, exposing the inside.

A second explosion blew a fireball up into the sky as the gas tank exploded. Debris seemed to be everywhere as pieces of the automobile fell back to the ground. Small fragments bouncing up and down on his van's roof made him worry that he might have parked too close.

The metal rubble that remained didn't even resemble a car. There appeared to be no trace of John; perhaps his body had vaporized, he thought. Lester laughed out loud and suddenly felt extremely relaxed.

Still laughing and feeling satisfied, Lester quickly drove away, positive that none of the neighbors had seen him. He was excited that he had completed vengeance against Chapadeau for squealing to the Mob about his embezzlement scheme. Tony Robelotto might catch up to him, but the financial damage he just did to the Mafia would haunt them for years.

He smiled and thought about the incredible amount of trouble Tony would go through trying to find his money without his high-powered CPA. Some funds he would never find and eventually they might go to the state of New York. John always kept his information secret; that was his protection from the Mafia. An anonymous phone tip to the FBI would further complicate Robelotto's attempt to locate his investments.

A short time later on I-95, thoughts of Nino Casatelli came into his mind. Maybe he should get another bomb and go to Casatelli's house in Lake Placid. Casatelli had been a constant thorn in his side ever since he told Chapadeau and Robelotto about his money laundering scheme he had hidden from the Mafia. The anticipation of blowing up Casatelli in his house excited him and he began thinking about how it could be accomplished. First, he would cut the phone wires, and then he would find the right location to place the explosives.

As he thought more about the plan, he realized that it wasn't realistic. Casatelli lived in the back-woods outside Lake Placid. It would take too long to get another bomb in Pittsburgh and take it so far north to his house. There was a better way to settle the score with Casatelli.

Time was crucial. Lester had planned to return to the hotel in Queens, but was now worried about how much the Mafia knew about his activities? After reconsidering, he decided not to go back since there were only a few items of clothing and a suitcase. They could be replaced. The City was a risk. It wouldn't take long before Robelotto would have his people watching all the airports in the New York and New Jersey area.

Another suitcase and some clothes were all he needed, and he had them in his flop house where he had lived for the past month. Lester changed interstates and drove west in the direction of Scranton, PA, where his other belongings, including a rifle, were hidden under the bed. He smiled in anticipation of his new plans.

It was nearly 7:30 p.m. when Lester finally arrived in Scranton. It had been nearly twenty hours since he left the hotel and drove up to

Connecticut to kill John Chapadeau. Exhausted from climbing the stairs he just wanted to collapse on his bed. The walk up to his fourth-floor room seemed to take an eternity.

The door was unlocked, and he assumed he forgot to lock it when he left several days ago. He turned the knob and pushed the door open. Startling him, were three of Tony Robelotto's goons. Too tired to run, he just sat down on the bed and wondered if they had discovered the hit on Chapadeau. There wasn't enough time for that, he haughtily thought.

"Where've you been Lester?" asked the man next to the door. Lester knew him from their days as union truckers. A thug who ran the Teamsters Union in upstate New York, Louie always wore a faded blue shirt with jeans. Bowlegged, he walked more like a cowboy than a trucker. "The boss wants us to take you for a ride and find out where you put his money. It's better that you come clean cause if our CPA finds it first, you're dead."

Lester suddenly felt an enormous sign of relief, because it was clear they didn't know he had blown Chapadeau to bits hours earlier. His feelings changed quickly as one of the thugs grabbed him by his hair and pulled him up.

"Ok Lester, it's time to leave," the thug released his hair and shoved him towards the open door. "You need to explain a few things to us. For one thing, Mr. Robelotto is very interested in learning about where his money is being stored. Chapadeau seems to think you stiffed the boss and that's not good."

They stayed close to Lester making sure he didn't attempt to get away before they put him in the back seat of their car. Too tired to think straight about their intentions, gruesome thoughts filled his mind as they left the area.

CHAPTER 2

Scranton, PA.

S NOW BLANKETED RON HARRISON'S CAR WINDOWS. A glance at his watch confirmed that it was nearly midnight, two hours since Lester Fetor had been picked up at the flophouse where he was staying and taken to Polsinilli's Restaurant. Leaning back against the seat Ron continued waiting, resisting the temptation to clean off the windshield. A faint vision of a flashing "OPEN" sign was all he could see.

An FBI agent for five years, Ron was a 1988 Olympic bobsled athlete and knew Lester Fetor from his activity with the Bobsled Association. He tried to imagine why three known Mafiosi, who worked for Tony Robelotto, had driven Lester to Polsinilli's, a popular meeting place for the syndicate in the Scranton, PA area. He had received a call in the morning to keep Fetor under surveillance. The FBI wanted to learn more about his current activities. Within a day or two Ron suspected his supervisor would give him the order to arrest Fetor.

He had spent hundreds of hours studying the FBI's records of mobsters living in the northeast region of the United States. Most had relocated to the affluent vacation spot along the shores of Lake Hurley, since the early sixties. The shadow of the Appalachian Mountains provided them with privacy and the convenience of less than a two-hour commute to New York City. Late at night it was common to observe known mobsters from Las Vegas and Hollywood slipping in and out of local nightclubs.

It worried Ron that the Mafia might execute Lester to prevent the FBI from putting together all the pieces of the Olympic Bobsled Association's corruption puzzle. Time was running out. The Bureau had many unanswered questions about what Lester and other officials may have done with the Association's records and Olympic funding.

They knew some funds were in local banks, but their efforts to trace the majority of the money had been unsuccessful. The Internal Revenue Service assisted in locating people who made significant donations to the Association's Olympic fund. Several hundred thousand dollars had been discovered, but that only represented about ten percent of the total budget.

John Chapadeau, the Association's treasurer, managed to keep their financial transactions and records so secret that neither the FBI nor the IRS could determine how the money was used. The FBI also suspected Lester hid other funds for Mafia clients in Swiss accounts.

A car horn caught his attention and he could see a taxicab pulling up to the restaurant. Mounting snow on the windshield blocked Ron's vision so he opened his frosted window a crack just in time to see Lester clamber into the waiting cab. It sped away in the direction of Scranton. He presumed that Lester was returning to the flophouse where he had moved after the Mafia's anger over the horrendous amount of publicity surrounding his alleged misuse of Olympic funds.

Publicity for the Mafia was intolerable, but even worse, they were convinced Lester had been skimming their funds. They had paid him to deposit drug money along with the Bobsled Association's funds in Swiss accounts.

While doing surveillance during the past year, it surprised Ron how much Lester had aged. His brown hair had turned nearly all gray and he was often unshaven. His clothing – once flamboyant had become wrinkled and mismatched. The changes suggested that Lester had been trying to evade the mob.

That was almost impossible to do in the United States, and Lester couldn't go to the FBI for protection in return for information because if the Mafia even suspected such a thing, they would torture, then kill him. They might not wait to find out where he had hidden the money. Ron suspected that Lester's only chance for survival would be to go to Europe, retrieve the currency he had stashed, and then create a new identity.

After Lester's cab departed, Ron got out of his car and entered the restaurant. The three Mafiosi were sitting at a table close to the end of the bar. Ron noticed a large, nearly empty bottle of Chianti at their table. A waitress took his order for coffee and a roast beef sandwich. The three men had lowered their voices, but he could still hear them discuss their meeting with Lester. One suggested that they should take Lester back to the "boss" and let him decide his fate.

"Not a good idea," replied the man with a large scar on his left cheek. "The boss don't want him at his place unless he says so."

"I think we need to find a private place where we can question him more and put on a bit of pressure, so he'll tell us how to get Tony's money."

"He ain't going to tell us."

"Oh yeah, if I use pliers on his fingers he might figure out that it would be better to give up the money, because if he don't, something worse will happen," said the man with the scar.

The short man looked off in the distance then said, "You know the Boss will want him whacked." He poured the rest of the Chianti in his glass then snapped his fingers to get the waitress' attention. As she turned, he motioned to bring another bottle. A look of smugness emerged on his face indicating that he knew exactly how the Mafia boss would react.

"I ain't making that decision," replied the man with the scar. "Let's stay in the City tonight, so we'll be able to get back here in case Robelotto tells us to get rid of him. Lester knows his time is running out and he might take off again."

"Watch your mouth. You better show more respect for the boss. If he ever heard you call him by his last name he would have you whacked!"

"Yeah, yeah I know. I never talk that way around him." The small man's face grew taut and he slid back in his chair, looking very uncomfortable. He puffed on his cigar while his eyes shifted back and forth between the two men.

Ron suspected that a chill had gone through the man's body as he thought about the serious mistake he made. Ron carefully turned his back to their table.

"Don't get in the habit, cause if you ever slip and he hears you, it's all over. You'll only have to slip once!"

"Yeah, yeah I know."

Suddenly the third man stood up, completely ignoring the new bottle of Chianti. "We better get going or Fetor will disappear now that he knows for sure the boss is coming after him for the money. I'll bet the asshole spent the money. It's a sure thing, you can bet on it."

The man with the scar poured himself another glass of wine. "Sit down. There ain't anything we can do tonight. We need to find a place, maybe a warehouse, where we can put some pressure on him. The boss wants his money. If there's any chance of finding it before he dies we better do it. You know we'll be in trouble if we don't put some real serious pressure on him."

"So, where can we take him?"

"Tony has a vacant warehouse on the East Side. Let's check it out early in the morning to make sure it's not being used and then we can come back and get him." said the man with the scar.

The waitress returned with Ron's sandwich and refilled his coffee cup. He grew concerned about Lester's fate. If they took Lester, the FBI might not find him in time and would lose any opportunity of locating the missing money. In a way Ron thought that Lester deserved any torture the Mafia would use since the government couldn't do the same.

Since it was nearly two a.m. the three Mafiosi decided they needed to get back to the city and get some sleep. They dropped money on the table and left the restaurant. Ron watched them through the front window until their car was out of sight before leaving. In the morning, he would call the Bureau in Philadelphia to see if they wanted to have another agent pick Lester up for questioning to avoid disclosing his FBI status.

He left the restaurant and drove past the flophouse to see if Lester's car was still parked in the same place. It had not been moved and a parking ticket was barely visible on the windshield under the wiper, partially covered with fresh snow. Ron returned to his hotel, hoping to get some sleep. It had been days since he had gotten a full night's rest. He suspected that his chances of a good night's sleep were better than Lester's.

Lancaster Street - Scranton, PA

The cold air in the room woke Lester early before daylight. Still tired, he pulled the covers up to his chin attempting to get warmer, so he could sleep longer. After several minutes he knew it was futile, his feet were cold and there were too many distractions on his mind.

He knew he had to get out of the country quickly and get his money before Robelotto's goons killed him, but the urge to take care of unfinished business had to be done. He needed to get a fake passport and some better clothes after he took a final trip to Lake Placid. He smiled as he thought about how he would pay back the other people who screwed him.

Daylight began creeping through the broken venetian blinds and Lester could now see around the room. Plaster was missing from the walls in several places and the door had several small holes punched through the thin wood. Dead flies seemed to be everywhere and cobwebs covered the curtains that looked as if they had not been cleaned in years. Roaches slithered along the baseboards sending chills up his spine.

He reached for a cigarette while he thought about the money he placed in Swiss accounts. It would put him on easy street for the rest of his life, if he could get to Switzerland within a few days. He imagined sexy young women attracted to him while he lived a wealthy life style in seclusion and not worrying about Tony Robelotto finding him. Robelotto! He couldn't get him out of his mind.

Rolling over, he buried his head in the pillow thinking about the three mobsters taking him to Polsinilli's Restaurant to interrogate him; suddenly perspiration began oozing from his forehead. He didn't want to die. Clear visions of different ways the Mob could assassinate him wouldn't go away and began to torment him.

Thoughts of a Mob member he knew getting shot in the back of the head while he and others watched flashed through his mind. The Mafia had many bizarre ways to rub someone out and none of them were nice. He sat on the bed and reached for another cigarette.

He knew one thing for sure that would never happen again; he would never trust a friend. Never, ever would he trust anyone! Trusting his close friend Nino Casatelli was destroying his life and probably would get him killed.

There was no question in his mind that Casatelli went to Chapadeau and Robelotto hoping to replace him and collect the five percent commission for carrying the cash to Europe and depositing it in Swiss accounts. Only Chapadeau and he knew where the accounts were, and now only he knew. Lester vowed that somehow before he left the country he would give Nino what he deserved. Time was a problem and he would have to do it very soon, before the Mafia found him. It haunted him that he had millions in Swiss bank accounts and he had to live like a vagabond.

Shawn Murphy was also on his list of people he wanted to repay. Murphy, the Olympic Coach had figured out his scam to embezzle funds from the Association and reported him to the FBI and the Olympic committee. Lester was confident that Murphy didn't know about the Mafia funds. Before he went to Europe he would settle with each of these bastards.

It was 6:15 a.m. and there was no chance he would ever go back to sleep. Better that he left early because they knew where he was staying. Who was he kidding? They would know wherever he was hiding in Scranton.

Lester packed the few belongings he had, rolled the rifle in a blanket, and went to the front door of the building. Standing back in the shadow of the doorway he looked up and down the street to see if the Mafia had left someone to watch him. His legs quivered and moisture on his back soaked his undershirt. Cautiously he glanced around again before carefully starting down the snow-covered steps being careful not to fall.

Paint on the woodwork outlining the front door was nearly all gone and chunks of wood were missing from the casing indicating years of little protection from the severe weather. It seemed to match the rat's nest room he rented. Setting his tattered suitcase on the sidewalk, he glanced around nervously then took out a pack of unfiltered cigarettes and lit one while carefully holding the blanket covered rifle. The smoke forced him to cough uncontrollably for several minutes until his throat settled down. He attempted to muffle the sound by holding his coat over his face.

After wiping the tears from his eyes with the back of his hand, he slowly walked to the car. Obsessed that someone was watching, he couldn't resist looking at every car on the street.

Once he reached his car, he took several minutes to clear the snow from the windshield. The parking ticket aggravated him and prompted a string of vulgarities. "You lousy God damn cops have nothing to do but harass people. What a bunch of bastards." Forgetting that someone might be watching, he stood there for several minutes staring at the ticket.

After getting control of his emotions, Lester took another quick look around the area checking for cars with no snow on their windshields. He yanked the ticket from under the wiper and tossed it on the street. The rear car door creaked from the lack of lubricant as he tossed the rifle then his suitcase on the seat. He could see snow through the rusted van's body under the door. Once again, he quickly scanned the other parked vehicles one last time and then got into the vehicle.

"This is how it's done," he thought to himself. "A hitman will now shoot, or my car blow up when I turn the key." Unable to move or think, he sat motionless behind the wheel, terrified, waiting for some sudden type of explosion. His hands shook so uncontrollably he couldn't hold onto his cigarette and crushed it in the ashtray. Tears slithered down his face.

Visions of Chapadeau's car explosion raced through his mind. What would it feel like? Would it hurt? Would he even know what happened? He closed his eyes certain that they were out there watching. When it was over they would call Tony and give him the good news.

Despite the extreme cold temperature, sweat beaded on his forehead, and he could feel his heart pounding. His eyes burned as sweat from his forehead trickled slowly down his face. He thought about another car explosion he once witnessed. Vino the Horse had repaid the Mafia all the money he had stolen, but they killed him anyway. It was a horrible sight watching a friend get blown into tiny fragments.

Lester opened his eyes and wiped the burning moisture away with the back of his sleeve, then looked around once again to see if Robelotto's men were watching him. Not seeing anyone still didn't give him a secure feeling. His undershirt was now completely saturated.

Afraid to start the car, he got out, opened the hood to see if wires were connected to the starter, then he closed the hood and knelt to look under the frame. Not seeing anything, he wiped the snow off his pant legs and got back inside. He knew there were many places that a package could be hidden, and he wouldn't find it unless the car was put up on a lift. People working for the Mob weren't careless.

Frazzled, he took a deep breath and with a trembling hand, inserted the key into the ignition, closed his eyes and turned it. The starter hesitated and then slowly turned over. The cold battery finally coaxed the motor to life.

He sat motionless for several seconds with his eyes closed tight, waiting for the detonation. But, nothing happened. Several seconds passed before he opened his eyes and looked around to see if someone was nearby with a remote waiting to detonate a bomb. Every car on the street appeared to be unoccupied and nobody was visible from any windows overlooking the street.

He lit another cigarette and thought that he should have been relieved, but knew it was too soon to be certain that he was in the clear. After waiting nearly ten minutes for the car to warm up, he felt more confident that it was not rigged.

"Holly shit," he yelled in excitement. "Those bastards probably thought I was too scared to skip town. Surprise, surprise," he yelled.

Lester eased the car out of the parking spot and slowly drove down the street. Being extra cautious, he went past the entrance to the interstate, then doubled back to see if any other car had vacated a parking space on the street. None of the other cars had been moved.

There would be very limited time to complete his plan. Casatelli would have to be dealt with before he could go to Europe and withdraw the funds from the Swiss accounts. Focusing on the expressway he kept reminding himself to drive carefully to avoid attention from the police. Cold chills ran down his back every time a dark Cadillac passed him.

Hunger pains began to get on his nerves after an hour, so he gave in and left the Turnpike to get something to eat. He turned onto Route 17 and located a small diner that truckers would go to regularly. Inside, it looked like it hadn't been cleaned in years and was badly in need of repairs.

Not the type of eating establishment that the Mafia would visit unless they saw him.

Sitting near the back of the diner he could watch the parking lot and feel comfortable that he wouldn't be seen through the window. He quickly glanced around the joint to see if he could leave by a back door. The kitchen was behind him, so he figured that if they came in he would leave from there.

After ordering black coffee he lit a cigarette and thought about his plot. He took a deep drag and blew smoke out through his nose, closing his eyes and visualizing the look on Nino's face when he settled the score for squealing to Robelotto.

Albany, NY

Lester parked in the long-term lot at the Albany County Airport and then went to the Dollar Car rental counter inside the airport terminal. To reduce the chance that someone might recognize his car, he decided to get a rental for the quick trip to Lake Placid. He used his U.S. Bobsled Association credit card to rent the car but reminded himself to make sure he paid the bill with cash when he returned it the next day.

In a hurry, Lester quickly shoved the items he needed into the rental car. Included with his suitcase, were a set of cross-country skis, the Winchester .25-06 rifle with a variable 3-9 power Leupold scope, and a box of 180-grain, high-velocity, hollow-point bullets. Lester liked the Winchester rifle. It was capable of hitting targets at extraordinarily long distances with lethal accuracy and still have enough force to kill a large bear. Carefully, he put the rifle on the back seat under a blanket to avoid someone seeing it and to make sure the scope didn't get out of adjustment.

Snow had already begun to accumulate on the nearby Adirondack Northway, the super highway connecting New York with Canada. The rush hour traffic was moving at a snail's pace as workers in the Albany area headed home. The weather forecast on the radio warned that the area could receive eight to twelve inches of snow by morning. Luck was with Lester as the worst part of the storm was predicted to move east of upstate New York into Vermont.

Glancing into the rearview mirror he noticed a state police car directly behind him. From the mirror his eyes shot down to the speedometer to see how fast he was going. Ten miles under the speed limit in a snowstorm was reasonable. He was using the middle lane and not holding back traffic. Fear gripped him as he wondered if someone at the airport might have seen him put the rifle on the back seat and called the police with a tip.

That wasn't possible. Nobody was near him in the parking lot, but why would a trooper follow him so close he wondered? Moisture on his forehead began to slide down into his eyes, making it difficult to see. Using the back of his jacket sleeve, he wiped the salty dampness from his eyes and face. Not seeing any cars in his right-side view mirror he put on his directional and eased into the right lane. If the trooper followed, it would mean he was going to be stopped.

The police car stayed in the middle lane and he could see that the trooper was talking on his radio. Suddenly, the red lights began flashing as the police car sped by and moved quickly up the Northway ahead of him. Picking up his speed he thought it would be better not to drive too slow and attract attention. When the police car suddenly left the interstate at the Saratoga Springs exit, he let out a sigh.

The lack of traffic made the ride monotonous and his mind kept drifting back to his troubled past. Suddenly a tractor-trailer truck passed him throwing snow and slush onto his windshield hampering his vision. Startled, he was brought back to reality. He exited the expressway onto Route 8, near Chestertown, to buy gas, coffee, and a sandwich. After paying, he walked outside the convenience store to stretch his legs for a few minutes. Feeling rested he got back into the car and drove back to the expressway. A road sign indicated he was 78 miles south of Plattsburgh.

Later, a large highway sign promoting gas and food caught his attention and brought him back to his current task. The exit for Plattsburgh was one mile ahead. After three hours of driving, Lester got off the Northway and drove into the parking lot of the first motel he saw. He parked in the rear of the hotel then went inside to register.

Chapter 3

Plattsburgh, NY

THE PIERCING SHRILL OF THE ALARM CLOCK continued until Lester was partially conscious. Groping in the dark he fumbled to locate it and turn it off. Forcing himself up, he got out of bed and stepped into the shower. Lester's brain was full of doubt as he thought about what he was about to do, but there was no second-guessing. The adrenaline in his body built as the excitement of his plan came together in his mind. His heart thumped as he dressed. Within minutes he was ready and stepped out into the pitch black, sub-zero air.

The extreme cold air hurt his throat forcing him to take short breaths. When his eyes adjusted to the darkness he noticed that the car windows were covered with a thick frost. He started the motor and began scraping ice off the windshield, as quiet as possible, to avoid alerting anyone inside the motel. When he finished he left the motor running and went back to his room to make sure he hadn't forgotten anything. After looking around carefully, he lit a cigarette and went back to the car.

There were no other cars on the road as he drove onto the Adirondack Northway's southbound entrance. The snow had stopped falling and the roads were already plowed. At the Keeseville exit he left the Northway and went west on Route 86 in the direction of Lake Placid. It was 4:10 a.m. The radio D.J. said the temperature was 10 degrees below zero. Not unusually cold this time of year in the Adirondacks. Lester suspected that it would be even colder when he reached the higher elevation near Lake Placid.

He looked at the shirt and jacket he was wearing. They were cheap used clothing he bought from a Salvation Army store in Scranton. The thought of wearing second hand clothing irritated him. Before his problems with the Mob, he wore only the best, always in style.

Driving past the Whiteface Mountain Ski Center, one of the 1980 Olympic venues, Lester turned south a short distance from the complex onto Riverside Drive which would take him to Route 73. The clock on the dashboard now displayed 4:42 a.m., right on schedule. At Route 73 he turned left and went east driving past the road leading to the Olympic bobsled track at Mount Van Hoevenberg. Two minutes later he passed Nino Casatelli's ranch house. There were no lights visible from the road.

It was back about 400 feet from the highway and difficult to spot unless you knew it was there, because it was partially obscured by trees. The green cedar shake siding helped the house blend in with the evergreen trees surrounding it. He remembered that Nino wanted a house with four bedrooms, a family room and a patio so he could inflate his ego even further.

I should nail the doors shut and set fire to the God damn building and let him die a slow death, he thought. Anger surged within Lester as he glanced at the house. He avoided the tremendous urge to turn into the driveway and confront Nino right then. No, he had to be careful or the police would get him and his plan to get the money would cease to exist.

Lester got a glimpse of Nino's 1967 Mustang parked under the carport. Seeing the car angered him even more. He gave Nino the cash to buy the bright red sports car. A short distance past Nino's driveway he turned right onto Mountain Peak Lane, a narrow dirt road. After driving nearly half a mile, he stopped his car in front of a dilapidated old farm house. Paint was non-existent after years of abuse from the punishing cold temperatures and the exorbitant wind. The front porch had separated from the main section of the house and was partially collapsed.

The land surrounding the house was covered with more than two feet of undisturbed snow, indicating that no one had been near there all winter. The road had been plowed wide, giving him ample room to leave the rental car on the shoulder. He checked the time again just before he got out. It was 4:51 a.m. It would be a couple of hours before the sun arrived and daylight would emerge over the mountaintop. The radio station in Lake Placid said the temperature was 14 degrees below zero.

Snow blowing across the road indicated that there was a bitter breeze which would make the wind chill lower than the temperature. He would have to be extremely careful to avoid frostbite. Now wasn't the time to take chances. He felt confident that once he got into the trees, the wind would not be a factor, but 14 below zero was still a concern.

Lester took his shoes off and put on heavy wool socks under his cross-country ski boots. Looking into the mirror he studied his face. Black whiskers mixed with white matched his exceptionally long hair. It had been nearly three months since he had his hair cut. Large bags under his eyes from the lack of sleep, made him look like an old man. Feeling the muscles in his arms and on his chest he decided that when he got to Europe he had to get back into shape.

The new type of cross-country skis he purchased in Scranton were perfect for this task. They were made for the backcountry, shorter and slightly wider than normal, with metal edges similar to downhill skis. Designed for deep snow usually found in the peaks of the Adirondack Mountains, they were perfect for the type of terrain Lester had to trek.

Lester took the skis out of the trunk, stood them in the snow bank, then reached for his rifle and loaded five hollow-point bullets. The bolt slid forward with ease, locking one round in the chamber and then he slid the safety on. Plastic sandwich bags over the end of the rifle barrel and the scope, secured with tiny metal twists, would keep snow off. Satisfied that the rifle would stay clean, he slipped his arm through the sling and placed it on his shoulder.

The glacial frigid air began to numb his face and the steady breeze made his ears throb in pain. He hastily put on his thick knit hat. For several minutes he held his ears with his hands in an attempt to relieve the pain. A pair of Thermasilk mittens with thin liners, designed for sub-zero temperatures, helped to protect his fingers.

He quickly placed them on both hands, then slid a ski mask over his face. Next, he took ski goggles out of the trunk and put them on over his knit hat. He quickly scanned the area for the lights of oncoming cars. Seeing nothing but darkness, he fastened his boots to the skis and climbed sideways over the snow bank.

Mountain Peak Lane was generally used only in the summer by hikers and Forest Rangers to reach the backside of Mt. Van Hoevenberg. It was plowed in the winter, although very few hikers used it during the severe cold weather. Certain that he would be alone, considering the hour and the temperature, Lester carefully determined which direction Nino's house would be and began skiing west through the field. Heat, produced by the demanding exercise, slowly spread up his arms and into his upper body helping him to relax.

The arctic air plus years of smoking made it difficult for him to breathe deeply, forcing him to slow his pace to avoid having to pull in large amounts of oxygen that hurt his throat. The laborious task generated perspiration making it difficult to see out of the ski goggles. It took nearly ten minutes to cross the field and reach the base of the mountain and out of the ferocious wind.

Out of shape and overweight, the deep snow forced him to labor while he trudged his way up and around the side of the steep mountain following the hiking trail. Cloud cover made it difficult to see in the distance, but the bright white snow enabled him to continuously check his compass without a flashlight.

Despite the frozen air, the steady climb continued to make him perspire profusely. Finally, he reached an area where he could clearly see Nino's house. He removed his ski goggles and cleaned the moisture off so he had clear visibility. It was 5:53 a.m. It had taken him over an hour to reach the side of the mountain facing Casatelli's property. From this site he had a clear view of Nino's house. There were no lights on in the kitchen meaning that Nino was still sleeping.

Lester was uncertain about when Nino would get up. However, several times when he stayed overnight Nino got up at around 6:15 a.m each morning. The first thing he did was to make coffee, let the dog out, take a shower and then get dressed.

During weekdays Nino went into Lake Placid every morning to meet Roger Ferris for breakfast. Afterwards, Roger would leave for the Bobsled Association office, and Nino would open his store at eight o'clock sharp. He was never late.

What would he do if Nino didn't get up early to meet Roger for breakfast? With the bitter low temperature and severe wind chill he could only stay there for a short amount of time. If Nino didn't get up early, he would have wasted all this effort for nothing. It would serve him right for not taking the time to plan this right. No, he thought, Nino would get up, let the dog out and then he would take care of the bastard.

Constantly wiggling his toes helped keep the circulation going and partially warmed his feet. He checked his watch again. It was 6:18 a.m. and the cold temperature began to really bother him. Darkness still blanketed the hillside. Lester knew it would be at least another hour before the sun would begin to reflect off Nino's kitchen window.

Suddenly, a light came on inside the kitchen and he instantly forgot the effects of the artic cold temperature. Lester slid the rifle off his shoulder, stomped his skis down in the snow setting them. He reached out and shook the nearest branch to remove the snow and then leaned up against the tall pine tree.

He removed the two plastic bags from the rifle and put his right mitten inside his coat pocket, leaving the Thermasilk liner on to protect his hand from the rifle's icy steel trigger. He raised the rifle, looked into the site and searched for Nino.

The scope was set on nine-power, giving him the highest magnified vision possible. It enabled him to see inside the kitchen as if he were standing a short distance outside the window. Moments later, he watched Nino walk into the kitchen and go directly to the sink to get water for the coffeemaker.

"Come on you son of a bitch, forget the coffee and let the dog out so I can get a clear shot." Thoughts of payback raced through his mind. His smile began to fade away as he became more impatient, forgetting the severe cold.

Lester positioned the rifle on the large branch to give him stability, and then slowly moved the cross hairs along the window until they came to rest on the right side of Nino's chest. He couldn't shoot now because he was using a hollow point tip and it would break into fragments when it hit the glass, forcing him to take a second shot. That could ruin any chance of killing him.

He slid the safety off to be ready when he got the opportunity to take a shot. Suddenly, Nino walked over and opened the sliding glass door to let his dog out on the patio. He quickly slid the door shut and stood inside waiting for the dog to urinate, not giving Lester enough time to shoot. Lester's heart raced and he started to hyperventilate. Unable to hold the rifle steady, he lowered it and closed his eyes attempting to calm his nerves.

Come on, God damn it; don't blow your only chance to fix this bastard, he thought. Get a grip on yourself. He hesitated for an instant to calm himself, then replaced the rifle on the branch. Suddenly, the dog turned and ran back to the house. Nino slid the door open as the dog ran in the direction of his legs.

Lester quickly sucked in a bit of air, exhaled, held his breath then gently squeezed the trigger. An earsplitting blast shattered the frigid silence on the hillside. The recoil of the rifle instantaneously moved him backwards shaking snow from the tree on him.

In less than a second the .25-06 bullet reached Nino's chest. The 180-grain bullet ripped through Nino's flesh and bones without any resistance. The impact hurled his large body back and up against the wall, before collapsing onto the floor.

Through the scope, Lester peered into the family room. Blood was spurting out of Nino's chest and pooling on the floor. The dark red color of the blood contrasted against the bright beige carpet under Nino's twisted body. The backs of his legs were pressed on the floor and his upper body was turned onto his right side. A small portion of Nino's back was completely blown away.

He could clearly see that the blood had stopped oozing so he assumed that Nino was dead. Suddenly, he felt dizzy and nauseous. His knees wobbled as his body became covered in a cold sweat. Lester leaned the rifle against the tree. His body started shaking uncontrollably and then he began to vomit. He had seen people get killed by members of the Mob in many different ways, but this was the first time he actually shot someone himself. He leaned against the tree to steady himself while he cleaned his chin to avoid the vomit from freezing on his face.

Nearly five minutes passed before he was able to pick up the rifle and look through the scope to see if anyone else came into the room. Suddenly, fear began to manipulate his emotions as he wondered if someone might be in the house. If they were, he would try to shoot them as well to prevent them from calling the police.

Occasionally, Nino would pick up a girl at one of the bars in town and they would stay over night. Finally, he decided that nobody was there or at least didn't hear the shot. He estimated that he was nearly 400 yards away and the snow-covered trees had muffled most of the noise.

Ten minutes later, the frigid air began to chill Lester severely. After taking one last look into the scope, he put the rifle back over his shoulder and began skiing back in the direction of the car. Going back down the grade allowed him to work faster enabling him to generate some heat in his body.

Lester was convinced that Nino deserved to die. The bastard ended his money laundering deal and ruined his life when he squealed to Tony Robelotto and John Chapadeau. Now, he had to find a way to hide from the Mafia and the police for the rest of his life. What the hell; even if the Mafia did kill him, he had gotten revenge against two of the bastards. Now he had to take care of Murphy.

A shrieking siren in the distance broke the dead silence and he instantly stopped skiing. He began to panic thinking that maybe someone was there and called the police. The siren stopped and then started again. It was a fire siren, not the police. His legs were weak, and he realized that he was hyperventilating. The fire engine sirens became faint and he realized the fire was in a different direction. The scare hurried him along the trail leading back to the car.

The tracks he made an hour earlier were nearly filled in by drifting snow. The brisk wind from the north was making it difficult to progress with any speed, and the struggle began to deplete his energy. His legs were exhausted and his back ached, making him wish he were in his car. At the edge of the woods near the vacant house where he began, Lester waited impatiently for several minutes. Hidden by shadows of the trees, it was critical that he made certain no other vehicles were nearby. The pain in his feet from the bitter cold was torture. Resisting the temptation to rush over to the car, he waited minutes longer studying the snow that had drifted in the road looking for fresh tire tracks.

Satisfied that there were none, he hurried to the car and put the rifle and skis into the trunk. He started the motor and pushed down on the accelerator to warm the engine faster. His feet were numb so he took off the ski boots, but left on the wool socks.

It was nearly 15 minutes before the pain in his toes began to ease. He put on his shoes and drove back to Route 73, turning east in the direction of Interstate 87. Once his body got warm he smiled, thinking about the two bastards he had gotten even with for squealing on him. That would leave just one person, Murphy!

Chapter 4

Route 73 – Upstate New York

A STEADY WIND BLEW SNOW ACROSS THE HIGHWAY as Lester drove down the steep, twisting road and around the bend where the highway twisted alongside two small lakes. The road and the lakes were nestled between two large mountains with tall vertical stone sides. The one-mile stretch was like being in no-man's land.

Known as Cascade Lakes, the first lake was only 500 feet at its widest point and less than 100 feet in many sections. It was rumored to be so deep that no one was able to measure it. He recalled hearing stories from folks in Lake Placid about people who had drowned in the cold deep water when their horses and carriages went off the slippery dirt road as they traveled between Lake Placid and Keene. In the late nineteen-thirties, the road was paved, and guardrails were installed. Nobody really knew for sure which stories were rumors, myth or real, but he knew that it was a treacherous stretch of highway in the winter.

Deep snow banks covered the guardrails located only two feet from the narrow edge of land separating the highway from the narrow shoreline. Snow blowing across the lake's frozen surface created a sudden whiteout, making it impossible to see the road.

Suddenly, the car skidded toward the edge of the road and slid into the snow bank stopping him instantly. Several minutes passed before the gusting wind eased enough for him to see that he was stuck in a drift next to the guardrails.

He shifted into reverse and pressed down on the accelerator, but the car didn't move. After several futile attempts to back the car out, he realized that it was useless to keep trying. Thoughts of how to escape raced through his mind. If he couldn't get unstuck, he decided that he would use his skis and go to Keene where he could catch a bus to Albany.

The small village was only seven miles away and downhill most of the way. If he had to, he could take the rifle and throw it out onto the lake where it would quickly be covered with snow. It would sink to the bottom when the ice melted in the spring.

Lester opened the door and waded through the deep snow shouting obscenities into the gusting wind as he attempted unsuccessfully to remove the snow from behind the wheels with his foot. Above the howling wind he heard a loud scraping noise and looked up to see a dim flashing yellow light and headlights through the pelting snow. It was a state highway snowplow moving in his direction. When the truck got close he waved his hands over his head and motioned to the driver to stop.

"What the hell are you doing out on the highway at this hour of the morning in this weather?" asked the driver.

"I'm on my way to Albany. I just got a call from my sister at the hospital telling me that our father had a massive heart attack. The doctors don't expect him to live more than a few hours," Lester said, trying his best to act distraught. "Oh God, if I can't see him again before he dies I'll never forgive myself for not trying."

"Oh shit! I could get fired for towing you out, but there comes a time when you have to do the right thing."

The driver and his helper got a chain then moved the large truck up to the car. The enormous truck towed the rental car out of the snow bank onto the highway without any difficulty.

"If you drive into another whiteout, just stop for a few minutes. Don't worry about anyone running into the back of your car. Nobody will be on the highway," said the driver, thinking that nobody would be that stupid.

Lester insisted they take twenty dollars for helping and thanked them. It worried him that the two men could identify and place him near the murder scene. There could be no more mistakes or the authorities would be hot on his trail.

He got back in the car and continued driving south on Route 73 in the direction of Keene. As soon as the highway truck lights disappeared in the rearview mirror, he stopped and got out of the car. Wasting no time, he opened the trunk, pulled out the skis and boots and heaved them over the guard rails. They instantly disappeared in the snow on the lake. He kept the rifle to use it for another task he had in mind.

The bitter cold wind blew the car door shut as he got back inside. Lester increased the heat and then turned on the radio. After several minutes he located one station from Plattsburgh. The high mountain peaks prevented him from receiving any other radio signals. During a break in the music the D. J. gave the temperature. Seven below zero with a wind chill of minus 26 degrees. Wow, he thought, a heat wave.

The blowing snow eased up once he drove beyond the lake. The mountain walls and trees helped prevent the snow from drifting on the highway. His eyes strained to see the road which twisted like a winding snake. The steep grades of the hills forced him to drive much slower than usual and he was concerned that he was still in the area in the event the police discovered Casatelli and might look for the perpetuator.

Keene, NY

As he navigated the last hill from Lake Placid, Lester could see the town of Keene in the distance. Suddenly his stomach began to growl reminding him that he hadn't eaten since the previous evening at the small convenience store.

He stopped at the local grocery store and parked near the side of the building to look around and see if there were any police vehicles in the vicinity. Keene was a small village with a population of about eight hundred people, during the winter season, so it would be difficult to hide a police car.

The only other businesses in Keene were a gas station and tavern that were closed at this hour. Not seeing any police vehicles gave him a feeling of relief as he went inside. He ordered coffee and a roast beef sandwich to go. While waiting, Lester picked up a box of jelly donuts covered with powdered sugar and put them on the counter. Across the room in the store he caught a glimpse of himself in a mirror. Looking closer, he saw a face that was aged by huge dark circles under his eyes and a cluster of deep wrinkles.

Thinking about how grubby he looked made him realize that he hadn't changed his clothing since he left Scranton. The shirt under his armpits was moist and the odor was repugnant. Lester walked over to the display shelf and picked up a can of Gillette spray deodorant. Looking around he noticed that the only other person in the store was the clerk who had her back to him. He quickly removed the cap and sprayed a quick burst under each arm then returned the container to the shelf.

When the sandwich was ready he paid the clerk for the food and left. Nearly starved, he ripped the bag open and began eating the sandwich, spilling gobs of Russian dressing down the front of his shirt as he drove toward the interstate. The girl forgot to enclose napkins which irritated him, but he couldn't go back. He finished the sandwich and reached for the jelly donut box.

A highway sign up ahead relieved his anxiety. The entrance to Interstate 87, the main route to Albany and New York City, was within a half mile. He smiled as he drove onto the southbound ramp, knowing the state highway would be clear, and he would have no problems reaching the airport in Albany. The cruise control was set for the speed limit. The risk of having a trooper stop him wasn't worth the few minutes he would save by driving faster. His nerves were shot and he needed to calm down. Racing down the highway would only add to his stress.

Main Street, Lake Placid, NY

Roger Ferris left his apartment and walked to the Mountainview Diner on Main Street in Lake Placid to meet Nino. Roger always arrived at quarter-to-seven and read the morning paper with a cup of coffee while he waited for Nino. The diner was a favorite gathering place in the morning for local people in Lake Placid. It was rare to see a tourist in such a "greasy spoon."

Roger looked up at the clock on the diner's back wall covered with years of crud. It was very odd that Nino was late. Maybe his car battery was dead, or he got stuck in the snow. He looked at the phone booth, then decided to wait a few more minutes before calling. Then it occurred to him that Nino's current girlfriend might have stayed over, so he decided not to call. That was about the only reason he would skip breakfast without call-ing. Good for Nino! He's starting the day out right!

Opening the morning paper he began reading the sports page and quickly forgot about Nino. There was a small story about the FBI's inves-tigation of the Association's missing funds. There was nothing new in the story, so he switched to the local news section to catch up on the gossip while he ate his breakfast and finished his second cup of coffee.

When Roger finished, he tossed his money on the table and walked down the street to his office. A smile formed on his face when he looked at his desk. The day before he had purchased a large nameplate that read U.S. Bobsled Association Executive Director. He reminded himself to call Nino when he had a moment to tease him about being late. Nino would brag and give him all the little details about what happened with the sexy girl he had dated for the past two weeks.

CHAPTER 5

I-87 Adirondack Northway

LESTER CONTEMPLATED DRIVING THE RENTAL TO New York City. He felt extremely uncomfortable since the mob knew what type of vehicle he drove which would make it easier to locate him. Right now he needed to find a place to stay for a few days while he took care of some unfinished business and then he could rent another car.

But, first he had to deal with Shawn Murphy. It was questionable as to who he hated most, Murphy, Casatelli or Chapadeau. Murphy ruined his deal with the U.S. Bobsled Association by reporting him to the Olympic authorities and the FBI. But, Casatelli and Chapadeau told Tony Robelotto, New York City's Mafia Don, that he was skimming their money. The Mafia was more terrorizing to him than the FBI. While in Albany he would find a way to kill Murphy.

Thinking about Chapadeau made him chuckle. The rat-faced weasel got just what he deserved. Lester suspected Chapadeau was also skimming money from the Mafia, but there was no way anyone would ever prove it. Well, he taught the egotistical bastard a lesson. The explosion was still vivid in his mind. He shuddered each time he thought about killing him.

If he had more time he would have done it Mafia style. After Chapadeau left for work he would have detonated explosives in the house while his family slept. Wait a couple of weeks then kidnap Chapadeau while he was still grieving, slowly torture him and then slit his throat. There just wasn't enough time to do it right.

Thoughts about how to disappear occupied his mind as he drove towards Albany. The first order of business would be to get rid of Murphy, get a fake passport and some cash, then go to Europe and empty his Swiss account. He couldn't stay in Europe more than a week. Casablanca sounded like a good place to lay low.

The Mafia wouldn't expect him to go there, and Africa was a continent with lots of places where he could vanish. In Zurich he could rent a car and drive to Gibraltar, then take a boat to Tangiers. After he took care of Murphy he needed to grab a flight to Frankfurt. It would be too risky to fly to Zurich. The Mafia could track him down too easily. In Frankfurt he would get on the train to Zurich, so they couldn't trace his steps.

The drive to Albany lasted two hours. He decided to return the rental car so his van wouldn't be discovered in the parking garage. If the police found his van it would be easy to identify the rental he was driving. He decided to drive his van south and rent another car closer to the city.

After returning the rental car at the airport he went into the men's room and attempted to wash his face. The combination of white power from the donuts and Russian dressing made a mess on his shirt so he zipped up his jacket to avoid attracting attention.

He decided to leave the charges on the Association's credit card, instead of paying cash. It wouldn't make any difference now if they knew he charged the rental to the Association plus he was low on cash. By the time they got the statement, he would be out of the country.

Thoughts about Murphy occupied his mind and he wondered if the rumors about him having a close relationship with the Soviets were true. It really frustrated him when Murphy made arrangements for the Soviet Bobsled team to visit Lake Placid on a cultural exchange without telling him or Casatelli. He read about the exchange in the newspaper. Murphy acted as if he didn't exist and he was infuriated that Murphy ratted him out to the Olympic Committee and the FBI.

"That son of a bitch will never know what hit him." He lit a cigarette and gritted his teeth while thinking about Murphy. "I'll take care of him tonight."

Spotting a pay phone, he dialed Murphy's number and Murphy's wife answered. Lester said he was a friend from the Bobsled Association and wanted to say hello to her husband. She said Shawn was on the West Coast with the Air Force and would be home in a couple of days. When she asked who was calling he hung up.

"Shit," he bellowed in frustration. Now he needed to forget Murphy and drive on to the City. He located his van in the parking lot, paid the parking fee with the Bobsled Association's credit card, and drove south on I-87 in the direction of the City planning to stop on the way to get a rental.

His mind was so occupied during the drive that it seemed like only minutes had passed and was surprised that a sign up ahead showed the last tollbooth on the New York State Thruway. He paid the toll and continued south on I-87, then onto I-278. Eventually, he got off on Grand Central Parkway without getting a rental. A Ramada Inn was only a few miles up ahead on the same block where he had stayed several other times when he flew out of La Guardia Airport. Nobody would recognize him there. To be safe he would eat in his room. Lester pulled into a strip mall that had a liquor store and small market. Peanuts on the shelf caught his attention. They would make a good snack so he grabbed a large bag, then purchased two bottles of French wine and a corkscrew. He was pleased when he arrived at the hotel. The parking lot was nearly vacant so he assumed there wouldn't be too many people inside.

After registering, he went back out to the parking lot to get his suitcase. The van was parked under a security light where he could observe it from his room after dark if anyone went near it. He stood adjacent to some large shrubbery examining the parking lot for Robelotto's men. Not seeing anyone he decided to walk in the direction of his van. Suddenly, thoughts of Casatelli filled his mind. He felt very apprehensive and his legs became chilled and weak.

The scene of Casatelli falling on the floor with blood gushing from his body flashed through his mind as he envisioned himself being shot by someone from the Mob. Now his legs felt like they were loaded with cement and refused to move.

He was doubly concerned about his van because he had half a kilo of cocaine with a street value of over $50,000 hidden inside the driver's door panel in place of speaker components. It was enclosed inside a green plastic bag with duct tape wrapped around several times to protect it. The hydrochloride was 92 percent pure, and the baking was done in Colombia. It was compressed to the size of a telephone book cut in half.

After several minutes Lester felt confident nobody was watching and he regained his strength. He walked slowly to the van and took out the suitcase then went up to his room to call Roger Ferris. He would offer to sell Roger the cocaine for what he had paid -- $8,500. Normally, he would sell it to Nino for $15,000 who in turn sold it a gram at a time for a grand. But Roger could never pay that much. The cash would be more than enough to get him to Europe and the Swiss accounts.

There was no need to unpack so he tossed the suitcase on the spare bed, then called Roger at the U.S. Bobsled Association office. It always amazed him that the Association hired Roger. He must have given the Association, a world-class snow job to get hired as the executive director. Lester knew the Association didn't have a clue about what was going on around them.

"Hello."

"Roger, I need some cash in a hurry. Can you get your hands on eight grand by tonight?"

"Where do you expect me to find that amount of cash?" Roger shook his head in disbelief that Lester would ask him for that much cash.

"Listen to me carefully. I've got half a kilo of uncut cocaine that I paid eight and a half grand for. It's worth 50 to 60 grand on the streets."

"Shit man, I can't get my hands on that kind of money. Where the hell did you get that much cocaine?"

"Never mind that. Look, I need the cash right away! Just go over to the Lake Placid Trust and draw the cash out of the Association's account," Lester stood up with the receiver in one hand and waved his other arm around in a circle attempting to control his anger. He couldn't believe that Roger was questioning him.

"Listen to me, God damn it, just get the cash. Stop worrying and go do as I said."

"What the hell is the matter with you Lester? I can't do that. John will go berserk when he finds out, and besides there's only $3,200 left in that account."

"What the hell happened to the rest of the money?"

"Hey man, you know how they are. Nino withdrew some last week to pay for equipment. The checkbook for the Key Bank account is at his house. Do you want me to drive over there and get a check for what's left?"

A cold sweat trickled down Lester's back. He could visualize his plan falling apart because Roger suddenly wanted to do things legally. Thoughts of Robelotto's men finding him in New York began to cram his mind. He had to get Roger moving and quickly.

"No. I don't want Nino to know anything about this. There's a little over five thousand in the Citizen's National account. Take out the five G's in cash and bring it to me in the City. You can have it for that amount."

"Oh, man I'll get my ass in a jam if I get caught doing this."

"Are you completely stupid? Just bring the five grand and in less than two weeks you can turn it into fifty grand and replace the money. This stuff is pure shit, straight out of Columbia!"

"What about Nino? I don't want him getting pissed because you gave me the deal and not him. He'll beat the crap out of me if he ever finds out," Roger paused. "You know, something strange happened this morning! Nino didn't show up at the diner for breakfast. And when I called the house, no one answered."

"Screw Nino," Lester screamed into the phone. "Are you going to get the cash or not? You better get off your ass because the bank closes at four."

"Okay, okay. I'll go to the bank. Where can I meet you?"

"Meet me at 10 p.m. tonight at that Holiday Inn in Queens where we stayed when we got back from Switzerland, remember?"

"Yeah."

"I'll be waiting in the bar."

"That doesn't give me much time to get to the City."

"How much time do you need? It's only 3:00 now. Figure a half-hour to get the cash from the bank and you still have six hours to drive down with a half hour to spare."

"Yeah, I guess you're right. But that's a long ride. I should stop at Nino's house and find out where he's been all day. He might be sick."

"Look, you asshole, forget Nino," screamed Lester in frustration. "If you stop at his house he'll want to know what you're doing and then you can forget the cocaine. I'm talking fifty grand here. Why can't you just do what the hell I tell you?"

"All right, all right, don't panic. I'll get the cash and meet you at the Holiday Inn. What's the phone number of the Inn just in case I get held up?"

"I'm not staying there and there's no phone where I'll be waiting. Just be at the Holiday Inn in Queens at 10 tonight with the God damn money!"

Lester hung up the receiver and set the alarm on the clock radio for 9:15 p.m. After all the turmoil he had been through, he desperately needed rest. Feeling exhausted, he couldn't concentrate on anything for more than a couple of minutes.

Years of heavy drinking, smoking cigarettes, and rich foods were taking their toll. Sixty pounds overweight and being out of shape made him look nearly 10 years older than his 50 years. Wanting to rest, he flopped down on the bed and within moments he fell asleep without eating the peanuts or drinking any wine.

The alarm woke Lester and he cautiously pulled the curtain back to peek out into the parking lot. There didn't appear to be anyone waiting in a car. He put on his jacket and stood outside in the shadows for several minutes making sure it was safe to get in his van. It was 9:40 p.m. He would have enough time to drive through the Holiday Inn parking lot and check the parked cars to make sure that no one was waiting for him there.

I'm becoming paranoid, he thought, and for a good reason. Tony Robelotto was not a merciful man, especially if he had been double-crossed. Tony would have his men torture him until they got the Swiss account numbers, and then they would kill him. And if Tony suspected that he was trying to skip out of the country without giving him access to the money, he would have his men kill him and just write off the cash. It would be a lesson to others who might get the same idea.

He also worried that Roger might have stopped at Nino's house and discovered his body. Roger would panic. The police could be waiting for him at the motel, or worse, some of Tony's men. His nerves were shattered and his stomach churned, making him wish he had some antacid.

The parking lot was nearly full, so he drove slowly around several times, checking cars before parking near the lot's only entrance, where he could observe cars entering. It was now 10:10 p.m. and he began to squirm in his seat, cursing himself for not getting something for his stomach. His heart began to race as he continuously searched the lot and checked his mirrors for anything suspicious.

Maybe Roger had stopped and found the body. No, he wasn't that stupid. He knew it would be in his best interest to do what Lester told him. The traffic probably held him up.

Minutes later Roger drove into the lot in the Association's van and parked in a spot four aisles away. Lester grabbed his .357 pistol, then got out and walked hastily to the rear of the van. He stood still for several moments to see if anyone was watching before he slid alongside Roger's van and opened the passenger side door.

"God damn it! You scared the shit out of me," Roger's face lost its color. "What's with the gun?"

"A couple of Robelotto's henchmen are looking for me. Casatelli and Chapadeau told him I've been skimming money off the top of their Swiss account. The sleazy bastards! After all that I did for them. Especially Nino! I picked that bastard up off the street and set him up." Lester's face was bright red. "I'll tell you something else you don't know. I set John up with the Mafia to launder their cash and those two bastards turned on me!"

"You know how much I hate guns and I can never seem to get away from them. Put the damn thing away and stop waving it in my face. I had to drive all the way down here with a pistol that Nino left under the seat. Don't worry; I'm not going to be a problem."

Lester looked at him and began laughing. Suddenly, he stopped and the expression on his face turned to antagonism as his twisted mind got serious again. "I don't trust anybody except you," he lied. "Do you have the cash?"

"Yea, I've got it, but why do you need it? Are you leavin' the country?"

"I don't know yet." Lester avoided eye contact. "Don't say nothing to nobody! You got that?" He pulled out a cigarette and lit it with his free hand. Once again the gun was pointed in the direction of Roger as he looked around nervously making sure there wasn't anyone near the van.

"Don't point that thing at me! Jesus, why do you have to smoke next to me? You know I hate the smell of cigarettes." He waved his hands then leaned back in his seat attempting to keep the smoke out of his face.

"Really, you little twit, you don't mind smoking pot, but cigarettes drive you nuts." Lester opened the window and tossed out the cigarette. "Where's the dough?"

"I got it, I got it, here. Don't worry; you know you can count on me."

Roger handed him the envelope and Lester looked inside to be sure it was there, but didn't count it. He was confident that Roger wouldn't be stupid enough to cheat him.

"Good! Now back out carefully and drive over there to my van, and I'll get the stuff for you," Lester pointed to where his van was parked.

Roger pulled up behind the van and waited while Lester removed the green plastic bag wrapped with gray duct tape and returned to his van.

"This is almost 100 percent pure, so be sure to dilute it in half if you use it," Lester said, and handed the bag to Roger. "There's 50 grams. If you're smart you'll get a grand for each one. But it's worth a hell of a lot more if you take your time and distribute it right. Sell smaller lots for more cash. Now get your ass out of here! Drive slowly, but not too slow so you don't attract any cops! If you get caught with that much cocaine you'll spend the rest of your sorry ass life in the pen."

Lester watched Roger pull out onto the street and waited until his tail lights disappeared before getting into his van. He went to an all-night convenience store and bought a large bottle of Mylanta. When he got back into the van he opened the bottle and drank several large gulps, then returned to the Ramada Inn.

Chapter 6

Warrensburg, New York

Four hours later Roger drove past the Warrensburg exit on the Interstate. The package of uncut cocaine sat on the passenger seat hidden under a newspaper. He looked at the clock on the dashboard and was surprised that it was nearly 3 a.m. In his head, he calculated that it had been over 11 hours since he had left Lake Placid. The long drive and lack of sleep were catching up with him. A parking area was just ahead so he pulled in and parked near the rest room.

There were very few cars on the Interstate and the rest stop was vacant. He picked up the paper to look at the package of cocaine and contemplated trying a small sample after he used the restroom. Rushing back to the van he took out a jackknife from his glove compartment, deciding to try a tiny hit to celebrate his good fortune. The blade cut through the duct tape with ease. Patiently, he peeled the plastic back, exposing the hydrochloride. It was too valuable to waste so he was extraordinarily careful not to spill any. Thanks to Lester, he was looking at about $50,000.

Excitement built as he slid his tongue over his lips anticipating a small sample. Just enough to get high and keep him awake for the next couple of hours. He opened the glove compartment and took out his bag of works, placing it on the seat.

Like most drug users, Roger carried a Zippo cigarette lighter, a spoon, a small eyedropper, several small pieces of cotton, and a syringe in a bag, his "works." Roger was never without it. It contained everything needed for a quick fix.

Carefully opening the bag he removed the eyedropper, and took it into the rest room. The hot water was only room temperature, too cold to generate any warmth; nevertheless, he filled the eyedropper and returned to the van. Carefully he cut off a small section of the narcotic and placed it in the spoon. Next he added a bit of water, then cautiously set the lighter on the floor to heat the metal spoon to melt the substance. Within seconds the water turned milky. He placed the cotton ball into the mixture and laid the spoon on the van's console so it wouldn't spill.

After looking around to make sure no one was coming, he then pulled out the syringe and slid the tip of the needle into the cotton ball. Slowly, he pulled the plunger back, drawing the freshly mixed cocaine up into the instrument. A smile of enjoyment filled his face as he looked at the syringe and realized he had a little more then he planned.

Lester's warning to cut the dose flashed through his mind, but he was confident the increase would just give him a slight extra high and take him a little tad longer to come down. Why not? He wiped his tongue over his lips in anticipation.

The button nearly ripped off his left sleeve as he rushed to expose his arm. A large rubber band, which he twisted with a pencil, was used to shut off the circulation, forcing the vein to bulge and make it easier to inject the needle. The vein swelled and hardened instantly as he reached over with his other hand to pick up the syringe. In his excitement, he didn't notice the New York State Police car entering the parking lot.

The syringe pierced his skin with no resistance, sliding easily into the vein. He began to tremble and hastily forced the plunger down. In one motion, he emptied it. The nearly pure substance was more than he had ever taken and it entered his bloodstream so fast that his body began to quiver.

Suddenly, he went into shock and his heart began racing, faster and faster. His body shook violently and then huge amounts of perspiration emerged from his skin soaking his clothing. Roger clasped his chest in a futile attempt to stop the relentless pain. Unexpectedly, he felt nausea and began vomiting. Within moments, he was dead.

The trooper left his patrol car and went into the men's room. When he returned the driver of the van wasn't sitting behind the steering wheel. Since there were no other cars in the parking lot and the driver hadn't gone into the restroom, he walked over to check the van. Roger was sprawled out on the seat with the syringe still in his arm.

Ramada Inn, Queens, New York

Lester woke up thinking about the several trips he had taken, at the Association's expense, to see if he could get through customs without any problems. His Olympic Bobsled credentials worked as well as having a diplomatic visa. The scheme was perfect and soon he was traveling to Europe on a regular basis, on the pretense of looking for sponsors for the Association. On each trip he carried large amounts of cash for the Mafia and deposited it into Swiss bank accounts. Eventually, the Mafia trusted Lester to place millions into seven different banks.

The Mafia paid him the usual five percent, but after several months, Lester came up with another scheme. He concocted a story that two custom agents in West Germany figured out what he was doing and agreed to let him continue if he gave them five percent. Chapadeau wasn't happy about paying 10 percent to hide the money in Swiss accounts, but believed he had no other choice.

Lester opened his own Swiss account and began depositing his share with the additional five percent, which would accumulate into a sizable amount of money over the next couple of years. The big mistake he made one night, when he was intoxicated, was bragging about it to Nino.

Lester knew that it was only a matter of time before the Mob would locate him. The recent ordeal at Polsinilli's restaurant was enough to convince him. Once Tony decided he wanted his money they would torture him until they got their money and then kill him. His only hope now was to get out of the country immediately.

He placed his suitcase in the van and drove to the airport. It excited him to purchase a one-way ticket to Frankfort, Germany using cash to avoid leaving a trail for the FBI.

CHAPTER 7

The Pentagon

SHAWN MURPHY SAT AT HIS DESK, LOOKING around the small office that had been provided for his new assignment with Special Operations at the Pentagon. In his position he would also be available to help other government agencies whenever there was a request. Shawn would also maintain a second office at the Air Force Base in Schenectady, NY near his home.

Holding back the desire to laugh out loud, Shawn smiled as he thought about his new assignment. It was almost perfect. He would be doing the type of work that he enjoyed the most and would have some excitement with the job. For once he could be creative and do what he was trained to do, be a Public Affairs specialist.

The only drawback would be the long separations from his wife, Angela. She would stay in Albany where she worked in the insurance business. He'd get used to it but suspected it would be more difficult for her. This was the way of life for people in the Navy. Six months at sea and six months home. That's the way he would have to accept it if he wanted to work at the Pentagon.

As a Public Affairs specialist working for Special Operations on the national level, he would be available to move around outside of ordinary assignments. At his former job in Schenectady, his supervisor, Sergeant Olive Hanson, had made his life miserable when he returned from his special duty assignment as an Olympic Coach. He had traveled with the team throughout Europe for several months and she was bitter because she had to do extra work in his absence.

When the Air Force temporarily appointed him to the Pentagon again, so he could be assigned to the CIA, Olive became enraged. She had her own worries now. The Air Force was accumulating evidence to prosecute her for destroying official papers. Documents that had reassigned Shawn to the CIA for a previous mission had disappeared.

Olive's court-martial would begin within a few weeks and she was on the edge of a nervous breakdown. The bitter woman had devoted her entire life to the military and now it looked certain she would be dishonorably discharged with no pension or even worse, time in a military prison.

The soft ring of the telephone interrupted Shawn's reflections. It was General Sam Abbott's secretary advising that the general wanted to meet with him. Special Operations in the Air Force was directly under his authority. Shawn liked the man, who was open-minded, and understood the public affairs business. He knocked on the general's door.

"Come in, Shawn."

Abbott walked around the desk to greet his new staff member.

"Welcome to Washington." A smile formed on the tall man's face as he walked up to Shawn. "Have you been able to find an apartment, or are you still staying at Andrews Air Force Base?"

"I'm at Andrews, but I've located a small apartment in Georgetown that will be available on the first of the month." Shawn remained at attention. "Angela and I will keep our home in Schenectady where I'll be doing most of my work."

General Abbott gestured with his hand for Shawn to relax and sit down at the small conference table. "It's clear to me that your new assignment is directly related to your former involvement with the CIA," Abbott smiled which assured Shawn that his new boss was in agreement with the arrangements. "I really don't know too much about what happened except that you helped smuggle Boris Yegorov, a Soviet metallurgist, into the United States."

"Yea, we sure did, and I still wake up at night once in a while thinking about the wild incident Professor Bodynski and I experienced."

"Why did you help him to defect if it was so dangerous?"

"In exchange for helping him defect from the Soviet Union, Yegorov agreed to divulge the secret alloy composite to the CIA and the Navy."

"Okay, but why were you involved in such a risky mission. I would think that the CIA would have used some of their agents to help him defect?"

"Because Boris Yegorov was once an Olympic bobsled coach and we had a lot in common. The CIA believed it would be easier for me to get into the Soviet Union and help Boris without attracting suspicion. The CIA got a break when Professor Ray Bodynski, the Director of the U.S.

Bobsled Technical Committee and I were invited to the Soviet Union to be part of a sports cultural exchange. The CIA jumped on the opportunity and developed a plan to get the Soviet coach out of the Soviet Union before they killed him."

"Let's have a cup of coffee, then I want to hear more." The general got up and called his secretary on the intercom and asked her to bring them coffee. After she left Abbott turned to Shawn, "Now let's hear the rest of the story."

"We successfully smuggled Boris out of the country on a Russian fishing boat near Tallinn, Estonia. We nearly lost him while on the fishing boat," Shawn hesitated momentarily thinking about the ordeal. "A KGB undercover agent attempted to kill the coach and severely wounded him. The Navy sent a nuclear submarine to secretly rendezvous with us just off the coast of Norway. The plan was to have the sub take us to Virginia, but Boris' injuries were so severe the navy doctor didn't think he would survive the four-day trip."

"Why didn't they have a carrier meet the sub and fly him back?"

"I guess there were no carriers in the surrounding area; so to keep Boris alive; the Air Force used a C-130 cargo plane outfitted with skis to evacuate the coach. Our sub met an Air National Guard plane on the Arctic Ice Cap in an unbelievable rescue. The Navy nuclear sub pushed its observation deck up through the ice and the C-130 with skis landed next to it. We were transferred to the plane, which flew us to Albany, N.Y."

General Abbott raised his eyebrows and tilted his head. "How did you get him to a hospital from the C-130?"

"An ambulance met us at the airport and transported Boris to a local hospital in Albany. He was operated on an hour later and his life was saved. Unfortunately, the KGB killed Yegorov's wife and her parents several months before the CIA could carry out their rescue plan."

"Why did the Soviets want to kill him and his family?"

"Yegorov was half Latvian and half Russian. He hated the Russians because of their violent mistreatment of his family and the horrifying persecution of other Latvian citizens. In 1940, the Russians occupied Latvia and their soldiers openly tortured and robbed the people. The Soviets were also unhappy with his new bobsled program. He had convinced them to invest money in his program and he would give them Gold medals. In 1984, they only won a Bronze Medal during their first Olympic Bobsled competition at Sarajevo, Yugoslavia.

The Soviets had invested millions in his bobsled program and considered a Bronze medal a failure and an embarrassment. Of course, they had no idea that since the 1984 Olympics, Yegorov had secretly created an advanced alloy composite for use in bobsled runners."

Leaning back in his chair, the General appeared deep in thought for a moment and then he looked at Shawn with a serious expression. "What's the real story about the composite?"

"Yegorov was frustrated that the Soviets treated him so badly for not earning a Gold Metal. Soon he faded into the background and continued to secretly do extensive testing of his new alloy. When he believed he had perfected the alloy composite, without permission from the Soviet government, he went to East Germany and did private coaching with their bobsled federation. He tested a pair of runners made with his secret alloy and carefully recorded the results."

Abbott reached for his cup of coffee and took a drink. He quickly put the cup back down. "Ugh, the coffee got cold." He had an irritated expression on his face. "I assume these runners were better?" He got up and moved across the room and sat down on a small couch.

"Yes. Whenever they used these runners, the times were considerably faster. There was no question that the alloy was reducing the friction between the runners and the ice. He convinced the East Germans that the minor change in the shape of the runners was improving their times. Nobody suspected that the faster times were the result of the runners with the composite reducing friction drag on the ice. The East Germans paid him a large amount of cash for his training principles and several pairs of runners, none of which contained the secret alloy.

"Before returning to the Soviet Union, Boris opened a Swiss bank account and deposited the money to prevent the KGB from taking it from him. Boris knew the KGB would never let him keep the money, so he concealed the information about the Swiss account from his superiors."

Shawn thought for a moment before continuing. "He wanted to keep his new alloy secret. It could be used with other metals and alloys to reduce friction with water or ice, which would make it a precious and strategic commodity for warships. There was one thing for certain; he didn't want the Soviets, who had inflicted so much pain on his family and other Latvians, to get the money or the alloy secret."

"That's amazing. Where is he now?"

"I don't know, he is hidden in the witness protection program. The Navy considered his alloy to be a valuable breakthrough. But, when they attempted to get all the information, Yegorov was unable to recall his alloy's entire formula. Doctors suspect he is in the preliminary stages of

Alzheimer's disease. Nevertheless, the David Taylor Research Laboratory in Bethesda, MD is working with him to retrieve the complicated formula.

Robert Gilmore, a research physicist employed by the Navy, is convinced that the alloy will enable submarines to increase their speed and use less energy, as well as other benefits for Navy ships. Gilmore believes that when he is able to use a computer with the formula, many other uses for the alloy will be discovered."

"What is Yegorov's educational background?"

"He was educated as a physicist at the Zalkalana Institute in the Soviet Union. Yegorov was recognized as one of the foremost metallurgists in their country. He had also worked at the Soviet Military Research Center in Kiev and is recognized worldwide for his work with alloys and titanium used in their space program.

He became even more important because they suspected he had developed some type of an advanced alloy, a secret known only to him. The KGB wanted to get this information and he knew they would execute him once they learned the formula of his secret alloy. If they couldn't get the formula they would kill him anyway to prevent other countries from getting it."

Standing up, the general stated, "That's mind-boggling, yet typical of the Soviets."

He shook his head in amazement as he walked back to his desk. "Thanks for sharing that with me. I knew parts of the story and you're right it's unbelievable. Look at the clock. We should get some work done. I'd like to go over some assignments that I want you to complete."

"I appreciate you taking the time to review these with me. My former supervisor never had any interest in reviewing assignments."

"Shawn, I'm going to share something with you that I would normally never tell a subordinate." The smile left his face and his eyes appeared to be darker. "What I'm about to say must be kept confidential."

He walked over and shut his office door then returned to the table and sat down. After searching for words, he leaned forward, lowered his voice, "I'm fairly confident that Hanson will be found guilty and given a dishonorable discharge. Her former commander, Colonel Crosby, and his deputy, Lt. Colonel Fowlkes, will also be removed, and if I have my way, they'll be forced to retire immediately. Unfortunately, we don't have enough solid evidence to court-martial either of them."

"I'm glad to hear something's finally being done."

"Crosby has another worry that'll keep him awake nights. The accident investigation team uncovered another problem. They determined that the reason his plane crashed in Greenland, has been traced directly to pilot error. Crosby was completely responsible for the accident and he tried to cover it up."

Abbott stood up and looked out the window then added, "It seems that Crosby had a hangover the morning of the accident. From what I understand, it was a real throbbing hangover. So much in fact, the team is confident that he was legally intoxicated when he made the landing."

"That doesn't surprise me. There were rumors for a long time that he had a drinking problem."

"It's not a secret that the three of them were abusing their authority when they tried to prevent you from working with the CIA on the previous assignment."

The general turned around, smiled then said, "Now, let's get down to business."

Abbott went to a secured file cabinet and pulled out a fireproof metal container. "Take a few minutes and look through these classified documents. They contain information about the Soviets restructuring of their military. The Soviets are secretly making plans to send 11,000 troops to the Republics of Azerbaijan and Armenia to support the 5,000 troops stationed there to prevent ethnic skirmishes from erupting into a full-scale war."

"What do you want me to do with the information?"

"Nothing, I want you to read these files carefully and bring yourself up to date on what is going on in Europe." General Abbott moved some newspapers off the table to make room for Shawn to spread out the files. "Newspapers never give the public the real stories taking place around the world. They're in the business of selling newspapers, and more often than not, slant the news according to what a reporter personally believes or wants you to believe. Another problem: politicians don't want mainstream Americans learning the truth. But these files contain CIA reports, and they are as close to the truth as you're going to get."

"The Soviets are getting themselves in a delicate position with all the trouble they're having," Shawn said. "Besides being close to a civil war in Armenia and Azerbaijan, Yugoslavia is another hot spot they can't control. It's just a matter of time before Latvia, Estonia and Lithuania openly revolt for independence. When I was working in Latvia and Estonia in 1989, I thought it would be years before they would gain freedom from the Russians. But I had returned to the States for just a few months when the

East Germans tore down the wall. Like most people, I was shocked. The Soviets will have a difficult time maintaining control now."

"You're absolutely right, Shawn. Another factor is that they're in more trouble economically than most people realized."

"How do I fit in?"

"You'll be working as a reporter assigned to the Pentagon. Occasionally you might have to spend some time in Europe, including the Soviet Union. Your role in Latvia last year was perfect. You were secretly working for the CIA, but at the same time, a coach for the U.S. Olympic Bobsled team. The Agency is now certain that the KGB believes you were simply a bobsled coach. They're interested in using you in that role again."

General Abbott explained that in his meeting with the CIA he was informed that the technical information Boris Yegorov gave to the David Taylor Research Lab was not complete. He was also made aware that Boris had hidden documents with the complete information in Riga, Latvia near where he and Shawn once met.

During the next hour they discussed Shawn's role at the Pentagon. When they finished, Shawn returned to his office, thinking about Abbott's statement that his role as a bobsled coach was a perfect cover for the CIA. At 5 foot 11 inches, he weighed 200 pounds and suits had to be tailor-made to fit his enormous shoulders. The jackets were size 50 with a taper to fit his 36-inch waist. His appearance suggested he might be involved with professional sports, not the CIA.

Chapter 8

CIA Headquarters, Langley, VA

"I ceSpy" was the CIA's code name for the previous mission to smuggle Boris Yegorov out of the Soviet Union. Fred Unser was the CIA director of Europe which included the entire Soviet Union. He thought of the code name because of the connection to an Olympic bobsled coach used in that mission. He looked through the IceSpy file while he waited for Dr. Robert Gilmore.

Although, employed as a research physicist with the David Taylor Research Laboratory, Gilmore was also respected as one of the country's top tribologist. As the director of CIA operations in Europe, Unser had also worked with Gilmore the previous fall to determine if the alloy Boris Yegorov had developed was authentic. Gilmore and his associates at David Taylor considered the technology to be of huge importance.

A knock on the door interrupted Unser's thoughts. "Come in," he said.

Gilmore walked in. "How are you Fred?"

"I'm doing fine, how about you?"

"Okay. I'll feel better when we solve this problem."

"Yea, I know," Fred gestured with his hand for Gilmore to sit at the small conference table next to the window.

Gilmore watched him walk over to his desk to get the file. Unser reminded him of Abe Lincoln, but without a beard. "Yegorov's memory seems to be getting worse. We have about 90 percent of the formula, but Yegorov has drawn a blank on the rest, and without it, what we have is worthless."

"Damn it!" Fred cursed. "We spent a fortune putting this mission together and," then suddenly he began coughing and couldn't finish his sentence. A respiratory tract infection made his throat dry and irritated. He slammed the IceSpy file down on the desk with such force that some of the papers slid off onto the floor.

"He simply can't recall a couple of calculations," Gilmore said. "You should've been with us when we were working with him. He was so upset that he began to cry. I discussed the situation with a staff psychologist and it was her opinion that Boris is suffering from all the trauma he has experienced."

"There's no question the man's life has been hell, but there's too much at stake. We've got to get the information before the Soviets." Fred looked off in space for a couple of minutes until his throat calmed down then began speaking again. "If this formula is what you think it is we can't risk the Soviets getting it. If we both have it that is one thing, but if they have it and we don't it will be a disaster."

"This formula is real and it works. At this point in time, there is no way to even attempt to put a value on it. It's massive."

Fred thought about what Gilmore said, "We need to get as much information from him while we can. You never know when he might die from his illness and then we may never get the information. We really don't know if there is another copy of the formula that the Soviets might find!"

"It's sad to watch him." Gilmore paused for a moment. "I feel sorry for all the suffering the poor man has gone through."

"So, what do we do?" Fred asked. "Forget everything? I don't think so. We need to get this technology."

"Boris says that Shawn Murphy met with him last fall near the place where he hid the formula plus several samples of the alloy. I'm convinced that Murphy could find it."

"Where?"

"Someplace near Riga," Gilmore said. "Boris insists he could tell Murphy exactly where to find them. He claims they're hidden in a cave where he met Murphy and another agent who works in the Soviet Union. But that agent's cover was blown there, so he has been assigned elsewhere."

"Sending Murphy would be a tremendous risk," Fred said. "The KGB might figure out who he is and wait until he locates the information. Then they'll kill him, and get the formula in writing, with samples to boot."

"I'm only telling you the way it is! What'll you suggest?"

"I hate these kinds of decisions. But we have already spent a fortune and the military lost a C-130 on the rescue."

Fred rubbed his chin and reached for his pipe. After several minutes without speaking, he quietly said, "Let's meet with Boris and find out exactly where the container is hidden. Then we can look at the possibility of sending Murphy or perhaps someone else to find it."

They spent the next two hours discussing details of the mission. Both agreed that the risk was extremely high, but worth it. The two men agreed they really had no choice, but to try and locate the formula. It was much too precious to risk the Russians obtaining it. Gilmore left and Unser spent the rest of the day going over several possible ways to get someone in and out of the Soviet Union undetected. Regardless of the plan, the risk was incredible.

The Pentagon

Late in the afternoon Fred called General Abbott to brief him on the possibility that they might need Shawn Murphy for a few weeks.

"We've been expecting you to call," Abbott replied. "Obviously, I'm concerned about his safety. I understand the last little venture he was involved in became a very risky episode. Can you guys assure us that this one will be better managed?"

"You know that's not possible, but we'll have everything worked out in advance to reduce the danger we experienced the last time. There are no guarantees in this business."

"Well let us know when you've made a decision and I'll have him ready."

Abbott hung up the receiver and thought about the CIA using Murphy for another mission. He wasn't happy that it would be such a dangerous mission, but agreed with Unser's thinking that someone had to retrieve the documents and Murphy was the best choice. Unser had assured the general that he wouldn't let Murphy go alone and would send another agent with him. The CIA would create a plan for Murphy and another agent to enter and leave the Soviet Union undetected; not an easy task.

After thinking about his conversation with Unser, General Abbott called Shawn into his office.

"The CIA needs you to help find Yegorov's formula. They don't know the plan yet, but it'll probably involve you going back to the Soviet Union to locate the documents and the alloy samples that Boris hid in some cave in Riga. Are you comfortable doing this?"

"Sure, and I remember the place," Shawn said. "I met Boris there once. I didn't go inside the cave, but I know where it is located."

"How do you feel about going back?"

"It's not something that I really want to do, but I'd be interested in looking at their plan if you don't need me here in public affairs."

"Fred Unser said the mission wouldn't take too long, we can spare you."

"What's too long?"

"I'm not sure, but I'm under the impression that it would be a real short duration. He said maybe a few weeks."

"I hope so." Otherwise, I'll have some serious problems with my wife thought Shawn.

"So, are you getting acclimated to your new job?"

"Yes, I've been reviewing the classified documents about Azebaijan and Armenia, but it's almost the same as anybody can read in the New York Times."

"I know, but I wanted you to become familiar with world events because in Special Operations nobody knows where or when they'll be needed. We can discuss the mission in more detail after Unser gets back to us next week.

Shawn understood that he could be spending more time in the Soviet Union and other parts of the Eastern Bloc. After years of misery at his former job, he was thrilled to be back working in his former profession, espionage! The information contained in the files astonished him. How could national reporters write such inaccurate stories about current events? He suspected the general was right about the media.

A folder labeled "Yugoslavia" caught Shawn's attention. He opened the file and read the CIA report on the current situation. Anti-Communist backlash was growing against its leaders. Neighboring Romanians revolting and executing their dictator as well as jailing other high Communist party leaders stunned Yugoslavs. The CIA suspected that the violence and revenge in Romania would soon spread to Yugoslavia, a country known as a maverick and the most reform-minded communist nation in Eastern Europe.

Shawn thought about the Soviet plan to send more troops to the republics of Azerbaijan and Armenia. Soon, they would have to send more troops to Romania and Yugoslavia to help preserve communism there. The file included another problem area that concerned the CIA: Lebanon and Syria were lining up their armies against each other from East Beirut to the edge of the Bekaa Valley. The Lebanese were committed to evicting the Syrians who controlled two-thirds of their territory. The Soviets were committed to supporting the Syrian's efforts to maintain their presence.

The Soviet's military involvement in so many regions at the same time had to be placing a huge burden on their economy. The report indicated this pressure was seriously threatening the control over their communist empire. He recalled the Soviet Army patrolling the streets of Riga with tanks and armored cars during the fall when he and Professor Bodynski were setting up the mission to smuggle Yegorov out of the Soviet Union. The Russians were trying to starve the Latvians to pressure them into backing off from their rebellion.

Food was extremely scarce. Latvians stood in long lines at markets every day attempting to buy enough food to feed their families. While the Russians were starving the Latvians, the Communist Party stores were well stocked with food and meats. Caviar and other delicacies were abundant for well connected Latvians and Russians. Latvians roaming the streets in search of food intensified their bitterness against the Russian leaders.

Shawn chuckled to himself and thought about Lester Fetor and some of the other U.S. Bobsled officials. They seemed to have the same attitude toward bobsled athletes. Nothing was too good for the officials. They took trips to Europe on the pretense of searching for sponsors, lavish dinners in French restaurants, fine wine and lots of women at their pleasure. Several companions were involved in drugs and Association money was used to finance their addiction. He hoped that Ron Harrison and the FBI would be successful in obtaining enough evidence to prosecute them.

The office door opened, startling Shawn. He turned around to see General Abbott walking up to him. The information he was reading in the files was so interesting that he hadn't realized the general had left the room.

"My God, do you know what time it is?"

"No. I got so involved with these files that I forgot all about the time. My stomach is growling. It must be way past lunch."

"It's nearly 5:30 p.m. In a few more minutes you will have completely missed Washington's wonderful rush hour."

"I've been in the middle of its rush hour and I'm happy to miss it," Shawn said. "I hate to move at a snail's pace and listen to all those car horns blowing. But Washington's beltway isn't as bad as New York City's rush hour. That's the real nightmare."

"Let's secure these files in the cabinet and you can continue reviewing them next week. Fred Unser is meeting with us Monday afternoon at two to discuss Yegorov's problem with his formula."

Shawn felt as if he had overloaded his mind with too much information. He needed to find some aspirin soon or his head would explode. After taking several minutes to relax he returned to his office and began reading reports again. He decided to quit after a few minutes.

The general looked in Shawn's office, "If you're still planning on going to Schenectady this weekend, you should leave now, or you might miss your flight."

"I didn't realize the time; I'd better get going right now. I have the late flight to Albany, but need to pack some things."

"Have a good weekend and tell your wife I was asking for her."

Shawn left the Pentagon and went back to his apartment. The weekend would give him time to think about the mission. Eventually he would have to give Angela some indication that he might be leaving the country for a while. She wouldn't be happy, so he would have to wait and tell her when she was in a good mood. He didn't want to upset her.

When he worked for the CIA previously, he would often disappear for weeks at a time doing undercover assignments and was unable to contact her. It was too great a risk and a simple phone call might blow his cover. The stress on Angela got so severe that she developed an ulcer. Finally, she convinced him to leave the CIA and return to the military.

When he agreed to go on the assignment to help smuggle Yegorov out of the Soviet Union, she was angry and warned him not to get too involved with the CIA. He could still hear her yelling, "They get you to do one little job and then there's another and another. Suddenly, you'll be in so deep it'll be hard to quit again and I'm not going to let you ruin my health."

The flight to Albany would give him time to develop a story that she would believe. Angela frustrated him sometimes, but he would never be happy without her. Her genuine concern for him was always a turn on.

The cab ride to National was quick and he rushed up to the ticket counter to get on the flight. The hour and ten-minute flight gave him time to think about the mission and some ideas about how to gently give the news to his wife.

CHAPTER 9

Albany, New York

Angela was waiting for Shawn when his plane finally landed at the Albany County Airport. The flight was nearly 30 minutes late due to a storm that had already pelted the Capital District with 6 inches of snow. They left the airport in Shawn's Blazer and drove to Schenectady.

He offered to take her to the River Road House restaurant just as she had expected. Shawn hated airline food and always wanted to stop at his favorite Italian restaurant whenever he arrived from out of town. There was a plethora of Italian restaurants in the Schenectady area, but Shawn liked the food at the River Road House better than the other places and it was only a few miles from home. They ate there so often that the waitresses no longer needed to give them a menu.

The restaurant would be busy with its normal Friday evening dinner crowd, so Shawn called ahead to reserve a table. When they arrived, they were pleased that a table in front of the fireplace was reserved for them. Angela liked the romantic atmosphere created by the burning logs.

"Why is it named the River Road House?" asked Angela.

"Just a short distance away is the Mohawk River and what was the original Erie Canal"

"I never knew that." replied Angela

"That's why you married me. Because I know these things," teased Shawn. "Want to share a bottle of wine?"

"Sure, that would be nice."

Shannon has great Italian wine. I like French wine better, but I don't think I would ever convince her to provide French wine in an Italian restaurant!"

"No," said Angela laughing, "and I don't think you should suggest it either."

They ate their meal and brought each other up to date on their activities of the past two weeks. Shawn was surprised that so much snow had accumulated on the ground during the time he had been away. He gave Angela an overview of his new job, being careful not to tell her that he would still be doing an occasional assignment with the CIA. She wasn't surprised when he told her about Olive Hanson's court-martial and that Lt. Col. Fowlkes and Col. Crosby would probably be forced to retire during the next several months.

As they were driving out of the parking lot he decided not to lie and told her the truth about the alloy formula and samples that Yegorov left in Riga.

"There is a strong possibility that I may have to go back to the Soviet Union." He looked at Angela to observe her reaction before continuing. "Boris is having a problem recalling the entire formula."

"I knew this was going to happen. Those damn people never leave you alone once they get their claws in you."

"Come on, that's not really true. This is too important. We can't take a chance that the Russians will get the information."

"Why does it have to be you?" Without waiting for an answer she said, "You need to think about this a little more. I really don't know what happened on your last trip, but I'm well aware that it wasn't exactly as smooth as the CIA predicted."

"There were some problems, but nothing that they couldn't work out if I needed to return for a few days." Shawn carefully avoided looking directly at her. He was certain that she knew he was dodging the issue.

"On the last trip you told me it would be for about five days and then you disappeared off the face of the earth for nearly six weeks. I can't stand the suspense and don't say it wasn't a major problem. And now if you return only a few months later, don't you think they'll know who you are and what you're doing there? They'll be real happy to see you again."

"Well, it's too early to worry about it. I'll know next week when I return to the Pentagon. There is a meeting scheduled for Tuesday with General Abbott, the CIA people and me. I'll have a better idea then about what needs to be done. In the meantime, don't discuss what I told you with anyone."

"Who do you think I'm going to tell? The girls at work? They could care less about the shit you get involved with." She moved away from him and looked straight ahead avoiding eye contact. The look on her face was much more expressive than anything she could say.

"I know, but it's important that you don't discuss this with anybody. People always tell their spouses and they tell someone they work with, on and on it goes. It can travel and you never know who might be listening."

"Yeah, I know. You've told me this a thousand times and I'm sick of hearing it. Don't talk to me."

After about twenty minutes Angela calmed down and moved closer to Shawn. She rested her head on his shoulder indicating that her mood had changed. He turned up the romantic music on the radio. They both enjoyed the soft music. The conversation with General Abbott nevertheless occupied his mind. The possibility of returning to the Soviet Union excited him.

The bright sun shining through the bedroom blinds woke Shawn early so he decided to get up and clean the snow from the driveway. He was nearly finished when Angela opened the door and yelled. "Someone murdered Nino Casatelli!" Angela shouted several times before Shawn turned off the snowblower. "It was just on the radio. Someone murdered Nino Casatelli! Oh my God, I hope these people aren't after you too."

"What people are you talking about?"

"You know what I'm talking about. I'll bet those people in the Mob who took control of the Association had something to do with this. I knew that sooner or later they would begin to take more and more control."

"Stop it. Unless you know something for sure don't be making accusations." He knew she was right, but didn't want her to get alarmed.

"While you were gone I got a strange phone call. Someone said he was from the Bobsled Association and wanted to just say hello. I forgot you were in Washington and said you were on the West Coast. When I asked who was calling, he hung up. I felt very uncomfortable at the time, but forgot to tell you. I don't trust these people in Lake Placid."

The news concerned him, she was right, even if he wouldn't admit it. Angela followed him inside and looked over his shoulder as he checked the Gazette's morning paper, but found nothing.

"They must have found the body early this morning, because the paper doesn't have the story. I'll call the Association office and find out what they know."

Shawn phoned the Bobsled Association in Lake Placid but nobody answered. This was strange, since Roger Ferris should have been working on Saturdays during the bobsled season. Curious to find out what was going on he decided to drive up to Lake Placid and do a bit of investigating. After breakfast he left, assuring Angela that he would be home before supper.

The previous twelve months for the Association had been one of chaos. Shortly after the 1988 Winter Olympics, when Lester and Nino had taken control of the Association, there had been nothing but problems. The Association's funding was nearly gone and it appeared to have been squandered by the numerous trips Lester and Nino took to Europe on the pretense of searching for sponsors. Athletes were receiving less and less support from the Association and Lester opposed any type of request from them for additional equipment or training. The athletes were forced to privately secure their own sponsors to raise money to help them prepare for the Olympics.

Rumors were flying around town that drugs were easily available from either Nino or Roger. The morale of the organization had reached an all time low and many of the talented athletes began to leave the sport in frustration. The large numbers of volunteer coaches like Shawn were gone now because Nino made it clear that he didn't want any help.

Normally the board of directors of most Olympic organizations would have prevented the corruption that the Bobsled Association was experiencing. Lester avoided that when he took control of the votes and selected directors who were connected to the Mafia.

When Shawn arrived at the office, he found the door locked and the lights off. That puzzled him. He drove to the bobsled track at Mount Van Hoevenberg hoping to visit with some of the athletes who were racing. The race was finished, but he located one of the bobsled athletes.

"What's the story with Nino?" asked Shawn.

"Who t'hell knows what's going on with this bunch of bastards? I hear that someone shot him at his house. No big loss if you ask me." He didn't know why the office was closed, but suspected that there were a lot of serious problems.

"Where's Roger?"

"Nobody has been able to locate Ferris all morning and the police suspect that his disappearance might be connected to Nino's death. In addition, nobody knows the whereabouts of John Chapadeau or Lester Fetor."

Several athletes shared stories about their own negative experiences with the officials. Whatever the outcome, he was certain it was mob-related. As Shawn returned to his SUV, he saw Ron Harrison drive into the parking lot. He asked Ron if he had heard about Nino.

"That's why I'm here." he replied. "Get in the car and let me bring you up to date with what's happening."

"It's good to see you," Shawn said. "It's been a long time. I think the last time I saw you was at the Olympics in Calgary."

"It was. You look great, Coach. You must be doing a lot of training, to stay in shape."

"Yeah, I keep at it. Last month I finally earned my sixth degree Black Belt in karate, a lotta hard work. So, what's the deal with our friend, Nino?"

"I want to hear about what you were doing last year before I tell you about Nino. I heard rumors that you were involved in some deal to help a Soviet coach defect. Is there any truth to that?"

Shawn briefed Ron about his trip to the Soviet Union with Professor Bodynski and how they helped smuggle Boris Yegorov out of the country. "Holy shit, that's really wild." The story astonished Ron.

"What happens now?" he asked.

"I don't know what the CIA and the Navy Department are planning to do with Boris now," lied Shawn.

"That's too bad." Ron said. "Are you still involved with the CIA?"

"Not right now. I have a new assignment with the Air Force in Washington that allows me to move around the country and I'm available if they need me. What's the scoop with Nino?"

"I don't know. I was in Lake Placid looking for Lester. The last time I saw him was in Scranton. When I finally got the word to pick him up for questioning, he disappeared. I know that Tony Robelotto's men are pressuring him, but I don't know why. I have a feeling it is drug related or has to do with money. What else would they have in common? Have you heard about Roger Ferris?"

"No. Who'd he rob?" Shawn asked, the sarcasm dripping.

"He won't be robbing anybody anymore. The State Police found his body in an Interstate rest stop. Cocaine overdose. Damn syringe was still in his arm. They think there's a connection between the two. I'm on my way to Lake George now."

"Do you mind if I tag along? Maybe we can help them put some of the pieces together. We know more about their activities than they do."

"Sure, damn, it's a wonder that they haven't tried to kill you. You're the only person in the Association who's made any serious effort to stop the corruption."

Shawn shook his head. "Lester and Nino once threatened to have my legs broken, but backed off. I know they'd like to get rid of me. That's why I was so happy when the FBI had put an undercover agent in the organization. I suspected it was you and was happy when I found out my thoughts were right."

"Thanks, Shawn. Glad you have so much confidence in me, well, let's get going. I want to head back to Philly after I finish talking with the State Police."

Shawn agreed and followed Ron south on the highway to the State Police station near Lake George. The trooper who discovered Roger's body recounted with the zone sergeant what they knew about the overdose.

"We estimated the package of cocaine had a street value of 50 grand or more. Rumors about drug trafficking among bobsled officials were common," the sergeant said. "When the troopers searched the van they discovered several discarded international airline travel schedules and used tickets. We'll use them to piece together Ferris's movements during the past several months."

"Who was doing most of the travel?" asked Ron.

"Most of the used ticket stubs were in Roger's name, but two had Lester's name."

"That's interesting," replied Ron. "FBI agents are looking for Lester to question him." Ron and Shawn supplied the two troopers with some inside background information to help their investigation. Shawn wanted desperately to help them put the corrupt officials in prison.

After meeting with the troopers, Shawn left to go home. He looked at his watch. It was nearly four p.m. There was no time to waste, because he and Angela had reservations at Mallozzi's Villa Italia at 6:30 p.m. They loved the Villa's pastries and always brought some home for Sunday morning. Later they planned to watch a movie at the local mall.

During the drive back he attempted to put the pieces of the two mysterious deaths together. Nothing added up. The answer continued to elude him, so to get the Association's problem off his mind he began to focus on his new job in Washington. Shawn looked forward to spending the evening with Angela. It would be a long time before he would be able to return to Schenectady, and they needed this time together.

He thought about the possibility of Angela occasionally coming to Washington. They could spend some time together and would give him the opportunity to show her all the historical sites.

Chapter 10

Washington, D.C.

Shawn was pleased that U.S. Air's early morning flight from Albany to the nation's Capital was on time. An airport shuttle took him to the Pentagon. On his desk was a message to call Fred Unser.

"Good morning Shawn." The cheery voice was General Abbott's secretary. Fred Unser called. He wants to meet with you tomorrow afternoon to discuss the new mission and some other items. He offered to drive here and meet you at your office."

This delighted Shawn. If Unser was willing to meet him in D.C. it must be important. Shawn didn't enjoy driving in the heavy, fast-pace traffic on I-495 to CIA Headquarters in Langley, VA.

Unser was the CIA's Director of Operations in Europe. He was a tall, thin, subtle man capable of doing whatever was necessary to accomplish a mission, including killing people. He was single and definitely married to his work. Shawn suspected that he was very lonely. Fred was a quiet man who dressed well, but never flashy.

Shawn liked him and often thought that they had similar personalities and beliefs. Unser had put together the plan to smuggle Boris out of the Soviet Union. Not an easy mission and it didn't go as smooth as the CIA had planned. Shawn shivered when he thought about it and how they had managed to keep one step ahead of the KGB. It was a trip he wasn't enthused about repeating.

When they met the next day, Fred discussed the CIA's plan to get Boris's documents out of the Soviet Union. He told Shawn that they would assign Amos Kelly, an agent who specialized in this type of operation, to work with Shawn. Unser gave Shawn a file with Kelly's background and special qualifications. Several things about Kelly caught Shawn's attention. He was a skydiver, had a Black Belt in martial arts, and was a skilled survivalist; qualifications comparable to his own.

An experienced skydiver who still did some parachuting, Shawn's logbook included 236 free-falls, many from altitudes higher than 10,000 feet. Survivalist training was another of his specialties. His uncle Irvin, a Mohawk Indian, spent summers during Shawn's teenage years teaching him how to survive in the wilderness when they traveled through the Adirondack Mountains on foot, searching for brook trout and wild berries. The military had refined his survival skills and he was confident that he could handle anything the CIA might have in mind.

"Do you plan to have somebody inside the Soviet Union to work with us?" Shawn asked, as he put the file back in front of Unser.

"Yes. Merrill Wojcik will be our contact for you and Kelly. Merrill has been working in the Soviet Union for several years as a journalist. He writes for the New York Times covering international news and is aware that we'll be sending two people there for a couple of days. We'll make all the necessary arrangements to get you and Kelly into the Soviet Union undetected, and then Wojcik will work with you there. He'll be your only contact and will help you leave the country."

"How do we get into and out of the country undetected? Or maybe I should ask, how do we get in and out, alive?"

"Those questions haven't been worked out yet. I have some of my people looking at ways to accomplish this," Fred said, as he looked away from Shawn with a concerned look on his face. He picked up a pipe from the desk and put it in his mouth without attempting to light it, then turned back to face Shawn. "I know the initial plan doesn't sound very practical, but it'll fall in place once we explore all the possibilities."

"I have all the confidence in the world that your people will come up with a practical plan," Shawn said, trying to look reassured. "But I have to admit I'm a little apprehensive."

"You should be," Fred replied. "Your survival will depend on you and Kelly being alert all the time. People who get too confident lose respect for danger, make mistakes and eventually get into trouble. I don't have to remind you that the punishment for spying is death. Usually they make sure it's not a pleasant way to die."

Unser and Shawn discussed several matters that needed to be completed. The plan required Kelly and Shawn to go to the Air Force base in Schenectady to train with the life support team. The preparation would not only help them get into peak physical shape, but would bring them up to date with current Air Force life support equipment. New technology created a lot of changes in survival training and both men needed to become proficient with the new apparatus.

The plan for Shawn to train at the air base in Schenectady was exciting. He knew the news would make Angela happy. Fred told him that Kelly was divorced, so he didn't mind staying at the Officer's Club for a few weeks while they took the refresher course.

Unser returned to CIA Headquarters in Langley and Shawn studied the files that General Abbott had given him the previous week. He had summarized several items that needed attention and prepared a background paper for the general. Special Operations included several departments and Shawn was assigned to Public Affairs. His qualifications for the assignment were excellent. While working in Schenectady he received recognition for his ability to create good publicity for the military.

Working at the Pentagon was much different than working in Schenectady. The pace was fast and the majority of the military people assigned there were more interested in advancing their careers than properly performing their jobs.

It amused Shawn to watch people trying to be in the right place at the right time. The most important rule was to always be politically correct. Captain Theresa Hamilton was the supervisor of Public Affairs at the Pentagon and it didn't take Shawn long to realize that she was working in this position for only one reason. Hamilton was looking for a better job to help advance her career.

She was a party animal and made sure that the proper people knew she could be very friendly. She was often seen late at night in bars with married officers who had influential positions. Her lack of qualifications really didn't matter, because Chief Kevin Robbins and Sergeant Stanley Staskowski really managed the Public Affairs section.

The chief and Staskowski were qualified and did an excellent job at overseeing and controlling public affairs for the Air Force at the Pentagon. The two men had a lot in common. They went to the same high school in Louisiana and joined the Air Force shortly after they graduated. The chief was in his mid-fifties, although he looked fifteen years older and Staskowski was ten years younger. They shared three vices that made them trusted buddies. Gambling, alcohol and fast women. Captain Hamilton didn't keep close tabs on their work, assuming that they would do whatever was necessary to get the job done.

She allowed them to travel around the country seeking assignments that needed their expertise. Not surprisingly, the searches often took them to areas such as Las Vegas or Reno. Suddenly, gambling casinos were being built all around the country giving them a lot of different places to schedule work assignments.

At a national conference for military members working in public affairs, Shawn once criticized the luxurious locations selected by the national leaders. He suggested that less expensive sites would allow the air bases to utilize their funding better to meet their goals.

During their first meeting in Washington, Robbins and Staskowski made it clear that Murphy shouldn't expect the type of special treatment he had previously received from the Air Force, when he was an Olympic coach. It was no surprise to Shawn that neither of them liked him.

Their attitude and jealousy made him laugh, reminding him of his old boss, Olive Hanson. One nice thing about the military was that sooner or later these types of people were usually exposed. It had taken nearly six years, but Olive was in the process of getting what she deserved. A common expression was, "What goes around, comes around," he thought.

Robbins and Staskowski had heard about Shawn's impeccable reputation. They were concerned that he might expose their budget abuse to their superiors. If the wrong people discovered that they used government funding to pay for their travel expenses, to gamble, they would be reassigned or worse, court-martialed.

Murphy knew he wouldn't be a part of their tight-knit group. He suspected that they would flood him with difficult work assignments and make sure that General Abbott was aware of any mistakes he made. They might even create some mistakes, just to put him in his place.

Another concern was his connection to the CIA and several high-ranking officers in the Air Force. Chief Robbins was worried that the general might put Murphy into a position to authenticate what he and Staskowski were doing, which would give the general documentation to remove them both from the military.

Shawn was unaware that Chief Robbins decided to devise a trap to get rid of Murphy before he could give the general damaging information. If his plan worked there would be no assignment with the CIA.

CIA Headquarters, Langley, VA

Fred Unser entered his office at CIA Headquarters. During the entire drive from the Pentagon to Langley, he thought about ways to smuggle Murphy and Kelly in and out of the Soviet Union. His mind kept coming up blank. This frustrated him because he usually worked these problems out easily. He looked at the messages on his desk then opened the file cabinet and pulled out several cases that had presented similar dilemmas. Three hours later he was still without an idea. Each case he studied presented different scenarios that were difficult to repeat. Frustrated, he put the files back and secured the cabinet. Too tired to return phone calls, he decided to go home and get a good night's sleep.

Fred drove back to his condominium in Chesapeake Beach. Within minutes he had taken off his clothing and stepped into the Jacuzzi. With the lights turned down, he relaxed in the warm water. The slurping noise of the return line normally annoyed him, but tonight he didn't hear anything. Hot water rushing through the spout onto his back did wonders for his tired body. He liked the Jacuzzi's temperature lower than most people, so he could stay in for long periods of time. Unable to concentrate any longer he dozed off. Nearly 20 minutes later he suddenly woke up. While asleep, he had been dreaming about Murphy and Kelly. The answer, crystal clear, had come to him.

Sitting on the edge of the Jacuzzi, he envisioned his plan. The CIA had been successful with similar types of clandestine entries into the Soviet Union and into Bulgaria. But this wasn't an elementary covert operation and couldn't involve military planes. There was only one person to call. A retired CIA agent he knew who was now working for an American commercial airline that flew cargo throughout Europe.

Fred shut the Jacuzzi off while making a mental note to send an agent to the Soviet Union to meet with a contact who would get them into the Soviet Union. He also needed the contact to help develop a strategy to get Murphy and Kelly out of the country alive. Feeling much better, he went to bed still thinking about the plan.

CHAPTER 11

Albany, New York

JOHN BRENNER WENT INTO THE EVIDENCE STORAGE room and signed for the package of cocaine that had been taken from Roger's van. He and his partner, Joe Knapik, received an early morning phone call from State Police investigators detailing Ferris's suspected overdose. When the forensic scientists arrived at the scene, they began to identify and itemize the evidence. Two other troopers from the crime lab had already dusted the van for fingerprints. The troopers left the gun where they found it to avoid any chance of contamination.

Brenner and Knapik used rubber gloves to protect the evidence and themselves. They found the loaded snub nosed .38 pistol under the driver's seat. Joe carefully removed the pistol, still inside its holster, from the springs. Duct tape had been used to secure the weapon up under the seat. He removed the bullets and placed them in a plastic bag. The used travel stubs, bag of works, plastic bag of cocaine, bullets, and gun were carefully placed in a steel container to be transported to the lab.

The items would be taken to the State Police Crime Laboratory in Albany. Rigid state police procedures regulated the way evidence had to be stored and released to forensic scientists for analysis. The data compiled would be used by the state police investigators to help solve the crime, and later as evidence for prosecution.

Plastic wrap and duct tape used to cover the cocaine brick would be tested and checked for fingerprints. Brenner was confident that he and Knapik would be able to produce enough evidence to help McHugh and Siler solve Ferris's mysterious death. He also suspected they would uncover additional evidence, which might help the FBI solve Nino Casatelli's murder.

"Joe, I'm taking the cocaine down to the drug testing room and have the fingerprint guys check it and the pistol for prints. I bet they'll discover that the gun has been used in some other crime that involved the mob."

"So what else is new?"

"You think? There has to be a connection between Ferris's overdose and the Casatelli murder. It's too much of a coincidence. The FBI is involved so you can be sure that both deaths are likely to be connected to the Mafia. Otherwise the FBI wouldn't have any reason to be investigating."

"While you're gone, I'm going upstairs to get the body fluids and the autopsy report. The pathologist should be finished with both by now."

Knapik went to the autopsy room and picked up the fluid samples and the report. On the way back to the lab he read the autopsy report. It confirmed that Ferris died of a massive overdose of cocaine. The pathologist wrote that Ferris had used cocaine for an extended period of time. He had several other puncture marks where he had injected drugs into his veins, in addition to popping it under the skin and snorting it through his nose. Brenner and Knapik were confident that Ferris had abused cocaine for years; however, they suspected the evidence would prove his consumption had escalated.

Knapik returned with the body fluids and began running tests on the blood and urine in a gas chromatograph. The instrument measured the exact level of cocaine and the purity of the drug.

The gas chromatograph had been used at the state police laboratory for a number of years. Its manufacturer had recently made several state-of-the-art improvements that permitted the crime lab to run sophisticated tests on all types of fluids. It would also identify amphetamines and any other drugs in the body. Amphetamines and other drugs would be easy to identify since they often stayed in the body for up to three or four days.

Joe put the blood and urine samples in the machine, and then opened the file on Ferris that he and Brenner had compiled. After about 20 minutes, the sound from the gas chromatograph caught his attention as it began printing the report. He turned sideways so he could read the computer printout as it came out of the machine and dropped to the floor. Their suspicions were right on the money!

Brenner carefully weighed the cocaine substance once again before removing a small trace to analyze. The weight matched the figures recorded on the evidence sheet when the people in the storeroom previously inventoried the package. It weighed 18.4 ounces, about half a kilo. The street value was high enough, he thought, for someone to murder even a close friend.

After recording the weight and measurements on his evidence sheet, John took the package down the hall to the fingerprint department.

The lab technician sprayed liquid nitrogen on the package to instantly freeze the glue on the duct tape. He then lifted the tape one section at a time, carefully placing each piece upside down on a strip of decontaminated plastic. The duct tape gave them a perfect set of fingerprints. The prints would be scanned into a computer and checked for identification.

Prints from the gun and other evidence would also be searched in the computer for identity and comparison. The mystery was unfolding as the evidence analysis neared completion.

Chapter 12

Las Vegas, NV

A MERICAN AIRLINES FLIGHT 825 LANDED AT 11:10 a.m. Shawn's plane was filled with people heading to the nation's largest computer convention. Nearly 1,000 military personnel and 9,000 civilians would be present. The conventioneers would spend four days attending a variety of seminars. Several hundred company representatives would provide information about new equipment and ideas for upgrading current equipment. The real purpose of the trade show was to sell state-of-the art products.

Captain Hamilton reluctantly approved Chief Robbins and Sergeant Staskowski's request on the condition that the entire Public Affairs staff attended. She was concerned that General Abbott would criticize her for letting the two men cover the convention themselves. The general had made it clear he didn't want that pair given any future assignments at resort hotels unless the work was genuinely military related. After receiving a complaint regarding drunken behavior during their last trip to a city that featured a casino, the general stated he wouldn't tolerate another such fiasco.

Robbins and Staskowski had given Hamilton a detailed proposal outlining the importance of generating positive publicity about military personnel who were computer experts. The promotion would give recruiters a boost in their efforts to attract high school students who were looking for careers in the computer marketplace. The media attention they would receive from attending the convention would give a strong message that Air Force training could prepare individuals for jobs in the civilian workplace. A high-paying position in the computer industry was a goal for many young

Americans. Robbins and Staskowski had assured her that Public Affairs at the Pentagon would be regarded as ingenious for creating the media blitz.

The chief suggested that they might even receive an award for the interest they would stimulate among students. He promised her that the benefits for recruiting would be enormous. Staskowski included a chart in their proposal, highlighting the financial value of the media coverage. The publicity meant thousands of dollars of free advertising and would be worth ten times the cost of their trip.

Hamilton also wanted to use the trip as a mini-vacation at the government's expense. She made arrangements to have one of her former boyfriends, an F-16 pilot, stay with her during the convention. She was a beautiful woman with blond hair, blue eyes and dark features, who devoted time every day to aerobics and fitness training. Many men were attracted to her and she had a small book full of names that she carried with her everywhere. Shawn suspected the Public Affairs team wouldn't see much of her during the trip.

He caught the shuttle from the airport to the Sands Hotel. The lobby was filled with people arriving for the convention and long lines of hotel guests were registering. It took almost an hour to get his key, after which he went to his room to unpack and take a shower. After checking his watch to see what time it was in Albany he decided to call Angela. She was happy that he had arrived without any problems and he assured her that he would call each evening.

Shawn joined Chief Robbins, Sergeant Staskowski, and Sergeant Molaine Taylor who were in the bar, taking advantage of happy hour. They were making plans for the evening and were not in a hurry to talk about how they would cover the first day of the convention. Which casinos to visit was their main concern.

Molaine amused him. She was rather tall and wore her hair in a style that didn't meet military regulations. She had worked at the Pentagon for nearly ten years in a variety of clerical jobs. Captain Hamilton had recently promoted Molaine to her current position to help her friend.

It was the right thing to do, she had explained, and attempted to convince everyone that she had helped Taylor because the promotion was deserving, and not because she was a friend. Those who had worked with Taylor knew she was totally incompetent and thought that it was a typical decision of Hamilton, who most considered to be dysfunctional.

"Have a seat, Murphy," Robbins said and pointed to the vacant chair at their table. "I've been thinking about what we should do. I want you to spend a couple of hours inside the convention hall and get a story about the work involved to set up this show. Interview some Air Force people who are attending and get their comments about what they expect to get out of the convention."

"Take Taylor with you so she can learn how to interview people." Staskowski turned to Robbins looking for approval.

"That's a good idea, Stanley," Robbins said.

Neither he nor Staskowski wanted Murphy or Taylor on the trip, but Captain Hamilton insisted that they take part because it would help build a good team relationship.

"I can't tell you'all how much I appreciate this," Molaine said, slurring her words. "I need to go upstairs and get my pad and pen. I'll be right back, Shawn."

She finished the rest of her drink and walked out of the bar. Staskowski waited until she was out of hearing distance and turned to Murphy.

"The chief and I know what your little game is all about and if you get out of hand we'll make life miserable for you. Do you understand?"

"Not really!" replied Shawn. "Why don't you educate me so there'll be no misunderstanding?"

"Look you wise ass, don't get smart with me. I've been at this game too long to have someone like you waltz into town and think you can take over our section."

Staskowski stood up and took the napkin holder and ashtray and put them on the empty table next to them. Shawn studied him trying to understand why he was clearing the table. Staskowski was 6 feet tall and appeared to be solid, but Shawn noticed that he had large love handles and his upper arms were slender, suggesting he was not in good physical shape.

Staskowski returned to the table and stared at Shawn for a moment. He hesitated before speaking again. "I understand that you gave General Abbott your opinion of the chief and me."

"He asked me questions and I gave him answers. Honest answers. That's my job. Should I have lied?" Shawn leaned forward and stared at Staskowski suggesting that he wasn't intimidated.

"I didn't trust you from the moment that I heard you were being assigned to our section," Staskowski's face was bright red indicating that he was about to lose control of his emotions.

"What's the real problem Stanley? Are you afraid that people might find out that you're a phony?"

"Yeah, I'll show you who's a phony. I think you're a spineless son-of-a-bitch. You told the old man that you didn't approve of what we were doing. If you don't like what we do, then tell us, unless you don't have the balls."

"Stanley, you didn't ask me, but I'll give you something to think about. First, he asked the question, not you, and he was told the truth. Second, you are way too small to talk to me this way."

Shawn stood up and stared menacingly into Staskowski's eyes. Neither the chief nor Staskowski said a word. Shawn leaned over towards them. "You two drunks are a disgrace to the military."

Shawn shook his head and bit his lip, then left for his room. He called Molaine to tell her that the plans to interview people had been canceled, then unpacked his luggage. When he was finished he laid on the bed thinking about his encounter with Robbins and Staskowski. Later, Captain Hamilton called and said she wanted to meet everyone in the lobby at eight in the morning to set up a schedule.

Curiosity finally got to Shawn, so he changed his clothes and went downstairs into the casino. A glass of dry red wine was just what he needed at the moment. Not too far from his seat at the bar he could see Robbins and Staskowski gambling at the dice table. When he finished the wine he left the bar and stood in the background watching the two men. Both appeared to be intoxicated. A short time later they added more charges to their credit cards.

He overheard Robbins tell Staskowski that he had lost more than $3,000 and if he didn't win the money back his wife would divorce him. It was common knowledge that his wife had warned him that she would leave him if he continued to gamble.

When the group met the next morning, Hamilton suggested that they go over to the side of the enormous lobby and sit around a large coffee table to make plans. Once everybody was comfortably seated, Sergeant Staskowski stood up and faced the group.

"I need to apologize to Sergeant Murphy," he said, looking down at Shawn. "Last night I called him a spineless son-of-a-bitch and I'm sorry for being so unprofessional."

"Thank you, Stanley," Shawn said. "That was kind of you." He assumed that the chief must have lectured him for being so stupid. Robbins was much calmer under pressure than Staskowski. Shawn was certain the chief had warned Stanley that threatening and calling him the obscene name wasn't very smart. Staskowski stared at Shawn and his neck began to redden.

"Do you have something else to say to me?" Stanley asked.

"I said, thank you. What else do you want me to say? You called me a filthy name and threatened me. Did I say anything that wasn't appropriate?"

"That's enough. Stop this right now. Stanley sit down." Captain Hamilton said, exasperated. "This is insane. We're here to build good relations with each other and this is what you do?"

"Okay, okay," Chief Robbins stood up and put his arm on Stanley's shoulder. "Relax everyone, before this gets out of hand. We need to get our priorities back on track."

Thereafter, the chief took control of the meeting and finished making plans for the day. They spent 20 minutes working on a strategy to gather all the information they would need during the next three days. Murphy and Taylor would work together, and the chief and Staskowski would work together. The captain would move back and forth between the two teams giving support as needed.

Hamilton reminded everyone that she wanted them to have a good time, then reiterated it was important that they needed to get along for the sake of the team. Choosing her words carefully, she repeated the general's warning about gambling or drinking excessively. She avoided looking at the group, but everybody knew she was talking about Robbins and Staskowski.

Shawn thought about the possibility of another assignment with the CIA. It couldn't come fast enough for him to get away from the dysfunctional people on the Public Affairs team.

Chapter 13

Riga, Latvia, USSR

ERRILL WOJCIK LOOKED OUT THE WINDOW OF his hotel room watching the Soviet pedestrians. He had left Moscow a day early because he needed the extra time to locate some quiet places to meet with the contact Fred Unser was sending to brief him. The room and furniture were typical of Soviet hotels, old and worn. It was evident that at one time, the Riga Hotel had been an elegant spot. It was sad how much it had deteriorated.

Merrill had already located the tiny microphone the KGB had placed in the ceiling. He was amused because CIA agents and people working for them would never discuss anything in the room that could tip off the KGB. The bug would help him to give the KGB data that would support his cover.

He continued looking out the window, studying the parked cars. The snow banks were piled high, making it difficult to find parking space and had forced him to park nearly two blocks from the hotel. This worried him because he couldn't check his car from the hotel window. The streets were covered with drifting snow driven by a bitter wind belting the entire northwest of the Soviet Union.

Merrill wasn't really sure why he was in Riga. Unser had sent him a message stating that an agent who worked in Romania would contact him there at the Riga Hotel on the afternoon of January 27th. Wojcik had lived in the Soviet Union for nearly twelve years, working as a news correspondent for the New York Times. An unpretentious person, he wore wire-rimmed spectacles and looked more like a country doctor than a reporter. Merrill took his job as a journalist seriously, and was respected by the other foreign correspondents. He was also very effective in his part-time capacity with the CIA, a role that was carefully concealed from the Times management. Working in the Soviet Union also benefited him, because he had relatives who were from the Ukraine region.

Barely 5 foot 8 inches tall, he was pale and gaunt. His ordinary appearance allowed him to blend in, and he was a master of both English and Russian, a skill required for CIA undercover agents. Merrill located and visited several relatives still living near Kiev when he first moved to the Soviet Union. Because of this, the KGB began interrogating them, but once they were satisfied that he was really just a foreign news correspondent, they stopped. Now he visited his relatives whenever he was in Ukraine. The visits helped solidify his cover. Nevertheless, he was certain that the KGB were watching him, and sometimes they assigned someone to tail him for weeks at a time. He was always careful not to do anything to make them suspicious.

Merrill did his best to write news stories that were both accurate and pleasing to Soviet authorities. His job as a correspondent would be limited if he upset them, and sometimes he found it difficult to not be honest. Merrill spent a lot of time in the two republics gathering information for the Times while keeping the CIA current with everything happening in that region. He was proficient in writing and speaking several Russian dialects, and his ability to blend in without alerting people was extremely important. His current assignment dealt with President Mikhail Gorbachev's policies in the republics of Armenia and Azerbaijan. The Soviet Union was split between the hard-liners and the Gorbachev backers. The political split was widening and becoming more intense as the Russian economy worsened.

It was nearly dinnertime when he heard a soft knock on his door, waking him from a nap. A young woman was standing at the door with a small attaché case. A thick, dark overcoat and a scarf covering her head were damp from the wet snow. Her beauty startled him and he couldn't help but stare, then he suddenly realized that he hadn't greeted her.

"Dohbriy vyeh-cher (Good evening)," Merrill said, as a smile began to form on his face.

"Spaseeba. (Thank you) Dohbriy vyeh-cher. My name is Natasha. I work as a news correspondent with the Chicago Tribune. I was told that you were staying here."

"Come in Natasha. I am delighted that you are here in Riga. Are you covering a news story?"

"Yes. I'm here on a special assignment," as she stepped inside and took off her coat and scarf, which Merrill hung on the tiny coat hook behind the door. "I have come to Riga to write about the shortage of food. The paper wants fresh stories about the large number of people waiting in lines to buy provisions. There have been plenty of stories about the lines, but they want something on what Latvian women are doing to help make the food go further."

"Perhaps I could help you with the story. I have several friends who live here in Riga. We could visit them tomorrow and you could see firsthand what they are doing to stay healthy with less food. Have you plans for dinner?"

"No. Could we dine and visit?"

"Yes. That would be nice."

"Have you been to the states in recent months?"

Merrill was acutely interested in her answers. He assumed that she was his contact, but because she was so young and attractive he was uncertain. The KGB frequently used young women to expose the identity of the CIA and other foreign agents. After a few drinks men often got careless and couldn't resist the women who deliberately wore revealing clothing. The CIA described them as high tech prostitutes who were experts at obtaining information from agents. They had the ability to listen and remember a tremendous amount of detail. Being skilled at gathering information from what they had heard, also knew that what wasn't said, was often just as important. They would go to extremes to obtain results, even go to bed with someone.

"No. I met my family in England last year for a holiday. Have you?" she asked, smiling as she crossed her legs and adjusted her skirt without making eye contact.

"No. I haven't been back in years," Merrill replied as he studied her. "My work here keeps me so busy that I don't even think about returning. All my close relatives are dead, so I don't have a reason to visit."

He estimated that she was in her late twenties, extremely young if she was in fact with the CIA. It wouldn't take long to find out.

"Let's find a restaurant and have dinner," he said.

"That's a good idea. I'm really starved. Can we eat here in the hotel?"

"If you insist, but I would rather go to a quaint little restaurant on the other side of the city," he said.

Merrill preferred to leave and then he would be able to tell if the KGB was following them when they took the subway. He intended to change routes several times making it difficult should they tail them.

"I'm comfortable wherever you choose," Natasha said, smiling at him and now making eye contact.

Merrill held her coat and she extended her arm so he could help her. She buttoned the garment and placed the scarf on her head to protect herself from the winds that were still blowing violently outside. They took the elevator down to the main lobby and walked up the street to the nearest subway entrance. Snow was now falling and accumulating on drifts built from the winds that had been blowing for days. People were struggling to get out of the bitter cold air.

Merrill led her down the subway entrance stairway and they stood on the platform waiting for the next train. The platform was crowded with people eager to get home, but nobody was within hearing distance. The concrete walls on both sides of the tracks were covered with thick frost and ice reminding travelers of the extreme bitter cold temperatures.

Taking a chance that she was his contact he made the first move. Leaning down he whispered, "It'll be better if we act as if we're a couple."

Natasha snuggled up close to Merrill and rested her head on his shoulder giving the appearance that they were on a date. He stood still, cautiously watching everyone waiting for the subway, wondering what she was planning to do when unexpectedly, she whispered into his ear.

"Fred Unser asked me to give you his regards," she said smiling, looking him in the eye.

"Just my luck!" he said quietly with a chuckle teasing her. "I knew it was too good to be true that a young beautiful woman would walk into my life."

"Please!" She laughed at his remark then got serious. "We need to go somewhere where we can talk without anyone observing us."

"I know just the place, but not until after dinner. Do you have a room at the hotel?"

"Yes. I have a room one floor down from you."

Within a few minutes the noisy subway train arrived, filling the entire area with fog-like vapor as the heat from the train mixed with the cold damp air. They got on, and sat near the back of the car until the train reached the center of the city, he gestured that they get off. They stood on the platform a short distance from each other to avoid the appearance that they were together. Another train going in the opposite direction arrived within minutes and they got on, carefully watching to see if any other person did the same.

They rode on the subway until everyone who got on the train with them had gotten off. Just to be safe they changed directions one more time and then found a restaurant that wasn't too crowded. Merrill was increasingly nervous about being discovered. He knew what would happen if his cover was blown.

CHAPTER 14

Piskarevsyoye Restaurant, Riga, Latvia

D URING DINNER, NATASHA REVEALED BORIS YEGOROV'S INABILITY to recall all of his formula. Merrill tested her by offering her a glass of wine. She declined and didn't suggest that he might enjoy a glass. This assured him that she was the contact who Fred Unser sent to meet with him.

"Yegorov claims that he wrote the formula on paper and hid the document with small samples of the alloy somewhere near Riga."

"Why doesn't he just tell us where and I'll locate it?"

"He doesn't trust anyone except somebody by the name of Shawn Murphy. Unser is worried about getting the formula and samples of the alloy out of the country without the Russians discovering what happened."

"I've never heard of Murphy." He picked up his glass and took a sip of water trying to avoid staring at her. It was difficult for him to keep his mind on Fred's mission. Her face and body reminded him of a movie actress that he always admired.

"Is he working over here?"

"No. I don't know very much about him, but he and some professor from Syracuse University were part of the plot to smuggle Yegorov out of the Soviet Union last year. He credits Murphy with saving his life and will trust nobody else."

"I guess I'm confused. What's my role?"

"Unser believes it would be too risky to send Murphy back here through the normal methods, so he plans to have him enter and leave the Soviet Union undetected. Murphy is a former agent who on occasion does assignments for the CIA. However, he's in the Air Force and does public affairs work for Special Operations at the Pentagon."

"Isn't it a little risky to have him working on this type of an assignment?"

"Fred Unser has tremendous confidence in him. He and the professor were very successful with the mission to get Yegorov out of the country."

"Getting in and out of the Soviet Union undetected is almost impossible," Merrill said, shaking his head, trying to imagine how this could be achieved.

"They'll also have one of our agents working with Murphy."

"I don't care about that. How does Unser plan to get the two of them in and out without being discovered? If they get caught, the publicity created by the hard-liners will be devastating."

"You can be sure Unser has thought this through very carefully and he does have a plan in place to get them into the country undetected. Let's pay for the dinner and go somewhere else to discuss this. I feel uncomfortable discussing this here."

They paid the waiter and left the restaurant. The walk back to the subway entrance was extremely difficult. The temperature continued to drop as darkness descended. The strong wind that had tormented Latvians for days made the wind-chill unbearable and continued creating high drifts. Deep snow on the sidewalks and the gusting wind prevented them from walking briskly and it took nearly 10 minutes to reach the subway. The temperature inside the subway entrance was only 38 degrees, but it was a godsend to be out of the brutal wind chill.

Merrill suggested that they get off the train where he had left his car and then drive to a remote location where they could talk. However, he wasn't sure about how much comfort because heaters in most Soviet autos were not very efficient and barely defrosted the windshields in the frigid cold.

They got off and trudged two blocks through the snow to Merrill's car. She waited while he cleaned the snow off the passenger side and unlocked the door. He pushed the door through the drift as he opened it for Natasha. He went behind the car and carefully brushed the snow away from the exhaust with his foot, then got inside the Soviet-built automobile. The motor started on the third try and he smiled as he thought about his decision to replace the Soviet battery with a more powerful one from the States.

"It'll take the car about 10 minutes to warm up. Let's talk here, because it will be too difficult to drive anywhere."

"I don't think I'll ever warm up," Natasha said and pulled her coat tighter around her body attempting to keep out the cold. "I need to have my head examined for doing this kind of work. I have a law degree and should use it to get a job in the Caribbean."

"I've gotten so used to the cold that I don't even think about it," Merrill rubbed his hands together briskly to get the circulation moving. He strained to see if anyone might be watching.

They sat in silence for the next five minutes waiting for the car to warm. When the heat indicator on the dashboard began to register, Merrill turned the fan to high and warm air began blowing into the car. Carefully, he checked through the windows that were partially cleared of snow and frost to see if anyone was outside. The dim streetlights gave the snow a peaceful appearance as it fell to the ground. It looked relaxing and harmless, so unlike current day Riga.

Natasha looked at him and studied his small thin face. The spectacles he wore made him look studious. Fred Unser was right. No one would ever guess he was working for the CIA. The lines on his face gave her the impression that he was in his mid-fifties.

"The heat feels great," Natasha opened her coat and leaned forward placing her hands in front of the vent.

"It always takes forever for these Soviet cars to warm up."

"I must give you the information from Fred and then we should not be seen together," she said. "I'll stay in Riga and do the story about the Latvian's struggle to get enough food to feed their families."

"I'll write down names and addresses of a couple of people I know that you can contact for information," he said. "Now tell me how Unser plans to get two people in and out of the Soviet Union undetected and how do I fit into the picture?"

Natasha spent the next several minutes explaining the CIA's plan.

When she finished, he shook his head slowly thinking about the bizarre plan. "Those men must be completely nuts to even think of doing this. Okay, that's how they get into the country. How do they get out?"

"That's not worked out yet. I suspect they'll have phony papers and take a commercial flight from Moscow. I really don't know what they are planning."

Let me tell you what Unser needs. He needs to have his head examined. That's what he needs. My God! Does he really think that they'll be able to survive this?" Merrill said and shook his head. "Where does he get these people?"

Natasha laughed. "Now, this is what we need from you," she said.

"Yeah, I know. You want me to catch them," he replied laughing.

"You're close."

"Fred Unser wants you to pin point a safe location. You'll pick them up and drive to the place where the papers are hidden. When Murphy finds the papers, you'll help them get out of the country."

They spent the next 20 minutes discussing the location Unser had suggested. Merrill would have to visit the area to pick a safe and secluded spot. Their equipment would be hidden and left behind. Merrill would be sent money and measurements to buy clothing for Murphy and Kelly to change into when they were ready to leave the country. He would drive them to the place where the papers were hidden, after which they would leave immediately for Moscow. The plan was for them to arrive in the middle of the night, then leave the next afternoon before anybody had a clue to what had happened.

Natasha finished her briefing and they were about to return to the hotel when Merrill noticed someone standing on the street corner.

"Don't turn your head. Someone is standing under the streetlight watching us. Move close to me and pretend we're lovers."

"Are you serious?"

"Yes. Let me hug you for a moment. Then we should kiss. He'll think we're having an affair and are sneaking some time to be together." He was thrilled at the opportunity to embrace her even if it was only to let someone else think they were lovers.

Natasha moved over and kissed him as he pulled her tightly with his arms. Unable to resist the temptation to glance sideways to see if someone was really standing there, she moved her eyes and saw a man staring at their car. She suspected it was because the snow was melting off the windows, making the car look suspicious. Merrill waited a couple of minutes then told her they should leave.

"If he follows us, you go to the hotel and I'll get back on the subway and return later. He'll think I'm married and have a girlfriend who is visiting me."

They got out of the car and walked in the opposite direction to see if the man would follow them. He said good bye to Natasha then left in a different direction, disappearing into the darkness.

The man didn't follow either of them. Not wanting to risk being discovered he took the subway a short distance then returned to the hotel. He knocked on her door to let her know he was back. Shortly after, Natasha went up to Merrill's room to get the names and addresses of the people to contact for her story. When he finished giving her the list they made plans to meet again in three weeks when Merrill would have the information for Unser.

Chapter 15

Las Vegas, NV

Chief Kevin Robbins intently studied the woman working as the pit boss at the dice table. Down nearly four grand he was desperate to change his luck. For the past two hours he observed how she always glanced around the table twice, checking bets before she passed the dice to a player. As soon as she handed the dice to the thrower, she would check the bets once more, then didn't look at them again until the dice had stopped. He put a single $500 chip on his bet and waited until she handed the dice to Staskowski. Both men had been playing craps at the table for nearly four hours and had consumed an enormous amount of free drinks provided by the casino. Staskowski's earlier luck had changed and now he was losing nearly as much as Robbins.

Staskowski put a $25 dollar chip down over the pass line, then took the dice from the pit boss. A six was needed to match his first throw. The dice flew across the table as he screamed, "Bring some luck for Mamma!"

The dice knocked against the wall, rolled, tumbled, and then came to a halt with two and five face up. Staskowski screamed at the attendant. She looked up at him, wondering why he was yelling. It confused her.

Robbins watched her carefully as he slid his $500 chip back over the pass line. Distracted by Staskowski's yelling, the pit boss didn't notice, but Staskowski noticed. She slid another $500 chip to Robbins to cover his even number bet.

Staskowski and Robbins had agreed earlier to this ruse. They believed the distractions would prevent anyone from noticing that they were cheating. And when other players were throwing the dice, they would place a

$25 chip on the table instead of betting a $500 chip. The agreement was to pool their money and split the winnings at the end of the night.

Staskowski lost his turn to throw, and it was several minutes until Chief Robbins' turn to throw again. He gulped his scotch and water, then grabbed the dice. He placed a $25 chip on pass and looked at Staskowski who placed a $500 chip on the table. He cupped his hands together and began to shake the dice. His face got bright red as he began yelling and shaking the dice in his hands over his head, attracting attention from around the casino.

"Come on baby! Seven come eleven! Baby needs a new pair of shoes!"

Robbins threw the dice and they bounced off the opposite wall rolling out on the table. A five and three. He picked up the dice and repeated the maneuver shouting, "Baby needs an eight."

The dice bounced off the soft wall and rolled to a stop with the numbers one and three showing. The pit boss picked up the dice and gave them to him to throw once again. This time a pair of snake eyes rolled out onto the table. On the third throw, number seven came out, making him an instant loser and Robbins screamed that the casino was using loaded dice.

While the attendant attempted to calm him down, Staskowski moved his bet back inches to the no pass bet where he would win. The attendant told Robbins that if he had another outburst he would be ejected. She pulled in the chips from the losers and then gave Staskowski a $500 chip. When Staskowski reached for the chip, two enormous men on both sides of him told him to pick up all of his chips and come with them. Staskowski began to argue. The man on his left flashed a badge and the other large man grabbed his arm.

"Get your hands off me, you jerk!" Staskowski's words were slurred. "I'm a general with the Pentagon and if you don't take your goddamn hands off me right now, I'll make sure that military personnel will never be allowed to stay at your hotel ever again."

Chief Robbins looked over to see what the commotion was about and before he could move, two men were next to him. One of the men told him he had to go with them. The four men didn't speak as they escorted Staskowski and Robbins to the casino's security office. Staskowski yelled the entire way. Another man, holding a VCR tape in his hand, was waiting for them at the security office. He shut the door behind them, then instructed the men to let go of Staskowski and Robbins.

"We have both of you on tape cheating."

The security chief placed a tape into a player and the screen clearly showed Staskowski moving his bet.

"Now let's look at you from another angle," the chief of security said, looking at Robbins as he changed tapes.

They watched the second tape that clearly showed Chief Robbins moving his bets.

"Cheating at a casino is a crime," the chief of security said, looking directly at Chief Robbins. "The type of crime you may be charged with is determined by the amount of money involved. In your case it will be a felony since the amount is more than a thousand dollars."

"Those tapes don't prove a thing," yelled Staskowski, red-faced and having difficulty sitting up in the chair.

"Keep your stupid mouth shut, Stanley," Chief Robbins stared at him for a moment and then turned to the Chief of Security. "Sir, I'm embarrassed for both of us. Stanley isn't a general. He is a senior master sergeant and I'm a chief master sergeant. We both work at the Pentagon and we're here to do a news story about military personnel attending the computer convention. We got a little intoxicated and when we lost so much money we stupidly thought we could cheat and get it back."

The security chief listened to Robbins relate his story then asked, "Is there an officer in your group who I can release you to?"

"Yes, sir. Captain Theresa Hamilton is registered at the hotel. She's in charge of our group."

The security chief called Hamilton and suggested that she come to his office. "Your captain wasn't too happy, but she's coming to get you. We'll need your identification and after she gets here I want both of you to complete a written statement admitting to your guilt. Neither of you will ever be permitted to enter another casino that we own."

"I can't thank you enough, partner," Robbins said. "We're both highly embarrassed and I can personally assure you that this will never happen again."

"Look Buster, I'm not your partner. For your information, we own many of the casinos in the United States. We'll send this information along with your photos to every casino in the country so they'll be alerted. It will never happen again in one of our casinos."

The young pilot watched as Theresa slammed the phone back down on the receiver. "What's going on doll?"

"Those two goddamn idiots that I'm blessed with got caught cheating and are being held in the hotel's security office until I can go down and get them. I swear to God, they've got to be the stupidest assholes I've ever known. And, I've known some dumb ones."

Hamilton picked her underwear up from the floor, continuing to curse as she dressed and adjusted her hair. It would be hell for her when she returned to the Pentagon. The general warned her about Kevin and Stanley when she asked permission to let them cover the story at the casino. And now her career might be damaged because she let them talk her into doing the assignment.

Good publicity, my ass, she thought. The Air Force would be lucky if this stayed out of the paper. There would be no way to hide this from the general. It wasn't worth the chance. She decided that when she got to the security office she would order both of them to check out and catch the first flight back to Washington. Shawn and Molaine could finish the stories. She suspected that they were doing all the reporting anyway. Kevin and Stanley needed to get counseling and that would be the first thing she would do when she returned. It was very obvious that both were addicted to gambling and alcohol.

The Pentagon – Several days later

Shawn walked into General Abbott's office. The general was on the phone and motioned for him to sit down. He was glad to be back from the computer convention in Las Vegas, but the general wouldn't be happy about what happened. Shawn suspected that in all probability he would transfer Hamilton, Robbins and Staskowski. Molaine Taylor would probably be the only one to remain with Public Affairs.

"Welcome back, Shawn." General Abbott got up to shake his hand. "I wasn't surprised at what came up in Vegas. I'd discussed the situation with Captain Hamilton and made it clear that I thought those two would be a problem, but she assured me they would behave and not do anything to embarrass us."

"They need professional help and unless they get it, they aren't going to change."

"You're absolutely right. Well, that's not why I asked you to meet with me. Fred Unser and I met while you were gone and I agreed to release you to help the CIA locate Yegorov's hidden documents."

"Good. I'm eager to get started. What was decided?"

"You can go to the Schenectady air base tomorrow. Fred and an agent named Amos Kelly will meet you there. They want to get started right away. You and Kelly will have to take a survival refresher course at the base and get up to speed with the new technology they use today."

"Do you know when they want us to go to the Soviet Union?"

"No. You know how the CIA is. They don't give out too much information for fear of jeopardizing the mission." The general watched Shawn for a moment then added, "You should think about what you are about to get involved with before making a commitment."

"I have been thinking about this for a long time and unless something drastic changes, I'm ready."

Shawn spent the rest of the day completing his unfinished assignments. Later, he met with Captain Hamilton and briefed her about his temporary transfer to the CIA. She was still upset about the ordeal in Vegas and appeared to be in a fog. He suspected that she wouldn't remember what he had briefed her about and that in a couple of days she would be calling the general to find out where he was working.

CHAPTER 16

Schenectady AFB, NY – January 14, 1990

SHAWN MURPHY AND AMOS KELLY MET WITH Fred Unser at the Schenectady Air Force Base's survival training office. Fred explained that they would spend the next two weeks at the base becoming familiar with new survival tactics. During training they would make several high-level parachute drops from an Air Force C-130 cargo plane. The first jump would be at 10,000 feet and the following jumps would increase in elevation until they were able to jump from 37,000 feet.

They would wear special gear to protect them and provide oxygen. Night vision goggles would be installed in their helmets so they could see the surface where they would be landing. The goggles provided near-daylight vision even in total darkness. Each dual imaging system cost the Air Force $6,000 and was guaranteed to give optimum, "fail-safe" visibility under the worst conditions.

The jump suits were designed to protect them from the extreme cold temperature they would encounter. Each suit contained an oxygen system designed to last eight minutes. Colonel Roger Stoddard and his deputy, Major Jason Pollack, would teach them how to use the new high tech equipment.

"Getting both of you into the Soviet Union is going to require a lot of work on your part," Unser said, poker-faced. "Stoddard and Pollack will spend as much time as you guys need to become familiar with the new equipment and the conditions of the free-falls."

"What's the plan?" asked Murphy. "I still don't know how we're getting into the Soviet Union or how we'll get back out."

Unser looked at them for several moments, with a strange expression on his face before he spoke. Suddenly it occurred to him that they didn't know the plan. "You and Kelly will fly to London in one of our planes. There you'll be put into the cargo bay of an American-owned commercial airliner. You'll have a supply of oxygen and special cold weather clothing. Another CIA agent will board the plane as a crew member and during the flight he'll join you in the cargo bay to help both of you with your equipment."

"How long will we be in the cargo area?" asked Kelly. His eyebrows raised as he thought about the conditions.

"I can't tell you that information at this time for security reasons. When you reach the target area both of you will free-fall from about 37,000 feet in the middle of the night. One of our undercover agents working in the Soviet Union will meet you. He'll have a change of clothing and iden- tification papers."

"Where in the Soviet Union?" Kelly asked.

"You won't know any more until you're in the air. We can't take a chance of having any part of the mission leaked outside. The final portion of the plan is in the works and I don't expect any problems. You'll be briefed on the plane about what to do on the ground and what the arrangements are for getting out of the Soviet Union. For the next two weeks I sug- gest that you learn as much as you can from Colonel Stoddard and Major Pollack. There's no question that your lives will depend on your knowledge and use of the survival equipment."

Stoddard picked up a rifle with an unusual looking scope and a silencer located on the end of the barrel and stepped forward.   "This is a German counter sniper rifle," he said. "The stock is made out of a synthetic material designed to withstand lots of abuse. The scope probably looks a little different to you. It's a Blitz scope and can be used in total darkness. It's state-of-the-art."

Stoddard handed the rifle to Kelly, picked up another one and gave it to Murphy. Shawn was surprised at how light it was. The automatic rifle's magazine held 30 rounds. The weapon was well built and perfectly balanced. He looked at the telescope, then put the rifle in place against his shoulder. Turning away from the group, he pointed the barrel in the direction of a window. Shawn was surprised at the clarity of the lens and wondered if he would be in a situation where he would have to use it. Obviously, Fred suspected they might, otherwise it wouldn't have a silencer mounted on the tip of the muzzle.

"Do you like the scope?" asked Pollack.

"I'm impressed that it's so clear," replied Shawn.

"This system's advanced electronics will enable you to view your target in complete darkness," Pollack said as he watched Shawn appraise the rifle. "The silencer will be helpful too."

"Maybe we should take Jason with us," Shawn joked. "He can watch our backs and keep the Soviets off us."

"What're you nuts? You couldn't pay me enough to do this."

"I think it would be a blast," Stoddard said. "Jumping out of a plane in the middle of the night at 37,000 feet has got to be a thrill."

"Everyone in this room needs to remember one thing," Fred interrupted. "This is top secret and we need to be aware about how we discuss anything relating to this mission. I realize everybody is joking, but let's not forget this is a very serious mission. Murphy, Kelly, and our agent in the Soviet Union will be in jeopardy if any information about this mission leaks."

"We understand, and it won't leave this room," Stoddard replied.

"Roger do you have a schedule for their training?" Unser asked.

"Yes. Jason and I arranged for them to start jumping tomorrow morning. Our C-130's fly a local mission each morning at eight.

"We'll also do some night jumps the following week to get them used to using the night vision goggles," Pollack said, picking up a helmet with the special night vision goggles and handing it to Unser.

Shawn felt uneasy being around Amos Kelly and watched him intently. Kelly was in his early forties, about 5 foot 10 inches tall and had a medium build, but was very muscular. His file indicated that he had worked for the CIA for nearly 12 years and that was all Shawn knew about him. The man was very quiet and slightly distant. Shawn decided to try to get to know Kelly, since they would be depending on each other during the mission.

They spent the morning learning how to use the jump suits and the oxygen attachment they'd need on the high altitude jumps. At 11:30 a.m. Kelly and Murphy left with Unser to eat lunch. Fred wanted to review several items with them in private before flying back to Langley.

They got into Unser's rental car and drove to a restaurant near the air base.

The Skyport was a popular eating place for those who worked at the base. A table at the end of the dining room, where it was quiet, was not being used so they sat there. There were only a few customers in the diner, but Shawn knew that it would be crowded by noontime. He used to eat there when he was assigned to the base's Public Affairs section.

"I don't have to remind both of you that this assignment is going to be extremely risky," Unser said. "Pay close attention to whatever Stoddard and Pollack tell you because you're going to need all the help you can get."

"What's the date for us to jump into the Soviet Union?" asked Kelly. "I don't have that information yet."

"The final plans are still being planed. Don't worry, you'll have enough time to get ready."

Unser stopped talking as the waitress walked to their table, then resumed when she left. "I told you earlier that you will fly to London. That's all I can tell you at this time. When we're ready, I'll give you your final briefing. I also plan to have someone with the Agency travel with you and give you the rest of the information while you're in the air."

"How many days do you expect us to be in the Soviet Union?" While waiting for Fred's answer Shawn studied Kelly who was looking out the window as if his mind were a thousand miles away.

"We don't expect it to be more than four days. If we're lucky, maybe we can get you out in half that time. Don't worry about that. I won't let you go until we've got all the pieces of the puzzle in place."

They finished lunch and returned to the base. Fred left and Shawn walked into the survival training building with Kelly. He still had a strange feeling about the man and wondered if Kelly was just a quiet person. Perhaps as they got to know each other the uneasy feelings would go away.

Several days later, Shawn arrived home after a grueling training session. He and Kelly had spent the entire day outside with Stoddard and Pollack. The weather in Schenectady was cold and dry. Their early morning skydives from the C-130 were now from an altitude of 21,000 feet. The jump was a rush for Shawn, but the sub-zero air temperature really tired him out.

After showering, he dried off and examined his muscular body for new black and blue marks. Stoddard was pushing extremely hard in preparing them for the mission. At 8:00 a.m. each morning the C-130 left the Schenectady Air Force Base and climbed to the jump altitude. Colonel Stoddard had made arrangements with a farmer in a rural area west of Schenectady in Princetown to let Murphy and Kelly land in his hayfield. The farm was located outside the small town with no other homes within a one-mile radius. The desolate area was ideal because they wouldn't attract any attention from local residents.

The rest of the day would include equipment training and target practice with the rifles. During the day they ate survival food that they carried with them.

Now that Shawn was home, he was looking forward to eating a nice steak with Angela when she arrived. He looked at his watch. It was nearly 6 p.m., so he decided to rest and read the paper until her arrival.

Just as he sat down to read the sports pages, the telephone rang. Ron Harrison wanted to meet with him later in the evening, to bring him up to date regarding the FBI's investigation. Ron agreed to meet Shawn at his home later so they could relax and not worry about other people listening. Shortly after, Shawn heard the garage door open and Angela's car entering.

"Hi! Can you give me a hand with the grocery bags?" Angela looked tired. "What a day. I haven't stopped since this morning."

"You poor thing," Shawn chided. "At least you were inside."

"I forgot about your training. You must have been cold."

"That's an understatement."

"Were there any messages on the answering machine?" she asked.

"No. Who were you expecting to call?"

Angela had a curious look on her face. "I thought someone might have called with some news about who killed Casatelli or if they had found Fetor. That man scares me. I think he's a psychopathic nut. I hope you stay away from him." She was worried about Shawn being around him and some of his friends who were now involved with the Bobsled Association.

Shawn sensed that it was upsetting Angela so he decided not to discuss anything about Lester. He wasn't happy about Lester being involved with the Mafia and was concerned for Angela's safety. There were too many stories about how the Mob often did horrible things to family members of adversaries. Hopefully, the State Police could keep a good watch on his home, but he also knew they couldn't watch her all the time. She commuted in the morning from their home to work and back in the evening. This was a dangerous time, the Mob often killed people in traffic.

He had to get this out of his mind. The TV was on so he sat in the rocker and watched news. There was nothing new about the Bobsled Association, but they ran some old footage about Casatelli and Ferris. The State Police gave no updates on the story and there was nothing about Lester. He wondered where Lester was hiding and if the Mob was really looking for him. If that was true he knew it wouldn't take them very long to find him.

CHAPTER 17

Schenectady, NY

SHAWN LOOKED UP AND NOTICED ANGELA WALKING back into the room. "Ron Harrison just called and I invited him over around eight to bring me up to date about the bobsled investigation. We should eat right away if that's okay with you."

"I don't mind. Why don't you invite him over for dinner?"

"I didn't think of it and I didn't ask where he was staying, so I can't call him. I should invite Amos Kelly over for dinner some evening. I want to get to know him better. He's such a strange person. I can't explain why, but I still feel uneasy when I'm with him."

"You don't talk very much about him. What's he like?"

"Strange! I haven't learned anything about him except what I read in his file. He's very quiet. At times he seems to be totally inconspicuous. You know the type. When there are three or four people in a room having normal conversation, you suddenly realize that he is sitting in the background listening and not taking part in the conversation."

"I would talk to him and force him to take part."

"It's not that easy. Whenever you ask him a question he'll answer, but he never offers any information. He's always in the background listening and staring. This strange behavior makes me uncomfortable."

"Has he ever said anything to indicate what he's thinking about?"

"No. I can't put my finger on it. He's friendly. I just don't have confidence in him as a team player."

"What does he look like?"

"Average build. My height, black tight curly hair, brown eyes, no personality. He's an expert at survival, martial arts, and is as comfortable jumping out of an airplane as a duck is in water. I just can't put my finger on what's so different."

"Maybe you just need to be around him a little longer. Why not invite him over for dinner this weekend? He's probably the type of person who needs a lot of time to feel comfortable around people when he meets them."

"No. That's not it. We have been with each other now for a week and he's still as distant as he was when I first met him. I'll invite him for dinner just to see what his reaction will be, but don't be surprised if he declines."

Angela put the groceries away and began preparing dinner. Shawn leaned back in his chair and watched his wife move around the kitchen. Thin streaks of gray were creeping into her dark black hair. She was very conscious of how her hair looked and he suspected that soon she would be going to a hairdresser to get rid of the gray. She often teased him because he still had a full head of dark brown hair with no signs of gray. Shawn coyly suggested it was the result of hard work and proper nutrition.

Leaning back in the soft chair, he thought about Ron and the investigation of the Mafia thugs who had taken control of the Bobsled Association. The FBI was working with the New York State police on the investigation. The police had once planned to arrest both Casatelli and Ferris. Their deaths had to be connected, Shawn thought and wondered if the FBI had any real evidence connecting the two. He was looking forward to visiting with Ron.

Angela finished preparing dinner. During the meal they discussed a project that she was developing at work. They had barely finished when Shawn noticed a car slowly pass by their home. He got up and looked out the window just as Ron pulled in the driveway. Angela made coffee and the two men visited and exchanged stories about their involvement at the 1988 Olympics in Calgary. When they finished their coffee, Angela excused herself and began cleaning up the kitchen.

Shawn took Ron on a quick tour of their home before they went up to the library on the second floor to chat alone. "How is the investigation going?" asked Shawn.

"We think we know who killed Nino and supplied Roger with the cocaine," He then reviewed the circumstances with Shawn, informing him of John Chapadeau's murder and the FBI's belief that Lester Fetor was probably responsible for the death of Nino and John.

Ron hesitated for a moment before he spoke. "We have reason to believe he might attempt to kill you. He might become frustrated if he can't kill you and attempt to kill your wife. It would be in her best interest if she could stay somewhere else for a couple of weeks while you are gone." He also revealed the FBI believed that Fetor was running from the Mob because they were trying to kill him for stealing money from them.

"This is so weird," Shawn said. "Who would ever expect this to happen to an Olympic organization?"

"We obtained a search warrant last week and checked every square inch of the Association's office in Lake Placid for evidence."

"Did you really think they were stupid enough to hide drugs there?"

"Not really. But they were stupid enough to keep their drug records on the Association's computer. We had our computer expert with us and within minutes he cracked their password. Ferris kept a record of all the drug activity in Lake Placid for Fetor and Casatelli. The State Police were getting the warrants ready to search their homes and arrest them when the killings began."

Ron and Shawn spent the next hour discussing the Association's investigation. Ron described how the FBI gathered an extraordinary amount of evidence from the computer. Their expert removed the hard drive and connected it to one of their laptop computers. They copied all the files located on the Association's hard drive. Within an hour the expert printed up the files and was able to retrieve data that somebody had previously erased.

"I met with the two forensic scientists at the State Police laboratory in Albany last week. They gave me a copy of Roger Ferris's autopsy. I don't know how he lived to be in his thirties. They found traces of so many drugs in his body, I can't remember them all. Let me read the list to you," Ron pulled out some papers from his pocket. "Amphetamine, nicotine, diethylopropion, meperidine, caffeine, PCP, methadone, diazepam, prazemem, thioridazine, and of course a healthy dose of cocaine."

"Damn! What did he do? Use any drug he could get his hands on?"

"Apparently he used just about anything."

"I would have expected you to find a large amount of alcohol in his blood."

"They didn't find any. I guess it leaves the body within a short period of time. Unless he had used booze within a few days it wouldn't show. It didn't seem to matter. Apparently he was happy with any type of drug."

"When will you arrest Lester?"

"As soon as we find him. We have a warrant for him, but we've lost track of him. I was following him in the Scranton area and suddenly he just disappeared." Ron shook his head. "I'm really worried that he might try to kill you. I've asked the state police to keep a sharp look out for strange cars near your home. He might be stupid enough to attempt something."

Ron excused himself and left to do some work in his hotel room. Later, Shawn thought about Ron's suggestion that Lester might harm his wife. That's one method everyone knew the Mafia used to get revenge. He began to get more concerned about her safety. Thoughts about Lester getting involved with the Bobsled Association filled his mind. Soon he drifted back to the story Lester told him about when he met Nino Casatelli at Lake Placid in 1985.

Nino was racing bobsleds and living in cheap rooming houses. He worked odd jobs during the evenings to pay his living expenses and hitch-hiked to the bobsled track each day to train with a group of bobsledders in the same financial position. Shawn believed that it was unlikely that Nino would ever become competitive enough to race on the international circuit.

Lester met him one night at the Hilton bar. Nino had just gotten off from his job as a dishwasher, and had boasted that he had all the athletic skills to qualify for the World Cup circuit. He gave Lester a sob story about his dream of becoming an Olympian, but being unable to purchase proper equipment or pay his living expenses.

Nino explained, "It's a given that I would make the Olympic Bobsled team if I had two new sleds and didn't have to work every night to support myself. The real problem is that the Association is managed so lousy there isn't any money left over for the athletes. We have to pay for our own sleds and living expenses. Unless you're in bed with the big shots they give you shit equipment that nobody wants."

Lester said he listened with interest, because he was looking for a way to get involved with an Olympic sport to set up a money-laundering business for Tony Robelotto, the head of a New York City organized crime family. Lester was confident that he would get into Nino's head by offering to put a little money in his pocket. Lester became a sponsor of the Association and also provided Nino a modest allowance each week for living expenses so he wouldn't have to work.

Lester located a business owned by an elderly couple that wanted to retire and relocate to Florida. It was perfect for his plan. The business was located on the main street in the center of Lake Placid and it attracted both local residents and tourists. The deal included a grocery and a liquor store.

Lester recalled that he couldn't use his name on the application for a New York State liquor license because of his connection to the Mafia and past criminal record, so he put the ownership in Nino's name to avoid any problems. He arranged for Nino to secure a mortgage from a Mafia controlled bank in New York City and then gave him enough money to purchase merchandise to open both stores.

After two years it was obvious that Nino wasn't Olympic material. But, by then, the Mafia was using the stores to launder money and giving Lester five percent of the gross. He had grown impatient and wanted to find a way to move larger amounts of cash.

Nino suggested to Lester that they meet with Roger Ferris, the Bobsled Association's executive director. Roger agreed to work with Lester, provided that he got paid with cash so the rest of the Association's officials wouldn't know of his relationship with Lester. His simple scheme to gain total control of the Bobsled Association impressed Lester.

Lester put up the money and they purchased memberships for a large group of friends who lived in the Scranton, Pennsylvania region. The cost for becoming a member of the association was only $20. Lester arranged for two buses with the new members with proxies to attend the annual meeting. The group along with Lester and Nino carried their proxy votes to the election and gained control of the Association before anyone realized their scheme.

Next, they called another meeting and changed the by-laws to prevent anyone else from doing the same thing. Finally, they kept Roger as the executive director, appointed Lester as the Olympic team manager, and Nino the Olympic coach. All were paid a hefty salary and given a liberal expense allowance.

Lester then arranged for John Chapadeau to become the Association's treasurer. Chapadeau owned his own accounting firm in New York City, and nearly all of his clients had business ties to the Mafia. The new position enabled Chapadeau to set up a system to help Lester launder money for the Mafia in Europe. He smiled when he thought about how clever he was to outsmart the Association and authorities by appointing himself as an Olympic team manager.

CHAPTER 18

Riga, Latvia, USSR – January 29, 1990

ERRILL WOJCIK PARKED HIS CAR IN THE village square and walked to the Riga Hotel. He liked the Riga. Built in the early 1900's, the hotel's original decor had remained unchanged.

In 1940, Russians invaded the three Baltic countries and occupied them ever since. Their original reason for conquering the three countries was to control the ports and prevent the Nazis from having access to the Soviet Union. Their seaports were on the Baltic Sea and were prime locations for the Germans to invade, to give them easy access to Russia's mainland from the northwest. Fearing this, the Russians destroyed an immense number of buildings in the Baltic countries. Churches, warehouses, and schools were demolished to prevent the Germans from using them if they were successful in an invasion.

During this period, Russian soldiers searched every home and confiscated any valuables. Family artifacts that had been handed down for centuries were taken. Graves were dug open and robbed. Many caskets were left exposed and the Russians arrested anybody who attempted to cover the exposed remains. The uncovered graves were a horrific message to the Latvians.

Jewelry and other valuables were loaded onto trains and sent back to Moscow. An outrageous number of Latvian men were arrested, and then were either shot or sent to Siberia, where they spent years in confinement doing hard labor. Some actually spent the rest of their lives there. Families were split up and were never able to see each other again.

Merrill sat in his hotel room and thought about the severe conditions the Latvians had struggled through. The Russians took control of the Riga Hotel and all other businesses when they initially occupied Latvia. Russian

Army officers used the hotel as their living quarters and exotic entertainment was often provided to amuse them. When originally built, the hotel was very prestigious. Only the elite and their distinguished guests could afford to stay there.

After the war, the hotel, as all businesses in the Baltic countries, became state-owned property. In the Soviet Union, the government controlled everything. Most of the hotel employees in important positions were Russian. Latvians held positions that the Russians believed were beneath them. It was easy to understand why the Latvians hated the Russians. Merrill felt pity as he watched Latvians walk with their heads down avoiding eye contact. They still feared the Russians.

Times were beginning to change, however, Russian soldiers were highly visible on the streets, armored cars and tanks were a common sight, a separatist movement had arisen in Latvia. Legal documents had been filed in the International Courts by Latvians requesting the papers that Stalin used in 1940 be declared illegal. This had created a resurgence of hope for Latvians.

Merrill looked at his watch. It was 3:37 p.m. Outside he could see darkness immersing the city. Natasha's charm and youth had overwhelmed him, but he still knew very little about her. In fact, he didn't even know her last name. Time seemed to move at a snail's pace as he waited for her. Captivated and unable to concentrate on his work, he wasted much of his time daydreaming about her. Every few minutes he would look up at the clock as the hour drew near.

She was meeting him to learn the location of the landing area for Murphy and Kelly, which she would pass on to Fred Unser. Merrill spent several days scouting places. It had been difficult to locate a place in a remote area that had a large field surrounded by trees. To further complicate matters, the field had to be located under airline routes from London to Moscow.

Merrill finally located a landing position near Rezekne, Latvia. The area was flat and surrounded by trees, and about the size of a football field. It was in a desolate section where there was very little traffic during the day yet only a short distance from a major highway connecting Moscow and Riga. There would be little activity late at night during February or March.

The region had only a small number of residents who survived by growing flowers that they sold in Riga during the summer and fall. The extreme cold kept everybody inside at night unless there was an emergency. Merrill was confident that Murphy and Kelly could land without being detected, drive to Sigulda in less than three hours, and then they could be on their way home. He wondered what kind of plan Unser had worked out for them to get out of the country.

Natasha called at 6 p.m. and told him she was registered at the hotel. They chatted for several minutes and then agreed to meet downstairs for dinner at 7:30 p.m. Merrill was extremely lonely. Talking with her was exciting and his mood skyrocketed as he thought about being with her again for the evening.

He took extra time to be certain that he looked his best. An average-looking man, he always dressed neatly with expensive shirts and fine tailored suits. After shaving extra close he put on his best suit. Carefully, he scrutinized himself in the mirror and brushed a little powder into the lines under his eyes, around his mouth, and upon his brow. Then he fixed his tie just so and combed his thinning hair, using a little water to get every strand into the right place. Satisfied that he was ready, he splashed on an ample amount of cologne and left the room.

Natasha was waiting for him in front of the hotel dining room. She smiled and surprised him by leaning forward to kiss him lightly on the cheek. He wondered if it was inspired by their profession. They wouldn't discuss any arrangements he had made while they were at the hotel. That conversation would take place when they were alone.

"You look lovely, Natasha." He touched her shoulder lightly and gazed at her face, reminding himself to keep the relationship professional. His knees felt weak as he admired her attractiveness.

"Thank you. You look ever so charming, just as I remembered from my last visit."

"I have made arrangements for us to be seated in front of the large window overlooking the park," Merrill said taking her arm, leading her into the dining room.

The table he reserved was located next to a large window allowing them to watch the snow falling outside. Young children were ice skating on a small pond across the street in the city park.

"Oh Merrill, the view is breathtaking," she said. "It's gorgeous. I can understand why you enjoy visiting here. The architecture of the buildings is so beautiful. I love the old designs."

"Riga was founded in the year 1202," he said. "I must take you for a ride around the city and show you the many different forms of architecture that have arisen during the past several centuries."

"I would enjoy that."

A waiter interrupted them to take their order. Merrill waited until he left, then leaned forward and whispered. "I'd like to order some wine to celebrate your return visit."

"Perhaps just a little."

"Which do you prefer? Dry or sweet?"

"Dry."

"I prefer dry also," he smiled as he made a hand gesture to the waiter.

They enjoyed their dinner and finished the bottle of dry red wine. Deciding to skip dessert, he put money on the table and they left the room. Merrill walked her to the lobby suggesting that they get their coats and meet near the front door in five minutes.

The cold air outside the hotel encouraged them to walk swiftly to the car. Merrill was thankful that he had managed to park in the village square just outside the hotel. He started the motor and apologized to her for having to sit in the cold car.

"I would rather be here in the cold than in some building where the KGB might be able to listen to our conversation," she said. Her eyes searched the area to see if anyone might be watching them.

"It won't take long for the motor to heat up. It isn't as cold as it was the last time we sat here."

"Don't worry about me; I'd rather be certain that nobody can hear us."

"How's Fred Unser?"

"He's okay. He sends his regards with the usual reminder to be careful."

"I know. Fred is always concerned about us. I've never known anyone so compassionate, yet able to do whatever it takes to get the job done. I haven't seen him in years."

The car finally began to warm up. Merrill decided to not drive to another location and take a chance of losing the excellent parking spot near the hotel. The instructions that he wrote were in the form of a news story, to prevent the KGB from learning the real truth should they search Natasha.

The story was about peasants who lived in the rural section of Latvia. It explained how they had survived by planting and growing flowers, potatoes, oats and barley. The news report was very positive and wouldn't draw any suspicion from Russian authorities if they discovered it. It would also provide her with a real human life story that the paper could publish as filler for some future edition.

Merrill cleverly included several latitude and longitude positions. Each position referred to various parts of the region that were written in the story. One position described a stone farmhouse that was built in the fifteenth century. Another gave the exact location of a building that dated back to the twelfth century. Merrill identified a large potato field that would be used to grow an enormous crop in the spring.

This information wouldn't be used in a newspaper; however, it would give Unser the exact spot for Murphy and Kelly to land. On a separate piece of paper he gave Natasha the specific location in code. He warned her to keep the small piece of paper in her pocket and to destroy it once she had it memorized.

"We can return to the hotel," Merrill said, disappointed that their business was finished. "Perhaps we can have a glass of wine before we retire for the evening?"

"Yes. That would be nice."

The frigid air nearly numbed them as they hurried across the village square to the hotel. A steady wind made the short walk nearly unbearable. Once inside the hotel lobby they felt the rush of heat pouring out from an ancient steam heater. They walked into the bar, where a small band was playing, and sat at a table in a corner of the room. Merrill chose the table because the area was dim, and they wouldn't attract too much attention.

The wine warmed them and helped them to relax. They talked about where they had grown up in the states and finally Merrill built up enough courage to ask her to dance. Slowly, they moved around the room holding each other tightly as the band played a popular Russian waltz. Finally, Natasha rested her head on his shoulder molding her body against him. The band played several slow waltzes and he wished the night would last forever.

Merrill noticed the smoke-filled room was occupied primarily with Russian Army officers. It was amusing to watch them and their companions. He suspected some were with their wives, most of which were excessively overweight, and a large number were with their mistresses. It was easy to determine who the girlfriends were. They were 20 years younger, slender and very attractive. Merrill explained that it was common in the Soviet Union for men to have a lover. Natasha remarked that it was sad that the majority of the women there were obese and they looked very unhappy.

They enjoyed a second glass of wine and then danced together again while the band played several more waltzes. The soft music and the wine made them both feel mellow. It was nearly 10 p.m. when Natasha looked at her watch and reluctantly suggested that it was getting late. She reminded him that she needed to get up early and take the train to Moscow to catch her flight to the states. Neither spoke on the way up to her room. He wondered if he would ever see her again.

When they reached Natasha's room he turned to face her and smiled as he looked into her blue eyes. Her long black hair made a striking contrast against her smooth white skin. The stirring was involuntary but strong. After telling her how much he enjoyed the evening, Natasha leaned forward and kissed him lightly on his mouth. They embraced for several minutes until she moved back slightly.

She smiled and squeezed his hand, "Would you like to come in for a few minutes?"

Surprised, Merrill took the key from her and unlocked the door. Once inside Natasha turned on a small lamp and went into the bathroom. He was filled with mixed emotions, unable to determine if she invited him in to be polite or if perhaps she might be attracted to him. When she walked out of the bathroom, he could not believe his eyes. She had brushed her hair and removed the bulky sweater, revealing a white silk blouse with the top four buttons undone.

"You're so quiet. Are you disappointed?"

"No. I'm overwhelmed," he said, reaching out to touch her, but she moved away out of his reach. She smiled and shut off the lamp. He watched her move toward him in the dark. Neither spoke.

For several minutes, Merrill held her close, stroking her back. He worried about getting involved with a woman working with him. The fact that he knew very little about her began to trouble him and suddenly he moved back at arm's length, holding her face in his hands.

"Natasha, do you think we should be doing this?"

She put her finger on his lips then kissed him passionately. He lost all ability to rationalize as she began undoing the buttons on his shirt. When she began to run her fingers over his chest he no longer cared what was right or wrong. Merrill caressed her neck and shoulders then let his hand slide below her back.

"You feel so good," he whispered.

She wrapped her arms around him drawing him closer. Her boldness startled him. Moving back slightly, she finished unbuttoning his shirt. While she stroked his chest, he awkwardly undid the rest of the buttons on her blouse. They helped each other undress and then moved onto the bed. He held her tightly as they kissed passionately. Merrill was oblivious to everything else during the next several minutes.

It was nearly midnight when she woke him. They embraced and kissed and then he went to his room. He tossed and turned reliving the experience in his mind until he fell asleep exhausted.

Chapter 19

Schenectady AFB, NY

S HAWN STUDIED THE TINY COMPUTER CHIP USED to create and send infrared signals. A miniature strobe light powered by a nine-volt battery produced the signal, which was strong enough to be picked up by a satellite orbiting the earth. Major Pollack spent nearly an hour showing Murphy and Kelly how to program the computer chip to change the signal. It would be pre-programmed and used only in the event of an emergency during their escape from the Soviet Union. The computer transmitted long or short infrared signals. They could use Morse code or create their own code to send messages.

"Each of you take one of these and make your own program," Pollack said and handed them a nine-volt battery and a miniature signal device with the computer chip. "You can change the signal from a long to a short by simply using a dime."

The major took a dime out of his pocket and showed them how to change the signal. Once the code had been set, the miniature device would transmit a pre-set message through the infrared signal by attaching a nine-volt battery. The CIA would make arrangements to have the information sent to their rescue team in Finland the moment the satellite received the signal. Pollack reminded them that it should be used only in a case of life or death.

"Keep in mind that if our satellite can read this, the Soviets can also read it," Pollack said soberly. "Within minutes they'll also know your location. They might not understand the code that you send, but it doesn't matter. They will know exactly where you are. Don't use this unless you really have a serious problem and you're close to the border where we can get help to you."

"Why do we need to be near a border?" Kelly asked.

"You need to be near whatever border you plan to cross to escape. If you're too far from the border, the Soviets will get you before the CIA."

"I didn't know the plan to get out undetected included crossing a border." "I don't know what the plan is, Amos. My assignment is to provide both of you with the necessary equipment to help you survive and escape regardless of the plan. Even the best thought out plans can go bad. Nobody can predict exactly what will happen and you need to be prepared."

"I'll feel more comfortable having some way to contact our people," Shawn said. "I went through this once before with Professor Bodynski when we were in the Soviet Union being pursued by the KGB. There was no way we could get a message to our side. That's a terrible feeling. I'll feel much better having the infrared signal."

"Who's Professor Bodynski?" Kelly asked.

"The technical director of the United States Bobsled Association who went to the Soviet Union on a sports cultural exchange with me last year."

"Oh yeah, I remember reading about you two in the Agency's file. As I recall you got chased out of the Soviet Union."

Shawn studied Kelly intently as he spoke and didn't reply to his sly remark. He had a strange feeling that Kelly was either jealous or perhaps bitter that he and Bodynski were involved with the CIA's assignment to get Boris Yegorov out of the Soviet Union. This not only confused Shawn, but it concerned him that Kelly would be discussing it openly in front of Major Pollack. He made a mental note to discuss the incident with Fred Unser when they were alone.

"If you think you're going to be captured, try to get rid of the computer chip so the Soviets can't send the signal and tempt the CIA to try an impossible rescue. It would create an international incident. The Soviets would use this to promote their assertions that the United States is increasing their efforts to spy on them."

"They are!" Kelly stated and chuckled.

"I don't think we need to get into this discussion," said Shawn, who was annoyed by Kelly's attitude.

"Are there any more questions about the infrared signal device?" asked Pollack. Neither Shawn or Amos spoke. "Good, let's look at the Global Position System. You will hear it referred to as a GPS. All of our airplanes and ships use the GPS to determine their exact location. It also sends a signal to an orbiting satellite. The satellite will return a signal to the GPS telling you exactly where you are located."

Major Pollack held up a hand-sized GPS that they would carry with them, then handed it to Shawn so he could study it. He was amazed that it could provide them with the type of information they would need. About the size of a pack of cigarettes, it was small enough to fit inside a jump suit pocket and only weighed about ten ounces. The case was made of hard plastic, making it quite durable in the event he had a rough landing after jumping from the plane.

"How long will the battery last?" asked Shawn.

"We'll install a new one just before you leave. It should last for several months unless you forget to turn it off. If left on, it will last about a week. Long enough to meet your needs."

Major Pollack finished their Global Position System training and reminded them that in the morning they would be jumping from 30,000 feet. Before they left the base, Shawn invited Kelly to have dinner with him and Angela, but Amos said he had other plans and left without an explanation. His indifference and unfriendly attitude disturbed Shawn. On the way home, he thought about some of Kelly's remarks during the past several days.

When he got home, he called Fred Unser. They discussed Kelly's attitude and Fred advised Shawn to continue the training and avoid any conversation about their work in the presence of Stoddard or Pollack. If the opportunity arose, he suggested that Shawn should engage Kelly in a discussion about the United States spying on the Soviet Union. Fred was interested to learn more about Kelly's attitude of the CIA's policy and was also disturbed that he spoke freely in front of others. He told Shawn that he would do an internal investigation to learn why Kelly had become so outspoken, or if indeed he had a prior history of this.

Chapter 20

Boston, Massachusetts

Lester got off the bus, hailed a taxi and gave the driver instructions to take him to the Days Inn near Logan Airport. He decided not to fly from Hartford since the cost for the short flight was extremely expensive. The flight from Boston to Brussels was scheduled to leave early the next morning and he would take a shuttle from the hotel to the airport. His plan was to eat a quiet dinner in his room and watch TV.

He didn't want to chance being located by Tony Robelotto's people. In Hartford he purchased a small amount of clothing to take to Europe and planned to buy more once he arrived in Casablanca.

Thoughts of the future occupied his mind. In a couple of days he would withdraw a million dollars from his Swiss accounts and disappear. He planned to rest for several months, and then in time, maybe start a business, earn a modest income to keep from being bored. Perhaps a small tourist hotel with a nightclub would be possible. This had always been a dream, but he was in no hurry. Enjoy the good life and look around for the opportunity to buy some property at a good price, he thought.

If anyone asked about his background he would tell them that his wife died recently, he was distraught and had to get away. Tony Robelotto would never suspect him to be in Casablanca, and he would be close enough to Switzerland in case he needed to conduct bank business. Yes, that would be a great place for him to live.

The taxi arrived at the hotel and Lester went inside to register. He took his suitcase and went to his room on the fourth floor. Inside he put the luggage on the bed and called the front desk to order dinner. Steak and a bottle of fine French wine. Tonight he would celebrate.

He hung up the phone and without unpacking laid down on the bed. Normally, no one beats the Mafia out of money, but he had! His three Swiss bank accounts contained over four million dollars. The majority came from the cash he had skimmed off Tony Robelotto. The rest was from the Bobsled Association.

He snickered as he thought about bobsled association's president, Wilbur Hippenbecker. The man didn't have a clue. Lester suspected that John Chapadeau also had taken his share of money from the Association. Wilbur worked for a finance company in Rochester, New York, but had no control of the Olympic funding or the private donations the Association received. Lester and John didn't agree on most things; however, they did agree to keep Wilbur in the dark when it came to finances. Whenever someone needed money, John's typical response was that the Association was broke, and Lester had been successful in forcing out the majority of the board of directors and replacing them with his cronies.

Once he had absolute control, he began to change the Association's by-laws. The first change was to give himself the authority to spend up to $30,000 without board approval. This allowed him to travel to Europe whenever he needed to deposit cash for Robelotto. Usually, he took his young mistress and showered her with expensive gifts that were charged on the Association's credit card. Then he would give the receipts to Wilbur and tell him the gifts were for potential sponsors. Wilbur would simply shrug it off, but John knew better. He also knew better than to question Lester.

There was a knock on the door.

"Who is it?" asked Lester.

"Room service. I have your dinner Mr. Fetor."

"Just a second." Lester got up and looked through the security opening then unlocked the door.

The waiter wheeled a cart with Lester's dinner into the room. "Just leave the cart right there and I will take care of it."

Lester pointed to a spot in front of the television set, tipped the attendant and closed the door after he left. He picked up the bottle of French wine, removed the cork and poured a glass. Holding the wine up high in the air; he made a mock toast to Nino and John.

"You bastards got just what you deserved for screwing up my life."

He drank it in one gulp and poured another.

"This one is for you Robelotto. You lousy bastard."

Too bad he couldn't shoot Tony, he thought. But it would be just about impossible and, in any case, wasn't worth the risk. He had beaten the

Mafia Don at his own game. That was good enough. This was going to be a great night. As the past few week's events drifted through his mind, he snickered and poured another glass of wine.

Nino and John turned against him and squealed to Tony, but he had gotten his revenge. He laughed when he thought about shooting Nino, and blowing up John's car with him in it. Yeah, he'd gotten his revenge… and Tony's money. Tomorrow he would be in Europe and in a few days… Casablanca!

Lester finished eating his steak and drank the remaining wine. Why not cap the evening with some real fun he thought. He grabbed his coat and left the room to get another bottle of wine at a liquor store down the street from the hotel. Rather than use the elevator, he used the stairs in case he had been followed. The stairs entered the lobby across from the elevator and he could observe if anyone might be watching.

The lobby was empty and the clerk paid no attention as he walked quietly to the door leading outside. Deciding that one bottle might not be enough, he purchased two at the liquor store and left. Standing outside the building he watched three prostitutes who were working the corner. Maybe I should have a little fun on my last night in the States, he thought. Moments later a car stopped and after a brief conversation one girl left with the driver. He walked over to them.

"Hi, what's happening?"

"Depends on what you want to happen," said the blonde, who looked as though she might be a teenager. "Are you looking for some company?"

"How much?"

"How much do you have?" she replied, laughing. "Do you want someone for a short visit or for the night?"

"What do you charge for the whole night?"

"Four-hundred, but nothin' kinky. Where ya staying?"

"Right here at the hotel." Lester pointed behind them.

"You have the cash?"

Lester pulled out his wad of one-hundred dollar bills and thumbed through it to impress her then put it back in his pocket. "Yeah, honey I've got the cash. Are you interested?"

She squeezed the back of his arm and smiled. "I'm always interested in big guys like you. What's your name sweetie?"

"You don't need that, just be at my room in 10 minutes." Lester gave her his room number then left. The lobby was still empty when he returned so he used the elevator. When he reached his floor he held his finger on the button prepared to shut the door if someone was waiting outside the elevator. The hallway was empty so he went to his room. 10 minutes later there was a knock on his door.

She smiled and rubbed his crotch as she entered the room. Lester looked out into the empty hallway then shut the door and turned the lock. She took off her coat, revealing a short dress that was low cut and showed off her cleavage. This was a perfect way to celebrate his last night in the United States, Lester thought. He opened the bottle of wine and poured two glasses.

"I need to get paid first."

Lester laughed. "Do I look like the kind of a man who'd take advantage of a pretty lady like you? If you're as good as I think, there'll be a bonus in the morning."

Lester gave her four one hundred-dollar bills.

"What's your name?"

"Maxine, but everyone calls me Max. I don't have a last name. And don't worry about how good I am. I'll make you feel so good that you'll wish you could stay with me for a month!"

Lester laughed again. "We'll see about that," he said as he handed her the glass of wine. "Take off your clothes so I can see what you look like."

"Slow down big fella. Let's go slowly so this'll last all night. I want that bonus."

"You will if you can do what I want."

"Remember, nothing kinky."

"Who cares about kinky," he said as he pulled her to him and began unbuttoning her dress. "I just want to get laid, Max." Up close in the light she didn't look quite so young. She looked much older than he thought earlier while under the streetlight, probably because of a hard life and drugs.

Max put her arms around him, caressed his back then pressed her lips on his neck. Her wet kisses sent shudders through his body in anticipation of what would follow. She moved back, stepped out of her dress and stood nude in front of him, waiting for his approval. He smiled as he moved his hands over her breasts, then quickly undressed.

They got on the queen size bed and suddenly without warning Lester jumped atop her and forced her legs apart, ramming himself into her. Like a teenage boy rather than the middle-aged man he was, Lester's thrusts were frantic. He was consumed by his excitement and within minutes he spent himself. Feeling drowsy from too much wine, Lester curled up alongside her and dozed off.

Thirty minutes later when Maxine moved to get up, Lester awoke instantly. He didn't trust her and suspected that she might rob him and slip out of the room.

"Where are you going?" he asked.

"Relax, sweetie. I'm just going to the bathroom."

She shut the door, and he listened to find out if she was telling the truth. The toilet flushed and in a minute or so, she was back in bed with him. After several moments he began to fondle her breasts and she pushed his hands away. Lester was furious and grabbed her breast and began to twist her nipple.

"Stop it, you bastard. That hurts."

"You little slut. You agreed to sleep all night and that includes sex whenever I want it."

"You got what you paid for, and I agreed to only spend the rest of the night to keep you company. That doesn't mean that you get to screw me all night."

Max moved to get out of the bed, Lester grabbed her and threw her back down on the mattress. She slapped him in the face and slid off the bed, surprising Lester.

"Get a life you asshole!" she screamed as she grabbed her clothing off the floor. Max pulled her dress down over her head, picked up her coat and headed for the door.

"You aren't going anywhere, you little slut."

Lester got out of bed and grabbed her by the hair, pulling her back from the door. His temper was out of control and he punched her cheek with a tremendous force knocking her backward into the dresser. Holding her by the hair, he slapped her face several times then ripped off her dress.

Blood began flowing from her nose and mouth as she slid down on the carpet where she laid unconscious. In a rage, Lester picked up her dress and started tearing it into shreds. Then, in a fit of temper he looked at her then leaned down and punched the side of her face several times. Her body was a mess. Blood covered the carpet and her face was swollen to the point that she would be unrecognizable to friends.

If he stayed he would risk getting caught so he had to get out of there fast. He picked her up and placed her on the bed face down so she wouldn't choke to death from the blood or her vomit. Using a strip of cloth from her dress, he tied her onto the bed, her wrists secured to the back bedposts and her ankles to the front bedposts. He stuffed a washcloth in her mouth and wrapped it securely with one of the strips of cloth from her dress.

Satisfied that she was secure he went into her purse and took the $400 he'd given her earlier as well as another $300. She began to mumble, so he slapped her head several times until she was unconscious again. He gulped down the rest of the wine and stared at her motionless, nude body with her legs spread-eagled. Laughing, he jumped atop her and with a vengeance, raped her from behind.

It took only a couple of minutes to pack his things. He opened the door slowly and checked to see if anybody was outside. The hallway was empty so he put the "DO NOT DISTURB" sign on the doorknob and shut the door. At the stair entrance on the first floor he opened the door slowly, watching to be sure the desk clerk didn't see him. Nobody was at the front desk so he left the hotel and hailed a cab.

On the way to Logan Airport he noticed that there were no hookers standing on the street corner. Hazards of the job, these sluts expect a little rough treatment. That's why they get the big bucks, he thought. It was 4:15 a.m. He would get an early breakfast and wait for his flight. By the time the cleaning people in the hotel found the whore, he would be out over the middle of the Atlantic.

Lester walked into the terminal at Logan and purchased a first class ticket to Brussels. His flight was at 7:10 a.m. which gave him time to relax and read the paper while he ate breakfast.

Turning to the sports page he located a small story about the murder of the Bobsled Association's treasurer, John Chapadeau. Police suspected that the assassination was mob related since Chapadeau worked closely with Tony Robelotto.

Lester laughed to himself thinking that killing Chapadeau worked out better then he ever thought it would. The police were looking at the Mafia, and not him.

Chapter 21

Lake Placid, NY

Ron Harrison unlocked the front door of the Bobsled Association's office. With him were four other FBI Agents. It was 6:30 a.m. on Tuesday, the third week of February. They planned to search the Association's office for financial records and any evidence of drug dealings. Earlier in the month, they had seized the computers and obtained several files revealing narcotics traffic. Numerous files had been deleted, but the computer experts were able to retrieve the ones that had not been written over. One contained a list of people distributing cocaine for Nino.

After Nino had been murdered, the FBI searched his home and store for evidence. They found enough proof to link him to the drug business in Lake Placid. Records indicated that Roger Ferris was his main distributor. The FBI traced the transactions to Lester, but were unable to connect any other Bobsled Association members. Ron wondered how the three were able to conduct such a large scale operation under the nose of Wilbur Hippenbecker and the athletes.

On Monday morning, Ron and the agents obtained a court order that went to several banks in Lake Placid and Plattsburgh. The IRS had supplied a list of banks and account numbers for the Association, and the FBI seized all the accounts. Now they were searching for any financial records that might be in the office. Ron suspected that the records were never kept in Lake Placid.

While they searched the office, other agents in Rochester were searching the home and office of Wilbur Hippenbecker, who insisted that he had never seen the records that all the financial documents were kept by John

Chapadeau. The agents found it hard to believe that the president of an Olympic organization did not have any control over its finances or books.

Ron opened Roger's desk drawer and searched the contents. A letter from a company that donated bobsled team jackets to the athletes was on top of the paperwork. He read the letter, then slammed the drawer shut with such force that it startled the other agents. After walking around the room for several minutes he handed it to the nearest agent.

"Read this God damn letter," Ron tossed the letter on the desk in front of the agent and walked across the room trying to control his emotions.

"What's wrong with this?" the agent asked. "They donated fifty down-filled jackets for the athletes, coaches, and officials. I think it's nice."

"Oh, it's nice. Would you believe the Association officials told us they purchased the jackets and we had to buy them from Roger for 90 bucks? We were told that the company sold them to us at their cost below the retail price of $160. What a bunch of bastards. I can't feel sorry for John Chapadeau. That guy was miserable and never allowed us to get money for anything. He always said, the Association's 'broke.' Yet when it came to spending Association money, he and Lester seemed to have plenty available."

They searched the office for several hours and were unable to locate anything with financial information, except the one letter from the manufacturer of the jackets. Unsuccessful, they left Lake Placid and returned to Albany. Ron was frustrated because he knew that John must have kept records somewhere. He couldn't believe that a CPA wouldn't have a record of the $1.5 million that the Association received from the United States Olympic Committee, sponsors, and private donations.

The IRS was able to search their computers for companies and individuals who donated money to the Bobsled Association. They knew how much money was given to the Association, but were unable to determine where it had been spent. Travel and expense records were taken from Roger Ferris' files several days after he had been found dead. The FBI had obtained copies of the credit card transactions and copies of bank statements. They added all the income they were able to identify and subtracted what they could verify was spent. There was at more than half a million dollars that they could not trace.

The Association had several credit cards, all overdrawn or at their maximum credit ceiling. Ron knew that the finance company Wilbur Hippenbecker worked for was one of the Association's major creditors. It wouldn't take the company very long, he suspected, to learn that Wilbur had managed to overextend the Association's credit and they would probably fire him. He couldn't understand why Wilbur had allowed the others to manipulate him so easily. It frustrated him that Wilbur could turn his back to misdeeds just so he could maintain the title of president of an Olympic Association.

Ron decided to phone the United States Olympic Committee's financial director to encourage them to begin an official investigation of the Association. The majority of the Association's funding came from Olympic donations and the rules governing the use of the funding were very strict. He suspected that the committee had been very lax in their management of the money supplied to the Bobsled Association.

"This is Albert Marcott. How may I help you?"

"My name is Ron Harrison. I'm with the FBI and we're investigating the Bobsled Association. There are many problems with the way its finances have been handled and we need the Olympic Committee's help."

"Uh, I don't think we should get involved, Mr. Harrison. You see, uh, if the media learned of this it would create an abundance of bad publicity which could be very detrimental to our fund-raising efforts. You know the press would take this and make it a major news story. It would have a disastrous effect on our future fund raising efforts."

"Well, Mr. Marcott, let me share this with you. So far we have been able to determine that the Bobsled Association wasted nearly a half a million and there is another half a million missing. Does that bother you?"

"Of course, but look at our position. We provide the Bobsled Association roughly one million dollars, the rest of their funding comes from sponsors and private donations. A million dollars is only a modest part of our overall fund-raising efforts. If it gets into the papers that we are investigating the Association, it'll have a very dramatic affect on our entire fund-raising efforts. That might cost us millions. We would be wise to write off the million the Association may have wasted, squandered, or misappropriated, or whatever they did with it. The bottom line is... we can't afford to get involved."

"That may be your choice. But think about this for a moment. The FBI is in the middle of two murder investigations and a death from an overdose of cocaine. All three were officials of the Association. We have evidence that they were operating a drug ring from the Association's office. If that's not enough, we're fairly certain that more than half a million dollars is missing. Now, what do you think the press will write when this story is released and the U.S.O.C. didn't want to get involved because it was only a measly million? I suspect your fund-raising efforts will be dramatically affected anyway, but that's your choice. I hope you have a nice day, Mr. Marcott."

"Hold on a minute. Please understand that you are hitting me with some pretty shocking news. Yes, you're correct. We do need to get involved. I wasn't aware that drugs entered into this. Please give me your number and I'll get back to you within the hour."

Ron gave the director his number then hung up. He was disgusted that the U.S.O.C. was only interested in how the truth might affect their fundraising efforts. Twenty minutes later Marcott called him back.

"We are sending a financial swat team to Lake Placid to identify the missing money and hopefully learn where it has been spent."

"I'll provide you with a team of experts to help with the investigation. We have an attorney who is a specialist at conducting inquiries. I'll ask him to go to Lake Placid and take testimony from the athletes and coaches to help you ascertain where the money was spent."

Ron thanked him and hung up the receiver. He felt some satisfaction; however, he was frustrated about Marcott's original attitude. It was obvious to Ron that fundraising for Olympic sports was big business and appeared to be more important to them than preparing athletes to win!

Having a U.S.O.C. attorney would help with the investigation. He would be apt to have the confidence of the athletes and they might be willing to give him better information. The attorney would also be able to spend time questioning the athletes and coaches, allowing him to work on the criminal side of the case. Ron thought about the pandemonium that would take place in Lake Placid when the public discovered the U.S.O.C. and the FBI were investigating the United States Bobsled Association for financial misconduct. This was something that had never happened. He phoned Shawn Murphy.

Shawn was sitting at the kitchen table reading the newspaper when the phone rang. Ron gave him a quick summary of his conversation with Albert Marcott and brought him up to date with the FBI's investigation of the officials. Ron expressed concern that the U.S.O.C. might not provide the effort required to uncover the entire truth. They might only attempt enough to give the appearance that they were genuinely concerned.

"We'll have to wait and see if they're really looking for the truth or only interested in doing enough to make themselves look good," Shawn said. "Did you find Lester?"

"Not yet. The word on the street is that Tony Robelotto has everybody in his organization looking for him. We need to find him first or else he's dead. Robelotto put a hefty price on him."

"Where do you think he's hiding?"

"That's the problem, Shawn. If we knew, we would have him."

"Maybe he left the country. He used to brag about going to the Caribbean. Maybe he's hiding in the Virgin Islands."

"I don't think so. I think Lester's still around. It's not a question of finding him. The question is… who'll find him first?"

Ron hung up and thought about Shawn's suggestion that Lester might have gone to the Virgin Islands. He would have the FBI look at the airline flights from Miami and other cities that routinely flew to the Islands. They should start with the day John was killed. Time was running out and he needed to find Lester alive.

CHAPTER 22

Riga, Latvia, USSR

THE DISTURBANCE OUTSIDE THE HOTEL WOKE MERRILL much earlier than he had planned. He looked over to the nightstand at his travel alarm clock and groaned. It was only 6:30 a.m. Plans to stay in bed until mid-morning and catch up on the loss of sleep the past few days were now ruined. He got out of bed and went to the window. Slowly, he pulled the drapes back to see what was making the loud noise. It took a couple of seconds for his eyes to adjust to the bright sunlight.

The city square was crowded with hundreds of demonstrators carrying signs denouncing the treatment they were receiving from the Russians. Latvians were showing the frustration they had endured during the past 50 years. They had lived in terror since the Soviet occupation in 1940. Fifty years later large trees were growing next to the looted grave sites. The Russians had never allowed the Latvians to properly re-bury the caskets. The overgrowth of brush in some areas made it impossible for Latvians to locate their relatives. During the past year, Latvians had become more open about their hatred of the Russians.

A large number of Russian soldiers remained in the background waiting for orders to quell the disturbance. Chills went down Merrill's back as he peeked out. The soldiers were equipped with assault weapons. He noticed that many had their fingers positioned on the triggers suggesting that they might fire at any moment. Suddenly, he thought about Natasha's plans to leave the hotel early and return to the United States.

He called her and her phone rang several times before she answered. "Dohbrayi ootra."

"Dohbrayi ootra, Natasha."

"Oh, I couldn't imagine who was calling me so early."

"I enjoyed being with you last night, Natasha," he said feeling flushed about the understatement. "There is a problem and I think you should change your schedule."

He described the disturbance in the city square and suggested she call Moscow to change her flight to the next day when it would be safer to leave the hotel. She told him that she would make the call and then come to his room to watch the demonstration. Merrill decided to take a quick shower and shave before Natasha came. Their lovemaking kept playing over and over in his mind, the thought of her soft, sensuous body intertwining with his, and how she took the lead in making love to him.

The rushing water from the shower drowned out the loud noise in the street. While rubbing soap on his body, he imagined what it would be like to caress her body in the shower. Suddenly, a knock on his door brought him back to reality. Not realizing he spent so much time thinking about Natasha, he reached up to shut off the water and grabbed a towel. He dried off quickly and went to the door with the towel wrapped around his waist.

"Who is it?" he asked without unlocking the door.

"Natasha."

He quickly opened the door.

"Ha, I caught you in the shower," she teased.

"I didn't realize how long I was in the shower. It will only take me a minute to get dressed." His cheeks became a bright crimson as he pulled his towel tighter around his waist. Avoiding eye contact, he turned, opened the dresser and picked up a clean set of jockey shorts. He placed the underwear under his arm, grabbed his trousers off the chair, and then turned to go back to the bathroom.

"Your face is bright red," she giggled, realizing that he was embarrassed to be caught undressed. "Where are you going?"

"To get dressed."

"It didn't bother you last night to take off your clothes and make love to me. Why are you embarrassed now?"

"I don't know. I guess it's... I really don't know." Suddenly he felt like a young school boy being caught undressed in the locker room.

She walked towards him and took his pants and underwear, placing them on the chair next to the bed. "I'm sorry. I didn't mean to embarrass you," she said and looked up at his face, then leaned against him, fingering the edge of the towel. I didn't sleep very well. Thoughts of what we did kept me awake most of the night. I wished you had stayed all night."

"I had the same problem." The towel fell to the floor as he put his arms around her. "It's been a long time since I made love with anyone."

"You made me feel so good. It's been a long time for me too."

He kissed her tenderly, searching her mouth with his tongue. For a moment she surrendered to his desire, savoring the security she felt wrapped in his arms. Surprised at the intensity of her own response, she pushed him backward until his legs reached the bed and he was forced to sit.

Merrill reached to pull her next to him, but she defiantly slid to the floor between his thighs. She took hold of him, and kissed and licked him. At first she seemed to be teasing, but gradually her tongue and lips moved more forcefully, more insistent. Merrill lay back on the bed losing awareness of anything, but the overwhelming pleasure. He sank his fingers into her hair guiding her into a rhythm that would quickly send him out of control.

Natasha's moans excited Merrill even more. Suddenly she began stroking him more forcefully with her mouth.

"Oh God!" he cried, as his entire body quivered with pleasure.

To his surprise, she continued holding him in her mouth until he spoke.

"You are an amazing woman," he whispered pulling her up to lay beside him. They lay curled together, both of them breathless.

He stroked her cheek and murmured: "You didn't even take your clothes off."

She smiled and moved his hand from her face, sliding it under her knee length skirt. Merrill couldn't hide his surprise when he realized she wasn't wearing pantyhose, but rather a garter belt held her stockings that only reached to her thighs. As she continued lying on her side, he gently rubbed her buttocks enjoying the silkiness of her skin. In a motion she sat up and whisked her sweater over her head. Merrill felt his pulse quicken as he stroked her breasts. He unzipped her skirt, slipped it off her hips and then sat up to maneuver it completely down her legs. Feeling a desperate urge to please her, he began nibbling the flesh exposed above her stockings.

Suddenly, there was the sound of gunfire outside the hotel. People were screaming. They moved off the bed and rushed to the window, peeking from the corner of the drapes. Russian soldiers were shooting at the people who were running for their lives. Six bodies lay motionless in the snow. Merrill and Natasha were speechless as they watched three more fall.

Within minutes more soldiers arrived in trucks and began firing at the crowd. Suddenly the shooting stopped and they began to circle the rest of the Latvians remaining in the street. The soldiers arrested those who were unable to get away. Sixteen dead bodies were now visible and there was no way of knowing how many others were injured.

Natasha stepped back from the window trembling. "I just can't believe this."

"I know, but you must remember where we are," he said and put his arms around her, holding her close. "We have an obligation to these people. We need to remember every detail and send the information to our papers in the States."

"Do you have a camera with you?" asked Natasha.

"No. When you're calm enough, we'll write down the events as we saw them happen. Then we'll leave as soon as it's safe."

"Where should we go?"

"I'll drive you to Leningrad. From there you can take the train to Moscow. I think you should return to Romania and put a story together for your paper. Once that's completed you should go to the States and brief Fred Unser about this."

"I can't believe those soldiers shot innocent people in the back."

"I know. Try not to think about them. I understand how you feel, but we must remain in the background."

She stepped back and wiped the tears from her face.

"I'm all right now. I need to get dressed and go downstairs to my room to write down what happened."

"I'm going with you. I don't think we should be staying in this room; the KGB might search all the rooms that have windows overlooking the square. I don't want them to think we might have seen anything."

Merrill got dressed and placed the few belongings he had in a suitcase and went to her room. They spent nearly an hour writing notes, then went downstairs to the hotel dining room. During breakfast they did not speak about the incident, knowing it was too risky. There might be someone there from the KGB or the Secret Police. It was nearly 10:30 a.m. when Merrill thinking it would be safe, suggested that they go back to his room.

He wished he could resume the lovemaking they began before the gunfire started, but he knew it would be useless. She was too upset. Merrill wondered if they would ever be together again. At least, he would have some wonderful dreams that would last him a long time.

Merrill slowly pulled the drapes part-way back and looked out into the street. Nearly everyone was gone except several soldiers standing on the corner. He assumed that they were on guard in case protesters returned. Judging from the frost still on the cars in the square, he suspected that the temperature must be around zero. The soldiers were swinging their arms attempting to keep warm. Looking upward he noticed that the sky was covered with clouds.

"The weather doesn't look good. I think we should check out right after lunch."

"Are you sure it's safe for us to travel together?"

"I think it's safer for us to be together than apart. I'll drive you to Leningrad as we planned and you can take the train to Moscow."

"Where will you go?"

"I'll return back to Kiev," he replied deep in thought. "Yesterday you said Shawn Murphy and Amos Kelly were the two people who would be jumping from the airplane."

"Yes."

"I've never heard of Murphy, but the name Amos Kelly seems familiar. I'm sure I've heard of him."

"He's worked for the CIA a long time."

"That's not where I heard of him. I know I've heard his name mentioned and it was here in the Soviet Union."

Merrill didn't say anymore. Deciding that when he got back to Ukraine he would try to figure out where he had heard about Kelly. For some strange reason he thought it was from someone in the underground. He was sure that eventually he would recall it because he almost never forgot a name.

When they checked out of the hotel shortly after lunch, the street was nearly vacant. Bloody snow was visible in several places. They got into his car without looking at the soldiers, trying not to be noticed. The car started after several attempts and he waited until the car warmed up enough to melt the frost off the windshield.

Merrill drove out of the city in the direction of Estonia, hoping to reach Leningrad by nine… 300 miles, no expressways, and seven to eight hours of driving. He couldn't take a chance on the authorities grabbing Natasha. In Leningrad he would catch some sleep, then continue south to Kiev. That drive would take several days, he wasn't looking forward to the fatiguing trip.

CHAPTER 23

Schenectady, N.Y.

THE THUNDER OF THE C-130 ENGINES MADE it nearly impossible for Shawn and Amos to discuss last minute plans on the plane with Colonel Roger Stoddard. It was nearly 10 p.m. and the pilot was preparing for a routine take-off, but for Shawn and Amos Kelly it would not be routine. They would be making the final jump of their training, at 37,000 feet in frigid temperatures in the dark.

Stoddard was attempting to approximate the actual conditions of their jump in the Soviet Union, if possible. The plane would fly to New York City and then return to the vicinity west of Schenectady. It was a rural farming area that would give the flight crew enough time to reach 37,000 feet. Currently the temperature outside was 12 degrees above zero. The climate in Schenectady was almost the same as it would be in the section of the Soviet Union the two men would enter.

This was their fourth parachute jump wearing the flight suit that had been specially designed for NASA. The heat in the back of the plane was turned down to simulate what the temperature would be in the cargo bay of the commercial airliner when they flew into the Soviet Union. The outside temperature tonight at 37,000 feet was estimated to be 45 degrees below zero.

Both men wore a special heated underwear suit containing a carbon filament that would keep their body at a minimum of 68 degrees. The underwear worked on either AC or DC current. On the plane, they were plugged into the aircraft's DC system until it was time to jump. Just prior to jumping, they would have to plug into a battery pack attached to their jump suits. The batteries would work for three hours. They needed only 15 minutes.

Stoddard was sitting in his web seat reading a magazine. Shawn looked at the oxygen mask sitting on the seat next to him. It was plugged into the plane's internal air system ready to be turned on when he needed to breathe oxygen. Everyone would breathe air from the plane's oxygen supply once they reached 10,000 feet. When the C-130 reached jump elevation, Stoddard and the loadmaster would switch their oxygen line from the plane to a six-person portable oxygen console. The console allowed them to move around and assist Murphy and Kelly as they got ready to jump.

Shawn and Amos were wearing state-of-the-art advanced breathing regulators connected to the plane's oxygen system. A quick disconnect fitting allowed them to instantly switch to the twin-50 personal oxygen system attached to each suit. Just prior to jumping, they would switch the connection and breathe from their self-contained system. The high altitude regulator would supply them with 100 percent oxygen to prevent them from experiencing hypoxia, a condition that affects humans when their body receives an inadequate amount of oxygen. The body slowly shuts down the thinking process and within a short amount of time, the mind will become disoriented.

Shawn had seen training films that contained actual radio recordings of jet pilots who didn't use their checklist to prepare for flight. On a few occasions, some forgot to turn on the oxygen prior to take off. They quickly became disoriented above 10,000 feet. The films contained actual conversations of other pilots attempting to convince them to turn on their oxygen. The pilots without oxygen reacted like a person who was drunk. Within a short period of time, they would crash. Air Force instructors always showed the films to those receiving altitude chamber training or whenever they needed to be re-certified for flight status.

Hearing the conversation of people just prior to their deaths was something that Shawn never forgot. Leaning back against the webbing he closed his eyes and thought about the first time he received training at an Air Force altitude chamber. It seemed like yesterday. Something he would never forget, however, he carefully thought about each part of the exercise he was about to do to survive the jump.

The never-ending vibration from the four engines seemed to work as a mild tranquilizer. Shawn leaned back against his web seat, closed his eyes, and visualized preparing for the jump. Piece by piece, he mentally began to put on the equipment. Once he was dressed, he imagined he was standing at the door of the C-130 ready to jump. It seemed effortless in his mind to move around with all the bulky clothing that he would wear for the actual jump. As if in slow motion Stoddard smiled and motioned for him to jump. This time there was no sound as he dove straight down toward earth at 120 miles an hour. He changed positions and imagined he was floating downward then drifted off to sleep.

The loadmaster shut the plane's rear door, bringing him back to the present. Shawn looked at his watch. It was 9:55 p.m., the day after Valentine's. He thought about the roses and card he had given Angela. She always got excited when he gave her flowers.

Suddenly, the plane lurched ahead as the pilot turned toward the runway. The increased noise level prompted him to check his ear protectors. Within seconds the plane was accelerating down the runway and then he felt it lift up into the air.

The clock was now ticking. Shawn looked across the cargo area and noticed Kelly staring at him. Smiling he gave a thumbs up signal to him. Amos returned the gesture without a smile. Shawn closed his eyes and leaned back into the web seat thinking about him. Kelly was definitely an odd person. Shawn had made several attempts to invite him to dinner and each time Kelly gave an excuse why he couldn't come. He had never said or done anything that could have been interpreted as hostile or negative, but apparently he just didn't want to develop any type of comradeship. This seemed to be odd since they were involved with such a difficult and hazardous mission. Their survival and the success of the assignment might depend on each other.

Shawn noticed Colonel Stoddard putting on his oxygen mask. The loadmaster was already wearing his, and Shawn assumed they must be reaching 10,000 feet. He looked at his watch. It was now 10:25 p.m. They must be nearly to New York City he suspected and would be turning around shortly to head north.

He grabbed his helmet and stood up. Stoddard walked over to him and helped him fasten the hood of his parka over his helmet and night vision goggles, while the loadmaster assisted Kelly. It was important to obtain a perfect seal on the suit to prevent air from entering. Even a tiny amount of air entering would quickly lower body temperature creating medical problems. This could prove fatal.

His parka was secured and he sat back down on the web seat, inhaling slowly to get acclimated to the breathing apparatus. It was very similar to wearing a scuba diving wet suit with oxygen tanks, and only took a few seconds until he was breathing normally. The pressure gauge was now reading 11,000 feet. The plane banking, indicating they were changing course.

Shortly after the plane turned, he could feel pressure as the plane began to climb upward.

Shawn wondered if they would be in the cargo area for nearly the same amount of time when they left London or wherever the CIA decided to start the mission. Stoddard had done an excellent job with their training. He thought about Amos and himself crawling through the snow, simulating what they might have to do in the Soviet Union. Major Jason Pollack trained them to make snowshoes out of evergreen boughs in the event they would have to escape through the Soviet Union's northwest into Finland, something Shawn hoped he would not have to do.

He looked down at the German countersniper rifle with the silencer that was on the seat next to him. During the past three weeks he had fired several hundred rounds with the rifle and was very confident with it. The scope cost several thousand dollars, but was worth every dollar. He had used the rifle during late night training sessions to fire at targets in total darkness. Major Pollack was right. It was definitely an incredible weapon.

Shawn took out his GPS unit and examined it. It was difficult to hold while wearing the thick gloves needed to keep his hands warm. He looked at the device and from its readings; he estimated that they were about 70 miles from the drop site. It was fascinating to Shawn that the GPS was so accurate. He remembered Colonel Stoddard's advice about how it could be instrumental in keeping him alive.

He thought about the computer chip and the nine-volt battery that he and Kelly carried with them in case they got into a situation where they needed to send a signal to get them out of the Soviet Union. Shawn hoped that they would never be in a situation where they had to activate the chip. A quick glance at his GPS showed that they were now within 50 miles of the target. Stoddard and the loadmaster attached a safety cable to themselves to prevent accidentally being sucked out of the plane when the jump door was opened. As an added measure, Shawn and Kelly would wear a special parka that covered their entire faces except their night vision goggles. Tonight's jump would be the coldest the two men had experienced. The combination of sub-zero temperature and wind chill could make it around 100 degrees below zero as they plummeted downward.

Murphy and Kelly stood up and began to put on their parachutes. Stoddard helped Shawn, and the loadmaster assisted Amos with his. After the parachutes were securely fastened, they unplugged their air line from the aircraft's portable oxygen console and began using their self-contained breathing apparatus.

Once the oxygen system was changed, Shawn reached down and picked up his rifle. The jump suits were outfitted with special connectors to keep the rifle fastened to the suits during the long descent to the ground. They would not be able to use the rifles in the event someone was firing at them from the ground. The intent was to allow them to carry the weapon, without it interfering with their landing, to be used only in a life or death situation once they were on the ground.

Shawn and Amos moved towards the rear of the plane and waited for the loadmaster to open the jump door. Colonel Stoddard made a motion with his hand indicating to the loadmaster to raise the door, and both men moved closer. The light over the exit was still red. Seconds later it turned green and Shawn rolled out of the plane headfirst with Kelly seconds behind him. He could feel the intense pressure as he dove toward the ground.

What was only a few seconds seemed like an eternity while Shawn's eyes began to acclimate to the extreme dark surroundings. At 37,000 feet he could see the curvature of the earth. The sight nearly took his breath away as he looked in amazement. The scene quickly disappeared as he continued to free-fall downward at an incredible speed. Though the pilot had assured them no other air traffic was in the area, he strained his eyes, worried that a plane headed towards the Albany Airport might pass near them.

Tonight he and Amos were parachuting into a desolate area in Princetown, west of Schenectady. Stoddard changed the position each time to prevent them from becoming accustomed to a location. At each nighttime jump, someone met them with a car with the lights off to simulate meeting their contact in Latvia.

Shawn managed to flatten out his body and change to a prone position. This slowed his descent and allowed him to look at the instruments on his arm. The GPS indicated that he was right on target, although he still couldn't see the red light indicating where to land. The intense wind created incredible pressure on his neck as the helmet with the night vision goggles cut through the pitch dark sky. Seconds later, he caught a glimpse of Amos about 200 feet away.

Shawn moved his left arm in front of his night vision goggles and checked the altimeter. The dial dropped past 15,000 feet. In less than three minutes, they had fallen 23,000 feet. He kept his arm in a position where he could monitor his altimeter constantly. The red light marking where he and Amos should land still wasn't visible. Off in the distance he could see the lights from Schenectady and Albany. Directly below him a few scattered lights from rural houses broke up the darkness. At 8,000 feet, still no red light.

He watched the dial on the altimeter continue to drop. At 5,000 feet he pulled the ripcord. The chute opened and the pressure from the air gathering inside felt as if he had applied huge brakes. Suddenly, he spotted the red light and he realized that he was slightly off course. Amos's chute was off to his left and he appeared to be right on target. Shawn maneuvered his chute to change directions and continued to descend in the direction of the red light.

At 2,000 feet he could clearly see the field and the blinking red light. The field he would land in appeared to be much smaller than the others they had used in the previous training exercises. Groves of trees surrounded the area. At 1,500 feet he could see Major Pollack holding the signal light. He was clearly visible standing in the snow covered field. The white background enabled Shawn to see as if it were in the middle of a cloudy day.

Within minutes, Shawn and Amos were on the ground. The nearly 15 inches of deep snow, made it somewhat difficult to collect the chutes. Once they had picked up their chutes, they went to the car and stuffed them into the open trunk. The two men got inside and the Major drove the military vehicle out onto the deserted road.

"What a rush," Amos yelled.

"It was incredible," Shawn replied. "I had a difficult time locating the red light until I got down to about 5,000 feet."

"That's because I didn't turn on the light until you opened your chutes," Pollack said. "When you make your jump in the Soviet Union, your contact won't signal you until he can see your chutes. That's why we spent so much time training both of you how to use the instruments. You'll need to have faith in them as they'll be your only ticket to reaching your target. The person meeting you will probably be hiding in the cover of trees until he sees your chutes."

"I'm ready," Shawn said.

"Likewise. I think we're in as good shape as we can get," Kelly said. "We need to talk about where we'll be going when we meet our contact, so in case something happens to you, I'll be able to complete the mission."

"I can't explain just exactly where the documents are hidden," Shawn said. "I know the general location, but I'm not sure where they are inside the cave. I believe Fred Unser is planning to have me meet with Boris just before we leave."

"I should be with you when you meet with him since I'm part of the mission."

"I don't think he'll talk to me in front of any other person. He's paranoid about who gets the information. The CIA has changed his appearance and Fred doesn't want to take a chance of anybody exposing him. The Russians would try to kill him in a heartbeat if they could identify him. I'll mention it to Fred if you want me to."

"No, let it go. You need to share the information with me just before we do the mission in case something happens to you. What if your chute doesn't open or you get shot when we land? The mission is too important to risk not completing it successfully."

"I guess you're right. I'll have to talk to Fred."

The drive back to the base seemed to take forever for Shawn. He felt very uncomfortable with Amos and wondered why he was pressing to get the information about Boris. When they arrived at the base, the three men took the chutes into the life support section. They went next door to the large hanger and attached them to a pulley, then pulled them up to the ceiling to dry out.

Shawn said good-by to both Pollack and Kelly, then drove home. He thought about next week when he and Amos were scheduled to fly to Washington to meet with Unser on Monday at Andrews Air Force Base to make the final arrangements for their trip. The parachute jump from such a high elevation had exhausted him, and he couldn't wait to get to bed.

CHAPTER 24

Schenectady, NY

S HAWN LOOKED AT THE CLOCK ON HIS dresser and cursed that he could not sleep longer. It was nearly 7 a.m. and he was still tired from the previous night's jump. The Bobsled Association's financial problems kept him awake throughout the night. There were too many questions still unanswered. Thousands of dollars of the Bobsled Association's money could not be located despite the efforts of the FBI and the USOC.

So much had happened so fast. The assassinations of Nino Casatelli and John Chapadeau, and the bizarre death of Roger Ferris. Perhaps the strangest piece missing in the Association's puzzle was the disappearance of Lester Fetor. How could he just disappear? Shawn promised himself to call Ron Harrison later in the morning to find out if the FBI discovered anything new.

After taking a relaxing shower, which relieved some of the soreness in his body, he made coffee and retrieved the Daily Gazette newspaper. He hoped to find a story that put some light on the Bobsled Association's problems. As he scanned the paper, Angela came in.

"You're up early," he said.

"I don't think so. It's nearly eight o'clock and if I don't leave soon, I'll be late for work."

Shawn looked at the clock and was surprised that it was so late already. Tired and sore from the previous night's training, he continued to move in slow motion. Angela, however was late for work and rushed around the kitchen pouring orange juice and making toast. Within minutes, she was kissing Shawn good-bye.

When he returned to the sports page, a headline caught his attention. "U.S.O.C. takes control of Bobsled finances." A strange sensation crept through him as he read about the Bobsled Association scandal. The story highlighted the Association's inability to account for nearly a million dollars in Olympic funding. USOC auditors expressed frustration about missing records and funds. They suspected that thousands of dollars were hidden in Swiss bank accounts. The story quoted Wilbur Hippenbecker as saying he had been completely left out of the inner circle of the Association's finances.

The reporter interviewed several athletes who stated that Hippenbecker had been an effective president until Fetor and Casatelli took control of the Association. During the past two years under their control, Hippenbecker had become a figurehead. Auditors noted that Hippenbecker no longer signed checks or negotiated for bank loans; that having been done either by Fetor or Chapadeau.

The story gave an accounting of money spent illegally. USOC auditors were able to trace some transactions from local bank records. Casatelli and Fetor spent most of the cash that could be traced, on trips to Europe. Credit card statements included first-class airline tickets, plush hotels, and extravagant restaurants. The reporter stated that the two officials were not alone on the trips since there were airline tickets for other people; mostly women. He also indicated that restaurant checks were outrageous and that the bills included expensive wines and champagne.

Shawn was interested in the portion of the story that indicated that most of the missing money was presumed to be hidden in the Swiss accounts. He had similar problems during his time as a coach at the Olympic Trials in Europe. Large amounts of cash stashed in German accounts came to his mind. He suspected that the FBI would never find the missing money or records.

Another related story included information about the drug transactions that were discovered by the New York State Police when they analyzed the Association's computer. Police said there was enough evidence to prosecute Ferris, Casatelli, Fetor, and Chapadeau. Unfortunately, all were dead except Fetor, and no one had a clue to his whereabouts. The FBI was searching for him and Shawn suspected the Mafia was also not merely looking, but hunting for him. Maybe they had found him.

If so, the chances were that nobody would ever find out. Fetor would likely be resting with Jimmy Hoffa somewhere. It was 9:15 a.m. He called Ron Harrison, hoping to hear some updated news.

All Harrison could tell him was that they had checked several more leads to the whereabouts of Lester Fetor, but had come up with nothing. They feared that the Mafia may have found Fetor.

"I wanted to let you know that I'll be out of the country for a couple of weeks," Shawn said, over the phone

"Where are you going?"

"I can't say for sure, but I'll be busy working on a project for the government. I'll call you when I get back. Could you call the state police and ask them to keep a close watch on my house while I'm away?" Shawn felt uncomfortable leaving Angela while he was away.

"Of course, they are watching for suspicious vehicles in the area, but I'll ask them to also keep an eye on your house."

Shawn hung up, feeling frustrated about the FBI's inability to locate Lester. He was tempted to tell Ron that he was going to the Soviet Union, but knew that he shouldn't tell anybody, not even Angela. She wouldn't really know what he was doing, though she probably figured it was something with the CIA, which was why she knew not to pressure him.

Shawn packed the clothing he would need for the next couple weeks, then called Angela at the insurance office in Latham to say good-bye. As usual she was busy handling problems that customers had with their auto insurance. She took a couple of minutes to chat, and then asked him to call her that evening after he arrived in Washington. His flight was scheduled to leave the Albany Airport at 11:30 a.m., not giving him anymore time to waste.

Kiev, Ukraine, USSR

Merrill slept for nearly 10 hours. The drive from Riga had exhausted him, but he managed to get Natasha to the airport where she caught a flight to Moscow. Later he slept for a couple of hours in his car until the cold woke him. He thought about Natasha and wondered how someone his age could fall in love with someone so much younger. God, she was beautiful. She had everything. A talented writer who seemed to know what international gossip would develop into a good news story. Natasha was perfect for the CIA. Her Romanian looks allowed her to roam around foreign countries without attracting attention.

He had to get her off his mind and go to work. But the more he thought about her, the more he realized he knew very little about her. Suddenly, it occurred to him that he still didn't even know her last name. She introduced herself to him as Natasha and he had gotten so caught up with her charm, he never thought to ask. It was critical that he had to get control of his feelings. Otherwise, he would be prone to making an error that could be tragic for both of them.

Merrill left his apartment to visit some friends who were part of the Ukrainian separatist underground. He had lived in that section of the Soviet Union for so long, he felt like a Ukrainian. They concealed their tremendous hatred for the Russians much like the people in the Baltic States, but he knew it was existent.

During the early 1930s the Soviet Government contrived a man-made famine in the eastern section of the Ukraine, resulting in the deaths of nearly 10 million Ukrainians. Soviet troops occupied the country in 1944 and there had been massive arrests and executions. During the years after World War II, people around the world eventually forgot that the Russians absorbed the Ukraine once a proud independent country.

Ukrainians didn't forget and secretly believed that the day would come when they would once again be free. Then, in the spring of 1986, the Ukrainian hatred of the Russians was rekindled during the world's worst nuclear power plant disaster. The meltdown at Chernobyl drew worldwide attention and sparked a resurgence of a separatist movement.

Merrill had spent most of his time in Kiev gathering news stories for the New York Times. His work as a correspondent was a natural connection to Ukrainians who wanted to spread their story to the rest of the world. He often received anonymous tips about dreadful things that the Russians were doing. Most of these stories were never used or he would have been expelled from the country. It was difficult to work and live with the occupied Ukrainians without personally feeling their anguish. The longer he lived in Kiev, the more he became a part of their culture.

The coffee shop was busy as usual. The morning regulars were eating and chatting about the weather, which was dismal at best. Merrill looked around for a moment, then spotted his friend and walked over to sit across from him. He always sat in the back facing the front, where he could watch everyone entering. The large window next to the table allowed him to observe the city park across the street. It always worried him that the KGB might be using electronic equipment to eavesdrop.

"Dohbrayi ootra," Merrill greeted his contact in Russian, then began to speak in English to prevent the regulars from understanding their conversation. "What's new with your efforts?"

"We are feeling a lot of pressure from the KGB. They arrested two of our people last week. It has been five days and no word about them. They could be imprisoned here, or perhaps they have been taken to Moscow."

"Do you think they will talk?"

"No. They would rather die than give information. But, they... they may have no choice. The Russians use drugs that force you to relax and answer their questions honestly." He took a long drag on his cigarette, releasing the smoke through his nostrils while his eyes continually searched the surroundings through the window.

"How much do your friends know about the movement?" Merrill felt uncomfortable questioning his friend like an investigator, but this was the quickest way to uncover information that might be helpful to him.

"Not too much. I worry more that they might give the Russians important names. They keep pulling people in to get new information. We must be very careful and keep a low profile. Enough about my troubles. Where have you been?"

"I had to run up to Riga on some business for the newspaper," Merrill said, and quietly shared the experience he had with Natasha. "I can't believe that she would be interested in someone as old and boring as me."

"You never know what women will do. Never! What's her name?"

"You know something strange. I only know her first name. She introduced herself as Natasha and I was so caught up with her that I never asked her last name. Now I feel foolish that I acted so irrationally."

"How long have you known her?"

"I just met her."

Merrill began to think about this question. Fred Unser told him that someone would meet him in Riga. He and Natasha spoke in the car and discussed Fred and their jobs with the CIA. She had to be clean. God, what if she were a double agent. How could he have been so stupid? His mind drifted as he thought about his situation.

After several moments of silence his friend touched his arm and said, "Zdrahstvooyti! Are you in another world?"

Merrill leaned forward and whispered. "Have you ever heard of an American woman named Natasha?"

The elderly man sat back and stared at him then looked around the room before he leaned forward. "Do you mean Natasha Lyubarsky?"

"I told you I don't know her last name."

"I have heard about an American reporter by that name. My people believe she's a KGB informant. I don't know her, but I was warned about talking with her. What did you tell her?"

"Nothing! We just had sex," Merrill lied. "That's all. Look I'm sorry, but I just remembered that I have a deadline on a story. I... I will meet you here tomorrow."

"If you don't see me here in the morning, you will know that I have gone to my place in the country until the pressure eases. If you come, make sure nobody is following you or they will arrest us both."

"I will be careful," he said and wished his friend well, then left the coffee shop feeling queasy and upset about the predicament he may have gotten into if Natasha was a double agent.

Merrill replayed in his mind all the conversations between himself and Natasha, trying to find something she might have said that suggested she was looking for information. Now it all made sense. She had sex with him to lower his resistance, so he would confide with her about what he was doing. The only information she needed for Unser was the exact spot where the two men would land. He told her about the cave and the plan to escape across the border into Finland.

He turned down a side street to be less conspicuous should anybody be watching him. How could he have been so careless? Roaming the streets, feeling helpless and stupid, he pondered his predicament.

It was critical that he send a message to Fred Unser and tell him of the possibility that Natasha might be working for the Russians. Then he needed to return to Latvia and select an alternate location for the landing site in the event that Natasha was a double agent.

It would be a miracle if he got through this mess without being caught by the Soviets. What a stupid thing to have done at his age, he thought. The thought of what might happen if she was a double agent began to upset him.

He decided that he had to redo the entire plan for Fred and not take a chance that he had blundered. There was too much at risk.

Chapter 25

National Airport, Washington, D.C.

THE STEWARDESS WALKED DOWN THE AISLE, REMINDING passengers to put their trays back and return their seats to the upright position. A voice on the loudspeaker told everyone that they were on the final descent and would land within 10 minutes. Information for several connecting flights was provided on the loudspeaker, after which Shawn heard the familiar thump of the landing gear moving into place.

He looked out the window and saw the Washington monument off in the distance. Landing at Washington National Airport was not very pleasant for him. Commercial pilots rated it as one of the most dangerous airports in the United States to land a plane.

The plane leaned to the left as it maneuvered into landing position. Moments later it touched the runway and began the slow process of moving across the taxi strip to the passenger terminal. Incoming traffic was backed up waiting for a plane that was still loading passengers to depart before they could move into place and let the passengers from Albany enter the terminal.

Shawn leaned back. Amos Kelly was still on his mind. People who train together for such a dangerous mission as theirs normally form a strong bond. The camaraderie creates a natural feeling of trust and commitment to the mission, which would be very important when they went behind the Iron Curtain. Not wanting to make any hard feelings between himself and Kelly, however, he had avoided talking to him about this.

Then again, maybe Kelly didn't trust him. Except for the one mission to smuggle Boris Yegorov out of the Soviet Union, it had been years since Shawn had worked for the CIA. Maybe Kelly simply didn't have confidence in Shawn's ability to carry out his part of the mission. But considering that the mission with Yegorov was so successful, there must be something else, he thought.

The plane taxied up to the passenger terminal. Within minutes the 737 was positioned at the ramp and passengers began to exit. Shawn left the terminal and hailed a taxi. The cab ride to his apartment in Georgetown only took 20 minutes. He paid the driver and went up the steps to his temporary home. The one-bedroom residence was all he needed, since he spent most of his time traveling with his new job at the Pentagon.

Looking around he noticed that dust had collected on everything while he was away. He wasn't looking forward to cleaning the small apartment. Maybe he should look around and find someone interested in doing some house cleaning for him. Angela wouldn't like that, so he forgot the idea. The stack of mail that had collected while he was gone contained nothing except junk advertisements. Thumbing quickly through the pile he found nothing of use, then tossed the entire stack into the garbage. His official and personal mail was delivered to him at his office.

After a quick shower and a change of clothing he backed his car out of the garage and drove across town to the Pentagon. There was a note on his desk from General Abbott to call as soon as possible. Shawn hung up his overcoat and dialed the general's phone number. A secretary answered and said the general was in a meeting and told Shawn the general would meet with him in two hours. Looking at his watch, he made a mental note to be there at three-thirty. He hung up the receiver then picked it up again and called Fred Unser at Langley.

"Shawn. It's good to hear from you. I spoke to Colonel Stoddard this morning and he said that the training went well. Did Amos come back to D.C. with you?"

"I really don't know where he is or what his plans are. That's why I called you. He hasn't changed a bit. In fact, he's been downright unfriendly, and I would even describe some of his behavior as a bit strange."

"Why do you say that?"

"He's avoided any casual conversation and shunned all my invitations to have him visit my wife and me for dinner. I don't know anymore about him now then when I met him."

"I really don't know him either. His CIA service records show that he's highly qualified for the mission and he has an incredible amount of experience working behind the Iron Curtain. So, from what you're saying I assume you didn't engage in any conversations that would have revealed more about his political beliefs?"

"You hit that on the nose."

"Well, then do you think you might want to withdraw from the mission?"

"No. The information we're after is too valuable to scrap the mission. I'm simply saying that he's strange and I don't feel comfortable with him. I just thought you could give me some information that would help me understand him."

"I don't know what to say, Shawn, except that his record speaks for itself and that I feel confident he'll get the job done."

"That's the bottom line and I can accept that. I'd just feel better if we were able to develop a bond of trust between each other."

"You might be surprised and see it happen during the mission."

"You could be right," said Shawn, who thought otherwise. "When should I be at Langley?"

"I would like to have you over here next week so we can do the final training, and our people can brief you and Kelly on the assignment."

"I'll be there. Do me a favor and talk to some people who have worked with Kelly. You might dig up something that will at least explain why he's so withdrawn."

"Okay. I'll do that. Take care of yourself and I'll see you next week."

Shawn hung up. While reading his mail, he received a call from General Abbott's secretary. The general was ready to meet with him.

"Come in, come in. Please shut the door," he said. He called his secretary, asking her to hold his calls. "Well, how do you feel? Did the intense training make you feel as if you are getting any older?"

"Boy, I'll say it did. It's the day after a training exercise that you realize how old you are!"

"When will you be leaving for Langley?"

"I have to be there next week. I suspect we'll execute the mission the following week. Hopefully, I'll be back here to work in three weeks."

"By the time you come back, there'll be a lot of changes in Public Affairs. I'm in the process of revamping the entire section."

"What's going on?"

"Nothing except total incompetence." General Abbott shook his head, making a face. "In all the years I have worked in the Air Force I've never had the number of bungling idiots that I currently have in Public Affairs here at the Pentagon."

"I realize that it's not widely accepted in the military to criticize superiors; however, I have to agree with you," Shawn said, then he hesitated, thinking carefully about the correct words to use. "In my opinion, Captain Hamilton doesn't have a clue as to what Public Affairs is all about."

"That's obvious, now. I know what happened. The supervisors at her last assignment wanted to get rid of her so they gave her glowing references."

"I'm not surprised. Unfortunately, this happens all the time in the military. Is there another place she could be assigned where her abilities would be an asset?"

"Where?" Abbott said and leaned forward on his desk. "She's a social buff… a real social buff. Where in hell do you assign a social buff in the military? In the Officer's Club," he replied answering his own question. "It's a wonder she hasn't developed some kind of social disease. I'm told that she has slept with nearly every pilot in the Air Force."

"There have been several work assignments she has gone on for us and there has been someone different each time traveling with her. I felt that it was none of my business as long as she didn't interfere with the stories we were working on at the time."

"Well, we can't let her continue to operate this way. She should be managing the section and not using it to promote her social life," Abbott said as he leaned back into his chair. "Frankly, she can't manage her own life let alone supervise a national Public Affairs Department. My people are working on a transfer for her."

"What about Chief Robbins? I heard that he got into a lot of trouble."

"That's the understatement of the day." Abbott rolled his eyes and leaned forward speaking in a soft voice said, "We discovered a story in Robbins' computer that was very critical of the Air Force doing clandestine missions in foreign countries with the CIA. He used your name for the by-line and we suspect he was planning to release it to the media after you began the assignment with the CIA."

The information upset him and Shawn quickly envisioned being arrested and imprisoned in the Soviet Union. "A story like that would have a serious effect on us while we are completing the mission."

What a bastard, thought Shawn. "I hope that you're planning to discipline him!"

"His retirement papers are currently being drawn up. There are other problems. He can't seem to stay away from booze and gambling tables. His wife left him after he accumulated thousands of dollars of gambling debts on his credit cards. I guess she surprised him on one of his trips and caught him with some young bimbo. I swear to God, some of these people think when they reach forty, they have to prove something to the world. The only thing they really prove is their stupidity."

"What about the other two characters in the section?"

"They're also leaving," Abbott said as he rolled his eyes. "We got them all at the same time. Stanley Staskowski is being reassigned to Lackland Air Force Base as a billeting sergeant for basic trainees. I guess he had a slew of gambling losses on his credit cards too."

"I heard the same thing. I also heard through the rumor mill that his wife left him. Will Sergeant Molaine Taylor stay in the section?" Shawn asked, hoping the general was also planning to move her.

"She's history. God, what a waste she was. We discovered that Hamilton allowed her to take college courses during the day when she was supposed to be working. Too make matters worse, Hamilton requested that Taylor be given an award for her work," Abbott said as he sat on the edge of his chair in anger. "This is a perfect example of how affirmative action can be abused. She sneaks out during work hours to complete her degree, then Hamilton wants to give her an award!"

"What are your plans to rebuild the section?"

"We've already hired someone to replace Hamilton. He should be on board by the time you return. I plan to move you into the Chief's position. We're still working on replacements for the other two."

"I appreciate your confidence." Shawn smiled knowing that the public affairs section would finally get rid of the incompetent people who were managing the organization.

"Don't let it go to your head," General Abbott said teasing Shawn. "I'm pleased with your work and I'm confident you will train the new people well and put this section back on track."

They spent the next half-hour discussing several changes the general wanted. Shawn left feeling much better. It always amazed him how the government managed to let incompetent people rise up in the ranks.

CIA Headquarters, Langley, Virginia, a week later

Shawn drove to Langley to meet with Fred Unser at CIA Headquarters. It was Monday, the first week of March and the warm air suggested spring. He shivered as he thought about how cold it was in Schenectady. Angela had complained on the phone about the snow storm they had gotten over the weekend. Most of the snow in Washington had already melted.

He took his time and enjoyed the countryside. The thought occurred that when he retired, Virginia might be nice to relocate to and avoid the harsh winter in upstate New York. What a contrast to the North Country.

They were still blanketed under a foot of snow in Schenectady, but here in Virginia along the beltway, green grass was starting to appear.

Shawn recalled a vacation he and Angela took to Virginia Beach one fall. They were there one week after the tourist season, not only had great weather, but the price of nearly everything was reduced since it was their winter season. This week would not be a vacation, he thought, bringing his attention to what would take place during the next several days.

The mission would be dangerous for him and Kelly, however, sharing the risk with Angela made him feel more uncomfortable. She would have fits if she really knew what they planned to do in the Soviet Union. He still didn't know everything about the mission. The only thing he knew for sure was how he and Amos were getting behind the Iron Curtain.

The purpose of the mission was to recover the written alloy formula Boris Yegorov had hidden in a sandstone cave. The formula was buried in a plastic container with samples of the metal compound. Shawn was confident that he could locate the container with very little difficulty. What he didn't know was how they planned to get Kelly and him out of the Soviet Union once they had the documents and composite samples.

He was uneasy thinking about what would happen to them if they got caught. They would face a long prison sentence, if they were lucky. Death was also a possibility. The Soviets wouldn't be happy, knowing the formula was in the hands of Americans. Trying not to think about being caught, he shifted his thoughts to how Fred might be planning to get them out from behind the Iron Curtain.

Suddenly, it occurred to him that he still didn't know for sure where they would enter the Soviet Union. He turned on the radio to a soft rock station to try and relieve his mind. As he listened to the music, he began humming. A short time later he realized he was thinking about the trip again and was glad when he saw the beltway sign for Langley.

Shawn arrived at CIA Headquarters within ten minutes and was escorted to Fred Unser's office. "Nice to see you." Fred stood up and came from behind his desk to greet him. "Did you have a good trip down from Schenectady?"

"Yes. I can't believe how much closer to spring it is in Virginia, compared to upstate New York."

"I know. This is a great part of the country to live in. We still have the change in seasons, yet we don't have the harsh winters or summers." Fred motioned for Shawn to sit and then returned to his desk and sat down. "Where's Amos?"

"I don't know. The last time I saw him, we were in Schenectady and he said he would meet me here."

"I haven't heard from him in nearly a week," Fred said. "Did he say that he might be going somewhere other than here?"

"Fred, like I told you, Kelly is a very strange person. He hardly spoke to me while we were training. I don't know if he had a chip on his shoulder or if he resented having someone in the military working with him. I really get the feeling that he thinks that I can't perform up to his standards because I'm not full-time with the CIA," Shawn said, feeling uneasy about speaking so negatively about him. "We never developed a friendship and for some reason I don't trust him."

"Well, without Kelly there's very little we can do today. Why don't you come back here tomorrow morning around nine? In the meantime, I'll try to track down Kelly. We've got a lot of work to get done in the next few days."

"When will we start the mission?" He sat up in the chair eager to hear Fred's response. Maybe Fred would finally tell him when it would start. Lester Fetor's disappearance was bothering him and he wanted to get the mission completed so he could get back quickly.

"Next week."

"I understand exactly how we get into the Soviet Union and that we'll meet someone there who'll take us to the cave, but how will we get out of there?"

"I can't give you that information yet," Fred said. "For your safety, we won't tell you until you're aboard the flight which will take you to your drop zone."

"It would be nice to know how we'll reach safety."

"I know how you feel, but if we tell you in advance you'll be thinking about that and not the mission. Don't worry, we'll take good care of you. Now go back to your apartment and get some rest."

Shawn left Fred's office and drove to Georgetown. He unpacked his suitcase and called Angela at her insurance office.

"Hello there," Angela was happy to hear that Shawn had been holding for her. "Where are you?"

"I'm at the apartment. Wow, it's really warm here. Maybe I'll sit on the veranda and get some rays."

"Oh. That's tough work. Don't get sunburned," she teased. "How long before you start your assignment?"

"I don't know for sure. I suspect about a week."

"So, has Kelly gotten any friendlier?"

"No, in fact he didn't show up today. I spoke to Fred about him. He didn't say too much, other than that he has an impeccable record with the agency. I could tell though that Fred was upset about what I told him and the fact that Kelly hasn't called for several days. Listen, I think it would be better if you stayed with your mother until I get back or until they arrest Lester."

"I don't feel very comfortable about this situation, Shawn."

"Angela, you wouldn't feel good about anything I'm doing with the CIA. Let's talk about something different."

"Well then, when you finish your little trip, I expect you to take me to Orlando for a couple of weeks."

"Orlando?" Shawn teased. "Let's go some place different."

"No. I want to go to Orlando. I know you don't like it, but I enjoy the theme parks. I don't know why I listen to you."

"You know why. You let me vent my frustration, and then you make me do whatever you want."

"That's not true. By the way, a bunch of women from work are going to the River Road House tonight."

"What's going on at the Road House?"

"We're going to celebrate the birthday of a girl who works for us in claims. Too bad you're out of town. I'll tell Shannon you asked for her."

"Yeah, you do that."

"Do you have a phone number for me in case I need to reach you when you're gone?"

"I won't have one. Just call Fred if you really need to contact me. You have his number."

"I would feel strange calling him and would do it only for an emergency. Don't worry I won't bother you, just do whatever you have to do," she said and slammed the receiver down on the phone.

Shawn smiled to himself. They had been married long enough for him to be used to her Italian temper and he understood that she was just upset about the mission. He didn't blame her; he was uncomfortable about it himself.

Chapter 26

Riga, Latvia, U.S.S.R.

K GB Commandant, Georgi Pasevs sat at his desk looking over a report that had just been handed to him by Nikolai Kravchuk, his vice- commandant. Georgi thought that the file on Boris Yegorov was dead, but once again it was a hot topic. The KGB's failure to stop the Americans from escaping with the defecting coach had cost his predecessor his life. Georgi knew all too well, the penalty for failure and he was not happy to have the problem resurface. He drew a blank about how to proceed with the situation.

"Yegorov must not have taken his secret formula with him," Nikolai said quietly, not wanting to upset Georgi, who had a reputation of shooting his subordinates if they agitated him. "Our informant says that Natasha Lyubarsky met with Wojcik who is working for the CIA. The report says the Americans are planning to have someone jump from a plane into Latvia at night."

Georgi interrupted him. "Do you think that I am stupid and cannot read this report?"

"No, commandant, I was only trying to help you." Standing erect, he began to tremble while he waited for what would follow next.

"Then shut up so I can read it," Georgi shouted and glared at him, then turned to continue reading the report. "The formula is in a sandstone cave. There must be a hundred of those in Latvia. The report does not say when they plan to make the jump, but it must be soon. Find Wojcik and bring him to me."

"Yes, Commandant. I will call Kiev and have him picked up at once."

Nikolai left the commandant and went to his office to call Kiev. He was told that they had been watching Wojcik because he had been meeting with members of a Ukrainian underground movement. They had suspected he was only involved to gain information for his newspaper, but now it appeared he might be working for the CIA. Nikolai was told that Wojcik had disappeared and they suspected he was in Riga. He had told a colleague that he was taking a short holiday and would be back in a week.

Nikolai asked to have the file sent to him, then told the agent to call him personally if they spotted Wojcik back in Kiev, then went to tell Georgi what he learned. He stood outside for several seconds to gather his thoughts, then knocked on Georgi's door and asked for permission to enter.

"Come in. What do you want?"

"I called Kiev and the CIA's man who met with Natasha is missing. They think he might be here in Riga, so I will have our people begin looking for him as soon as we get his file. I was given a description of him and his file will have a photo."

"What does he look like?"

"Middle age, 5 foot 8 inches, brown hair, thin, about 72 kilograms. He wears wire-rimmed glasses, very quiet, and keeps to himself. Seems to appear wherever there is news in the making. I guess that is why he works for a large American newspaper," Nikolai said, waiting a moment to see if Georgi wanted to comment. When the commandant didn't speak, he continued, "Our contact Natasha Lyubarsky only knows where the Americans will land after they jump from the plane. She did not know when."

"The information is useless unless we know when, Nikolai!"

Georgi slammed his fist down hard on the desk. "Find Wojcik and bring him to me. Act as if your life depends on it. Get the woman, too. What is her name?"

"Natasha Lyubarsky. I will have her located at once and then bring both of them here."

Visibly shaken, Nikolai left Georgi's office and started to work on locating Wojcik. He knew exactly what Georgi would do if he failed. The commandant would never accept failure. He could not forget the scene when Georgi had two agents brought to KGB Headquarters. They had done nothing wrong, except to do the impossible for the Commandant. Georgi had them taken to the basement where prisoners were interrogated and tortured. Moments later he shot both agents in the back of the head, claiming they had committed crimes against the Soviet Union. Georgi then blamed them for a mistake he made to prevent his superiors from learning the truth.

Nikolai Kravchuk had his people call in all KGB agents on duty to be briefed about Wojcik and Lyubarsky. It was made very clear in the briefing that Georgi was agitated and would not accept failure from any agent. He didn't have to remind them what that meant. After the briefing, he sent agents to the train station, the port, subway, and the Riga Hotel. Visitors normally stayed at the Riga, which was the only decent hotel in the city.

Nikolai was concerned about his own future. Walking down the hallway, he carefully avoided eye contact with anyone. He knew precisely what he would do if his agents failed. It had to be either himself or Georgi, and he would make sure that he got to the Commandant first.

CIA Headquarters, Langley, VA

Fred Unser had just sat down at his desk when his secretary called to say that Natasha Lyubarsky was waiting to see him. He had been waiting to hear from her and was eager to obtain the information she was bringing to him. Not wanting to keep her waiting, he went to the door and welcomed her into his office.

"It's good to see you again Natasha," said Fred, who couldn't resist staring at her. "Here have a seat. You look great."

"Thanks. You look terrific yourself, Mr. Unser." Unable to relax, she sat in the chair waiting for him to lead the conversation.

"Please, call me Fred," he said, feeling uncomfortable and thinking he might look foolish to her. "How was your trip?"

"Tiresome. I've been traveling a lot recently for the newspaper and then the trip here. I'm ready for a vacation," she said smiling at Fred, hoping he would not keep her long. "I have the information from Wojcik. Do you want it now?"

Fred was a bit surprised at her direct question.

"Why yes, let's see what Merrill selected."

Natasha pulled out the paper on which Merrill had written the fake news story. She leaned forward and wrote the exact location on the back of the paper.

"Do you have a map of this area in Latvia?" she asked.

"I do," Fred said as she pulled out a file folder and removed an aerial map of the location Wojcik had suggested for the landing. A couple of lines, drawn with a pencil, pinpointed the spot.

"This appears to be a very desolate area, just as we requested," he said.

He studied the map for a minute and asked her several questions about homes in the area, then made small talk about her job with the newspaper.

"When do you plan to return to Romania?"

"I plan to stay here for a week to visit family. Will you need me before I leave today?" She leaned forward indicating that she wanted to stand up and leave.

"No. The information you gave me was enough," he said smiling, hoping to relax her.

Natasha appeared to be extremely nervous. Perhaps being inside CIA Headquarters was in itself nerve-wracking for her. He understood that most people were uncomfortable working with the CIA. They generally did it either for money or for the love of their country. She was obviously helping them for the money.

"I hope that in the future you'll be agreeable to other short assignments that we might have for you."

"I would be interested as long as they don't interfere with my work with the Chicago Tribune. I would be fired instantly if they ever knew I had visited you."

Maybe that's why she's so nervous, he thought. She's right. Most newspaper employers who discovered that one of their journalists was working for the CIA would fire them immediately, unless it were one of the tabloids. He suspected a tabloid would pay her much more than she was making from the Tribune.

"I understand, and we have taken every precaution to prevent that from happening," Fred said as he walked Natasha to the door.

He returned to his desk and made a phone call downstairs to alert someone he had arranged earlier to follow her. Natasha was stopped by security as she entered the main lobby and was asked to wait while their agents checked a car in the parking lot for a bomb. After a couple of minutes, she was told there had been a false alarm, and it was safe for her to leave. Natasha rushed to her car and drove out of the parking lot, unaware that someone was following her.

Satisfied that he had taken the proper precautions, Fred began to enter the information Natasha gave to him into his computer. Suddenly, he remembered he had a meeting with Murphy and Kelly. He returned the file for the mission to his desk drawer and locked it. Murphy and Kelly were waiting for him in the small conference room when he arrived.

"Where were you yesterday, Amos?" his tone of voice indicating that he was annoyed that Amos did not call with a reason.

"I apologize," he said. "I got the dates mixed up and thought the meeting was today."

"In this business we don't get times or dates mixed up. There's no excuse for missing a meeting. You should have called. Are you feeling all right, or having any problems that I should know about?"

"I feel fine, and no, I don't have any problems. Like I said, I just got the date mixed up. It'll never happen again."

Fred dropped the issue and began to brief the two men about the mission dubbed 'The Inside.' They spent nearly three hours working out the details about where they would land and how their contact would signal them. Colonel Stoddard and Major Pollack had used the same type of signal each time they made the night jumps from the C-130's in Schenectady. The plan was quite simple.

Shawn was concerned that if something happened to Wojcik prior to their jumping there would be no back up. Unser assured him that there would be an emergency plan, but insisted that they continue with the current strategy to be sure they were ready. After the briefing, Unser told them to be back the next day at 9 a.m.

"What do you have planned for tonight?" asked Fred, curious to see if Kelly planned to spend some time with Murphy.

"I plan to work out in the Agency's exercise room and then get something to eat," said Murphy, who then turned to Kelly. "How about you, Amos?"

"I'm tired. I'm going to grab something to eat and watch a movie at my place."

Fred thought about Kelly's reply, then left the conference room and returned to his office. He was concerned that Murphy was right that Kelly didn't want to spend any time with him.

Atlantic City, NJ

Pauli DeSarbo walked across the room to the closet and got his suitcase. He laid it on the bed, then opened the cover and looked at the special compartment it contained. On the bottom was a lead case, built to secure a revolver and silencer, on top was a plastic container that held fishing lures. The lead case was overlaid with plastic to hide the bottom container in the event customs or airport personnel checked his luggage. X-ray machines would not reveal the lead-coated compartment that gave the appearance of fishing equipment. He even carried a small rod in the suitcase.

DeSarbo had the suitcase made several years ago to carry the tools of his trade, a Smith & Wesson .22 caliber revolver and silencer. Unlike most hit-men working for the Mafia, DeSarbo didn't like the powerful .357s, preferring the smaller caliber, which made little noise, and was very effective at close range, where he did most of his work.

A professional hit-man, Pauli was considered by many to be the best in the business. Insiders had claimed that DeSarbo was involved in the Jimmy Hoffa incident. Pauli was not a member of the Mafia; however, he made his living from the Mob by hunting down and killing people for them. He only rubbed out people who Mob hit-men were unsuccessful in eliminating. The word on the street was that when everyone else had failed, Pauli DeSarbo was the man for the job.

A quiet distinguished looking man, who stood 6 foot 1 inch and weighed about 180, DeSarbo was a loner who never attracted attention. Nobody knew where he lived or where he vacationed. When his services were needed, the right people had a pager number to call. He was careful to protect his private life, to prevent some jealous Mob member from giving information about him to the police.

His fee included not only finding Fetor and killing him, but also taking photos of Fetor to prove he was dead. Pauli enjoyed taking the photos. That was his trademark. The gruesome photos proved he had completed the job. A $3,000 Nikon camera gave him the best photos a camera could produce. He prided himself on his photography skills. To protect his identity and his specialized service, he had invested in a small commercial photo lab to develop film and print photos. The equipment got very little use, since he only worked on two or three cases each year.

The tax-free income he earned from the Mafia was in the range of one to three million each year. DeSarbo lived in a very modest neighborhood in the suburbs of Atlantic City. He had moved back east from Las Vegas when Atlantic City got its first casino. Though not a high stakes gambler, he thoroughly enjoyed playing dice and betting on the ponies. Always careful to keep his profile low and in the background, he wanted others to believe he was simply a quiet businessman.

It had been nearly a month since Tony Robelotto had called him. Robelotto was enraged that his men were unable to locate Lester Fetor. DeSarbo's price for finding and eliminating Fetor was less than what Robelotto suspected was hidden in the Swiss account. It wasn't a matter of money. He could not afford to have people skimming from his organization and getting away with it. This would encourage others to do the same. No, the price would be worth it to teach others a lesson.

DeSarbo knew that people, especially those like Lester Fetor, do not just vanish unless somebody causes them to disappear. To find someone who has disappeared, you must think like a hunter. People are often like animals and the hunter must think like them. Fetor was a person who loved scum. The kind of person who would never have class regardless of how much money he might acquire. A careful check in Scranton, Pennsylvania where Fetor stayed in a rundown, disgusting flophouse led him to Fetor's hotel in Boston.

Pauli suspected that he might leave from Boston, to avoid the obvious airports like Kennedy and Newark. After several days of showing Fetor's photo to prostitutes he found one who had seen him. She told Pauli about how he had nearly killed one of her friends. He gave her a C-note and she took him to the hotel. A little more upscale, but not a hotel Pauli would want to visit.

Several people who knew Lester well had told Pauli he loved to travel with women and was known to take prostitutes to Europe on bobsled business trips to impress them. A known drug user and suspected of being a dealer, he was also very comfortable in flophouses and cheap hotels. While his trail was cold, it was not too difficult to follow. DeSarbo knew that sooner or later Fetor would be in Switzerland.

At age 60, his nearly all-white hair had replaced the jet-black of his youth. Pauli looked rather distinguished in his expensive suit as he picked up his passport and airline ticket in Newark. He had a one-way ticket to Zurich, Switzerland. It would be a great time of the year to be in Switzerland. The ski resorts would still be open, making Lester easy to find. He had always stayed at the best places when he traveled on bobsled business, but now that he was paying with his own money, he would probably stay at a low budget hotel near where the elite vacationed. Lester was known for boasting about the celebrities that he rubbed shoulders with whenever he was in Europe.

This would be an easy job. He was confident that he would find Lester and it would not take long. Most of his victims hid in large cities like Chicago or Philadelphia, but this job would be a vacation in Europe.

Chapter 27

CIA Headquarters, Langley, VA

Fred Unser looked up at the clock when his private phone rang. Nobody knew the number except CIA agents working in the field. It was unlisted and billed to a loan company with a post office box.

"Quick Loans, how may I help you," Fred answered.

"Fred, this is Merrill Wojcik. I think something's wrong with our little venture in the Soviet Union."

"Where are you? How did you get this number?"

"I'm in Finland with one of your agents." His hands were damp with perspiration. Even sitting in a CIA office didn't give him a feeling of security.

"Who's with you?"

"John Matulewicz."

"Let me speak to him."

"Hello, Fred. I used the private number because you need to get this information right away. Merrill just told me what's going on and there's a problem with the mission to get Murphy and Kelly into the Soviet Union."

"What's going on with Wojcik?"

"He suspects that the woman you sent to meet with him is also working for the Russians."

"Oh shit! Why?" asked Fred, who suddenly felt nauseous.

"I'll let him tell you."

Merrill told Fred about his short romance with Natasha and how she was extremely interested in any information about the mission.

"I don't have any proof, but it's too risky to take a chance. My Ukrainian underworld contacts suspect that she's working for the KGB. I don't have any way to check her out, but I have a bad feeling about her."

"This puts us in a difficult position. I'm all set to put two people on a plane and now you tell me that Natasha might have the Russians waiting on the ground for them."

"Not exactly. I've found a different location, which is also very secluded, on the same route. They should make their jump about seven to eight minutes later."

"Okay, give me the precise details."

After Merrill gave him the information, Fred asked to speak with Matulewicz.

"John here, what do you need from me, Fred?"

"We can't have Wojcik meet the two men when they land in Latvia because if he returns to the Soviet Union now, the KGB will find him, get the information from him, and kill him. We'll need you to meet Murphy and Kelly. Can you find a safe place for him to stay in Helsinki?"

"That's a given. Don't worry. I'll take care of him until it's safe for him to return to Kiev."

"Now, do you need any help getting into the Soviet Union?"

"Not a problem. I can get a visa from the Soviets to let me vacation in Latvia for a couple of days."

"I'll get back to you with more information," Fred said. "In the meantime, don't let Wojcik out of your sight."

"I don't think you have to worry about that for a while. He understands the seriousness of the situation and is terrified that the KGB will locate him."

Maybe this problem would turn out for the better, Fred thought. Already part of the escape portion of the mission, Matulewicz worked for a Russian tour boat company that operated a gambling cruise ship between Helsinki, Finland and Tallinn, Estonia. Every day, he was given entry into the Soviet Union for a short time, providing him the perfect cover.

Nearly six foot four inches tall with a large build, Matulewicz was as strong as he looked. His blonde hair helped him blend in with the Finns and other Scandinavians working on the tour boat. An expert woodsman known for his wilderness survival skills, he often took part in missions that involved the CIA in back-country situations. He had worked for the Agency for nearly 10 years, and truly enjoyed what he did.

Fred thought about Natasha and the problem with Kelly. Maybe Murphy was on to something. He called Gary Circe and the director agreed that Fred should continue as planned, and said that he would authorize the extra expense to have agents assigned to tail and investigate Amos and

Natasha. Circe cautioned Fred to be very careful not to give any indication to either Murphy or Kelly that something was wrong. They could always abort the mission just prior to the men boarding the plane in London, if necessary.

Just after Fred arrived home that night, he received a call from the agent who was following Natasha.

"Fred, you'll never guess where our newspaper girl is staying."

"Where?" asked Fred.

"The Seagull Hotel in Virginia Beach."

"That's not so strange. We own it."

"That's right, but we didn't make arrangements for her to stay there."

"Is that so? I wonder how she happened to go there." Fred asked, puzzled.

"Well, I checked and she isn't registered. And are you ready for this?"

"Just tell me."

"She's staying with Amos Kelly."

Fred was silent for a moment. Suddenly the puzzle of Kelly's odd behavior became quite clear.

"Stick to her like glue," he said. "I talked with the chief a short time ago and got permission to have a surveillance team take over. I'll also arrange to have another team watch Kelly for the next several days. Thanks for the info."

Fred was frustrated that after all the precautions they had taken, the KGB had managed to get inside their circle. On the other hand, it was a blessing that he knew all the facts. He would let Kelly and Murphy continue as if nothing had happened and would make sure that Kelly knew the original location. The only people who would know the real location would be Matulewicz, Wojcik, and himself, plus the agent who would be on the flight. Fred had selected Brian Cooper to work with Colonel Stoddard on the plane, to help Murphy and Kelly prepare for the jump.

Everything else would be status quo. He would keep Kelly on the mission to prevent him from warning the Russians. The problem he had to work on was what to do with Kelly once they landed in Latvia. Since Kelly wanted to know the plans that would be easy. He would be given a different location for the cave and would have Cooper make sure he jumped at the first location. At some point he would have to inform Murphy and Matulewicz. That wouldn't be a problem. Cooper could take care of that with Murphy on the plane right after they left London. In the morning, it would be business as usual.

It was 6 a.m. when Fred Unser arrived at the office. Normally, he went to work before most employees at the huge complex, but this morning he was there an hour and a half earlier than usual. He tossed and turned most of the night. Wide awake and full of ideas, he finally got out of bed at 4:50 a.m. At 6:15 a.m. he was sitting in front of his computer working on the mission. There were too many unanswered questions. Just when he thought everything was ready, new developments arose. But this was to be expected in espionage. In fact, he didn't think he had ever worked on a case when something unexpected hadn't occurred. This was good in a way, since it forced everyone to keep on their toes and to plan on unforeseen problems. A mission without problems might not be so good, because they would tend to let their guard down. The problem with Amos and Natasha was just routine business.

At 6:40 a.m. he called Murphy at his apartment and asked him to come in earlier to meet with him at 8 a.m. After talking to Shawn, Fred unlocked his file drawer. Amos Kelly's file was in the front where he had placed it the previous evening. He began to read the background reports. Kelly had worked in both East Germany and the Soviet Union and had a total of 11 years working behind the Iron Curtain. Fluency in Russian and German made him perfect for the assignment.

Nothing in his file suggested that he might have compromised his duties. Kelly was not a flashy person or the type of person looking for the limelight. He was simply a quiet person, ready to perform whenever needed. Exactly what the CIA demanded of their agents. Fred thought about Murphy's complaint that Kelly was unsociable. Perhaps that was an indication that Kelly was trying to cover-up his guilt feelings.

Fred heard Shawn knock on his door. He was amused at his military habits. Normally, agents working for him simply walked into his office and greeted him, but not Shawn. Fred looked up and told him to come in and take a seat. He glanced at the clock and noticed it was 10 minutes to eight.

"Good morning," Fred got up and closed his office door. "Sorry to get you up so early. I must share some information with you."

Fred sat down at his desk with his back to Shawn, looking out the large window. Without turning around, he began to speak.

"I have to tell you something that I've never had to tell anyone working for me in all the years I have worked for this agency."

Fred turned around in his chair and faced Shawn. It was obvious that there was a serious problem. "Excuse me," Fred picked up his pipe and lit the half burned tobacco. He always smoked the pipe whenever he had to think out a serious predicament. "You need to know that there may be a problem with Amos Kelly. We don't have proof yet, but it appears that he may have provided information to a KGB informant about the mission."

"What do we do now?" asked Shawn.

"We have several choices. The two main ones are to either abort the mission right now, or continue as if nothing has happened. If we continue, it'll require some serious changes in the plan."

"Such as?"

"If we make any changes right now, it will tip Kelly and the Russians that we're aware of what they are doing. To prevent this, we'd have to continue with the plan until the last possible moment, and then remove Kelly when he wouldn't be able to inform the Russians. That would have to take place after you're on the plane, scheduled to make your jump."

"That's cutting it close," Shawn said. "If he goes on the plane, how will you control him?"

"Have you told him anything about the cave?"

"No. He's asked a couple of times, claiming that he should know so that if I got killed, he could complete the mission."

"We can give him erroneous information about the location where you are going to jump out of the plane. I've decided to find another place where our undercover agent will meet you. Our contact in the Soviet Union suspected there might be a problem, so he located an alternate spot."

"Boris said that there were hundreds of caves in that section of Latvia. I hope to hell that the Russians can't narrow down the number or I'll be in deep shit!"

"No, there are too many and besides, you're the only person who knows the exact cave. You'll be landing about a hundred miles from where the KGB will meet Kelly."

"That's fine, but what do we do about Kelly?"

"We could have the mission get screwed up on purpose," Unser said. "If we let Kelly think we're still going to the original place to meet with our contact, the KGB will be waiting there. We'll let Kelly jump out of the plane first, at the bogus location, then let you jump minutes later. You'll land where our contact will be waiting. Kelly will be at a remote location with the KGB and with no information. I can just imagine the confusion and anger when they meet him and it appears that he double crossed them. During that time you should be on your way out of the country."

"You mean you'll let Kelly escape?"

"If he's actually informing the Russians, think about the position he'll be in. It'll look like a double cross. The KGB won't be happy with a CIA

Agent who has taken money and given them bad information. If they don't kill him and he returns to the United States, we'll arrest him. He won't escape," Fred said and smiled.

"What about him giving other secret information about the Agency? You know, things like the names of undercover agents in Russia or Europe or other clandestine operations that you may be working on."

"He hasn't worked over there for several years and doesn't have any current information that will help them. I suspect that the KGB wouldn't believe him anyway. Remember, he took their money and gave them bogus information. No, I don't think he'll do very well once they catch him. They'll also be after his contact who made the arrangements."

After several minutes of silence, Fred asked. "How do you feel about the assignment now?"

"Well... obviously, I don't like the situation. This whole thing is about getting the formula out of the Soviet Union." Shawn thought about Boris Yegorov and the risks they had taken to help him escape. "I'm inclined to continue, because there is so much at stake."

"Then you'll do it?"

"I have to meet with Boris first. I need to be absolutely sure he can remember exactly where he hid the container with the formula and the pieces of the alloy composite."

"What makes you think he can recall that information? Remember, that's why you're going back, because he can't recall parts of the formula."

"I know that, but recalling the formula is a lot more complicated than to recall the location where he hid it, even if he wasn't in the beginning stages of Alzheimer's. I have no choice except to meet and talk with him. Otherwise we could spend months looking for the right cave and obviously that's impossible."

"I'll arrange it for this afternoon." Fred looked up at the clock. "It's 9:15. Why don't you go downstairs and get a cup of coffee in the cafeteria. Come back up here around ten so Kelly doesn't know you met with me."

Shawn left Fred's office feeling rather strange. He was aware of the danger when he agreed to take the assignment, but the risk had suddenly increased considerably. Unable to trust Kelly from the start, it would be a challenge to be nice to him knowing he was probably working with the Russians. And not only working with them, but attempting to endanger him by informing the KGB. The more he thought about Kelly, the madder he got.

He looked forward to meeting with Boris to learn how he was doing, and also to get some reassurance that the documents were in the cave. Shawn suspected that the Soviet coach was a broken man, with very little hope.

CHAPTER 28

Riga Latvia, U.S.S.R.

L ATVIANS CALLED THE KGB HEADQUARTERS IN RIGA 'The Corner House.' They often said that from the top floor one could see Siberia, implying that whenever a Latvian was taken there for questioning, if not killed, they were sent to serve time in Siberia. Inside the compound parking area, Nikolai sat in the back seat of his car, looking at a map, and placing red marks on the locations he thought might have sandstone caves. He planned to have his agents find as many as possible to get one step ahead of the Americans. It worried him that Georgi's reaction would be deadly, should the CIA get the documents and escape.

His driver sat patiently, not wanting to interfere with Nikolai's thinking. Nikolai was much different than the commandant, who often had violent outbursts. Every KGB agent working in Latvia knew that Georgi Pasvas covered up his incompetence by blaming subordinates. Nikolai folded up the map and slid it in his leather attaché case.

"Drive me to Dougavapils," he instructed. "I want to check out a place located in the country."

"Yes, Sir."

"Do we have enough gas?"

"Yes, Sir. I filled up just before you called for me," carefully avoiding Nikolai's eye contact.

He quickly thought about several other things he should do to prepare for the trip should the commandant question him further. "Good. When we get to Dougavapils, I will tell you where to go," Nikolai said.

He leaned back in his seat. Georgi Pasvas will have to be eliminated regardless of the success of this mission. Sooner or later the commandant would become too volatile and would have to take the fall. Now was the time for Nikolai to take control of the KGB's regional operation. The hour and a half-trip would give him plenty of time to think about his plan. Regardless of how he got rid of Georgi, everyone in the KGB would treat him like a hero. Nikolai smiled to himself in anticipation of how he would eliminate Pasvas and become the commandant.

Langley, VA

Shawn sat in the far corner of the cafeteria eating his breakfast, thankful that Angela was not with him. It would be difficult for him to conceal the problem with Kelly. A story in the Washington Post had caught his attention. Soviet troops were building up in the Baltic States. There were two pictures of the Soviet Army: one of tanks in Lithuania, the other of an armored car carrier in Latvia. The disorder behind the Iron Curtain made him feel uneasy. He hoped the military actions in Latvia would not complicate matters. Another story was about areas in the Soviet Union where non-Russians were rebelling against Russian occupation.

After looking at his watch he decided to leave, so he could be early for the meeting with Fred Unser and Amos Kelly. He didn't look forward to it. Regardless of what he had learned, he had to be friendly, and give the impression that he knew nothing about Kelly's connection to the Russians. In a way, he felt relieved. At least now he understood why Kelly kept his distance. Fred and Kelly were in the conference room waiting when he walked through the door at three minutes to ten.

"Good morning, Shawn. You're right on time. I like that," Fred said, careful not to suggest he had spoken with Shawn earlier. "Take a seat. We have a lot of work to do."

Shawn noticed Kelly was staring at him. "Good morning Amos."

"If you can call it that. I never feel good when I have to fight traffic early in the morning," Kelly said, then turned away, looking into space. "There's nothing like being in the country away from people."

"Well, let's get started on our little project," Fred said.

Fred briefed them about how they would enter the Soviet Union. Already familiar with this information, Shawn's mind began to drift and he thought about other events that might interfere with the mission. His biggest concern was what might happen once he got on the ground. He could visualize a group of angry KGB agents waiting with guns drawn, singing praise to Kelly for his role in their success.

"Shawn, I hope I'm not disturbing you!" Fred interrupted him, and Shawn realized that both of them were staring at him. His face flushed when he realized that they caught him day dreaming.

"Sorry. I was thinking about being cooped up in the back of the plane," said Shawn. "The last time I was in the Soviet Union, I spent a lot of hours inside a shipping crate with Professor Bodynski, Boris and another person waiting to be smuggled out of the country. It's a little hard to forget the experience and I was reminded of it when you told us that we would jump out of the cargo plane's lower compartment."

Fred continued his briefing. Shawn studied Kelly who was a graduate of Duke University with a degree in political science. He was a hard person to read, a strong type A personality and extremely aggressive, yet at the same time, very withdrawn. Fred looked at Kelly's cold black eyes and thought that he must have a split personality. The man was full of bitterness. Something must have changed his personality over the past ten years. The CIA did not hire people who were hostile. They did extensive personality testing before hiring and investing thousands of dollars to train their agents. Who knows what had happened to him. The only thing certain now was that he could not be trusted.

"I think that's enough information for today," Fred said. "You guys go to the gym and relax. You can't afford to let yourselves get out of shape while you're waiting to begin the assignment."

Amos immediately grabbed his coat and walked to the door. His eyes were closed and his hands were clinched in a tight fist as he walked down the hallway towards the elevator. Unser's an asshole, he thought. Maybe he'll finally wake up, when he learns that Murphy is being held by the Soviets on spy charges, and figure out that the CIA isn't so brilliant after all. This story will make the front page of every major newspaper in the world. I hope he and Circe get just exactly what they deserve for pulling this shit.

Once Kelly had left, Fred handed Shawn a slip of paper with an address on it. The note explained that Boris Yegorov would be waiting for him at 3 p.m. Perhaps after meeting with Boris he would have a renewed feeling of excitement about obtaining the secret formula. His enthusiasm had disappeared since he learned the truth about Kelly. He left Fred's office and went to his car to get his gym bag. A hard workout might help him get his mind off Kelly; and as Fred said, he needed to stay in top physical shape. There was no way of predicting what might happen once he got inside the Soviet Union.

After a strenuous workout, he called General Abbott, only to learn that he was in Texas attending a conference. His secretary said, "The general had selected a replacement for Captain Hamilton who would begin working the following week." Shawn already knew this, but was surprised when she added, "They decided to process Chief Robins' retirement papers."

"Is the general following through with his plan to move Staskowski?"

"Absolutely, he's being transferred to Lackland Air Force Base in Texas. Would you believe he had his congressman call the general to try and convince him to change his mind? I've never seen General Abbott so mad. But he politely shared with the congressman all the problems he had with Staskowski, as well as the rumor about Staskowski's venereal disease."

Shawn chuckled. "The trip to Las Vegas was too much of a temptation for a pair of gamblers like Staskowski and Robbins. Hamilton was really stupid to believe they would behave, and not embarrass the Air Force."

He said goodbye and went to his car. It was 1:30 p.m. when he finally drove out of the parking lot. Yegorov was living just across the state line in North Carolina. The Witness Protection Program had placed him in a house along the coast. The trip would take Shawn a little over an hour.

He mentally rummaged through the latest information about the U.S. Olympic Committee Bobsled Association's problems. According to a newspaper story, the USOC had gone to court and won control of the Association. Unfortunately, they were unable to locate any financial records of the more than half million in cash that was missing.

The FBI suspected that the Association's records were destroyed with John Chapadeau in the car bomb blast. The police still had no evidence to suggest who might have killed Chapadeau, although they suspected Fetor. They were almost certain, however, that Fetor had assassinated Nino Casatelli and had also supplied Roger Ferris with the cocaine that killed him. The police were still bewildered as to where Fetor might be hiding. They were not sure if he had simply disappeared, or if the Mafia might have killed him.

Shawn suspected that the Mafia might have located Fetor. They always seemed to find people who cheated them. Although he would never admit it, Shawn would rather have the Mafia locate Fetor than the FBI. The Mafia would make sure justice was served and he believed the judicial system would protect Fetor at an enormous expense to taxpayers. He also believed that Fetor had enough cash to hire an attorney who would get him released on some sort of technicality.

When Shawn rang Yegorov's doorbell, he heard movement and then noticed the drape covering the front window move. A moment later, the door opened and Boris rushed forward to hug Shawn. Tears formed in his eyes. He stood back and motioned for him to come inside.

"Zdrahstvooyti, zdrahstvooyti," Boris said. "I owe you and the professor for saving my life. I think about you all the time. You are well, yes?"

"Yes. I also think about you and the terrible time we had helping you escape from the Russians. You look well Boris, how do you feel?"

"I not so well. My mind, it fails me. I cannot remember things, and it upsets me very much. They tell me I repeat things all the time, but I feel well. How about you?"

"I'm well. I work in Washington now, which isn't too far from you. Now that I know where you live, I can visit you from time to time."

"I would like that. I'm a lonely man. Life isn't the same without my wife. I happy that you come to visit."

Shawn noticed a nurse sitting in the kitchen drinking coffee and went to introduce himself to her. She said she had been notified that he was coming to visit Boris. Nobody was allowed in the home, she said, unless arrangements had been made. Shawn asked if she would permit them a few moments of privacy and without speaking she left the room. He watched her go out on the patio where she couldn't hear the conversation.

"I must admit that I came to get some information from you Boris. I understand that you can't recall all the parts of the formula?"

"That is correct. Did I tell you about my wife and her parents?"

"Yes, I know," Shawn said.

"There's not much left now, for an old man like me."

"About the formula, Boris. I've been told that you wrote it on a piece of paper and hid it in a cave near Riga. Is that true?"

"Yes. I put the formula in a jar with pieces of the alloy composite. Nobody will find it!"

"But you said that you would tell me, right?"

"Yes, I only tell you. You are my friend. I hate the Russians. I never forgive them for killing my wife and her parents. Why do you come to see me?"

"Can you tell me where the formula is hidden, Boris? Where is the formula?"

Shawn felt tremendous pity for this man, who was once such a brilliant scientist. The Russians had destroyed his life.

"I need to know, Boris, because I plan to return to the Soviet Union and find the jar."

A glaze of moisture covered his eyes. "You must be careful. They kill my wife and her parents."

"I know Boris. But tell me where the jar is." Shawn asked again.

"Yes, you were at the cave with me. I hid it in the cave with the writing carved on the walls."

"The cave with the dates on the stone?"

"Da! That is the one," Boris replied. "The Russians will regret they kill my wife and her parents someday. The bastards." His face grew taut.

"Where in the cave? Where in the cave did you hide the jar?"

Boris described the cave to Shawn and helped him draw a small map that pinpointed the location. They chatted for another twenty minutes, then Shawn bid farewell. As he drove back to Georgetown, Shawn wondered if the information he had gotten from Boris was accurate. He recalled going to the cave with Boris and Professor Bodynski. The entrance had a collection of names and dates that people had carved into the stone. Shawn and the professor had only gone a short distance into the cave, however, because it was so dark.

When he returned to the cave he would have to take extra batteries for his flashlight, because Boris had said that the cave was nearly a half mile long and had several smaller tunnels that branched off in different directions.

Shawn reached the motel shortly after 6 p.m. and called Angela. They talked for several minutes, and then she read a newspaper article to him about the Bobsled Association. The USOC had been forced to provide funding to prevent the organization from filing for bankruptcy. He promised to call her in a couple of days.

CHAPTER 29

Zurich, Switzerland

Pauli DeSarbo looked out the window. The view from his room at the Royal Hotel was much more picturesque than the photos he had seen of Zurich. He studied the magnificent stone work of the centuries-old buildings across the street. A recent storm had left the city under a blanket of snow and he could visualize what it would be like in the mountains. For several minutes he watched people clearing the snow off the sidewalks, then decided to go downstairs and get a cup of coffee in the hotel restaurant.

Two days earlier he had located Lester Fetor drinking in a hotel bar on the other side of the city. Just as he suspected, Lester was drinking with a woman he had met in the bar. He was loud and boisterous. Pauli introduced himself to Lester and told him that he owned a string of hotels in the United States and Great Britain. Lester seemed interested when Pauli said he was planning to expand in Europe and was looking for an associate. Pauli chuckled to himself when he thought about Lester becoming a silent partner. He would definitely become silent, but not a partner.

Lester told Pauli that he was a retired businessman with no family and was simply enjoying himself for the first time in his life. He said he was looking for an opportunity to invest some money. They agreed to meet for dinner at a small restaurant, where it was usually quiet, so they could talk business without any interruptions.

Pauli picked up his Nikon camera, took a quick look around his room then opened the door and stepped into the hallway. If Lester asked why he had the camera, he would say that he had been photographing several sites suitable for locating a hotel. While walking towards the elevator he felt under his suit coat to make sure his Smith & Wesson was secure in its shoulder holster. The habit of rubbing his hand over his coat to feel the outline of the gun and silencer always gave him a confident feeling. Both were intact.

Stepping into the elevator, he pushed the button for the first floor, and looked at his watch. There would be enough time to sip coffee for an hour while watching people coming or going through the hotel lobby. Then he would walk to the restaurant to meet Lester. How easy it had been to locate Fetor. Mob fugitives like him were easy to locate if someone knew their habits. Lester was especially easy because he liked to drink and brag about himself. Pauli thought about Lester and wondered if he might have cash in his hotel room.

It was rumored that Fetor had over three million stashed away in Swiss banks. It would be nice if there was a large bundle, but that was not why he had been hired. Tony Robelotto was more interested in rubbing Lester out than getting the cash. Robelotto admitted that he did not know how much Lester had skimmed off him. Pauli suspected that at least a third of the cash was money that Lester swindled from the United States Bobsled Association.

While studying the people drinking in the hotel bar he wondered if they were on vacation, or perhaps business people who were relaxing after a busy day. Studying people to pass the time helped him to learn about different habits people had when they were traveling. A man sitting alone nervously sipping a drink caught his attention. The elderly gentleman acted as if he had done something wrong and was waiting for the police to discover him. Pauli looked up at the grandfather clock located in the corner of the room. It was 6:20 p.m. He finished his coffee and slipped into his heavy gray overcoat.

The street was quiet with only a few people rushing to get out of the cold. Light, fluffy snow was falling. The sidewalk was slippery and Pauli was glad he was wearing a pair of rubbers. They were good for safety and he could discard them later to prevent the police from identifying his footprints. He pulled his overcoat tightly around his neck and picked up his pace.

At 6:50 p.m. Pauli arrived at the restaurant. He opened the door and rushed inside, instantly feeling relief as the warm air eased the pain in his ears. After taking off his overcoat, he paused for a moment to look at himself in a mirror, making sure his coat and tie were adjusted properly. A sign over the door identified where the bar was located and he guessed Lester might be in there.

The room was crowded and noisy. It took a minute for Pauli's eyes to adjust to the light and then he spotted Lester near the end of the bar. For a moment, he studied Lester, who was talking with a different woman than the other night. Pauli walked closer to listen to their conversation.

Lester was telling her that he was an investor and was about to build several large hotels in Europe. He suggested that she meet him there the following evening for dinner. Pauli waited until he heard her agree, then walked up to them and patted Lester on the back.

Lester spun around quickly and smiled when he saw Pauli.

"Pauli, I want you to meet Heidi."

Pauli nodded then turned around quickly to prevent her from getting a good look at him. Lester reminded her they had a date for dinner the next night, then followed Pauli into the dining room. They selected a table in the corner where they could talk privately. Sitting with his back to the rest of the room, Pauli made it difficult for anyone to observe him discussing business over dinner with Lester. A young waitress greeted them.

"Good evening! May I get you a drink?" she asked as she handed them menus.

""You sure can sweetie!" replied Lester, grinning. "I'd like a scotch and water."

"Please give my friend a double scotch and I'd like a black coffee," said Pauli, who was pleased that Lester was ordering more liquor. This would make his job easier.

After the waitress left, Pauli turned to Lester. "I'm delighted that you could make it tonight. I like people who are on time."

"I got here nearly an hour early. I'm never late for a meeting. If I tell someone that I'll meet them, I'm there no matter what. Yes sir, you can bet the bank on it."

He will not make his dinner date tomorrow night. Thought Pauli.

"I plan to rent a car tomorrow and ride around Zurich to look at some sites to build a resort hotel," Pauli said. "Perhaps you would like to go with me?"

"Absolutely, partner. What time do you wana go?" His eyes were bloodshot indicating that Lester had been drinking scotch most of the day.

"About mid-morning? That would give us time to rest. There's no rush. Is that okay?"

"Yeah. I like to sleep late, then get something to eat before I start the day."

"Good. I'll rent a car and pick you up around 10:30 a.m."

The waitress interrupted them with their drinks and took their dinner order. Pauli watched as Lester gulped down his scotch. The veins in his cheeks were clearly visible despite his bright red complexion. It was obvious that he had been a heavy drinker for a long time. Lester continued to brag about how successful he had been as a businessman, attempting to convince Pauli that he would be a perfect partner.

"I want to build the type of resort hotel that will attract only the elite," Pauli said, amused that Lester was so gullible. "I'll put up the majority of the cash that is needed and I already have a bank commitment to cover the balance, but if you would like to invest a small amount and become a partner I would agree to it."

"Do you want me to manage a hotel?"

"Certainly, if that's what you would like to do. Do you have any management experience?"

"Hell, yeah. I used to own a small resort hotel and managed the United States Bobsled Association," Lester replied. Suddenly realizing that he just made a big mistake. He hoped Pauli hadn't seen any of the newspaper stories connecting him to the bobsled group.

"Oh, so you were involved with sports." Fetor's stupidity amazed Pauli. To make Fetor think he didn't know who he was, Pauli added. "Well, I never have enough time or interest to get involved. I don't even read the sports pages."

Dinner arrived and he ordered Lester another double scotch. Lester ate his steak like an animal. He was disgusting. Saliva dripped down his chin and bits of meat slobbered on both sides of his lips. When they finished eating, Pauli ordered Lester another drink while he sipped his coffee.

"How much money would you like to invest in the hotel?" asked Pauli?

"I could come up with two million real quick if I need to." Lester said, wiping his face with the cloth napkin. "I'd need to have something in writing to guarantee me as a partner and manager."

"That's no problem. We won't need any money for several months, but I'd feel more comfortable if I could see proof that you have that much cash at your disposal."

"No problem. As soon as we're finished I'll show you my bank statements. I only live a block from here. Between you and me, I have about four million in several Swiss accounts." Lester belched, then let out a big laugh as he imagined a cushy job where he could skim millions more in the future. His plans to hide in Casablanca would have to wait while he built a larger nest egg.

Pauli put money down on the table for the check and they left for Lester's hotel. The cold air encouraged them to walk at a fast pace. The hotel was only a short distance and within minutes they were in the lobby. The building was small and in the style of a typical low budget hotel on the west side of New York City. They walked past the desk clerk who was totally engrossed in a magazine and didn't pay attention to them. Lester's room was on the fourth floor, not too far from the elevator.

It took a couple of minutes for Lester to locate his key. The scotch was affecting his balance. Pauli took the key from him and opened the door. Lester staggered in and removed his coat dropping it on the floor.

"Sit down while I get my bank statements."

Pauli took off his coat and laid it on a chair near the window. He watched Lester pull a box out from under the bed and begin to search through it. This will be too easy he thought.

"Do you mind if I use your bathroom? Too much coffee."

"Na, help yourself partner."

Pauli shut the door behind him, pulled out his revolver and quickly screwed on the silencer. He waited a moment, then pulled the chain to flush the toilet. Instead of placing the revolver back, in the holster, he slid it inside his belt under his sport jacket. When he returned to the room, Lester was sitting on the bed sifting through several sheets of paper.

"Take a look at these!" Lester said with a smile, waving three sheets at him. "This should prove I've got plenty of cash!"

Pauli smiled as he looked at the statements. He would take them with him and give them to Robelotto when he returned to the States.

"What's that paper?" Pauli asked and pointed to a single sheet on the bed. Lester turned and reached to pick up the paper. In a split second, Pauli removed the revolver and fired a single round into the back of Lester's head. His hand never reached the document. The slug entered Lester's skull, instantly killing him. Pauli watched his body freeze for a moment then fall face first down on the dark blue quilt. Blood began to ooze out from the back of his head onto the bed.

Pauli unscrewed the silencer and returned the revolver to his shoulder holster. Several copies of bank statements were pushed to the floor when Lester's body began to twitch. It only took Pauli a couple of seconds to gather all the statements and place them inside his jacket pocket. There was nearly two thousand dollars in American cash hidden in a dresser drawer. He folded the stack of hundreds and slipped them into his pocket.

After a quick look around the room to be sure Lester hadn't written his name or any information about their discussions anywhere, he put on his overcoat. It took him several minutes to search Lester's pockets and around the room for information that might link him to the crime. He left a wad of Swiss francs in Lester's wallet.

Finding nothing significant, he reached inside his overcoat pocket and removed the camera. He tugged on Lester's shoulder so he would roll over on his back. The dead man's eyes bulged, suggesting that there was a lot of pressure inside his head.

Nothing works as good as a nice .22 caliber with a silencer, thought Pauli. Someone could have been standing right outside the door and they wouldn't have heard the shot. Pauli looked at the body of this disgusting pig of a man and thought that he had done everyone a big favor.

He took several pictures and then stood next to the door listening to be sure nobody was walking down the hall. Turning the knob carefully, he opened the door and peeked into the hallway. Seeing no one, he hurried to the stairs. When he reached the first floor, he opened the door slowly, looking around the lobby. The desk clerk was still reading his magazine, paying no attention as he slipped outside.

The temperature was well below zero and the wind was still blowing quite hard. It was too risky to hail a cab, so he pulled up the collar on his overcoat and walked as quickly as he could on the slippery pavement. He chuckled to himself as he thought about how easy it had been to blow Lester away. Not only had he completed the job, but he had also obtained the bank statements and some extra spending money.

In the morning he would take a train to Frankfort where he would catch a flight back to the States. Perhaps he would go to southern California, after he collected the balance owed him on the hit. A couple of months in the warm sun would be just what he needed. Maybe he would spend some time at the horse track.

Langley, VA

The ringing telephone woke Shawn. He reached over and picked up the receiver. It was Amos Kelly.

"Shawn, did I wake you?"

"Yeah. I got in late last night, but that's okay. What time is it?"

"About ten of eight. Do you want to get some breakfast?"

"Sure. Where?"

"In my hotel."

"How about 9 a.m.?" Shawn asked, wondering if Amos was suddenly being friendly because he suspected that the CIA knew he'd been working with the KGB.

Amos was waiting in the dining room reading the paper when he arrived.

"Good morning," Shawn said. "I can't believe I slept so late."

"You must have been tired. You said you were out late. Where were you?"

"I went downtown and had a few too many glasses of wine while I listened to some jazz," Shawn lied, covering up his visit with Boris Yegorov. "The music was great."

"What time do we have to meet with Unser this afternoon?"

"The message I got was to be at his office at two. I guess Gary Circe is supposed to be meeting with us."

"He isn't actually meeting with us. The Director simply sits in on such briefings if there's the potential for a serious problem."

"What type of problem do you think they're worried about?" Shawn asked, interested to hear what Amos would say.

"Us being caught in the Soviet Union without a visa. Then they would charge us with spying. Do you realize what the Russians would do with that story?"

Shawn studied Kelly as he explained how the international media would have a field day with a story about two Americans who entered the Soviet Union illegally.

"Circe will be in trouble with the president if this little deal goes bad," Amos said. "Presidents could care less about what happens to spies so long as they don't get any bad press."

"I can understand that, but frankly I'm more worried about my ass than theirs."

"Don't worry this job will be a breeze."

The two men chatted for another 20 minutes, then Shawn returned to his apartment. He shut the drapes and thought about the meeting with Fred and Gary Circe, wondering what the briefing was about. Maybe they would be getting their schedule. Hopefully, Fred would tell them what the plan was to get them out of the Soviet Union.

CHAPTER 30

CIA Headquarters, Langley, VA

Shawn showed his identification at the entrance of the Agency complex then drove to the parking lot outside of Fred Unser's office. It was the first week of March and snow still covered the ground. He wished it were a couple of months later. Thoughts about jumping out of a plane again in the cold made him shiver.

It was 1:30 p.m. He got there before Kelly or Gary Circe arrived, and he told Fred about Kelly's change of attitude.

"I'll bet he wants to make sure you're comfortable with him," Fred said, "so we don't change our plans at the last minute."

"But we have to change our plans or the KGB will be waiting for us on the ground! Right?"

"Yes. That's what we want him to think. Here's what will actually happen. Kelly will be the first to jump from the plane. You'll jump exactly seven minutes and ten seconds later. John Matulewicz will be waiting about 92 miles east of the original location. The KGB will catch Kelly, but we don't believe the Russians will tell anyone about the mission. They'll look foolish when they don't have you."

"You hope they won't have me!"

"There's no way they'll have time to change their plans quick enough to locate you," Fred said. "You and Matulewicz won't have any time to waste, because the Russian satellites will pick up a signal when you jump so they'll have an approximate location. You'll have to act quickly since you'll be much farther away from the caves than we originally planned. It's a good thing we didn't tell Kelly where the cave is located."

"I didn't think about it at the time, but the night he and I made our last jump in Schenectady, he wanted to go with me to meet with Boris. He said it was important for him to know the location, in case something happened to me so he could complete the mission."

"It was a good decision not to tell him early on. I'll give both of you a bogus location today so he can send the KGB to a different place. That'll give you and John more time."

"What happened to Natasha Lyubarsky?"

"She returned to her job in Romania as a correspondent with the Chicago Tribune."

"Didn't you have her arrested?"

"No. We didn't want to compromise the mission. It's better that she thinks we're still going along as planned." Fred picked up his pipe, stuffed some fresh tobacco into the bowl, and lit it. He leaned closer to Shawn. "Now and then we can give her incorrect information to mislead the KGB. It'll take them about a year to figure out that we know she's working with them."

"She must have been a real hot number for the guy in Latvia to go to bed with her!"

"There's no question about her looks. She's beautiful and so is her figure," Fred drew in on his pipe, blowing the smoke upward as he looked at the ceiling. "She's what I would call a knockout. Poor Wojcik."

"Poor! You should say lucky if she's that good looking."

"Remember this in case you ever get into that kind of a situation over there. If some great looking chick comes on to you, she has to be a plant."

"Don't worry about me. I think Angela has a sixth sense. She would kill me if something like that ever happened. All kidding aside, anyone with any common sense has to know that a young woman looking like Natasha doesn't fall for an older man in that short amount of time," Shawn laughed, then added. "Unless of course, the man is extremely wealthy!"

"That's for sure. Have you heard the latest on the Bobsled Association's saga?"

"No. The last I heard was that the FBI was still looking for Lester Fetor. He seems to have disappeared off the face of the earth."

"Well, I read an FBI report stating that Fetor's body was discovered in Zurich, Switzerland," Fred said. "Apparently someone shot him in the back of the head. The Swiss police believe it was a professional contract hit. There wasn't any evidence in the room. A real clean job."

"Well, that's all of them! They're all dead."

"What do you mean?"

"All of the bastards who were skimming money from the Bobsled Association -- Roger Ferris, Nino Casatelli, John Chapadeau and now Lester. They're all dead. It's an awful thing to say, but good riddance. Those guys set the bobsled program back about 10 years. They treated the athletes like dirt, and stole or spent all the funding, so they could live the good life. Maybe the Bobsled Association can rebuild and finally have a program where the athletes have a chance of winning an Olympic Medal."

"From what I understand staff from the U.S.O.C. has been running the Association all winter."

"I think you're right." Shawn said. "They removed Wilber Hippenbecker from his position and appointed a new board to manage the organization."

Suddenly, the phone rang, interrupting them. Fred's secretary said Amos Kelly had arrived.

Amos walked into the room.

"I waited for you in the lobby," Amos said to Shawn. "I didn't realize you got here so early."

"I got here early to chat with Fred about the problems the Bobsled Association has been having."

The door opened with no announcement and Gary Circe walked in with someone Shawn had never seen. Gary greeted everyone and introduced Brian Cooper. Brian was a CIA agent and would be part of the crew who would assist with the jump. He was just under 6 foot tall and his solid build gave Shawn the impression that he was in excellent physical condition. Cooper looked so young that Shawn wondered how much experience he had with the CIA.

"This is what you guys have been waiting months for." Fred moved around to sit on the edge of his desk.

"You'll be boarding a Southern Air 707 Cargo transport jet tomorrow at National Airport. The plane will land in London. You'll have a twelve-hour crew rest and then the plane will head to Moscow."

"Fred, what's the purpose of Southern Air's flight?" asked Gary.

"They're transporting an industrial air compressor that the Soviets contracted for from an American company. When Southern Air takes off at London they'll pressurize the plane until shortly before Shawn and Amos make their jump. Our undercover agent is already on his way to Riga, Latvia and will be waiting on the ground."

"Who's that?" asked Amos.

"I can't say right now. We'll reveal his identity just before you make your jump." Fred said, avoiding looking at Kelly. "If you two land exactly where you're supposed to, that person will be there waiting."

"Fred, what will you tell the media if this operation goes sour?" Gary asked, looking worried.

"We've prepared a press release just as we always do prior to an operation like this."

"What are you planning to say?"

"We'll deny everything. That's the standard practice of all countries whenever something goes wrong. If we have to, we'll negotiate for the release of Shawn and Amos. We know the whereabouts of many of their KGB Agents working in this country. We'll arrest a few, and make an exchange."

"The President will have a stroke if this becomes an international incident," Gary said, staring at Fred. "If they get caught the president will get rid of me, and you might as well forget your future with the Agency."

"I'm well aware of the situation. Trust me. We've double checked every little detail in preparing for this operation. The information we're after is well worth the risk. Whether we use the alloy or not, we can't afford to let the Soviets get the formula."

"I understand the importance of the alloy, but you can't argue it's not a dangerous endeavor. I've heard you say 'trust me' in the past and you've had to eat your words. We don't want this to turn into an international incident."

"Gary, we've been over this with a fine tooth comb and everything is all set. I'm confident that this will go as planned."

"I guess I'll have to trust you," Gary said, then went over to shake hands with Shawn and Amos. "I wish both of you the best of luck. Please be careful." He turned back to Fred. "Keep me informed of everything that's going on."

When Gary left the office, Fred got off his desk and walked around to his chair. "We'll leave here at 9:30 a.m. tomorrow and go over to National. Be here an hour early. And Kelly, make damn sure you're on time."

"Don't worry, I'll be here." The expression on his face denoted resentment for being singled out in front of Gary Circe.

"All right. I'll see you guys in the morning."

"What about a briefing on getting us out of the Soviet Union?" Kelly asked impatiently. He eyes fixed on Fred.

"That will be given to you en route to Latvia."

"Why not before? Don't you trust us?" He stared at his superior and appeared to be strung out.

The tone of Kelly's sarcasm was clearly evident, but Fred was determined not to give him any indication that they knew about his involvement with the Soviets. "Of course I trust you, but we still can't take a chance on the information leaking out."

"No shit! Do you honestly think we'll go around telling people?"

"First of all, don't ever talk to me like that again, or I'll have you disciplined." Fred said, wishing he could tell Kelly what he really thought. "Secondly, this is Agency procedure and you know it. You'll get briefed when it's necessary. I'll see you tomorrow and you better be on time. Now get out of here. Shawn, you stay for a few minutes. I need to finish discussing the bobsled situation with you."

Fred followed Kelly into the hall then shut the door. Turning to Brian he said, "Why don't you take off now. You'll need some time to get ready. Just make sure you catch the last flight to Albany tonight and that you're at the Air Force Base in Schenectady in the morning."

"Don't worry boss, I've got you covered," Brian said as he got up and shook both their hands and told Shawn he would see him at National the next day.

Fred was still aggravated that Kelly was pressing him for more information. "Now that Kelly has the date and the time you're jumping, he will probably call Natasha immediately so she can get the information to the KGB."

Fred sat down at his desk and picked up his pipe. He lit the partially burned tobacco, blew a large puff of smoke upward and then looked at Shawn. "Kelly's so guilty, he can't control himself. In less than an hour the KGB will know when he'll arrive in Latvia. They just won't know that he'll be alone!"

"Can you tell me how I'm getting out from behind the Iron Curtain or do you want to wait?"

"No. I'll tell you right now. Matulewicz will have snowshoes and will drive you to about 15 miles from the border of Finland. That's why you got the survival training with Colonel Stoddard and Major Pollack in Schenectady. After the plane is airborne, Cooper will give you written instructions about where you are to cross the border. He'll also give Kelly false directions. We want the KGB to think you guys are planning to fly out of Moscow, so make sure that he doesn't see yours. We'll give Kelly a fake ID, passport, visa and plane ticket. You'll be given other instructions about what to do if we need to come in to rescue you."

"Well, that was the original plan. I don't understand why Kelly has a problem with that."

"You can be sure the KGB is pressing him so they have time to beef up security in that region. Right now they don't have a clue as to just what the plans for escape are. If we gave them the information early they wouldn't believe it, but by letting them find out at the last minute it will throw them off."

"You're confident that everything has been worked out and I won't have a problem?"

"I meant what I said earlier. We have gone over everything with a fine tooth comb and I don't expect a problem, or we wouldn't go ahead with the mission. Are you comfortable with the directions Boris gave you to find the cave?"

"I know exactly where the place is."

"Good. You won't have much time to search for the formula. Remember, Kelly will tell the Soviets as much as he knows and they'll be searching for you."

"I know, but I think I can get it quickly, as long as Boris' directions are accurate. I hope his Alzheimer condition hasn't affected his long-term memory."

"You talked with him. What's your gut feeling?"

"I think he knows exactly where it is. Don't worry, I feel confident. If we jump on Friday night and get the formula early Saturday morning, I should get to Finland by late Sunday or early Monday. With any luck, I'll be back here by Tuesday. Right?"

"I would think so, are there any more questions?"

"No. Now, I'm going to go out and relax, and have a nice steak dinner."

Fred smiled and stood up, and shook Shawn's hand as he spoke. "Shawn, you'll do okay. I'm sorry that Kelly turned out to be a problem. We'll deal with him when the mission is over."

"What if he stays in the Soviet Union?"

"If he chooses to stay there fine, but I don't think he will stay there alive! I'm fairly certain about that, but if I'm wrong, we'll arrest him like I told you. Don't worry, he'll get what he deserves."

Fred watched Shawn leave his office, then sat down in his chair and closed his eyes. Kelly's involvement with the Soviets totally frustrated him. There could never be reason enough for someone to turn against his or her country. Regardless of the situation, he would make sure the mission went as planned, and in time, Kelly would pay dearly for becoming a traitor. Maybe the KGB was paying him a lot of money, but if they didn't kill him, he would make sure that the CIA did!

CHAPTER 31

Riga, Latvia, USSR

GEORGI PASVAS LOOKED UP AS HIS VICE-COMMANDANT, Nikolai Kravchuk, entered his office.

"Commandant, we just got a call from Natasha Lyubarsky. She said the two CIA Agents would land in a potato field near Vecumnieki. That is about forty kilometers southeast from here."

"I know where Vecumnieki is, you idiot. Do you know exactly where and when? There are hundreds of potato fields in that area."

"We have the exact location, but we are not sure about the time. We know they are planning to jump on Friday evening. I will have our people hidden around the area, and will grab them as soon as they land."

"No, you will not." Pasvas said and looked at his vice-commandant, shaking his head. "I do not want them to know you are there. We want the technology, not them. You have our people follow them back to Riga or to wherever they go. Put enough people on the surveillance so you can keep splitting up the tail.

I do not want them to suspect we are following them. Once they go to the cave and get everything, arrest both of them. Bring them back here for interrogation and we will separate them. I do not want Murphy to know we are working with Kelly."

"Yes, commandant. I will secure the farmhouse tomorrow so we will have time to check out the entire area."

"Make sure that you have a good understanding of all the roads in case they try to outrun our people. Make arrangements to have a couple of helicopters fly overhead to help with the surveillance."

Nikolai turned to leave. As he reached for the door, Georgi yelled at him. "What happened to that newspaper man who was working with the underground?"

"Wojcik. We still have not located him. Our people are searching here in Riga and in Kiev. We do not believe he was working with the underground, but he was friendly with some of the leaders of the Latvian Socialist State."

"He cannot disappear off the face of the earth, Nikolai. I want him brought to me!" He took a puff on his cigarette and began coughing uncontrollably. His eyes watered and his face got red. After several minutes he calmed down and mashed the cigarette in the ash tray.

"He may have left the country. We have searched his apartment and have someone watching it around the clock. We also have someone watching where he works for the New York Times. I am told that the newspaper has not printed any new articles with his byline for the past two weeks. Perhaps he has returned to America."

"I think he is hiding," Pasvas rubbed his chin. "The other correspondent, Natasha, who is working for us; have you talked with her?"

"No, commandant. I did not talk to her personally, but one of our agents in Kiev spoke with her."

"You idiot! I know you did not speak with her personally. What information did our people get from her?"

"Everything I told you came from her. She gave us the date, exact location and approximate time the two Americans will jump from the plane."

"Yes, yes. Find Wojcik."

Nikolai left the office quickly. Moisture was running down his back and his shirt was soaking wet from the tension of dealing with the commandant. The first thing he would do would be to get a list of people Wojcik was known to be friendly with in Riga and Kiev, then have their homes searched. He had to do something fast, because the commandant was losing his patience. Nikolai knew he would be blamed if they did not catch the Americans. Knowing the commandant's history made him afraid for his life.

He would have to put his plan in action soon, or it would be too late. Nikolai was confident that he would soon be chosen as the next KGB Commandant in Riga. The thought quickened his pace as he left the Corner House.

Schenectady AFB, NY

Dave Koltermann thought it was a perfect day for flying as he guided the Southern Air 707 cargo plane down onto the landing strip at the Schenectady County Airport. He listened as his copilot, Frank Kovacs, radioed instructions to the Air Force Base Operations office. There would be just a short wait in Schenectady while an industrial gas compressor was loaded. The Soviet Government was desperate for the 40,000 pound-compressor needed to compress natural gas for their heating plant in Moscow.

In Schenectady, they would also pick up Colonel Stoddard with equipment needed for the CIA's mission, and a CIA agent. Southern Air had been contracted to deliver the compressor to Moscow and, along the way, would be dropping off two people. They would leave Schenectady and fly to Washington where they would pick up the two men who were going to parachute from the plane.

Koltermann laughed to himself, thinking about the crazy idea the CIA had come up with this time. He was glad he was flying and not jumping out of the airplane somewhere in the Soviet Union. He removed his seat harness and asked Kovacs to go inside to operations and check the documents to be sure that all the paperwork they needed to enter the Soviet Union was in proper order. Concerned about the cargo he went to the rear of the plane to check on Mike Cristiano, his second officer.

Cristiano was watching the cargo handlers maneuver the gas compressor into position to slide onto the plane's roller bed. Once in place on the rollers the enormous industrial gas compressor moved forward with ease. Cristiano showed the handlers exactly where the crate had to be positioned in the center of the aircraft. Koltermann watched as his second officer instructed the handlers on how to secure the huge piece of equipment to the floor.

"Mike, I'm going inside with Frank. Make sure these cargo handlers leave the plane as soon as the freight is completely secured."

"We're nearly finished. I think Colonel Stoddard may have some equipment, but we can carry that through the crew door."

"Okay. Come in as soon as you can and we'll grab some coffee to take with us on the plane. The Air Force always has plenty, if you can stand drinking it."

Koltermann walked down the plane's stairs and stood on the runway looking at the row of C-130's on the parking ramp. It brought back memories of when he flew the huge birds as an Air Force major. He turned and walked towards the door marked "Operations." His youthful face and blond hair often gave people the impression that he was too young to be the pilot of the aircraft. He spotted Frank sitting at a table talking with someone.

"Dave, this is Colonel Roger Stoddard. He'll be assisting the CIA's two men on the flight."

Colonel Stoddard stood up and greeted Koltermann with a handshake, and invited him to sit down. "I was instructed to give you this information when you picked me up." Stoddard pulled out a sheet of paper and handed it to Koltermann.

The document instructed them to list both Stoddard and Brian Cooper as cargo handlers on the plane's manifest. "Who is Brian Cooper?" asked Koltermann.

"Never met him, I think he's CIA. He's flying with us to make sure the two men jumping don't have any problems."

"Where is he?" An uneasy feeling crept into him as he became aggravated that Cooper might be late and prevent them from leaving on time. He glanced around nervously to see if someone might be walking in their direction.

"Don't know. I got a call from Langley yesterday inquiring about when we were leaving Schenectady. I was told that Cooper would be here when we left and I haven't heard anything since."

"We're just about loaded now," Koltermann said and looked at his watch. "I hope he gets here soon."

Five minutes passed, and then Cristiano entered the room.

"Dave, someone by the name of Cooper is out on the plane. He showed me his identification and said he preferred to wait there."

"Now isn't that a surprise," Koltermann said facetiously. "Frank, is the paperwork all set?'

"All set. Since our other passenger is on the plane, we can get our coffee and leave," Kovacs said and picked up his brief case.

"Let's do it then. Mike, did you ask Cooper if he wanted anything?"

"I told him we're getting coffee and he said he didn't need anything."

"It's only about an hour and ten minutes to National. The galley gets supplied there so if he changes his mind, he can get coffee after we leave Washington."

They walked out to the plane to prepare for takeoff. Koltermann and Cristiano stood at the ramp for a moment reminiscing about their past when they had flown together in the Air Force. Cristiano had served with Koltermann at McDill Air Force Base as a flight engineer on a C-130 cargo plane for nearly two years. Koltermann left the Air Force and was hired by Southern Air. Later, he encouraged Cristiano to join him. Kovacs also was a former C-130 pilot, but had not served with either of them.

Cooper was waiting for them on the plane and once they exchanged greetings the two pilots returned to the flight deck to prepare for takeoff. Cristiano took Cooper and Stoddard to the forward cargo hold to secure their personal luggage and show them where they would sit. Stoddard had two large canvas bags containing the equipment for Murphy and Kelly.

"What about the clothing and the snowshoes they need to cross the border?" Cooper asked.

"I don't know anything about that end of the mission," Stoddard said. "Fred Unser told me to outfit them with everything they need to enter the country and to protect themselves. The GPS and infrared signal device are to help them in case they run into trouble and the escape route is changed. I guess your people will near the border in Finland waiting to help them."

"That makes sense. There is a contact person in Latvia who will be waiting for them and he probably has clothing," Cooper said and shook his head when he thought about Murphy and Kelly jumping from the plane at 37,000 feet into sub-zero temperatures. "It'll be damned cold at the height they're jumping. I get cold just thinking about it."

"They'll have their work cut out for them," Stoddard said and looked at Cooper. "They'll have very little information about which way the wind is blowing, or just exactly how hard. They'll have to check their GPS all the way to the ground to be sure they land where your contact is waiting for them."

Stoddard looked at Cristiano and asked, "What door will they be jumping from?"

"They'll have to exit from the aft cargo hold. When we leave National, I'll take you downstairs and you can check the area and leave the equipment there until you are ready for them to suit up."

"Where is the stairway leading to the aft cargo hold?" Cooper asked, looking around the huge plane not seeing any doors.

Cristiano laughed and said, "There's no door from the inside of the plane. I'll have to unscrew a floor panel. Then we can drop down to the cargo compartment."

"Drop down. Isn't there a ladder?"

"No. The aft cargo compartment is usually only entered from the outside. We load small cargo crates that are being shipped, and never need to go there during the flight."

"What about jumping from the door up here?" Stoddard asked.

"Too dangerous, it's too close to the wing. The suction of the jets could pull them into the engines. The aft cargo hold is perfect. That door is reconfigured to slide on a track making it easy to open and close during the flight. About 45 minutes before they jump, we'll go down into the cargo hold and put on oxygen masks. It'll take 30 minutes for the plane to de-pressurize, giving us plenty of time to get them dressed and ready to jump. After they jump, we'll shut the door and wait until the plane has re-pressurized. Once that's done, we can return upstairs and replace the floor panel. Nobody will ever know what happened."

"I hope not," said Cooper. "Will there be heat in the aft cargo area?"

"Sure. But when the door opens I suspect the cold blast of air that comes in will just about numb us so we'll have to wear jackets and gloves."

"What's the air temperature outside?"

"About minus 45 Celsius."

"What's that in Fahrenheit?"

"About 48 below. It's the wind-chill that'll do you in," Stoddard said. "I'm not sure, but the wind-chill will be about a 150 degrees below zero when they start their free fall."

"No shit! Well, I know one thing. You'll never have to worry about me trading places with one of them," Cooper said. "What will keep the Soviets from detecting these two guys when they get near the border?"

"They'll have two heat-loss resistant blankets," Stoddard said. "The paper thin blankets will help keep them warm whenever they rest plus they'll reflect heat sensors that might be in the wooded area near the border. By the way Brian, what happened to the original plan to have these two guys jump from the cargo hold of a passenger plane?"

"I guess that was the original plot, but it was too difficult to arrange. The flight crew would have to simulate a problem with the aircraft so they could de-pressurize and the passengers on board would have to put on oxygen masks before they could open the cargo door. We didn't want to have the crew upset and talking about what happened. The wrong people might learn about it.

We've done a lot of work with this airline and when we checked with them, we learned there was a company that wanted to transport an industrial gas compressor to Moscow. Normally, it would have transported it by ship, but the Russians needed it right away. It worked out well for us. It's sort of funny that the Russians are paying for the flight we'll use to drop our guys into their country undetected."

They could hear the plane's jet engines increase their speed and then begin to move forward. Cristiano interrupted their conversation and instructed them to fasten their seat belts. Koltermann guided the large cargo plane into position for takeoff, and waited for permission from the control tower. Moments later they were racing down the runway and then suddenly felt the pressure as the four jet engines lifted the plane upwards.

"We need to refuel before we leave National."

"I thought you were planning to refuel in London?" Kovacs asked.

"I was, but I'd rather have the extra fuel in case we hit head winds like we did on the last flight to Germany." Koltermann replied as he banked the plane to the south.

He continued to climb and leveled out at 28,000 feet. Looking at the clock on the instrument panel, he estimated their arrival time at National Airport would be 10:38 a.m. Hopefully, they wouldn't have to wait too long to get refueled.

Chapter 32

Washington, DC

Ron Harrison felt uncomfortable briefing the new FBI Director, John DiCocco. He sat on a small sofa in the reception room waiting to meet and give him the completed report on the U.S. Bobsled Association. The case had created a tremendous amount of publicity, and the Director wanted to be briefed personally. He thought about the strange direction the case had taken. Perhaps the truth would never be exposed.

The door opened, and a secretary told him the Director was ready for their meeting. He hustled into the large office and introduced himself to the FBI's most powerful man. DiCocco welcomed him, then pointed to a chair. Ron handed him the file and sat down. The Director opened the folder and began reading Ron's report.

"It's hard to believe that these people were stealing from the athletes," DiCocco said, shaking his head. "Was this Fetor as bad as you claim?"

"He was a real slime ball. This file only contains the crimes he's suspected of committing with the Association, but his police record goes way back. Fetor was just a small time crook with a long list of petty crimes until he got involved with the Mob. Later he took the fall for a Mob leader and went to prison for a few years. Since he never ratted on the Mob boss he was rewarded quite well financially. After that, he was in tight with the New York City Mafia. We believe Fetor was carrying large amounts of cash to Europe and depositing it in Swiss bank accounts."

"How did he get through customs without them finding the cash?"

"He used his Olympic bobsled credentials. Normally, they don't check at the border if you're an official. We discovered that he wasn't the only person doing this," Ron said and explained the rest of the scenario, including Fetor's cocaine dealings, the murders of Nino Casatelli and John Chapadeau, stealing money from the Bobsled Association and the Mob, and his eventual murder.

"He was a thief, and that's what eventually killed him. Most of the people in the Bobsled Association were aware of what he was doing, but were afraid to challenge him. His mistake was stealing from Robelotto. The Swiss police believe his murder was the work of a hit man for the Mafia, a real clean job. Nobody ever saw the killer and there were no fingerprints or any other type of evidence. He was shot in the back of the head with a small caliber gun, probably outfitted with a silencer since nobody in the hotel heard a shot. End of story."

"Not quite. What about the money that belongs to the Association?"

"Never found it. The Association's records were never located. They could have been in Chapadeau's car when it blew up. The fire was so intense that parts of the car frame melted."

"So the U.S. Olympic Committee just wrote it off?" the Director asked.

"No other choice. We suspected that the Association's financial information might have been hidden on Chapadeau's computers and we spent a tremendous amount of time working with the IRS searching with computers, but could never trace it. When we reconstructed his car we found traces of a laptop. My guess is he had all the information on the laptop that he carried everywhere. Unfortunately it was also with him when the car blew up."

"Who planted the bomb?"

"We believe it was Fetor himself. We searched a flop house where he had been staying and found a note with the names of Casatelli, Chapadeau and Murphy. The first two were killed and we think he ran out of time before he could kill Murphy.

The Director walked around his desk with the file and handed it to Ron. "I want to compliment you. You've done an excellent job on this case. I want you to meet with our public affairs people to put together a press release. We need to let the public know what has happened."

"Yes, Sir, it was a real pleasure meeting you, Sir!" A feeling of relief filled his body knowing that he was finished with the briefing and was about to leave.

"Likewise, thanks again." The Director nodded and returned to his desk. Ron left with mixed feelings. He was delighted that the case was finally solved, but still felt a great deal of sadness for the athletes who were working so hard to qualify for the Olympics. They always seemed to be the real losers.

Ron would never admit that he was delighted that bobsled officials were dead. He always had a bit of anxiety whenever he worked on this type of case. The Mob had plenty of money to hire notorious lawyers to get them acquitted. These guys were so lucky and often got away with murder. Literally!

Langley, VA

Fred Unser sat at his desk looking over several sheets of paper, then looked up at Kelly and Murphy.

"I don't have to remind you how dangerous this mission is going to be. If either of you have second thoughts, now is the time to speak up.

"Kelly?"

"Let's get on with it. Maybe Shawn has mixed feelings. If so, I'm prepared to do it alone."

"Shawn?" Fred was slightly amused with his statement and suspected Kelly was hoping Murphy would change his mind.

"I never had second thoughts. Once I agreed to the mission that was it. I want to get started."

Unser spent the next several minutes going over his notes. They would go to London and wait while the plane's crew got the required rest and then on to Moscow. Without Kelly knowing the truth, both would be given a fake set of instructions on how to get out of the Soviet Union once the plane left London. Shawn had already been given the actual set of instructions that would have him crossing the border north of Leningrad into Finland on foot. He would have to cover about eighteen miles on snowshoes. This had been the plan from the beginning.

The phony plan said that their contact would have clothing, fake identification, and airline tickets to fly from Leningrad to Helsinki, where the CIA would meet them, and fly them back to the States. Fred was certain that Kelly would be content with the alternative plan, and wouldn't suspect anything. However, he was worried about Murphy having to cover the 18 miles to the border on foot. Nevertheless, it was too much of a risk to fly him out.

The CIA was certain that the KGB would be checking the airports with every available KGB agent. Letting them get the phony instructions from Kelly would take some of the pressure off, since they wouldn't be expecting Murphy to cross the border at Finland. He was also working on another plan, but didn't want to tell Shawn yet.

Fred finished the briefing, and then walked both men out to the helicopter that would fly them over to National to meet the Southern Air Cargo jet. As they walked to the helicopter pad with Amos ahead of them, Fred slipped Shawn a piece of paper. The note had Fred's home phone number with instructions for Shawn to call him when he got to London.

Deciding not to return to his office, Fred went to his car then got on the beltway and drove to his condo. Over and over in his mind, he went through each part of the mission. Confident that nothing had been left out and that the mission would go just as planned, he reminded himself to pick up a bottle of brandy. The Jacuzzi would feel great tonight! Maybe he would finally get a good night of sleep.

Washington, DC

The air traffic controller at National Airport gave Dave Koltermann clearance to land. As he guided the plane downward toward the approach, Kovacs finished going through the checklist. They received instructions to use the east runway, taxi to the end, and then pull off where the helicopter was waiting with their passengers.

Koltermann guided the large plane to where they were to pick up Kelly and Murphy while Kovacs called for more fuel and had food service bring them coffee and snacks. The pilots decided to refuel the plane before letting the two men get on board. After 20 minutes, Koltermann sent Cristiano out to the helicopter to escort Kelly and Murphy to the cargo plane.

Minutes later they were racing down the runway. The plane lifted up from the pavement then banked east into the direction of Europe. Once they reached their flight altitude of 33,000 feet, Koltermann leveled off and told the people in the rear of the plane they could move around.

Colonel Stoddard walked over to Murphy and Kelly to show them their equipment bags. Together with Cooper they checked everything, and then the Colonel gave them a last minute reminder on how to use each piece, to refresh their memory. He told them that just prior to landing in London he would review the items in the bag once again. Shortly after they left London the next day, he would do another review.

"I don't want to irritate you, but your lives will depend upon your ability to use this stuff without having to think each time you need something," Stoddard said, still amazed that they were going through with the mission.

Riga Latvia U.S.S.R.

Georgi Pasevs sat at his desk reading the intelligence report given to him by Nikolai Kravchuk. The report stated that the two Americans would enter the Soviet Union southeast of Riga, Latvia. Something about the report bothered him. It had been too easy to obtain the information. Nothing had changed. There seemed to be a duplication of the information he had read in the last report. He also wondered why Kelly was so willing to sell information to the KGB.

It was unusual in his business for a CIA agent to offer information for a price. KGB agents in the United States had been investigating Kelly and had nothing negative to report. Georgi felt apprehensive about the situation, deciding for the time being he would go along with the plan to pay the second half million in Swiss francs. If Kelly didn't deliver Murphy and the secret alloy as he had promised, he could always change his mind and not pay the American.

Under pressure to solve the mystery of the missing alloy technology, Georgi began to feel the pressure from the stress. If he were unsuccessful with the case, his career might be ruined. Boris Yegorov's defection was the reason he was promoted from vice-commandant to the prestigious position of commandant of the KGB in Riga. His former commandant was executed when Murphy and Bodynski were successful in helping the former Soviet coach and metallurgist escape from behind the Iron Curtain.

KGB officials in Moscow made it clear that they would not accept failure in capturing Murphy when he returned to find the hidden papers with the formula and alloy samples. The report gave Georgi the exact location that Murphy and Kelly would land, but they still didn't know the day or time. He had instructed his vice-commandant, Nikolai to set up a surveillance team in the nearest farmhouse. KGB agents would be ready to follow Murphy and his undercover contact wherever they went. Nobody was going to screw up this mission. Anyone caught making a mistake would be executed… on location.

Georgi pressed down on the intercom lever and yelled. "Nikolai, come here at once!" He waited for several moments then began screaming as loud as he could, until his face turned bright red and sweat began to rush down his face. In a fit of outrage he got up and ran to Nikolai's office. The vice-commandant was not there. Standing inside the office he looked around and noticed that Nikolai's heavy overcoat was not hanging on the rack. Georgi went across the hall to Nikolai's secretary's office and asked where he had gone.

She told him that Nikolai had left earlier in the morning with his driver and said he would not be back until the next day. She did not have a clue about where or what he was doing. Georgi stomped out of the secretary's office. How dare Nikolai leave without telling him?

Georgi picked up the report from his desk and threw the papers across the room. His pulse raced as his mood worsened while he tried to remember his conversation with Nikolai. He had said nothing about leaving the KGB Headquarters with his driver. The report was too vague and he wondered if Nikolai had intentionally withheld new information and put a new date on the old report to fool him. Getting up from his chair, Georgi picked up the papers from the floor. He retrieved the old report from his file, lined up the cover pages and compared them.

The earlier report was exactly the same, except the time and date of the receipt. So, Nikolai was trying to keep him in the dark, he thought, as he checked the next two pages, which were also identical. His mood shifted as he realized that his vice-commandant was trying to deceive him. Why did these educated young agents coming out of Moscow always think they could fool him? He chuckled to himself when he thought about the tragic mistake Nikolai had committed.

Too many people in his past had underestimated his skills. They assumed his lack of education was reason to believe that he was incompetent. They should realize that he was a survivor, but they overlooked his years of experience. Nobody in the KGB moved up to a position of command, unless they were persistent, and watched their back. He might not have the polished education of the younger men, but he possessed something better. The street education he had, meant staying alive, something those new agents didn't learn in school.

When Nikolai returned he would begin street training. He thought about others he had trained in the basement of the KGB Headquarters. Latvians called the building made of concrete the KGB headquarters the 'Corner House' for a good reason. There were five floors above ground and two below. The basement had a torture chamber and several cells to hold people suspected of committing crimes against the Soviet government.

Georgi's predecessor built a special room in the far corner of the first floor to interrogate prisoners, but he often used it to question his own agents. He learned from his former commandant to take agents for questioning to that special soundproof room without windows. They rarely left alive. The official reason was that they had committed crimes against the Soviet government or had attempted to kill the commandant. Nobody ever questioned anybody.

Georgi got up from his desk and went back to Nikolai's office. He shut the door and began to search through the desk looking for a clue about what he was working on. After 20 minutes, he left frustrated and went back to his office. After sitting at his desk for nearly 30 minutes he called the day shift supervisor upstairs to meet with him. He made arrangements to have several agents search the city for Nikolai. Their instructions were to stay in the background and follow him. Every hour, they were to call the supervisor, who would keep Georgi informed.

The supervisor left to get the agents started, and Georgi leaned back in his overstuffed chair with his eyes closed, thinking about some possible replacements for Nikolai. Suddenly one choice came to mind. After pondering about the replacement, he decided to be extra cautious and do some more research before making final plans.

CHAPTER 33

The Pentagon

Fred Unser got out of the military sedan and rushed inside to meet with Admiral Mark Miller. Walking through the maze of hallways in the Pentagon took him nearly 20 minutes to locate the admiral's office. The building was so difficult to get around in that he hated to attend meetings there. Today he had no choice, the admiral had been working on a backup plan to get Murphy out of the Soviet Union if things didn't go as planned.

"Good to see you again, Fred," Admiral Miller said, as Fred walked into his office. "I thought we were finished with this project last year."

"I thought so too, but as I told you, there's a problem with Boris' memory."

"What a shame. After all that poor man has gone through. Is there any sign of improvement?"

"Well, physically, he's fine, but his mind, I don't think there's much hope," Fred said. He looked at the admiral who kept himself in excellent shape, something most high ranking officers in the military didn't bother to do. "Do you have another plan in place for Murphy and Kelly in the event we have problems?"

"Yes," the admiral said and walked over to a conference table. "Take a look at this."

The admiral spent the next 50 minutes reviewing the plan, then assured Fred that although it looked nearly impossible, it was in fact a solid plan. Fred liked the idea that an Air Force AWAC plane would be monitoring the entire operation from the time Murphy and Kelly jumped from the Southern Air cargo plane until Murphy got out of the Soviet Union. Unser assumed that Kelly would remain in the Soviet Union either by his own choice or that of the Russians. He was only going to worry about Murphy.

As soon as the admiral finished, Fred left the Pentagon. In a hurry to get back to his office, he fidgeted as the military driver drove him back to the helicopter. There was still a lot of work to be done to get the rescue in place. He would have a difficult time sleeping until that part of the mission was over, so he decided to go to Helsinki and wait for Murphy's return when the mission was finally complete.

During the ride back to Langley, he thought about the plan Admiral Miller had put together. Fred had a lot of faith in the electronics and technology that the Navy and Air Force would be using, but he was also a realist. Too many missions had gone badly in the past. It bothered him when he thought about some people who had been killed.

CIA agents are well aware of the danger whenever they accept a clandestine assignment. It still upset him terribly that the CIA didn't provide the back-up support he requested to help a female agent working undercover in Columbia. A female agent, who Fred was madly in love with, a dark secret nobody knew.

When a mission went sour, it wasn't because of technology or electronics, it was usually human error. When his lady friend was killed, it wasn't human error; it was a case of agency blunder. His supervisors took too long to make a life or death decision.

A minor mistake and the entire mission could be ruined. Just jumping out of the plane seconds early or late would make Murphy miss his contact by miles. The wind could be stronger than they had planned and he could be blown off course. Fred tried to take his mind off what could go wrong and concentrate on what still needed to be done. It seemed as if it had only been seconds since they left National Airport when he felt the helicopter begin to descend. Looking out the window, he could see the CIA headquarters in the distance. So engrossed in thought during the ride, he had lost track of time.

Fred changed his mind and left the complex without going up to his office. That evening after dinner he poured a glass of French wine and began reading the "Inside" file. Colonel Dean Armstrong would be the intelligence officer onboard the AWAC plane. Not being up-to-date on the AWAC, he opened a CIA manual that had information on the plane. It was a Boeing E-3A. Its top speed was 600 miles an hour and it cruised at 40,000 feet. Its radar range was 250 miles. That meant the plane could cruise in a circle around the Scandinavian countries and monitor all the action that might take place near the Finnish border.

The AWAC could stay in the air for 12 hours, which Fred assumed, would be more time than they would need if Shawn ran into a problem. It really didn't matter if they needed more time, because another AWAC plane would be ready to fly and continue observing. Its radar system could track more than 500 targets simultaneously, which meant that missions the Air Force might be monitoring wouldn't affect theirs. Having the massive computer overhead at 40,000 feet gave him some confidence, but there were still too many things that could go wrong.

In London, Brian Cooper would give Shawn the final information he needed prior to boarding the cargo jet. Brian needed an opportunity to talk with Shawn alone without anyone, especially Kelly. It was critical that they do nothing that could warn Kelly the CIA was on to him.

Fred decided that he would call Brian to be sure he was comfortable with his instructions, and totally aware of what Shawn's options were. He would give him a "heads up," that is, inform him of the Navy's plan to rescue Murphy if problems developed. Brian would have to visit the CIA office in London to get the new plan that had been secretly sent over night. This time Fred wasn't going to take any chances, like they did last year in Columbia, when the CIA failed to rescue his girl friend from the drug cartel in the jungle.

London, England

Brian Cooper looked over his instructions for Shawn and shook his head. The plan for Murphy and Kelly to jump out of the plane at the high altitude was insane, but the Navy's rescue scheme was worse. He read the message over a couple more times just to be sure he understood the instructions. Someone would have to be deranged, he thought, to think up a plan like the one he was reading. The boss must be out of his mind to go along with the Navy.

Brian was at a CIA office located in downtown London and used a safe phone to call Fred Unser at his home in Virginia. He wanted to be absolutely sure of a couple of things before briefing Murphy. Kelly's name was omitted from the message, and he wondered if that was deliberate, or just an oversight. Brian was certain that Fred wanted the man left in the Soviet Union and not arrested.

"Hello, Fred. Brian Cooper. I just reviewed your new instructions from Langley and wanted to double check, just to be sure I understand what you want done."

"Okay."

"You want me to let Kelly jump, even though we know he's working with the Russians?"

"That's right. He has to jump first at the original location. Murphy will go seven minutes and ten seconds later, and will meet our man at the new location."

"Why not let me arrest Kelly, and have our people pick him up here in London?"

"We don't have enough hard evidence to hold up in court. We have proof of what he's doing, but with the money he has stashed, he could get a good lawyer to get him off. I'd rather let the Russians deal with him when he arrives without Murphy."

"Okay. I'll make sure he jumps first if I have to push him out of the plane myself. Are you serious about the Navy's ridiculous plan to get Murphy if there's trouble?"

"I'm not too confident about it either, but unless you have a better plan, we have to do what they set up. Admiral Miller is confident it'll work. He claims that they have done this successfully in Viet Nam and South America. I agree that it sounds ridiculous, but I don't have any other choice."

"I'll wait until we are on our way to Moscow before I show the message to Murphy. Once he understands what to do, I'll destroy the message to prevent the Russians from finding it when we are in Moscow."

"I'm going to Helsinki and monitor the mission there. I won't get any sleep anyway, so I might as well be there."

"I think Murphy will be all right. I've talked with Colonel Stoddard, and he says Murphy has his act together. "

"I hope so. Thanks for calling. And be careful that you don't do anything to tip off Kelly."

CHAPTER 34

Riga, Latvia, U.S.S.R.

GEORGI LUNGED FORWARD WHEN HIS TELEPHONE RANG. It was the day supervisor with an update on the search for Nikolai. The police at the document checkpoint east of Riga told him that Nikolai had passed there early in the morning with his driver. He had offered no explanation about where he was going, and the police didn't challenge him.

The commandant directed him to have two agents wait with the police at the checkpoint until he returned. The agents should call them, and then follow Nikolai. Georgi hung up and went back to Nikolai's office to search it again. After nearly an hour, unable to find anything that would suggest where he had gone, Georgi turned on the computer.

He hated modern technology. The screen offered several options that totally confused him. After studying them for several more minutes, he called downstairs and requested a person who was familiar with computers to come up and help him. Within minutes, the computer man was knocking on the door.

"Come in," Georgi yelled.

"I was told to come up here and help you with a computer." The man was terrified to be in the same room with the commandant. He fumbled with the keyboard striking several wrong keys. Perspiration began to drip down his face through his heavy beard.

"Relax," Georgi said. "I just want you to look through Nikolai's computer and tell me if you find anything that suggests where he may have gone today. Then print up whatever he has written that might explain this."

"Do you have any idea about what I should look for?" he asked.

"No. But he may be guilty of committing crimes against the government so look for anything that may have my name, or the name of Amos Kelly."

"Yes, sir. This may take some time because there are a lot of files here." he said, avoiding eye contact with Georgi.

"I am a patient man. You do not leave here until you have something for me. Is that understood?"

"Yes, sir. I will do my best."

"I do not want your best, you little parasite. I want evidence to prove that Nikolai is committing crimes against the government or else I will charge you with being his co-conspirator. Do you have enough brains to understand that?"

"Yes, commandant. I will find something for you. I will search everything and have it ready before you leave today."

"Very good," Georgi said and returned to his office.

Frustrated and completely at a loss about what to do next, Georgi called his secretary and told her to contact him at the restaurant if one of the agents called, or if the computer man came up with any information. He lit up a cigar and left to get something to eat.

Each afternoon Georgi and his comrades met for lunch at the bar inside the Communist Party Hotel. He enjoyed the prestige showered on him by the local party leaders. The time spent with the influential men from the Communist Party helped solidify his power base in Riga. The combination of being the head of the KGB in Riga and close to party leaders was enough to frighten any sensible person who might have an interest in challenging him as the commandant.

Apparently, his vice-commandant wasn't smart enough to understand this, despite all his education. Some people only learned the hard way, he thought, and then again, some died before they ever learned.

Georgi's mind was far away from his friends as he thought about selecting a successor for Nikolai. This time he would select someone down lower in the chain of command who would appreciate working as his vice-commandant. Someone who would be extremely loyal to him.

He turned from his desk and looked out the window. The bitter wind appeared to have gotten stronger. Soviets on the street attempted to keep warm by pulling their clothing close to their bodies. So much suffering he thought, then returned his thoughts to a new vice-commandant.

Tallinn, Estonia, U.S.S.R.

John Matulewicz walked up to the counter and gave the man behind the window of the Russian Document Checkpoint his papers. The official thumbed through them without looking up or speaking. Satisfied, he returned them, and motioned to the window next to him where passports and visas were checked. Matulewicz shuffled over to the next window and slid the documents under the glass.

"What is the purpose of you entering the Soviet Union?" asked the woman behind the window without looking up.

"I plan to vacation for a couple of days in Riga and then go to Leningrad for a day or two to visit some friends." Matulewicz said, staring at her.

"Where is your declaration?"

"Oh, excuse me. I have it right here. I thought it was with my visa." He handed her the paper he was required to fill out, itemizing every item of value and the amount of currency he was bringing into the Soviet Union.

He quickly glanced back at the document checkpoint to see if the official was looking in his direction. The man was busy with another traveler, so Matulewicz reached inside his coat and pulled out an envelope. Looking at the women behind the counter he waited until she smiled and nodded, then he slid the envelope under his paperwork. She quickly moved the envelope into an open drawer, then stamped adabreniye, on the visa and declaration, approving his visit.

"You are cleared to board the boat once you have had your luggage checked." She returned his visa, passport and declaration. Her facial expression returned to normal. Expressionless!

Five crisp American one hundred dollar bills not only guaranteed her approval, but the hard currency kept his name off the books so authorities wouldn't be alerted if he failed to pass through a border checkpoint on his way back to Finland.

Matulewicz put his suitcase on the conveyor belt to be x-rayed. As always, he also needed to open his luggage so they could check inside. Finding nothing but clothing, they told Matulewicz he could board the vessel. After pausing for a moment to see if anyone might be watching him he walked up the boarding ramp of the George Ott. It was a Russian cruise ship that made the roundtrip everyday between Tallinn, Estonia to Helsinki.

He went up to the bar on the third floor and ordered a glass of beer. Looking around, he didn't spot anyone he recognized, so he picked up his drink and sat in an empty booth. He carefully studied the people in the bar to see if anyone was observing him. Confident that no one was following him, he thought about what he had to do in the next 24 hours.

First, he was to pick up a car with the necessary equipment the agents would need for their escape across the border. It was hidden for him in

Tallinn; from there he would drive to Riga and stay overnight. The next day he would go to the designated area to wait for Murphy and Kelly. Getting out of the Soviet Union, however, would be much more difficult than getting in. The snow would be deep in the area north of Leningrad, where they planned to cross the border into Finland.

The trip might take 15 to 24 hours, if there were no problems. Matulewicz knew very little about either Murphy or Kelly, and wondered if they were physically up to the demands of the trek. The instructions he received stated that the two men had automatic weapons. He suspected they would need them before they got across the border. If they were lucky enough to get across... His mind wandered and he watched passengers enter the bar.

Most were Finns going to Estonia to party. Tallinn, Estonia's capital, was well known for its many bars and nightclubs, which were immensely popular with the hard-drinking Finns. The bar was becoming noisy and crowded, so he finished his beer and went outside on the top deck into the cold air. He lit up a cigarette and watched the city of Helsinki disappear in the distance.

Finally, he was getting an opportunity to do what he was hired to do. A member of the Navy Seals during Viet Nam, he spent nearly three years doing missions behind enemy lines. His heart beat faster as he thought about the excitement of leading the two men to the border. The CIA hired him because of his military survival skills, but he was always used on much simpler missions. The excitement built inside him as he thought about the next couple of days. Slipping through the forest instead of piloting a ferryboat across the Baltic Sea would be the thrill he needed.

In Tallinn, he hailed a taxi to take him across the city to a private garage. After paying the driver, he unlocked the door and went inside to inspect the car that had been left for him. It was a large black Volga, the type often used by the KGB. It would intimidate the guards and police at the document checkpoints outside each city and they would probably just wave him through thinking he was KGB.

The keys were hidden under the passenger seat. He opened the trunk and checked the equipment, which included an automatic rifle with several hundred rounds of ammunition. It was all there. Shutting the trunk quickly he went to the driver's door, got inside the car and drove towards Latvia and the Hotel Lenin.

It was a three hour drive and he would have to go through two document check points. Normally, the check point guards never checked the car trunks, unless they got suspicious. Experience taught him to be calm and confident which helped to avoid any suspicion.

London, England

The alarm on Shawn's wristwatch woke him from a short nap. Darkness was closing in on the city. Going around the room he picked up the few items he brought on the trip and put them inside a small travel bag. The lobby was quiet with only one hotel employee behind the front desk. Kelly wasn't there. It was 5:30 a.m. and they were supposed to meet in front of the hotel's main entrance. After 15 minutes, Shawn used a house phone to call Kelly's room, but no one answered. He waited another 10 minutes before taking a cab to the airport.

Koltermann and Kovacs were filing flight plans. Colonel Stoddard, Cooper and Cristiano were sitting in the snack bar drinking coffee, but not Kelly. Murphy walked into the room and sat at their table.

Cooper looked up at him, "Where's Kelly?"

"Don't know. I waited for him, and then called his room. He never tells me anything."

"Screw him. If he doesn't get here in time, we leave without him. I told him last night to be here no later than 6:15 a.m. He's nearly a half-hour late."

"What do we do if he doesn't arrive by the time we're ready to leave?" Cristiano asked.

"I meant what I said. Screw him. We leave on time. The success of the mission requires the plane be in a certain place at the exact time we agreed upon and we can't let one person screw up the assignment. You don't have to worry about Kelly. If he doesn't show up, then he's probably dead."

"Not a bad thought," Shawn said. "Brian's right, he'll show up at the last minute without an excuse. That seems to be his style."

"I see him," Colonel Stoddard said, pointing to the front door of the terminal. "He's standing there looking for us. I'll go get him."

Stoddard walked out of the snack bar. Kelly was nearly halfway across the large terminal. They spoke briefly, then both men came back into the snack bar and sat at the table. Kelly didn't offer any explanation and nobody asked him. Shawn wondered if he had been meeting with one of his KGB friends or perhaps he had met Natasha.

Moments later, Koltermann and Kovacs came and told them that a crew bus would take them out to the cargo plane. As soon as they reached the aircraft the two pilots went upstairs to the flight deck to begin going through the checklist. Afterwards, Kovacs came to the rear of the plane to talk with Cristiano.

"Mike, Dave has ordered fuel and it'll be here in just a couple of minutes," Kovacs said.

"I'm just about done here, and will keep watch for the fuel truck," Cristiano said. "Did you order a de-ice for us?"

"Yes. We're on the list. I think there are three other planes ahead of us so we'll have to wait another 30 minutes."

"Will that take us off schedule?" Cooper asked.

"Nah. We can easily make up thirty minutes and even a bit longer if we need to. We're scheduled to cruise at about 450, but we can increase that by about 100 miles an hour, if we don't have strong head winds. Unless there's an unusual change in the weather pattern, we should have a tail wind while going east to Moscow."

Kovacs asked Cooper to come up to the flight deck and give him the exact location that the CIA wanted for the jump. Cooper followed him while Stoddard took Murphy and Kelly over to review their equipment. Once upstairs in the front of the plane, Cooper shut the door to the cabin.

"We've got a slight change of plan." Cooper handed Kovacs a slip of paper with two separate coordinates.

"Wait a minute." Koltermann got out of his seat and took the paper to look at the instructions. "We were told that there would be only one location. Why the sudden change of plans?"

"I can't tell you the entire story right now, but we have recently learned that Kelly is working with the Russians. We're going to let him jump out at the original location where the KGB is waiting for them and then have Murphy jump several minutes later."

"Oh, man! Just what I wanted to be a part of. Why do I have a feeling that this is going to be a bad flight?" Koltermann asked and stared at Cooper, unsure of what to say next.

"Nothing will point to you," Cooper insisted.

"Yeah, right. The Russians pick up Kelly, who has been deceived, and he won't tell them who dropped him off at 37,000 feet. I guarantee you that we'll have the only American cargo plane in Moscow. It won't take a lot of brains to figure this one out."

"I understand just how you're thinking, but this guy has been paid big bucks to deliver and he's not going to give them what they paid for. He will be lucky if he stays alive long enough to make it to the KGB Headquarters in Riga. Even so, they'll think he double-crossed them, and will be reluctant to believe anything he tells them."

Koltermann looked at Cooper and shook his head slowly. He was about to speak when the CIA agent put his finger to his lips signaling that they be quiet. Cooper walked back to the flight deck door and climbed part way down the stairs to see where Kelly was. Stoddard was still with both men in the rear of the plane, so Cooper returned to Koltermann and Kovacs.

"Dave, let me say this. My ass is on the line just like yours. If I really thought this wouldn't work, I'd get off the plane right now. I'm not excited about spending time in a Russian prison if this plan fails. You're right about the Russians knowing that Kelly will have jumped from this plane, but you also have to understand how they think. Even if Kelly tells them the truth they'll never let anyone know the Americans got someone into their country undetected. Trust me. Their only concern will be that Murphy is in their country, and they don't know where."

Kovacs interrupted him. "How do you know they'll think Murphy is there?"

"We're certain that Kelly told them everything he knew about the plan."

Koltermann sat back down in his seat to finish his checklist. "You work it out with Frank where you want Murphy to jump."

Cooper handed the paper to Kovacs.

"The cruise speed has to be exactly 400 miles per hour when Kelly jumps," Cooper said and looked at the co-pilot. "Will that be a problem?"

"No. I'll have to convert it to knots on the computer, but it will be exactly four hundred. Why must it be at that speed?"

"With the plane at that speed, when Kelly jumps out it'll take only seven minutes and ten seconds to be over our second drop site. We'll be using our handheld GPS units, but it'll help us if we can follow the minutes. That's easier because we'll be able to count down and have some warning that the second jump site is coming up."

"I can do it with no trouble, but I agree with Dave. I'm not happy about having this dropped on us minutes before we take off."

"I understand and appreciate both of you working with us. I meant what I said when I stated my ass is on the line too, and I plan to get back home real fast."

"I guess we're in this together, so let's get on with it," Koltermann said. "They're finished refueling and the de-icing truck is on its way. You'll have to excuse us Brian, so we can finish our checklist. We'll tell you when we're 35 minutes from the first jump so everyone can get on their oxygen masks. At 30 minutes from the target we'll begin de-pressurizing the plane."

Cooper thanked them again and went downstairs to where Stoddard was finishing his instruction to Kelly and Shawn. Kelly made several adjustments to his gear then sat down and closed his eyes. Cooper motioned with his head to Shawn to follow him to the rear of the plane.

"We're all set with the pilots. They have both locations. We just have to make sure that Kelly jumps at the first location or the entire plan is screwed up. There's no way we can hide either of you in the plane in Moscow if one of you doesn't jump."

"The way I see it, we have to make sure Kelly leaves the plane right on schedule," Shawn said. "One way or another. I could care less if he jumped without a parachute. How about you?"

"Not really, I hate traitors, especially when they endanger others, like he's doing to you. Unfortunately, our job is to make sure that he jumps on schedule. Cristiano just came back inside, so we should be leaving in a few minutes."

Brian looked over to make sure Kelly was still in his seat then turned back to Shawn.

"Here are the instructions for you to follow in the event you and Matulewicz have trouble at the border," he whispered. "Remember, you must be no farther than ten miles from Finland or we can't use the backup plan."

"What if we have trouble and I can't get that close?"

"Don't even think that way. I was told that you should be at least within ten miles. If you get into trouble say fifteen or so miles, don't give up. Send the signal anyway, but do everything in your power to get as close as possible."

The expression on Brian's face wasn't reassuring to Shawn.

"Oh, man," Cooper added. "I wish I could do more for you, but you're really on your own, and I admire you for having the guts to do this."

"Thanks, but for some reason, right now the plan doesn't seem as exciting as it was a few weeks ago. Don't worry. I'm a survivor. I'll do whatever it takes to get the job done, and I'll get over the border, one way or another."

"That's the attitude. I'm certain that you'll get back without any problems."

Shawn looked at the backup plan he had just been given. It was insane at best he thought, hoping he would never have to use it. Then Brian tapped him on the shoulder.

"Cristiano motioned for us to get into our seats. They must be ready to take off."

As Shawn fastened his seat belt he looked over at Kelly who was sound asleep. He put his own head back in the webbing and closed his eyes listening to the winding jet engines warming up. A few moments later, he could feel the plane moving into position for takeoff. They sat at the edge of the runway while Koltermann and Kovacs went through their final check. Suddenly, the jet started moving down the runway.

The final leg of the mission had finally started. Shawn's mind raced; there was no way he could sleep. He visualized the jump over and over, then thought about the cave and finding the alloy samples and formula. The trip to the border was something he didn't want to think about, not yet.

Chapter 35

Riga, Latvia, USSR

"Commandant, I have found the information you were searching for!" The man rushed into Nikolai's office without knocking, waving papers in the air. Georgi was startled when he heard the earsplitting voice.

"Good man." Georgi smiled and stood up to shake his hand. "Now tell me what you have."

"Nikolai has gone to Daugavpils. Tonight at about twenty-two or twenty-three hundred hours, there is a plan for two Americans to jump from an airplane into a field northwest of the city. I have the exact location for you. It was hidden under a secret name he used. I looked in a file he had named, 'rescue data.' "

"I do not give a damn about the details. Just give me the location you idiot, so I can get some people together to find him."

Georgi pulled out the paper Nikolai had given him earlier. The location on the report was near the city of Velikie Luki. So his vice-commandant had lied to him. Now he had proof that he was being deceived. Well, it would not work because he would also be at the correct site, and have a little surprise for Nikolai.

Georgi took the sheet of paper and began calling on the phone to assemble a small group of agents to go with him to Daugavpils located 12 kilometers south of Velikie Luki. So that was Nikolai's plan, he was going to capture the American, get the technology, and make him look incompetent. Well, now he would show his vice-commandant that he was stupid to double cross him. He had his ways to get information…

Georgi got out a map and began working out a plan to intercept Nikolai. A quick glance up at the clock on the wall told him it was nearly seven. There was no time to waste if he was going to set up his surprise before the Americans arrived. After calling his driver and instructing him to get the car ready, he ordered eight agents to accompany them to Daugavpils. He picked up his service revolver, grabbed his overcoat and rushed to the courtyard where the car was parked. When he got there, everyone was standing next to two vans with rifles and gear they would need for their operation.

Georgi stood in front of the agents for a moment then said, "We will be going to an area near Daugavpils to look for the vice-commandant. Nikolai Kravchuk has committed crimes against the Soviet government and must be arrested. Do you understand?"

The group of men mumbled, "Yes commandant" to satisfy their boss. Although they really did not believe Nikolai was guilty, none of them would dare to challenge Georgi, knowing it would be their death sentence. He gave his men several more instructions, then ordered everyone into the vans. Georgi got into his command car, and snapped orders to his driver. They drove out of the KGB compound and headed south on the highway leading to Daugavpils.

London, England

Dave Koltermann continued to guide the Southern Air jet upward as they flew over the English Channel. They had been approved to level off at 37,000 feet. It was difficult for him to focus on flying the plane, because he kept wondering if they would be flying back from Moscow after two days of crew rest, or if they would be detained. He didn't want to think about the situation, but couldn't get it off his mind.

Downstairs in the main cargo section Shawn watched Colonel Stoddard helping Mike Cristiano remove the screws to a section of flooring that had to be lifted up so they could get into the downstairs compartment. The height in the cargo area they would jump from was only five feet and would prevent them from standing up. He wasn't happy about being closed in, but it would only be for about 30 to 40 minutes. By the time he put the equipment on he suspected that his adrenaline would be flowing so fast that standing straight would be at the bottom of his list of concerns.

Cristiano picked up the piece of flooring that covered the three by five foot section and placed it behind some webbing to prevent it from flying around inside the plane if they experienced unexpected turbulence. Stoddard motioned for Shawn and Amos to come over to the opening in the floor.

"I want both of you to climb down into the cargo hold a couple of times so you'll be comfortable with your footing." Stoddard's voice was somewhat different suggesting to Shawn he was becoming apprehensive as the time drew near. "It'll be much more difficult when you have your equipment on, so you need to know where every step is. Mike and I'll be downstairs to help you and Brian will help steady you from the top."

Shawn waited for Stoddard and Cristiano to go down the hatchway, then he followed. The steps would allow only a small portion of his toes to rest on them. He understood Stoddard's concern. With the large jump boots and the heavy equipment it would be extremely easy to slip. They repeated the maneuver several times until both men felt confident about entering the compartment.

Stoddard wouldn't let them wear their gear while practicing. The five foot fall wasn't his concern, it was the possibility they might damage something if they lost their footing and crashed against the plane's frame. Shawn silently agreed. He had gotten this far and didn't want to take any chances of damaging equipment and having to abort the mission. It was 8:33 p.m. Less than two hours before they would have to de-pressurize the cabin.

Shawn went over to his equipment crate and opened the cover. He picked up the helmet with the night vision goggles and put it on his head. The goggles fit perfectly. There was no reason to check them again, must be nerves, he thought. After placing the helmet back in the crate, he picked up the German countersniper rifle and looked through the scope at the back wall of the plane. He practiced switching the lever from daytime to night-time vision. The automatic rifle felt very comfortable against his shoulder or against his hip. The silencer extended the barrel more than he would have preferred, but wouldn't be a problem.

Hopefully he wouldn't have to use the weapon. He put the rifle back and looked at the small computer chip. Colonel Stoddard walked up to him while he studied the device that would send an infrared signal to the satellite when it was connected to a nine-volt battery.

"I hope you don't have to use the infrared signal."

"So do I, Colonel," replied Shawn.

"Please, call me Roger."

"Just a habit that's hard to break after nearly 25 years in the military."

"I hear you. Listen, I want to tell you how much I admire you for taking this risk for your country." Stoddard smiled and added, "I know that you'll be pretty much on your own when you land."

Shawn look over at Kelly to be sure he was still in his seat and unable to hear them. "That bastard won't be with me, but I'll be okay. John Matulewicz is one of the CIA's best trained survival experts. He'll be with me from the time I land until I get to Finland. I don't have any worries about what happens on the ground, but to tell you the truth I'm wound up like a corkscrew right now. I just want to get started."

"I know. That's one of the hardest parts about combat. Most men don't fear it, but the wait can drive you crazy. Why don't you go over and try to get some sleep. I'll wake you and Kelly about an hour and a half before we begin to de-pressurize so you can get something to eat. Then we'll go through the equipment one last time."

"Say, Colonel, I mean Roger, could you do me a favor?"

"Sure. What is it?"

"I really don't know what will happen once I land. This is a real risky thing and I just realized I never thought to thank you and Major Pollack for the excellent training. When you get back, would you tell Jason that I really appreciate what he did for me?"

"I'll give him the message, but don't you worry. You're going to be just fine. I'm convinced you'll get the formula and will be crossing the border into Finland right on schedule." Stoddard smiled confidently not showing his concern.

The colonel placed his hand on Shawn's shoulder nudging him toward his seat. "Try to get some sleep. You have an hour. Take advantage of it. During the next two days, you'll need every bit of strength you can draw on."

Daugavpils, Latvia, USSR

The lack of street lights and signs made it difficult for Georgi and his driver to find the small country road leading to the farm where the two Americans were planning to land. The three-vehicle caravan had made several wrong turns, until they finally got directions from the local police department.

Georgi instructed the men in the vans to wait at the intersection while he and his driver drove up the dirt road with their lights off. They spotted Nikolai's car about a mile up the road, parked behind a small shed near the farmhouse. They sat in the darkness for several minutes, but were unable to see either the vice-commandant or his driver.

"Go back to the intersection," Georgi muttered unable to decide how to handle the situation.

Georgi instructed the agents to follow him back up the road and they parked about a quarter mile from the shed, near the top of a small knoll, out of site. From this location he could watch the entire area. He suspected that Nikolai and the driver would hide in the small shed until they spotted the Americans parachuting down.

There was no need to change Nikolai's plan. Georgi decided that he would be patient and wait until they made a move. Once the Americans had passed them, he would block the driveway, and have several agents arrest the vice-commandant and his driver. The other agents would go with him to follow the two Americans to wherever the alloy samples were hidden and then arrest the one named Murphy and the second man. This was working out very well. Perhaps he would get promoted to the regional office. He was tired of Riga and the Latvians. Georgi loved it when a plan came together easily. Nikolai was not so smart after all; he chuckled as he thought about how he got the information.

"These Americans are stupid to attempt something like this," said the driver without looking at Georgi.

"They think they are much smarter, but we have ways to get information. It is just a matter of time before we find one of their agents who is greedy. We shove some money in front of them and we get what we need. They are no different than our people."

"What kind of technology are they after?"

"I am not really sure, but it has something to do with making metals slide faster on ice or something like that. I do not really understand that stuff. My job is to catch them and in a short amount of time. I will do just that."

"You are the best commandant I have ever worked for."

"Thank you. When this case is over there is a good chance I will be promoted to the regional office. How would you like to move up with me?" Georgi looked over at his driver who was shocked that his boss was being so generous.

"Yes sir, Commandant. I have been waiting for a break like this. Yes, sir. I will go with you. You can be sure that there will never be another driver who can take care of you like me."

Georgi looked at his watch. It was now 20:40. He did not know just what time the Americans were scheduled to land and really did not care. He could sit there all night if he had to. Patience was something that he had learned to control. Nikolai would not leave without him knowing. The police had told him that the dirt road was a dead end, so Nikolai had no choice but to try to get past him and his men.

This would be a night he would not forget for a long time and he would make sure that all the other agents found out what happens if they ever try to double cross him. Somewhere over the North Sea Colonel Dean Armstrong sat at his desk aboard the AWAC looking at his computer screen. He had been monitoring Southern Air's flight number 4827 from London to Moscow. It was nearly 21:00 hours and in about an hour, he should receive a signal from the satellite indicating Murphy had jumped from the cargo plane. Colonel Stoddard would send an infrared signal as soon as Murphy jumped signaling the start of the mission. Armstrong knew that Kelly would leave the plane six and half-minutes earlier, but the CIA didn't want him tracked. That's all right with me he thought. That's the CIA's business, not mine.

Armstrong was the chief intelligence officer aboard the 78 million dollar aircraft. The AWAC aircraft was cruising at 40,000 feet at a speed of nearly 600 miles an hour. With no real destination, the surveillance plane was flying in a circle that covered nearly 400 miles.

Monitoring this mission for the CIA would be simple, Armstrong thought. Just another wacky clandestine job involving the CIA. What else could he expect? The CIA never asked the Air Force for help unless they were involved with something that wasn't exactly legal. One thing for sure. It was never boring to work with the Agency. He wasn't sure about what they were up to, but they sure kept things interesting.

Armstrong switched the screen and began to check other targets the AWAC was monitoring to be sure that everything was in order. His deputy concentrated his eyes on the main screen to allow him to focus only on the CIA's mission. Satisfied that the other missions were in check, he switched back to the Southern Air flight.

The plane was still over the North Sea, just about 300 miles west of Riga. It wouldn't take them long to reach the target. The cargo plane was cruising at 400 miles an hour, so it would reach the jump zone for the first man in about 45 minutes.

Armstrong noted on his log that there were several other vehicles in the area where the first man was to land and he assumed the Russians were prepared to capture him. Hopefully the CIA has their plans all in order and there would be no mistakes, which would lead to an embarrassing situation for the military.

CHAPTER 36

Southern Air flight 4827

SHAWN WAS DREAMING OF ANGELA WHEN COLONEL Stoddard woke him and said that it was time to get up and eat. They were about forty-five minutes from the target. He stretched, looked around the cargo area and noticed Kelly eating near the equipment crates. Cooper was near the back of the plane observing Kelly. Shawn assumed Cristiano was in the lower cargo hold attaching safety straps for the crew who would be assisting when they jumped. The choice of sandwiches wasn't very appealing, but he knew he had to eat something before he got dressed. There was no way to estimate when he would get the chance to eat again during the next two days. Stoddard had told him that there were several energy bars in his jump suit to help him through the mission. He hoped Matulewicz had made arrangements for provisions.

Cooper walked over to Shawn and quietly reminded him that Matulewicz would have a change of clothing, snowshoes and documents to carry for hotels. Without the visa issued by the Soviet government, which Matulewicz was to provide, he would have a difficult time getting through a document checkpoint. He finished eating a turkey sandwich and a banana, then opened his equipment crate. The first item he pulled out was the heated underwear and electric socks.

Once he had finished putting on the clothing he began strapping on his self-contained breathing system that would supply oxygen during the long descent to earth. Cristiano announced that they were now starting to de-pressurize the plane. This meant it was about 30 minutes to target for Kelly, except he didn't have a clue that he would be alone when he jumped out of the plane. Shawn slipped on his own oxygen mask, then plugged into a large portable unit in the back of the plane. The long hose would allow him to move around and finish getting ready. He and Kelly wouldn't plug into their own units until it was time to jump.

To prevent Kelly from getting suspicious, Shawn would disconnect from the plane's system and plug into his own when Kelly made the change. He would switch back to the plane's oxygen to conserve his own immediately after Kelly left the plane. The small units carried only enough air to last approximately 15 minutes under normal conditions.

Shawn knew, however, that the excitement would make him consume more air than normal, until he was able to calm himself during the long descent. During the training jumps, he practiced the breathing control he learned as a scuba diver. The extra clothing made him feel uncomfortable in the warm plane. He was concerned that he would begin to perspire and didn't want his clothing to get wet and freeze while he was free-falling in the sub-zero temperatures.

"Roger, I'm starting to get overheated and don't want to start sweating." Shawn looked at Kelly to see if he felt the same discomfort.

"I'll have Cristiano switch from heat to air conditioning until we go below."

Within a couple of minutes, Shawn could feel the cool air circulating around the cargo bay. He removed the rest of his equipment and clothing from the crate, placing everything on the floor. There would be no need for the computer chip and nine-volt battery during the free-fall, so he put them inside his flight suit and zipped the pocket. The GPS unit would be used several times prior to jumping so he put the GPS on top of the heavy parka that would be the last piece of clothing to put on.

A small pack would be on his chest instead of a reserve parachute. This was needed to carry extra supplies, including 200 rounds of ammo. He glanced down at his GPS. They were closing in on the drop site. The altimeter on his left wrist was steady at 37,000 feet. Shawn moved it to fit over his heavy glove. During the practice jumps he had kept it under his jacket sleeve and it had been difficult to read. He didn't want to take any chances tonight.

"Make sure you load your rifle and put the silencer on," Stoddard told Shawn and Kelly. "And it wouldn't hurt if you put two clips of ammo in your jacket pocket just in case you have to get at it in a hurry."

They nodded. Only 20 minutes until Kelly would jump. Shawn sat on the empty crate, closed his eyes and practiced breathing slowly. Slower and slower he sucked in large amounts of air. This would be the most difficult part of the flight. He expected that he would consume more oxygen than normal when Kelly jumped.

That could be a difficult scene. He was sure Kelly would try to make him jump first and he really didn't know how to avoid it without simply refusing to jump. This was something he wasn't going to worry about until it happened. Attempting to relax, he took in a deep breath, and slowly exhaled. Daugavpils, Latvia, USSR Georgi grew tired of watching the shed. There had been no movement since they got there nearly an hour ago. Nikolai's car was still parked in the shadow of the small building. The moon was nearly full and there were no clouds in the sky. The snow-covered field appeared as bright as if it were sundown. He got out of his car and looked up at the sky. Stars blinked almost indiscernibly; then a shooting star streaked overhead. But there were no blinking lights yet from airplanes.

Georgi put his cold hands inside his coat pocket, walked back to the waiting vehicles and told the driver of the second van to park it sideways across the road to prevent Nikolai from escaping. The driver would stay in that van alone and two of the agents would join the others in the first van. The extra two men would ride with Georgi in the back of his car. When it was time the driver of the first van would follow Georgi's car when they drove up to the shed. He planned to take the two agents to help him arrest Nikolai while the other six agents would follow the two Americans.

Georgi did not believe Nikolai's driver would interfere with them and decided to leave him alone. To protect himself, he knew the driver would give them statements to use against Nikolai. They sat there another couple of minutes and Georgi began to get nervous. Something was troubling him, but he could not put his finger on it.

"Something is wrong," said Georgi, speaking out loud to no one in general. "I can feel it in my bones."

"I think something is wrong too, Commandant," said an agent sitting in the back seat. "The report you gave us said an undercover CIA agent would be here to meet the two Americans. There is no one here except Nikolai and his driver, and nobody has driven down this road or we would have seen their headlights."

"You are right. Nikolai must be the person who is meeting them. There never was a CIA agent."

"Nikolai probably set this whole thing up and is getting paid by the CIA to take the Americans to get the technology, and then help them get out of the country," the agent said. "Look around us. There are no other cars except the vice-commandant. He must be working with the CIA. For all we know, the story he gave us about the one American being paid to help us was just a diversion. Nikolai probably plans to kill the CIA agent named Kelly to protect his story.

"You are right," Georgi said. "Nikolai would take the other man to get the information and then tell us that he got away, but he killed one of them. I knew Nikolai was doing something corrupt. He had this all worked out. The parasite was taking bribe money and planned to make it look as if I had been incompetent by letting the American get away. The traitor has been after my job for a long time."

"Maybe we should arrest him right now so he can not follow his plan through."

"That is a good idea. Then we can follow the two Americans to where Boris Yegorov hid the papers with the formula and the alloy samples." Georgi smiled at the agent. "I will give you the honor of making the arrest."

"Who will pretend to be Nikolai when the Americans land?"

"I will," Georgi replied. "I can speak some English. I will take them in my car to the caves and then we will arrest both of them."

Georgi left the car and walked back to the van to brief the other men about the new plan. They would drive up to the shed with their lights off and arrest Nikolai. He would be handcuffed and put in the van parked across the road. They would take both vans and Nikolai's car and hide them further down the road past the field, so the Americans would not know they were there.

Once Georgi had the Americans in his car, they would follow from a safe distance with their lights off. Georgi was exhilarated. The day had started out with a tremendous amount of frustration. Suddenly, it had completely turned around and he was about to become a hero.

"Drive forward to the shed with your lights off," Georgi ordered. "We are about to ruin Nikolai's sneaky little plan. That parasite is about to learn a very valuable lesson."

His driver started the car and began to move down the road in the direction of the shed. Seconds later the van followed. As they drove up to the car they could see Nikolai and his driver inside. Their car motor was running. Southern Air Flight 4827 Cristiano helped Kelly steady himself with all the bulky equipment. As soon as Kelly was in the lower cargo section with Cooper and Stoddard, Cristiano looked at Shawn and made a hand signal telling him to switch his oxygen hose from the plane's system to his own. When Shawn began breathing from the self-contained unit, he climbed down into the cargo section. Cooper was telling Kelly that he was going to jump first and Kelly began arguing with him.

"You do what you're told. My instructions were for you to jump and Murphy would be right behind you. That's the way it's going to be."

"Who made that decision?" asked Kelly.

"Fred Unser. End of discussion."

"I'm the senior agent on this mission and I think Murphy should go first so I can cover him if there's a problem."

"Three minutes to target," Cristiano yelled.

Cristiano pulled the pin and strained to slide the door open. Noticing that he was having difficulty, Stoddard rushed over to help him. The pressure from the frigid wind outside was incredible. Once the door was completely open, Cristiano slid a safety pin in place to prevent it from closing. Kelly stood at door's edge with his back to the dark sky. His hands were on the inside of the doorframe and he continued to argue with Cooper that Murphy should go first. It was difficult to hear Kelly yelling through his oxygen mask over the roar of the wind. Cristiano yelled twelve seconds and began to count down.

"Nine, eight, seven, six, five . . ."

Kelly reached over with his left hand and grabbed Murphy's parachute harness strap. Shawn slammed his hand down, trying to break Kelly's grip. Over the roar of the wind he could hear Cristiano yelling. Cooper punched Kelly in the stomach, forcing him to let go of Shawn's harness, and then he shoved Kelly backward into the dark universe. Out of the corner of his eye Cooper saw a blurred movement as Shawn grabbed Kelly's air hose, ripping the oxygen mask off as he fell from the plane.

Stoddard yelled to Cristiano to switch Shawn's air hose to the plane's system. He told Shawn there wasn't enough air for him to make the jump, then he took the portable tank off the pack strapped on Murphy's chest and climbed up stairs to refill it.

Cooper yelled to Shawn, "Kelly will become hypoxic from the lack of oxygen and won't be able to open his parachute."

"Yeah, I know. The poor bastard won't be able to spend the dirty money he got from the Russians. Tell Fred he won't have to worry about Kelly getting a good lawyer and beating a trial."

"Five minutes," Cristiano yelled.

Shawn attempted to slow his breathing down. He was now breathing in very short and shallow breaths as he thought about Kelly and was upset that Stoddard was gone with his air tank. He now had less than five minutes.

"Calm yourself down," Cooper yelled over the roar of the wind. "You did the right thing. That bastard sold all of us out to the Soviets and got just what he deserved. Quit taking short breaths of air. Suck in a large volume and hold it before exhaling."

Shawn was getting weak from fighting the wind rushing through the door and hung on to the doorframe to brace himself. Realizing this, Cooper helped move him away from the doorway and held on to his jacket to steady him.

"Four minutes," Cristiano yelled.

"God damn it, where the hell is Stoddard with my oxygen tank?" Shawn screamed.

"Don't worry. He'll get here in time, he's got to get more air in it. You don't want to end up like Kelly."

Shawn closed his eyes. His rifle was loaded and the silencer was attached. Was his Blitz scope on night vision? Opening his eyes again, he double checked the scope to be certain. It was okay. He felt for his night vision goggles on the front of his helmet. Calm down, he told himself, Stoddard had checked everything only minutes ago. Nothing had changed. He closed his eyes again waiting for Stoddard.

CHAPTER 37

Daugavpils, Latvia, USSR

NIKOLAI'S FACE SHOWED THE SURPRISE HE FELT when he saw Georgi and the van of KGB agents pull up next to his car. Georgi ordered him to get out of the car and put his hands up over his head.

"What are you doing?" asked Nikolai as he got out of the car.

"I must admit that it took a while, but I finally figured out what you were up to." Georgi motioned to one of his agents. "Take his gun."

"You idiot!" Nikolai protested. "The Americans are going to land any minute. What has gone wrong with you Georgi?"

"Did you really think you would get away with your little scheme?"

"What is wrong with you? You are acting as if you are completely insane."

"Well, my little smart one. If anyone is insane, it is you for thinking that you could get away with this greedy little deal."

"What are you talking about Georgi?"

"It is quite simple. First, let me ask you a couple of questions. Why did you give me a report that said the Americans were landing in a field near Velikie Luki?" Georgi asked, nodding to the agent who had removed Nikolai's service revolver and was waiting to place handcuffs on Nikolai.

"I admit I was trying to mislead you about where they were landing to make myself look better. I thought that if I could solve the case I would get promoted."

"Promoted where, to my job after I get executed for failure? You must really be stupid, and I thought you were so smart. I guess they did not teach you everything in school. Where is the American undercover agent who was supposed to meet the two men when they fell from the sky?"

213

"I do not know. I was never able to locate the man that Natasha said would be here to meet them. I am confused, because he was to provide them transportation, and give them supplies to get out of the country, after they got the papers with the formula and the sample composites."

"Do you really think I believe you? We know you are the man who is meeting them. You were going to provide them with transportation and you took the bribe money." Georgi's voice grew louder as his temper began to escalate. "Take him down the road and put him in the back of the van."

"You idiot," Nikolai screamed as the agent forced him into the back seat of his own car. "You will blow the entire operation with your stupidity."

"We will soon find out who is the idiot. You are fortunate that I do not shoot you right here for being insubordinate. In time you will pay for your crimes against the Soviet Government. Get him away from me right now!"

Georgi could still hear Nikolai in the distance as the car drove down the road. He ordered the vice-commandant's driver to wait in the van. Several of the agents went inside the shed with flashlights to make sure no one else was hiding there. They found a small supply of farming equipment, but no people. It was so cold they could stay outside only a short while before returning to the van. Georgi stayed inside his car with his eyes fixed on the sky in front of him.

"Georgi, that looks like blinking lights from an airplane over to the right," his driver said and pointed upward to a tiny blinking speck of light.

"Da! That has got to be them."

He got out of the car and walked around, stopping in front of the shed, followed by the rest of the agents. The snow was nearly four feet deep and trudging through it made them even colder. Within seconds they heard a thud over in the nearby field. It was as if something had fallen hard and fast.

For several minutes, they waited for Kelly and Murphy to come out of the darkness. When no one appeared, Georgi ordered his men to go across the field and look for them. Aided by portable searchlights, they spotted Kelly's mangled remains near a row of trees.

The site was gruesome. A couple of agents began to vomit. It was impossible to even try to make an identification of the body. Blood was oozing from several parts of Kelly's body. Both arms and legs were twisted in several directions, like spaghetti, no longer even looking like human limbs. His ribs, looking like ivory knives, stuck out through his jacket.

They heard heavy breathing and turned to see Georgi rushing towards them. The excessively overweight commandant struggled to get through the deep snow, and was exhausted when he reached them. Too short of breath to speak, Georgi reached out to the agent next to him for support and gestured with his flashlight. The agent took the flashlight and pointed it on the body.

"Roll him over," Georgi ordered between breaths, "and look for some identification."

The ghastly site of Kelly's body seemed not to disturb him.

"Apparently, he did not open his parachute," Georgi said. "Not a very smart thing to forget when you are falling out of the sky. See the rip cord. I bet he was dead when he left the plane. Nikolai must have sent a signal to the Americans, and they rolled this one out and did not let the other one jump."

The agents rolled the body over and removed his papers. Then they collected his rifle and other equipment. One of the agents put his hand under Kelly's clothing to feel the body.

"Commandant. The body is still warm. He must have been alive when he hit the ground."

Georgi thought about what the agent said.

"Yes, he must have been," Georgi agreed. "Perhaps they drugged him so he would not open his chute, then we would think it was an accident."

He turned to walk back to his car then stopped.

"Drag his body to the shed and we will have the local police pick it up. Maybe they can figure out what really happened to him when they do an autopsy."

It took Georgi nearly 15 minutes to reach the shed. His pants were drenched up to his crotch and his feet were numb. As soon as he got into his car, he took off his shoes and attempted to warm his feet. He sat there for several minutes with his eyes closed, trying to adjust to the pain in his toes.

"Take off your shoes and give me your socks," ordered Georgi. He put on the driver's socks, and then instructed him to drive over to the van where Nikolai was being held.

"Stop right here and wait for me," Georgi yelled. "I will only be a minute."

Georgi walked to the van and opened the two large doors on the side.

"You traitor. I do not know how you did it, but you warned the Americans that we were here."

"How do you think I could possibly warn them?" Nikolai demanded.

"I do not know how, but I do know that you are a double-crossing traitor who has committed a terrible crime against our government and you are going to pay for your greed."

Georgi pulled out his revolver pointing it at Nikolai. In a useless effort to protect himself, the frighten vice-commandant put his hands up in front of his face. Georgi fired one shot into the side of his head just above his right ear splattering parts of his head throughout the inside of the van. The bullet passed through his skull, and shattered the window behind Nikolai.

"Georgi instructed the driver of the van to take the body back to KGB headquarters then shut both doors and returned to his car. He sat for several minutes without speaking while gathering his thoughts about what to report about the incident. When he had everything worked out in his mind, he ordered his driver to take him back to Riga.

There would be no problem proving that Nikolai was working with the Americans he thought. They had Kelly's body with no instructions about where the documents were hidden. All the other agents could witness that there was no undercover American agent there, so Nikolai had to be working with the CIA. The parasite got just what he deserved. Georgi leaned back in the seat and closed his eyes to get some rest, confident that he would look good in the eyes of his supervisor.

Maybe not! He forgot that there might be another American with Kelly. The first thing he would do in the morning would be to start searching for him. Where should he start? His problems were not over. Nikolai really put him in a terrible situation. Once he got back to the 'Corner House' he would have several agents with search lights return to search the area for the other American. They would need to have helicopter support from the air.

Southern Air Flight 4827

"One minute to target!" Cristiano yelled.

Cooper stood on a lower step and yelled up to Stoddard, "Give me the God damned tank now. We can't wait anymore."

Stoddard was already walking toward him with the tank.

"It just shut off," Stoddard said. "Here, you take it and strap it on him."

Cooper grabbed the tank and rushed over to insert it into Shawn's harness.

"Forty-five seconds . . ."

Cooper fumbled with the top strap that was stuck on the harness and wouldn't slide out of the buckle. Cristiano yelled 30 seconds and began counting down. At 20 seconds, Stoddard rushed over and managed to separate the strap. Cooper slid the oxygen tank into place while Stoddard uncoupled the air hose from the plane's system and plugged it into Shawn's receptacle.

"Eight seconds . . ."

Cooper secured the clamp and slapped Shawn's back.

"All set," Cooper yelled and helped Shawn move to the door.

"Three, two, one, target!"

Shawn dove out headfirst with his hands over his oxygen mask and the night vision goggles to prevent them from blowing off his face in the sudden rush of air. They watched him disappear instantly into the darkness. After several seconds, Cristiano pulled the pin and slid the cargo door shut, then notified Koltermann on the intercom to begin pressurizing the plane and to turn on the heat in the back of the plane.

"If I ever hear someone counting down again, I think I'll beat the shit out of them," Cooper said, and the three of them laughed briefly. But their humor quickly vanished. They were very worried about Shawn.

They had good reason. As Shawn fell towards earth, the frigid air seeping inside his helmet was giving him a headache, and while the bulky jacket and the special clothing prevented him from freezing, his whole body was so chilled and he felt numb. He also noticed he was breathing air from his oxygen tank in rapid shallow bursts, so he tried to concentrate on controlling his breath, as well as keeping his hands and legs outstretched and his chest facing the ground. This would slow his speed and reduce the wind-chill that was probably way over 100 degrees below zero.

Moving his arm to the front of his face enabled him to check the altimeter. Now below 23,000 feet and he still couldn't see any lights below. The severe cold bothered him much more than it did during the training flights. There was no way to estimate the temperature. He hoped his hands wouldn't get numb and prevent him from pulling his ripcord when it was time. His breathing was much slower, giving him confidence that he wouldn't run out of oxygen.

He was now under 15,000 feet. Scattered dim lights in the distance were visible, but below it was still complete darkness. Straining his eyes, he attempted to see images of buildings or trees. He was now able to see open areas covered with snow beneath him. The altimeter read 11,000 feet. With the night vision goggles Shawn was now able to identify small buildings and groves of trees, but he still didn't see Matulewicz's red light that was supposed to be his signal. The snow was now very bright and he could see a farmhouse near the edge of the field. His altimeter showed 7,000 feet. He kept his left hand under his goggles to monitor the descent and began to move the fingers on his right hand to get the blood circulating so he could pull the ripcord.

At 5,000 feet, still no red light. He became concerned that something might have happened to Matulewicz and began to count down quickly, deciding to pull the cord when he reached 1,500 feet with or without a red light. His fingers were stiff, but were able to grasp the steel handle. At 2,000 feet, he changed his mind and decided to pull the cord. His hands were nearly numb and he wanted to have a few extra seconds in case he had trouble.

The cord didn't move the first time he pulled, so he relaxed for a moment and then yanked as hard as he could until the handle moved out slowly. Instantly he could feel the chute collecting wind, drastically slowing him down. He was falling straight down, indicating that there was no wind. At 1,000 feet, he began to steer toward what he suspected was an old farmhouse surrounded by a grove of trees.

Suddenly, he saw a blinking red light and began to maneuver the chute in the direction of the light until it was clearly visible. Matulewicz was in front of the grove of trees next to the field. Shawn directed his parachute toward him. At 500 feet, his night vision goggles were becoming too bright. The moon's reflection from the snow through his goggles intensified his headache and he began to squint to reduce the glare.

Matulewicz stopped blinking the light and rushed out into the field to help him. Shawn nearly collapsed in his arms. Too cold to flex his knees when he landed, he fell against the CIA agent, knocking him to the ground. The deep snow cushioned their falls, and within seconds Matulewicz began to help him get up.

"Are you okay?" Matulewicz asked.

"I don't think anything is broken, but I may have the beginning stages of frostbite. My entire body is numb."

They removed the parachute and kicked snow on it to prevent anyone from discovering it right away, then trudged through the snow to Matulewicz's car. The farmhouse was vacant, and the driveway hadn't been cleared. John opened the trunk and put Shawn's equipment in with the other supplies. He unlocked the car and helped Shawn take his heavy coat off and get into the front seat.

"Take your boots off, but leave your socks on. You should let your feet warm up slowly or you'll be in a lot of pain."

Matulewicz started the car and put the heater fan on low. The air was not warm, but a lot warmer than Shawn's feet. As Matulewicz turned onto a much larger road and went northwest, Shawn's feet began to get feeling again.

"This road will take us to Riga. I assume that's where you want to go."

"Yes. When we get to Riga, I'll recognize the roads and will be able to tell you how to get to the sandstone cave."

"How do your feet feel?"

"They are beginning to pain so they must be warming up. My hands were just as cold. I was worried that I wouldn't be able to pull the ripcord. It didn't open on the first try and my heart sank."

"I still can't believe you did this. There's no way you would convince me to do that jump. No way!"

"It's too late to second guess now. It had looked good on paper."

"What happened to the other guy?" Matulewicz asked. "When I was first briefed I was told there would be two people and then the last message said just you would be jumping."

Shawn told him the story about Kelly and how he had been paid by the KGB to deliver the papers with the formula and the alloy samples. Fred Unser had made other decisions about Kelly and didn't advise Shawn. After that, they drove for several miles and neither spoke. Finally, Shawn dozed off into a deep sleep. The severe cold had drained all his strength. They were about twenty miles from Riga when Matulewicz woke him.

"We're not too far from Riga. We'll pass through a document checkpoint in another five miles. It's nearly 2:30 in the morning. I don't think the guards will stop us, but you never know."

Matulewicz slowed down and parked the black Volga on the side of the road. He reached across Shawn, opened the glove box and took out some papers. After reviewing them, he handed three to Shawn.

"This is a fake passport that the CIA put together for you. It has your photo and a forged stamp showing that you're visiting Leningrad. There's also a visa and a declaration of your belongings. You'll have to change your clothes now so we can hide the ones you're wearing to prevent them from becoming suspicious."

Murphy took off his clothes and dressed in the ones Matulewicz had in the trunk. To his surprise, they were the correct size. He changed then tossed the clothing over the steep embankment and got back into the car.

"Here's the deal. Normally, the KGB drives black Volgas, so the guards and the military at the document checkpoint should assume we're KGB and will just wave us on. When we pass, stare into their eyes as if you are the meanest bastard in the world. They fear the KGB more than any other agency and won't want to confront us."

"And if they stop us?"

"We'll try to get through with the fake documentation. If they don't buy the papers just hang on to your seat because I'll take off like a bat out of hell. They won't have a vehicle here that can catch us. When we get to Riga, we'll have to figure out a plan to get another car. I can steal one if we have to, then ditch the Volga."

"Should we get my automatic rifle out of the trunk?"

"No. We don't want to get into a shoot-out with them. Trust me, we would lose."

Two men in uniform stood guard at the checkpoint. A steel bar across the highway prevented traffic from passing through from either direction. Matulewicz dimmed his headlights and turned them on bright again, motioning with his arm to raise the bar. The man next to the control simply nodded his head and raised the bar. Both guards waved at them as they passed. Shawn looked at them and nodded a gesture.

"It's clear sailing from here to Riga. We'll have to go through another checkpoint when we leave Riga, and another when we go into Leningrad and once again when we leave."

"It's weird how they're so obsessed in keeping tabs on all their people." Shawn was amazed at the checkpoints, although he remembered them the last time he and Professor Bodynski were in Riga.

"How much money did Kelly get from the KGB for promising to give them the formula?" Matulewicz asked.

"I'm not sure. There were rumors that he was paid a half a million and was to get another half when he delivered the papers."

"That's a lot of cash. I'm not surprised that he went for the money."

"Why do you say that?"

"The CIA doesn't pay anywhere enough for the kind of risk some of us take year after year. Maybe Kelly was going to take the money and retire."

"Well, the bottom line is if you're unhappy, you get out and do something different. I worked over here years ago and left. You don't sell out your country and the people who work with you."

"You're right."

Shawn put his head back on the seat and within minutes he was asleep. Matulewicz continued driving towards Riga. They had only a few miles to go.

CHAPTER 38

Helsinki, Finland

FRED UNSER TOOK A CAB FROM HEATHROW Airport and went straight to the CIA's office rather than checking in at his hotel. Wes Ryerson, the office supervisor, greeted him when he arrived.

"The AWAC is on the ground refueling and getting crew changes. Kelly and Murphy jumped right on schedule," said Agent Gina Helbling, who had just gotten off the phone.

"Gina, this is Fred Unser," Ryerson said. "He's director of operations for Europe."

Fred shook her hand.

"Where are the two men right now?" he asked.

"No one knows," Ryerson replied. "Colonel Armstrong said that they left the plane at two locations. Four vehicles left the area where the first person jumped and a single car left from where the second man jumped. That was all he could provide from the AWAC."

"Good," Fred said. "If Murphy and Matulewicz are on schedule, they should be on their way to the cave by now. They'll stay overnight in Leningrad and drive up towards the Finnish border tomorrow morning."

"What route do they plan to use to get to the border?"

"They'll go north to Wyborg, abandon the car and then go to the border on foot."

"That's about 20 miles," Ryerson said. "They'll have to be real careful when they get within seven or eight miles. That whole area is full of heat sensors and they'll have one hell of a time getting through undetected."

"We thought of that," Fred said. "They have paper thin heat resistant blankets which will reflect the sensors, but they'll have to travel at night to prevent being seen. There's no fence in that section of the forest, so we expect the Soviets will put a lot of effort into searching for them."

"Well, if anyone can do this, Matulewicz can," Ryerson said. "I've worked with him on a couple of assignments and he's like a bull. If it can be done, he'll do it."

"I hope so. The formula they have is worth a lot of money."

"What is it?" Helbling asked.

Fred gave a brief explanation, then chatted with them several more minutes. Jet lag began to fatigue him, so he requested a call if anything came up or if there was any word from the AWAC. He then left to check into the hotel, not expecting to hear anything until late the next night. Desperately needing rest, he hoped to catch some sleep before he would have to work on the project.

Riga, Latvia, USSR

Matulewicz drove by the Riga Hotel where Shawn and Professor Bodynski stayed on the last trip. It brought back many memories. He hoped that leaving the Soviet Union wouldn't be as difficult as it was for him and the professor on their last visit. Shawn gave Matulewicz more directions, and they headed northeast in the direction of Sigulda.

The Soviet Union's only official bobsled track was in Sigulda. They had another one in Siberia, which they kept a secret. That track had been dug out of the side of a mountain and was made of blocks of ice. Political prisoners were used to build and maintain the Siberian track. The one in Sigulda was made of concrete and had a refrigeration system to prevent the ice from melting. Shawn and the professor had spent several weeks there with the Soviet bobsled team.

Several sandstone caves were located in this part of Latvia. The one they were going to was about 10 miles from the bobsled track. Boris had met Murphy and the professor at the cave several times to discuss bobsled business. On the last visit Boris showed Shawn the cave, where he spent a lot of time exploring.

It was early morning and traffic was building. They were fairly certain that no one had followed them to Riga. The highway they used was M-9 and the KGB would have used A-215 that went between Riga and Daugavpils. Matulewicz and Murphy would have to be careful, because the KGB might be watching the caves. Shawn found the national park, where the sandstone caves were located, and had Matulewicz drive around the area first, to determine if the KGB was keeping an eye on it. There were no cars parked within a quarter mile of the cave where Boris hid the documents, so he and Matulewicz were confident that no one was watching.

Stopping the car near the cave, Matulewicz shut the headlights off. It was still several hours before daylight would arrive. Out of the trunk, Shawn took his rifle, flashlight, and compass. He checked the silencer on the rifle and put it on his shoulder then put the duffel bag back inside the trunk. Shawn took extra batteries for the flashlight and told Matulewicz to drive around for the next hour, then return to pick him up at the entrance. Checking around one more time, he was satisfied that no other cars had entered the park, so he slipped into the cave's entrance. It was 06:20.

Visibility for the first 200 feet into the cavern was very poor, but the light from the street lamp enabled him to continue without using the flashlight. He remembered names and dates were carved into the cavern walls as far back as the 1500s, but he didn't have time to look at them now. Pressed for time, he needed to keep following the tunnel so he could get back within the hour.

The farther he went, the darker it became until finally, he had to use the flashlight to find his way. He cursed himself for not thinking to bring the night vision goggles. Stoddard had provided them for the night jump from the plane, but they would have made the search in the cave much easier. Too late now to go back, he had to keep pressing forward.

The ceiling and walls were moist with condensation. It was very quiet and the sound of dripping water seemed to be heightened. It had been nearly 10 minutes since he started and his outer garments were already damp. Continuing on he looked for the fork Boris had described to him. The tunnel was becoming narrower. A thick collection of cobwebs hung throughout this section, indicating that nobody had been there for a long time.

Finally, he arrived at the fork. Boris's instructions were to go into the tunnel on the right for another 1,200 feet, then look for a large section of stone jutting out from the left wall. Checking the time; he discovered that it had taken him nearly 20 minutes. He hoped he would find the rock shortly, or he would have to go back and tell Matulewicz he needed more time. Stopping for a moment he searched ahead with the light. All of a sudden he saw a rock, jutting nearly four feet into the narrow passage, was just ahead. That had to be the one. The instructions were to feel for a loose rock located another six feet farther into the cave, down near the floor.

He found the loose stone and set the flashlight on the floor of the cave, prying the rock loose with his knife. The light began to dim indicating the batteries were nearly out of power, so he stopped and changed them. Finally, he worked the stone loose enough to grab the edges with his fingers. After several minutes it came out, revealing what appeared to be a plastic bag behind it. Shawn carefully pulled the bag out and removed a glass jar from it. Inside the jar was the paper with Boris' formula and the alloy composite samples. Holding the jar, he felt a cold chill when he realized he had finally located the formula.

Shawn carefully placed the jar inside his jacket pocket and began walking back towards the cave's entrance. After only a short distance he saw another fork ahead in the tunnel that he didn't recall seeing on the way in. Staring at the second passage, he noticed it was filled with a mass of cobwebs and knew he should take the other one. Then he saw another intersection. The cobwebs on the left had been disrupted and he could see his footprints in the damp sand, telling him that he was on the right track.

The soft sounds of footsteps crept up behind him, but before he could turn, a blow to his head, knocked him to the ground. His face hit the moist sand covered with a thick layer of dust, forcing particles into his mouth. He put his hand down to get up and out of nowhere a foot struck him in the chest launching him backwards into the side of the cave.

All Shawn could remember was his head hitting the stone wall. Moments later he could feel someone searching his clothing, but he was helpless to stop them. The person going through his pockets found the glass jar and pulled it from his jacket.

Opening his eyes, Shawn could see a large figure walking away from him. His head was pounding and his face throbbed in pain, but he managed to get to his knees. Pulling the German Sniper automatic rifle off his shoulder, he checked the silencer to be sure it was on tight, switched the scope to night vision, then he put the weapon up to his shoulder and looked through the scope. He could see the large frame of Matulewicz, the man who was supposed to be helping him, hurrying away.

The pounding in his head was enormous making it difficult to focus on the fleeing man through the night vision scope. Balancing himself on his knees, he began firing in the direction of the torso in front of him. He held the trigger and moved the barrel left and right until the gun would no longer fire. The rifle made very little sound as it projected its powerful rounds in the direction of Matulewicz.

The combination of the beating and the energy he had used to fire the rifle left him exhausted. He lay on the ground for nearly 30 minutes, not knowing if he had stopped Matulewicz. Finally, he picked himself up.

Unable to locate the flashlight, he trudged through the tunnel toward the light leading out of the cave. He had walked nearly 200 feet when he saw what appeared to be a body.

Matulewicz, lying face down with the glass jar still in his hand, nearly made it out of the cave. Shawn picked up the jar and put it back inside his jacket then began to search the dead man's pockets. He found the car keys and a wad of rubles. Inside his coat he found Matulewicz's passport and visa, but no papers for the car.

Shawn walked slowly out of the cave. There were no cars in the parking lot, but there were a few people around the park walking dogs. Even if someone were walking near the entrance, they would not have heard the silenced shots. The body was nearly 200 feet inside the cavern so nobody could have seen Matulewicz laying face down in the dirt. Shawn removed the silencer from the gun to make the barrel shorter and placed the rifle down his pants leg. His right elbow was pressed tightly against the stock preventing it from sliding down his trousers. He managed to get to the car with the rifle concealed. Making sure no one was watching, he unlocked the trunk, removed the rifle, and put it under a blanket, then put the jar inside a small duffel bag that had Matulewicz's change of clothes.

In the car, he sat for several minutes trying to figure out what to do. The only person who could help him get to the border was dead. This wasn't the way it was supposed to work out. His mind was racing, making it difficult for him to concentrate. In an attempt to calm down he took several deep breaths, then tried to remember what Fred Unser had said Matulewicz would do to get him and Kelly across the border.

He needed to get to Leningrad as soon as possible. From there, it was only 90 miles to Finland. It was obvious that he shouldn't travel during the day because of the greater likelihood of being stopped for something like a simple traffic error. His face and clothing were filthy. There would also be document checkpoints he would have to drive through. It would be easier if he did that during the early morning hours, when the checkpoint guards were more relaxed, late in their shift. In any case, he needed to find a place to park the car where he could sleep until nightfall.

It was now 08:30. Shawn started the car and drove carefully out of the park towards the outskirts of the city. There would be a document checkpoint about five or six miles from the urban area so he would find an area that wasn't too populated and hide there until it was safe to continue on. He decided to get the rifle and all the ammunition and put them in the front of the car under the blanket in case he needed them at a checkpoint.

Determined not to let himself be captured without a fight, he decided to do whatever it took to get away. If identified, he would attempt to out-run the authorities, set fire to the paper and throw away the alloy samples. It would be better to lose them than have the Russians get them.

Shawn used the road that went past the Soviet bobsled track in Sigulda, because he knew it would lead him to the main highway to Leningrad. He drove several miles, recognizing many landmarks from his previous visit. A short distance from Sigulda, he found an industrial area and backed the car into a small clearing near several vacant buildings. The area appeared as if it was once very productive, but now it was nearly empty. From there he would be able to watch for other vehicles that might drive down the lane.

It was now 10:15 a.m. and he was exhausted. Using snow, he washed his face and neck then combed his hair. Confident that nobody would find him, he locked the doors and moved the seat back to give him extra leg room. Almost immediately, Matulewicz entered his mind as he thought about what the man had done to him. It bothered Shawn that he had been forced to shoot him. It was easy for him to believe that Kelly was dirty, but Matulewicz! What the hell was a half million dollars going to do for him. Giving up everything, to live in a place like the Soviet Union for the rest of his life, for any amount of money didn't make sense to Shawn. His mind began to drift, and within minutes he was sound asleep.

Chapter 39

Sigulda, Latvia, USSR

A noise woke Shawn. Looking up he saw a truck parked less than a 100 feet from him. The lights were on and the driver was attempting to restart the vehicle. The driver made several efforts to get the truck started, but the truck would only backfire and quit. Finally the motor started and large bellows of smoke shot out of the exhaust. Several minutes later the engine quieted down and the truck began moving. He watched carefully as the driver turned the corner and disappeared from sight.

Shawn's hands were nearly numb from the long hours of being exposed to the cold air in the car. He had put on the gloves that were to be used when they crossed the border. They helped, but after a couple of hours without any heat in the car, his hands and feet were cold again. After starting the car, he removed his gloves and put his hands under his armpits to warm them while he waited for the motor to create some heat. It was only 4:10 in the afternoon, yet completely dark outside.

Driving out of the parking area, he headed for Leningrad. It was only about four miles to the document checkpoint outside of Riga. When he arrived, he slowed the car to a crawl approaching the guards. He blinked the headlights and they reacted just like the other guards at the last checkpoint. One look at the car and they simply raised the bar and waved him through. After nodding to them, he resumed his speed being careful not to exceed the limit. It would be foolish to take any chance of challenging the police.

Traffic was light on the way to Leningrad. There were many trucks but few cars. He took notice of the trucks hauling a variety of commodities. What caught his eye was the number of cattle trucks on the highway.

Unlike American cattle trucks the Soviet trucks were not enclosed. Cattle stood up in trucks that simply had very high wooden racks covered with canvas. He decided that when he got to Leningrad he would watch to see if these trucks passed through the city and went north. They might provide him transportation if he were unable to get out of the city any other way.

He would have to ditch the Volga. It would be too risky to chance that the KGB might find Matulewicz's body and be able to trace the car and the murder to him. They also would know that he would head for Leningrad. There were five million people living there so he could hide for a short while until he found a way out of the country.

If he were successful in getting through the document checkpoint he would stay there until the next evening and then try to get to the border. If he had to stay there another evening, it would make him late, and Fred would get fidgety. However, there was no other way that he could think of to get to the border any sooner without being caught.

Darkness was the only safe time for him to travel. He needed to be patient or he would make a mistake. It was nearly 3:00 a.m. when he drove up to the document checkpoint just outside of Leningrad. The guard was sleeping so he blew the horn to wake him. The frightened man jumped up and immediately raised the bar. Shawn stared at him knowing it would make him very uncomfortable. Chuckling as he drove away, he thought, if the guard only knew he wasn't the KGB, but a fugitive wanted by them.

He drove into the city completely unsure about where he should go. Crossing over the Niva River, he recognized the Winter Palace on the waterfront. Shawn recalled pictures he had seen showing Lenin's soldiers storming the palace during the Bolshevik Revolution in 1917. The architecture of the building was incredible. Huge marble columns lined the front of the long green building that once served as the center of government for all of Russia prior to Lenin.

He drove past the palace and the road went into Nevsky Prospek, the city's business section. Feeling uncomfortable about being seen in this area, he made a U-turn and drove back across the Trotsky Bridge. This section of the city was somewhat rundown and he thought it would be easier to locate a vacant building where he could hide inside until he could put together a realistic escape plan.

It was nearly 5:30 a.m. when Shawn drove past the Leningrad Hotel and noticed a large unfinished addition attached to the building. Streetlights made it easy to see without using his car lights. Getting out of the car, he walked around the wooden barrier and went into the vacant building. It looked as if workers had walked off the job many years ago and never returned. Unused bricks and lumber were still stacked around the unfinished project.

The top floor was five stories up and Shawn found what he assumed was at one time a temporary office for the government officials who might have been supervising the building project. The walls were not finished, but there was some insulation piled up in the corner. He decided that he would lay several strips on the concrete floor to cushion him and keep the dampness from chilling him while he slept.

He went back to the barricade and looked around to be sure nobody was nearby. Then went out to the Volga to remove all his equipment from the trunk and put everything behind the wooden fence. Before returning to the car he peeked through an opening in the barrier to be sure it was safe to leave. It was important that the car not be found nearby so he drove around the block and parked the car in the hotel's parking lot. Before locking the sedan, he looked around carefully then took the keys just in case he changed his mind about using it again and went back to the vacant building.

Lugging the equipment up to the fifth floor drained a lot of energy, so he decided to rest. Shawn pulled his heavy parka around him then made a nest out of the insulation. The building was cold and damp. The concrete walls were bare except for a small amount of heating and plumbing material. It appeared as if thieves have taken most of the electrical wire and pipes for the plumbing. He assumed they were stripped and sold for salvage. Not much different than what happens to vacant buildings in the States. He thought it was odd that the building had never been completed and simply left to decay.

The screeching sound of an electric tram stopping outside suddenly woke him. He couldn't remember when he had finally fallen asleep and checked his watch. It was nearly 9:00 a.m. and he had managed to get about three hours of sleep. Not enough, but it would help. Daylight was creeping into the small room. Getting up, he stretched and then walked around the top floor of the unfinished project.

Standing back from an open window casing, he could see the entire street where he had entered through the wooden barrier. Everything appeared normal. There was a police officer in the middle of the intersection directing the morning traffic. The cars crossing the bridge over the river were bumper to bumper. Several people were waiting for the next tram to arrive and others were hustling along the sidewalk. The brisk wind made the air colder, forcing Shawn to button up his parka and put on his gloves.

Looking in the other direction he saw several large Soviet Army buildings. The sign on the front gate identified the compound as a military medical school. It was difficult for him to see the entire complex from where he was looking, so he walked to the other end. Eleven buildings were inside the fence. At the extreme end of the compound was a large building nine stories high.

The street in front of the medical school was made of cobblestone. Like most of the buildings in the city, the street was probably several hundred years old. There was very little activity outside it so he went back to the window overlooking the river. Traffic was still heavy and he could see two small tugboats moving down the river. The traffic cop was now sitting in his car smoking a cigarette. The traffic was mixed with cars and trucks. Several military trucks pulling trailers like he had seen on the way to Leningrad caught his attention. They were transporting cattle and going north.

That might be a way he could slip out of the city. In the dark he could hide near the tram stop and when a cattle truck stopped for the traffic light, he could climb inside a trailer. It would be risky, but he suspected that the guards at the document checkpoint wouldn't be checking trailers. The cattle would be his only problem. If they were afraid of him they might panic and try to jump out through the wooden bars. Should the cattle panic, he would have to jump out immediately. He would have to be careful not to get caught between a steer and the side of the truck. Each full grown animal probably weighed about 1200 pounds he thought and could easily crush him.

He returned to the room where he had been sleeping and lay down again on the insulation. He opened a nutrient bar hoping it would satisfy his hunger. With his eyes closed he tried to visualize himself successfully reaching Wyborg and crossing the border on snowshoes as he nodded off to sleep.

Riga, Latvia, USSR

Georgi walked into the sandstone cave with a flashlight to check the body of the American his agents had discovered. Matulewicz's body was face down with three bullet holes in his back. The agent who had discovered the body told him that there were no papers or alloy samples to be found. But there were two sets of fresh footprints. This meant there had been another person in the cave with him.

A government physician estimated the time of death to have been early that morning. This meant that the killer had between six and seven hours to get away. Georgi surmised that the other person had to be the other American who had jumped out of the plane with Kelly. Now that he had the papers with the technology, he would try to leave the Soviet Union… but how?

By boat from Tallinn, Estonia or by air out of Leningrad or Moscow he wondered? These were the only ways a foreigner could leave the Soviet Union. The CIA must have provided illegal documents with a phony identification for their agent. However, Natasha had given them his real name, "Shawn Murphy." Though the KGB didn't have a picture or a description of him, he could have all border checkpoints stop any person who looked or acted suspicious.

Georgi gave instructions to the man in charge of the investigation to set up a checkpoint at each of the three areas the American might try to leave. It frustrated him that he was always so close yet never able to crack the case which had attracted the attention of his superiors in Moscow. He had his driver take him back to the KGB Headquarters in Riga.

If he didn't find Murphy soon, his days would be numbered. Something had to be done, even if he had to fake the report and say that Matulewicz was the person with Kelly and that he had destroyed the documents and the alloy composites.

Georgi read his intelligence report from Kelly again very closely. The escape plan indicated the Americans would fly out of the Moscow Airport. Maybe this was a diversion and they were planning to cross the border into Finland on snowshoes. He went over to the map on the wall and studied it for several minutes then called the agent filling in for Nikolai.

"Yes, Sir Commandant?" the man said, standing in the doorway, afraid to enter the office without permission.

"Get in here you idiot!"

"Yes, Sir."

"If you were an American who had managed to sneak into our country, how would you get out without getting caught?"

The frightened man thought for a moment, purposely not looking at his commandant's eyes, then replied. "I would make the opponent think I was planning to escape one way and then do something completely different."

"I think you are right Janis. Our report said they would fly out of Moscow, but I think they will cross the border on snowshoes and escape into Finland. I will have extra agents check all international flights from Leningrad and Moscow just to be safe. Did you have our people contact all the border checkpoints?"

"Yes. I also had them contact the document checkpoints on each highway entering all three cities and they are watching the trains from Leningrad to Moscow."

"Very good. If they catch any person who can't prove how they entered the country, I want them held until we can talk to them. Do you understand?"

"Yes, Commandant." Janis said, then hesitated. "Sir. May I have permission to speak freely?"

"Of course. What do you want to say?" Georgi said, glaring at Janis.

"I suspect that if the CIA is able to forge documents to get their people out of the country, they would also provide them with forged documents to let them move freely around the country. I really don't understand what our people will be looking for at all these checkpoints."

"You're probably right, but we still have to make the effort, or our people in Moscow will charge all of us with incompetence. Do you understand the penalty for this?"

"Yes, Commandant." He knew that he and many others would be charged with crimes against the government. If he were lucky, the penalty could be a long tour in Siberia, if not it would be death.

"I want extra people at the border checkpoint and at the document checkpoint at Wyborg. If Murphy goes to the border like we think, he will have to go north through that city. That's the only highway that goes directly to the border from Leningrad. I don't believe he will attempt to cross anywhere else since it's mostly wasteland."

"Do you think he might try to go by boat from Tallinn to Helsinki?"

"He might. Have our agents in Tallinn check all the fishing boats and the ships that are planning to cross the Baltic Sea in the next day or so."

"I will get on these right away, Commandant." Janis hurried out of the office delighted to get away from Georgi. It made him nervous to be anywhere around the commandant. Hopefully, the commandant would leave soon.

Georgi got up from his desk and looked out the window watching the snow that was beginning to fall. His nerves were getting to him. Pacing around the room he reminded himself over and over that he had to either locate Murphy or report to his superiors that the man in the cave was Murphy and he had not located the alloys or the formula. He would put in his report that Boris Yegorov may have lied about the alloy to convince the Americans to help him defect.

Helsinki, Finland

Fred Unser walked into Wes Ryerson's office and sat down in the chair next to his desk, while listening to the conversation Wes was having with

Colonel Dean Armstrong on the AWAC. Fred looked over at Gina who was sorting through a stack of files on her desk. Ryerson hung up the phone and turned to Fred.

"No word from Murphy."

"He should be at the border by now. Something has gone wrong. God damn it!" Fred got up and began pacing around the office. "I hope they're just hiding and waiting for darkness."

"Maybe they stayed in Riga until things cooled down," Gina said. "He's with John and there's nobody better than he is at getting through the type of terrain where they'll be crossing the border."

"Fred, Murphy might have been too tired to make the trip the same night he jumped from the plane. It has to take a lot out of a person to be free falling that far and through such cold conditions."

"Maybe you're right. If we don't hear something by tonight we'll know they're in trouble." Reaching into his pocket he pulled out his pipe and tobacco. Puffing on the pipe always calmed him, but it wasn't working this time.

"What'll you do if they contact you and say they are in trouble?" Wes asked.

"Matulewicz is not crossing the border. His job is to meet Shawn and take him north of Leningrad near Wyborg where he'll go alone on snowshoes to the border. It would be too difficult to conceal two people, but one person walking under a heat reflective blanket has a chance of not setting off heat sensors that are throughout the forest."

"What happens if he gets caught or is blocked from crossing the border?" It was too late to change the question, realizing that this wasn't a good time to ask.

"If he gets caught we lose the formula and the samples and we'll have to negotiate to try to get him released. We've thought of that possibility. It'll be a political nightmare and I'll be looking at a very early retirement. The president will have egg on his face. Now if Shawn gets within 10 miles of the border and gets blocked, that'll be different. We have a rescue plan all set to go and would be able to get him out within an hour or so."

Fred walked to the door and hesitated before turning the knob. "Call me at the hotel if you hear anything. I mean anything."

He walked out of the office and went to the bar in the hotel and ordered a glass of bourbon on the rocks. After paying the bartender he took a couple of sips then changed his mind. No need to fill up on alcohol he thought. Instead, he left and went to his room to rest.

Chapter 40

Riga, Latvia, USSR

J ANIS RUSHED INTO GEORGI PASVAS' OFFICE WITHOUT knocking. "Agents in Leningrad located a black Volga with a fake license plate. The car had been reported stolen in Estonia and they suspected Murphy might have used it. They had set up roadblocks in addition to adding more guards at all checkpoints."

"What about the railroad station?" Pasvas asked.

"They have that covered, Commandant. He cannot get out of the city. They said that there was blood on the seat of the car, which means he might be wounded. Maybe he had a shoot out with the dead man, and he was wounded.

"I think you might be right Janis. Perhaps he killed the other American so he could get the reward for the information. Maybe not. I do not know why he killed the other man, but do know that we have to find him real soon, or we will all be shot for failure."

"I'll bet he is hiding in Leningrad until he gets enough strength to move, or maybe he is waiting until things calm down."

"Call my driver. You and I are going to Leningrad tonight."

Janis left to do what he had been instructed, but he was not happy about riding for three hours with his boss. Who knows what he would do if things went bad in Leningrad. He instructed the driver to have the car ready, then called Georgi.

"Your car is all set to go. With respect to your decision, sir, may I suggest that I stay here to keep on top of things in case the American is not in Leningrad? I would be able to help you more if I were here in Riga."

"Perhaps you're right. Okay, you stay here and call the KGB office if anything comes up."

Georgi liked Janis. He seemed to be on top of everything. Nothing like Nikolai, who thought he was the smartest person on earth, but in the end he learned that he was pretty stupid. Maybe he would select Janis to be his new vice-commandant.

Leningrad, USSR

The city was covered in darkness. Shawn looked at his watch. It was only 4:30 in the afternoon. Standing near the window opening he watched the street intersection by the river. Traffic was bumper to bumper as people rushed to get home. Another cattle truck pulling a trailer was in the traffic and going north. If he were going to get on one, he would have to wait until late at night, or early in the morning when there was no one around to see him climbing on the trailer.

Shawn watched closely as the truck drove through the intersection observing that, like the other trucks, the driver was the only person in the cab. He would have to walk out from the tram stop, and climb up quickly on the back of the trailer. It would be too easy for the driver to see him in the mirrors if he attempted to climb over the side. If the cattle didn't stampede and alert the driver he could climb over the tailgate undetected.

For the next two hours he stood back in the darkness watching the street. There was a cattle truck about every hour. He suspected that they made many trips because they could only carry a small number of steers at a time. Shawn worried about where the trucks were going. Maybe the trucks were only going to the northern section of the city. If this were true, he would be in serious trouble and would not know how to get to Wyborg. There had to be train tracks leading north from Leningrad to Wyborg from the cattle yard. If so, he could follow them in the dark until early in the morning.

It was a risk he would have to take, because he couldn't stay much longer in Leningrad without being caught. To make matters worse, the provisions that Colonel Stoddard had given him were nearly gone. He decided to leave the city after midnight. Shawn walked briskly up and down the empty hallways attempting to keep warm. From time to time he would return to the window to check the street below.

Waiting in the cold building was unsettling his nerves so he decided to work on his equipment, taking apart his automatic rifle and cleaning it. When he changed the clip, he counted the remaining bullets. Fifteen rounds were fired at Matulewicz and he wondered how many hit him. Stoddard had only given him 300, so he was glad he hadn't used more.

He collected his GPS, the microchip, and the nine-volt battery that he needed, and placed them inside his parka pocket with the microchip transmitter. Reaching inside the pack he located the survival knife, put it on his belt, then picked up the rifle and went back to the window. Looking through the night vision scope, he checked all the dark shadows to see if there were any people waiting. Not a soul in sight. Then he carefully studied all the parked cars in the small parking lot.

It was now 11:20 p.m. His stomach growled; he hadn't eaten any real food for more than 24 hours. There were only three nutrition bars left, so he cut one in half and carefully wrapped the remainder for later. He decided to rest for an hour before going down to the street to wait for the next cattle truck, hoping that the trucks continued hauling cattle all night.

The cold damp air chilled his body so he pulled the heat reflective blanket around him and leaned against the wall attempting to keep warm. Without it he might freeze to death. Unsure what the temperature was he felt like he was in a refrigerator. He planned to put the blanket over his head and cut two small slits to see through and wear it when he got near the border. Closing his eyes, he thought about getting to the border of Finland safely.

While Shawn was resting on the top floor, Georgi and his driver crossed the bridge and drove by the uncompleted construction site. The KGB commandant had talked with the guards and KGB agents at the document checkpoint west of Leningrad on the highway connecting with Riga. They had not seen anything suspicious, but did recall the black Volga the previous night. They told Georgi that they had assumed the car belonged to one of the agents from Riga or Tallinn, and just waved it on.

Georgi instructed his driver to drive into the parking lot of the document checkpoint north of the city and wait while he went inside to talk with the supervisor on duty. No vehicle had passed through their checkpoint without them checking every person's papers. The guards declared firmly that they had opened all trunks and checked their contents. It would have been impossible for the American to pass through their gate assured the supervisor.

"You don't understand what kind of a person you're dealing with," Georgi said. "He killed one of his own agents and may have killed another one who was working with us. This man is very clever and very dangerous."

"We are checking every person and vehicle that comes to our checkpoint."

"Continue to do so."

"Sir, we check every person, every vehicle, every day. There is a lot of traffic passing through this guard post."

"I understand. I am just frustrated because we were so close to catching him and then he just disappeared into thin air."

"He is wanted for murder?"

"No. I do not care about him killing his own agents. He has very, very important papers, crucial to national security, and we cannot allow him to take them out of the country."

"I will call our document checkpoint north of Wyborg and warn them."

"Is there another document checkpoint before the border?" Georgi asked.

"Yes. The one above Wyborg is only 15 miles south of the border. There is another one at the border of course. We have guards patrolling the entire border and there are heat sensors throughout the forest. It would be impossible for someone to cross the border and not get caught."

Georgi asked him for some coffee and sandwiches for himself and his driver then went back to the car with the food. They sat in the parking lot watching the guards and KGB agents checking the vehicles as they pulled up and stopped. He could not understand how Murphy might have gotten past the checkpoint. Maybe he had not. They might be looking in the wrong place. Maybe Murphy set them up to think he was hiding in the area. Snow began to fall as a storm moved into the area.

It was nearly 12:30 a.m. when Shawn decided to get up and look out the window again. Snow was falling and beginning to accumulate. The streetlights reflecting brightly off the fresh snow would make it difficult for him to stay in the shadows. He went back into the room and got his rifle. If he stood back inside the room he could shoot out two lights and make the intersection dark except for the traffic light. No one would hear the shot with the silencer and by standing back in the room they wouldn't see the flash from the blast. Switching the scope to day vision he squeezed off a shot and the first light went out.

Stepping back away from the window, he stood still and listened for any sounds that would indicate someone saw the light go out. After several minutes he raised the rifle and took out the second light. There were no cars passing through the intersection. The light changed several times with no vehicles going by so he decided to leave.

Back in the room he carefully folded up the blanket and put it inside his parka pocket then several clips with about 100 rounds of ammo and put them inside his pants. It was important to have the ammo with him just in case he had to ditch the bag with the snowshoes. He took the parka off and hung the rifle upside down on his shoulder and put the parka on over it to keep it concealed and dry. The stairs were slippery with ice that had collected from condensation so he had to be extra careful not to fall and damage any of his equipment.

When he reached the street level he stood near the door for several minutes, watching intently for anyone outside. Not seeing anyone he then walked over to the wooden barrier and looked through the loose boards where he had entered earlier in the morning. The street was empty and the snow had begun coming down harder. Judging from the tire tracks in the street it was nearly two inches deep. He climbed through the barricade and crossed the street. There was nobody nearby, and no cars.

When he got to the tram stop, he hid behind a small building with a bench for passengers to sit on so nobody would see him. During the next hour he watched as only seven cars and two trucks drove through the intersection. He would have to be ready to run if a cattle truck came when the light was green. The snow was deep enough to slow the traffic so he assumed that even if the truck didn't stop he could grab the rear gate and hang on until he could pull himself up inside.

Excitement built each time he saw lights coming over the bridge, but his hopes would fade when it wasn't a cattle truck. There hadn't been a truck during the past hour and half and he wondered if they drove this late. He would have to be patient, but it didn't look good, and his feet were getting very cold.

Shawn checked his watch. 1:40 a.m. Moments later he heard the sound of a truck laboring up the small incline of the bridge and could see its headlights as it drove towards the intersection. He moved out from the back of the tram stop and walked slowly towards the street corner. Luck was with him; it was a cattle truck and the light turned red. The truck driver slowed the rig and stopped waiting for the light to turn green.

He watched the driver put a cigarette in his mouth and light it. Moving quickly Shawn went to the rear of the trailer, put his bag over the tailgate then climbed up inside. The cattle began to move around nervously as he stood in the corner near the head of a steer with long curved horns. They moved around attempting to get away from him until the driver started forward through the intersection. The movements of the truck forced them to settle down to keep their balance.

Shawn stood still so as not to disturb the cattle. Before long, they were calmed down so he squatted down to keep the wind and the driving snow off of him. The metal sides of the trailer were only about four feet high and the rest was made of wooden poles. He felt sorry for the cattle. These conditions were unfit for any animal. The steel floor had no bedding and the urine and manure that had accumulated was frozen to the bed making it difficult for them to stand. The odor wasn't very strong since it was an open trailer and everything froze within minutes.

The slow moving truck made several more stops as it arrived at red lights. By now the cattle seemed to ignore Shawn. They were too busy trying not to fall. His legs got tired from squatting so he would alternate standing up with his back to the wind whenever there were no cars following. It seemed to take forever to get out of the city and the combination of the wind and the heavy snowfall was making him miserable.

Several miles outside the city he felt the truck begin to slow down and he got up to see where they were headed. A short distance down the road was a document checkpoint. Sooner or later he knew that they would pass through one. Sliding his arm out of the parka he removed the rifle then put the parka back on keeping the lens cap on the scope. Pushing the steers out of the way with his hand he moved to the front wall of the trailer to prevent the guards from easily seeing him. The cattle got restless again and he hoped the Soviets would think that was normal because they were checking the trailer.

He slid down inside the corner and held the rifle tight to his body under the parka and waited. Soldiers came out of the guard shack and he could hear instructions being shouted to the driver. Snow covered the cattle and had accumulated on his knit hat and around his shoulders helping to conceal him. A guard walked around the truck and then stopped at the tailgate of the trailer, peering through the legs of the eight cattle Shawn watched the man wiggle the chain giving the impression that he was checking the trailer. The guard glanced inside for a second then returned to the front of the truck. The soldier wasn't serious about checking either the truck or trailer because he had not used a flashlight, which was fortunate for Shawn.

He could hear voices near the gate, but couldn't understand what they were saying. The conversation didn't appear to be excited so he assumed they were just chatting to kill time. Hopefully they wouldn't stay too long because the cold air was brutal.

The truck left the checkpoint minutes later. From his hiding place Shawn watched the guards rush back into their office. When he thought it was safe, he stood up to stretch and moved to the rear of the trailer so he could climb over the tailgate if the truck went to a slaughter yard.

Otherwise he would stay in the trailer unless it left the main highway and went a different direction. North was the only way he could travel.

Helsinki, Finland

Fred Unser woke up in the middle of the night thinking about Murphy. He looked at his watch. It was nearly 2:00 a.m. No one had called from the CIA's satellite so he got out of bed and dialed the number. Ryerson answered and told him that they still hadn't heard anything from the AWAC.

"Sir, I'll call you the moment I hear something, good or bad."

"I know. I'm not checking up on you. It's just my nerves. I'm real worried about not hearing from him or Matulewicz."

"You won't hear from them until they get over the border unless they have a problem. So no news is good news," Ryerson said.

"You're right, I hope. Either of them could send a signal with their transmitter if there was a problem. But they should have been out of there yesterday. Something isn't right. This part of the mission has not gone according to what we had planned."

"Is there any chance they might attempt another way out of the country?"

"No. They only have enough supplies for 24 hours. Except for the car, the only transportation they have is a pair of snowshoes. Matulewicz had the choice of crossing with Murphy or returning to Tallinn if nothing had happened to expose his cover. There's a problem. I can feel it. Well, I'm going to attempt one more time to get some sleep. Make sure you call if something comes up."

Ryerson assured him he would call and hung up the phone. He was concerned himself because this wasn't like Matulewicz. The man was an expert in the woods and he hoped that nothing had gone wrong. Leaning back in the chair, he began wondering what might have happened to the two men.

Chapter 41

Leningrad, USSR

GEORGI PASEVS WATCHED AS THE CATTLE TRUCK vanished in the darkness, then went inside the guard shack for more coffee and sandwiches. He asked the supervisor where the cattle were being taken and was told to a slaughter yard south of Wyborg.

"What happens there?" asked Georgi.

"The cattle are slaughtered, then the meat is packaged, loaded onto trains and sent to Leningrad and Moscow. Why do you ask?"

"The American could hide on the train. Yes?"

"Yes, but why?"

"Maybe he knows we don't check the meat cars very well."

"Not possible. The meat is loaded on the cars and then the doors are locked to prevent people from stealing the meat. If he hid in a freight car he would be frozen like the meat."

Georgi picked up his fresh sandwiches and went back to the car thinking about what the supervisor had told him, but didn't completely agree with the explanation. He set the food down on the seat and told the driver to catch up with the cattle truck and follow it to the slaughter yard. The roads were not plowed and he knew the driving conditions would stay that way until early the next morning. The only tracks on the highway were from the truck.

The chauffeur drove as fast as he could in the snow that now was nearly five inches deep. Up ahead they could barely see the dim rear lights on the vehicle. When they got within view they could see the cattle standing in the back of the trailer and then Georgi thought he saw something move near the tailgate.

"Get closer. I just saw something," he said, straining his eyes to look through the heavy snow falling.

Helsinki, Finland

The cup shattered against the hotel wall spilling coffee on the wallpaper and the hardwood floor. It was 3:20 a.m. and Fred Unser was frustrated that there was no word about Shawn Murphy. There was too much invested in this mission. Failure would put him in a bad position with Gary Circe, who had warned him that he would not accept another failure.

The president's people were planning his re-election and couldn't afford any more bad publicity from the CIA. Maybe it was time to retire. He had given a lot of thought about resigning and moving to South America. Costa Rica would be a perfect place to spend the rest of his life. Away from espionage and away from presidents and directors.

Unser's stomach was killing him; he had no antacids to relieve the pain from the Finnish coffee that he had consumed too much of during the night. Unable to sleep for more than 20 minutes at a time he felt awful and resisted the urge to call Ryerson again to check on Murphy and Matulewicz. He was good at giving his agents advice about getting out when the job became too strenuous on the mind, but he couldn't seem to follow his own advice.

Looking out the window, he gazed into the darkness that covered the city. Feeling helpless, he shut the curtain and returned to bed hoping to get some sleep.

North of Leningrad, U.S.S.R.

Shawn watched the Volga move closer to the trailer. The car had been following for several minutes, but made no attempt to pass. They must have seen him when he moved to the front of the trailer, he thought.

Feeling uneasy he opened his parka and slid his automatic rifle out. He felt the silencer before switching from single fire to auto, and then positioned the scope on night vision. Afraid to stand up he moved slowly on his knees in a crouched position behind the nearly frozen cattle. When he reached the tailgate, he peered over the top and looked at the car that was now only 50 feet behind the trailer.

Georgi's hand was franticly pointing at him, indicating to Shawn that he had been discovered. Assuming it was the KGB in the car he put the rifle on the tailgate and fired a blast into the car's windshield. The Volga instantly slowed down and swung into the snow bank on the side of the road. Shawn quickly grabbed his bag, climbed over the tailgate and jumped onto the ground. The cattle truck continued moving at a slow pace so he was confident that the driver was unaware of the shooting.

The car headlights were still on, but the motor had stalled. Two bodies were sprawled across the front seat riddled with bullet holes. He opened the door cautiously and shut off the lights. Both men were dead and blood was flowing down their bodies onto the floor. Reaching over the body of the driver, he shut the ignition off and removed the keys.

Shawn put the bag with the ammo and snowshoes on the back seat then unlocked the trunk. It took nearly 20 minutes to pull both bodies out of the car and place them in the trunk. He didn't want to leave them on the side of the highway, and thought the extra weight would help the car have more traction in the snow.

He carefully disposed of the large shards of glass from the windshield and then started the motor. The front of the car was stuck in the snow, but he told himself not to panic. Volgas were the Soviet's luxury car and had a lot of power. Back and forth he rocked the car, eventually making headway. After a couple of minutes he was able to free the car. Nevertheless, without a windshield his visibility was very poor. Driving down the middle of the road enabled him to make out the tire tracks of the truck which were barely visible. His compass confirmed that the road was still going in a northerly direction.

It was now 4:30 a.m.; he would have to abandon the car shortly before people began commuting to work. Almost certain that Wyborg would be the next small city, he knew there would also be a document checkpoint. He had driven through several small villages that had no traffic lights or streetlights. Nobody was driving on the highway that was now buried deep under the snow. Shawn kept his speed at about 20 miles an hour. Any faster and he couldn't see the sides of the road.

Noticing a bag on the floor, he reached down and picked it up. Perhaps it contained food. The last bit of nourishment since he had left the other car was half of an energy bar and had nothing to drink. There were two sandwiches and a cup of black coffee that was partially spilled. He picked up one sandwich and took a bite. It was made with some type of greasy cold cuts and gobs of butter.

Extremely thirsty, he took a large gulp of the coffee and nearly choked. It was ice cold and very strong. Despite its horrid taste his body needed the liquid so he continued to sip it.

By the time he reached the outskirts of Wyborg it was nearly 5:00 a.m. No other vehicles were on the highway and the snow had completely covered up the tire tracks of the cattle truck and trailer. He pulled onto a side street and parked the car on the edge of the road. The coffee was gone so he got out of the car and packed the cup with snow and put it on the floor under the heater to let it melt.

The gas tank was half full so he kept the car running with the heater on. Still hungry he ate the other sandwich while waiting for the snow to melt. The car began to warm up now that the wind wasn't blowing through the broken windshield. Concerned about his location he took out the GPS and checked his position. He was about 23 miles southeast of the Finnish border. So close he could probably smell it he thought, yet it might as well be a 100 miles away.

Shawn waited until the snow melted and then drank the water in the cup. It was nearly 5:30 a.m. and he knew people would begin driving to work in Leningrad. He had to get just a bit north of the city before traffic began moving so no one would see him. The cold air chilled him as he drove back onto the highway. Driving conditions continued to deteriorate and the heavy snowfall showed no signs of easing.

Twenty minutes later he suddenly saw bright lights up ahead. It had to be the document checkpoint and he hoped that the guards were inside and hadn't seen his headlights. He turned them off and sat there for several minutes watching to see if a vehicle with lights would drive towards him. The snow continued to fall, making it difficult to see anything except very bright lights.

It would be nearly impossible, he thought, for them to see him with the snow falling so heavy. After he drank the rest of the water, he threw the cup on the floor then got out of the car. It took him several minutes to adjust the straps of snowshoes and put them on. When he felt comfortable with them, he took out the rifle and covered the scope with the lens cap. He put his gloves on and placed the rifle over his other shoulder upside down, then climbed up over the snow bank leaving the car running with the lights off.

About a thousand feet off the highway were railroad tracks that headed north towards the border. He began following the tracks now buried under the snow. There were snow banks on both sides of the track so he knew that trains passed through there on a regular schedule. If one came along he might be able to conceal himself then climb onto the side and ride for several miles to get closer to the border.

The snow shoes were cumbersome at first, but became easier to use as he got accustomed to the odd feeling of having his feet spread and having to pick them up higher than normal with each step. It took nearly an hour before he could see, off in the distance, the document checkpoint. He could scarcely see the gate, but couldn't see any activity.

He could see the land on both sides of the track drop suddenly so he stopped to study the terrain through the snow. It appeared to be a wide river and he was crossing on a railroad bridge with no side protection. He took out his GPS and checked his location again, calculating that he was about 16 miles from the border. Too close to take any chances. Once he reached the other side of the river, he would have to take out the heat reflective blanket and cut two holes to see through.

It would be safe to stay on the tracks until daylight and then he would have to go into the woods. Shortly, the authorities would find the Volga and the KGB would have helicopters looking for him by daybreak unless the snow continued at the rate it had been falling since midnight.

Once he got to the other side of the bridge, he took the blanket out of his pocket and used the knife to cut two small openings. His knit hat was soaking wet, so he threw it away and pulled the parka hood up, then adjusted the blanket over his head, letting it drape over his body. He checked his compass and then left the tracks. The deep snow forced him to use so much energy that he had to stop every hundred feet and rest. It was much deeper in the woods than on the railroad tracks. The snow made it nearly impossible to see where he was going so he had to continually check the compass to be sure he was going north. At about 9:30 a.m. daylight had settled over the area making it much easier to see.

The snowfall began to ease and which could mean trouble for him. If the storm completely cleared the Russians could set up a massive search for him. A quick check of the GPS showed that he was about 12 miles from the border. Estimating that he was moving about a mile each hour, he hoped that with the snowfall diminishing he might be able to go faster, but he was also becoming very tired.

At noon he was 12 miles from the border and his legs were beginning to cramp. Leaning against a pine tree, he took out his last power bar and ate it. Looking around the area he saw nothing but trees. The snow had stopped completely. Shawn assumed that by now the authorities had found the Volga. They would be unable to see his tracks, but common sense would tell them he was going north and soon border patrol soldiers would be following the railroad tracks looking for his trail.

He rested for a moment then checked his compass and started walking as fast as his cramped legs would allow him. It would get dark shortly and he still had to go closer to the border. If he didn't go about three miles further, any rescue attempt would be nearly impossible.

The odds of him getting over the border in the dark were very slim. If the Soviets came after him with snow machines they could easily follow his footsteps with their headlights. If he was lucky there might be only a couple of machines and he might be able to shoot the drivers and drive a machine to the border.

During the next hour, his cramps became worse and when he checked the GPS he had only gone a half a mile. He rested briefly. Time was running out and he began to panic. Talking to himself to calm down, he tried to forget the pain. Somehow, he picked up his pace, and by 2:00 p.m. he had covered another three-quarters of a mile. But 20 minutes later he heard a helicopter and knew they were searching for him. He moved into a heavily wooded area.

The helicopter passed about 500 feet overhead. They would return as soon as they realized his tracks didn't leave the thick evergreen cover. The trees would give him some protection. He took the silencer off the automatic rifle so it wouldn't restrict the rounds when he shot at the chopper.

After switching the scope to daytime vision, Shawn removed the partially used clip and inserted a new one. He looked around to see if there was a clearing that he could use to signal the CIA. A small clearing was about a quarter of a mile ahead. The sound of the helicopter was now in the distance. By moving several feet, he could look up through the treetops. The chopper was moving very slowly so he knew they were searching for his tracks. They might also have a heat sensor that couldn't get a reading because of his heat-reflecting blanket. Taking out his knife he cut a large slit so he could pull the blanket over his head to give him better visibility. Within minutes he saw the chopper. It looked like a troop carrier so he assumed it was filled with soldiers.

He waited until it was nearly overhead and opened fire emptying the clip within seconds. As he removed the clip and inserted a new one, he saw smoke shooting out of the rear of the engine. Twisting to get a better shot, he began shooting again until he unloaded the clip. The helicopter began to lose altitude and he watched it roll sideways, then plummet toward the ground, disappearing behind the tree tops. Seconds later he heard a tremendous explosion, and saw a huge burst of flames shoot upward into the sky, followed by intense black smoke.

Hustling as fast as he could, he moved in the direction of the small clearing in the forest. Moving the snowshoes through the deep snow was now pure torture. He reloaded, then put the silencer back on. If the Soviets sent soldiers on skis it would help prevent them from identifying where shots came from.

Twenty minutes later, he reached the opening in the thick timber. Standing on the edge he surveyed the clearing; he estimated that it was only 400 feet wide, but wide enough for the CIA to pick him up. It was now or never. He had to use the information Cooper had given him on the plane. He had been told that if he believed it would be impossible to reach the border and he was at least within the 10 miles, then he should use the backup plan. The GPS showed that he was a fraction more than 11 miles. It was 2:50 p.m. and it would take at least another hour and a half to get within 10 miles. Close enough he thought.

It was just a matter of time before the place would be crawling with Soviets. He looked around for a better place to conceal himself. A large section of thick brush across the clearing would be perfect. He walked around the clearing under the cover of the treetops so as not to leave a trail that could be seen from the air.

The thick underbrush was covered with snow so he was careful not to move the branches and knock any off to alert searchers. He pulled out his microchip and attached the nine-volt battery to it. Though it made no sound he knew the signal was going to the satellite and would bounce back to an AWAC plane. Standing still for several minutes he listened for sounds of another helicopter, but the only sounds were the soft whispers of the wind moving through the trees. It was 2:55 p.m.

He decided to make a small pad to stand on so he could move around quickly if he had to shoot in different directions. Using his snowshoes, he matted down the snow in an area about six feet in diameter. Being careful he used his knife to remove snow from the branches overhead to prevent it from falling on him if he accidentally bumped the brush. The branches were so thick with snow that it was impossible for him to look through them to see if anyone was coming, so he would have to rely on sound. But this also meant that the Russians wouldn't be able to see him from a distance.

Shawn closed his eyes and thought about what he should do if the CIA didn't attempt to rescue him. The papers and the alloy samples were in his jacket pocket inside the glass jar. If the soldiers got close enough to capture him, he decided to use his lighter and burn them. Better not to give them the information if he couldn't give it to his own country. The samples, he would toss into the deep snow and hope they wouldn't see them. He looked at his watch again. It was 2:57p.m. Time was crawling like a snail. There was nothing more he could do except wait.

CHAPTER 42

Helsinki, Finland

WES RYERSON ANSWERED THE PHONE LISTENING TO the caller for several minutes, then hung up. Fred looked at him wondering if it was the AWAC.

"That was Colonel Armstrong," Ryerson said. "They got a distress signal from Murphy at 2:55 p.m. He's about 11 miles from the border. A Soviet helicopter crashed about a mile from his present location only minutes before he sent the signal, and the AWAC people think Murphy may have shot it down."

Oh, shit. Fred thought about the situation for only a moment then said, "He's really not close enough to where we agreed to rescue him, but we have no choice. Call the airport and tell them to get the two planes ready. I'll call the Navy. Gina, get the car ready to go to the airport. I want to get on the C-130 that'll be making the rescue."

As soon as Fred finished talking with Admiral Miller, he rushed out to the parking lot. When they arrived at the airport, the Agency's C-130 gunship was running and the crew was going through their final checklist. Fred watched from the car as the plane crept forward in the direction of the taxi strip.

The CIA had purchased two C-130s and converted them into gunships. They are armed with a 105mm Howitzer cannon, a Bofors 40mm cannon and a pair of 20mm Gatling guns. Each Gatling gun can each fire 2,500 rounds of ammunition per minute. A 30 second blast from its weapons could hit every square inch of land the size of a football field.

Usually they kept the planes in South America to use in their operations there. The commander of the gunship division was very uneasy about flying along the border of the Soviet Union. After several meetings with Fred and Gary Circe, he agreed to take part in the backup rescue mission. Fred had hoped they wouldn't have to use the plane.

The inside of the plane was filled with high-tech equipment and ammunition crates. Designed to support rescue missions in Asian countries, it afforded the quickest way to destroy all human life in jungle conditions. Standard procedures required the Air Force to send in fighters to protect the plane during military operations because C-130's can't defend themselves from enemy missiles. The CIA also used this plane for rescue missions or assaults to support covert operations.

There would be no F-16s or A-10s to assist the CIA crew this afternoon, making the mission a very high risk. The CIA and the Pentagon couldn't risk starting a skirmish with the Soviets along the Finnish border. If the plane were shot down, the information released to the media would state that the crew was on a routine training mission and flew into Soviet airspace accidentally. The C-130 gunship's pilot, John Mahan, was one of the best in the business and had flown more than 100 assault attacks with the CIA.

Fred was banking on Mahan's ability to hit hard and fast, then disappear. Though the action could cause an international incident, he had no choice. The information Murphy had was too valuable. The thought went through his mind that perhaps Murphy might not have it. He didn't want to think about that. This was no time to second guess. It would be a disaster if the Soviets got the alloy.

Fred walked over to an Air Force C-130 parked near the operations office of the Helsinki Airport. He saw Colonel Brian Gomula come out of the plane. Fred identified himself, and the colonel invited him in the plane. Gomula was the pilot and Colonel Verle Johnston was the co-pilot. Their mission was very simple. They had to rescue Murphy.

"You got here just in time, Mr. Unser," said Gomula. "I'm getting ready to brief the crew."

They went to the rear of the plane where the crew was waiting. The colonel went through their normal briefing, then introduced Fred who explained the mission and the importance of the alloy they were trying to obtain. The look on their faces told Fred that they were thrilled to be taking part in a clandestine CIA operation. Once Fred finished, Colonel Gomula briefed the crew about the actual rescue mission.

"The AWAC received a signal from Murphy at 2:55 p.m.," Gomula said. "His position is about 11 miles southeast of the border and 12 miles northeast of Wyborg where the border patrol is stationed."

"Has there been any activity with the Soviet Air Force?" asked Mark Schaible, the loadmaster in charge of the actual rescue. "We won't stand a chance if they send planes with missiles."

"According to the AWAC, the only plane activity has been the helicopter that they believe was shot down by Murphy. The intelligence officer suspects it was carrying border patrol troops. The chopper crashed 16 minutes before they received the signal from Murphy."

"Do we have to air drop the equipment to Murphy?" asked Schaible.

"No." replied Gomula. "The Navy has already fired a Tomahawk missile. The warhead has been removed and the Fulton Recovery System has been packed into the compartment where the explosives are normally attached. There are instructions with the special suit in case Murphy has forgotten his prior briefing on the rescue operation."

Gomula went on to explain that the Tomahawk could travel up to 2500 miles and be programmed to land within 100 feet of its target. It was launched underwater from a submarine located in the Baltic Sea. The missile was traveling at 550 miles an hour and would land within minutes after the CIA's gunship had strafed the entire area surrounding Murphy.

"If there are no more questions, we need to get up in the air and fly a rotation near the border so we can move in right after the missile has landed."

Gomula and Johnston went to the front of the plane and Fred stayed in the back with Schaible. Moments later they were moving down the runway. Fred sat in a webbed seat wringing his hands. His nerves were shot and he felt helpless. Leaning back in the seat with his eyes closed he tried to envision the rescue attempt.

Wyborg, USSR

A high-pitched squeal caught Shawn's attention. Listening carefully, he finally realized it was the sound of snowmobiles. His fingers and toes were growing numb and he wiggled them to stimulate the circulation. For the past hour, he had been fighting sleep. Now he was wide awake knowing that the Soviets were on their way to capture him. He took out his knife and removed more snow from the branches surrounding him to get better visibility.

The snowmobiles sounded far away, but he knew it wouldn't take them long to reach him. It had been nearly 30 minutes since he had sent the signal to the satellite and he wondered where his rescue plane was. His rifle was ready with the silencer in place, and he moved around to warm up his body. The snowmobiles grew louder. Peering through the brush he searched, but was still unable to see them. His rifle had a full clip and he took out two other clips from the bag and put them in his parka jacket. He had just switched from automatic to single shot when he saw the first snowmobile coming in his direction.

He centered his scope on the driver's head, but was unable to hold onto the target because the snowmobile moved so fast. Moments later the snowmobile slowed down and he got the chance to fire. The bullet shattered the driver's face guard and he fell off the moving snowmobile, which twisted and rolled over on its side and became quiet. Suddenly, the other snowmobiles went silent. Shawn figured the other drivers were trying to determine where the shot came from. Having a silencer was a great advantage.

Nevertheless, it would only be a short time before they split up and came at him from several directions. Then he would be finished. Looking around for another place to hide he decided it was best to make a stand where he was. Reaching into his parka pocket he took out the tiny micro transmitter and pushed the send button.

"This is Murphy. Soldiers on snowmobiles are attacking me. I think there are 10 machines."

Shawn stood motionless, hoping to avoid exposing his location to the Russians. Time was now critical. His mind raced as the seconds ticked away. Thoughts of Angela kept floating in and out of his thoughts, and he wondered if he would even get to see her again.

Overheard at 4,000 feet along the Finnish Border

Brian Gomula and Verle Johnston listened to Shawn's message relayed from Colonel Armstrong in the AWAC. They were flying at 4,000 feet, 20 miles west of the Soviet border waiting for their orders.

"What time is it?" asked Gomula.

"15:36," replied Johnston.

"The gunship should be going in . . . within the next 10 to 12 minutes," Gomula said, hesitating briefly as he mentally calculated the speed of the Tomahawk missile. "I figure the missile will land at about 15:47. We'll have just enough time to make one or maybe two passes. If we miss the balloon we can't go back. The Russians will probably have fighters with missiles there by then. Regardless, by 16:00, it'll be too dark to see the balloon."

"I hope to hell we don't get shot at," Verle said, considering the possibility of being involved in an international incident.

"I read you."

Gomula and Johnston were quiet as they continued to fly a wide pattern that covered a 75-mile circle. They were prepared to switch directions at a moment's notice and cross over the Soviet border to make the rescue. Gomula looked at his watch again as tension continued to build. It was now 15:43. The missile should be landing soon.

Both men quietly worried that their mission might create an international incident. Although it was on their minds, they were committed to the rescue regardless of the risk or repercussions. Each remained focused on their mission, trying not to think about the possible consequences.

Wyborg, USSR

Shawn heard the snowmobiles moving closer. Closing his eyes he tried to relax while waiting for the Soviet patrol. He was prepared to use the rest of his ammo to protect himself. Reaching into his left hip pants pocket, he felt for the cigarette lighter in case he had to burn Yegorov's papers then he reached inside another pocket to be sure the small alloy composite samples were still there.

He switched the rifle back to automatic and took off the silencer to get the maximum firepower. His only hope was to hold them off with the rest of his ammunition. If he could do enough damage to them, he might have a chance since it was almost dark. Then he might be able to sneak over the border in the dark. It was his only chance.

Moments later, he heard the sound of a snowmobile and then he saw the machine moving slowly in his direction. Kneeling on one knee he aimed the rifle at the driver. Then two more snowmobiles came into view. Shawn opened fire and shot all three drivers in quick succession. Before he could reload, gunfire came from a different direction. Bullets penetrated the brush, knocking snow and small branches down on him. Suddenly, he was hit in his right thigh, nearly knocking him over. Blood gushed onto the snow. The fire continued, and he fell forward flat on the snow to avoid being hit again. When the shooting stopped, he inserted the clip and returned fire.

They fired back quickly and he knew they would keep him pinned down until he ran out of ammo, then close in on him. It was now 15:45. He pulled out his micro radio and turned it on.

"Where the hell are you? I've been hit," he yelled. "I'm nearly out of ammo and I'll have to burn the papers if you don't come and get me right now."

His leg was warm and wet. He took his knife and cut pants leg slightly to see just how bad his leg had been damaged. The blood made it impossible to check the wound so he rolled over and waited until he either heard or saw something.

AWAC

Colonel Armstrong listened to Murphy's transmission. He felt frustrated because the radio Shawn had could not receive messages. Armstrong relayed the message to the C-130 gunship then checked the computer. The Tomahawk missile was 82 miles from the target. It was time for the gunship to strafe the area surrounding Murphy.

"This is AWAC-7," he radioed the gunship, "Do you read me, forty-niner?"

"Forty-niner, we read you AWAC –7," replied Mahan. Excitement built in the former FBI agent as he thought about crossing the Soviet border and starting what could become an enormous international incident. The other thought was that the Russians could send in missiles and shoot him down.

"Move in at once. The Indian is now 78 miles west-southwest and will reach target at 15:47."

"We're on our way," said Mahan, making a sharp right bank toward the Russian border.

"You are six minutes from target. Drop to 700 feet and make two passes. Repeat, stay at 700 feet. The Indian will pass under you at 550. Do you read me?" Colonel Armstrong asked?

"Affirmative AWAC-7. We are descending to 700."

"Forty-niner, you're four minutes to target. I show you 16 miles from the border."

"Roger that, AWAC-7. We have a visual," Mahan replied. He could see the border patrol building off to his right. "We now have the target in sight. We're at seven even, AWAC–7, and are making the first hit."

"Forty-niner, we just picked up six helicopters on the monitor. They are nearly 20 minutes away. There are 16 snowmobiles in the woods surrounding Murphy. He is on the northeast edge of the woods. Make sure you don't fire too close to him. Repeat, Murphy is on the northeast edge of the woods. Do you read?"

"Affirmative," Mahan replied. "Murphy is northeast on the edge of the woods. We are making a left bank and holding."

Armstrong studied the computer screens keeping track of the six helicopters and the location of the Tomahawk missile. Timing would be tight he thought. There would be no room for mistakes or any type of delay. He watched the CIA gunship on his screen crossing the Soviet border.

Chapter 43

Langley, VA

Gary Circe read the report just handed to him. Shaking his head he thought about the consequences if Fred Unser's plan failed. It was too late now to have second thoughts about approving the mission. He called his deputy and told him to prepare a press release that would address an incident should the rescue fail.

"Under no circumstances will we admit that we were involved in any type of rescue mission," Circe hesitated for a moment then continued. "We don't know who Shawn Murphy is and the CIA is not involved in any type of clandestine operation. We suspect the Soviet government is creating this story to support their claims that our agency is engaged in efforts to help the Baltic countries separate from the Soviet Union."

Circe instructed his deputy to send him a copy of the draft the moment it was completed, then he called the White House to make them aware of the situation. A call he did not want to make. Their press agents would be busy creating a different interpretation of the events. The CIA was not in a good position. He would be vulnerable and the center of criticism from the president if his people were unsuccessful in getting Murphy and the documents over the border.

Leaning back in his chair he thought about the information Murphy was bringing back to the United States. The risk was very high, but still believed it was worth the efforts. He hoped everything would work as planned to prevent an embarrassing situation for everyone.

Wyborg, U.S.S.R.

John Mahan held the CIA's C-130 gunship steady in a left bank then gave his chief gunner, Greg Rainer the order to fire. The gunship fired into the wooded area at the rate of 3,000 rounds every 30 seconds. Mahan kept the plane in a tight left bank while Rainer continued firing into the wooded area.

Down below on the ground it both startled and exhilarated Shawn as he rolled over on his back and pressed his hand on his thigh to help slow the bleeding. The plane made a tight circle as it showered the area with bullets. The tops of the trees began to fall as if a violent windstorm were passing through. Shawn struggled to crawl out into the small opening, so the pilot would see him and not fire too close.

The plane made two passes and on the second turn Shawn could see the pilot. He got up on his knees and waved his arms. Mahan saw him and gave a thumbs up as he passed overhead. After the second pass was completed, Mahan leveled the plane off and turned back to Finland. It was now silent in the woods around Shawn. He hoped the gunship's fire had killed all of the border patrol soldiers pursuing him. It was now 15:46 and darkness was quickly creeping into the area.

Less than a minute later, he heard the Tomahawk missile scream into the middle of the clearing, landing less than 150 feet from him. Struggling to his feet, he dragged his rifle and walked on the snowshoes to the missile buried under nearly two feet of snow. Blood continued to flow out of his leg, leaving a dark red trail behind him. Stopping twice to get his wind, he continued, knowing that the C-130 would be coming real soon and he would only have one opportunity.

Colonel Armstrong had already given Gomula and Johnston instructions to approach from the northeast at 450 feet to make the pickup. Johnston watched carefully for the small blimp so they could change course.

Shawn reached the missile and began to dig the snow away. Reaching the bulkhead he opened the compartment and pulled out a large package. The balloon was packed on the top. After yanking it out he found the harness attached to the rope. Struggling against time and pain, he forced himself to take off the snowshoes and strap on the special outfit. Time was running out and he began to feel dizzy from the loss of blood. He had to get the balloon inflated or the C-130 rescue ship couldn't pick him up.

Once the zipper was up, he screwed in the four bottles of helium and instantly the balloon took shape. In less than a minute the miniature dirigible climbed upward, pulling 525 feet of rope. Too weak to stand, Shawn sat on the ground waiting for the plane.

Gomula spotted the balloon on his right. After instructing Johnston to call Schaible and tell him to get ready for the pick-up, he banked the plane and began to descend to 450 feet. He completed the turn and focused on the balloon ahead.

"Don't miss, Brian," Verle yelled. "I just got a call from the AWAC. Six helicopters are less than 60 miles behind us. They have got to be loaded with missiles, so we can't make a second pass."

"I know, Verle. It's going to happen on the first try. Tell them to get ready, we're seconds away."

Colonel Gomula lined up the plane's nose where he assumed the cable was under the balloon. He slowed their air speed to help reduce the jolt to Murphy. It was difficult to see the cable until the last second because its diameter was so small. Hoping that the wind wouldn't suddenly blow the miniature dirigible in another direction he held the plane at 450 feet, closing in on the target. On the front of the plane's nose were two long metal bars with their tips spread in a V-formation.

Suddenly, the familiar sound of a C-130 reached Shawn's ears. Forgetting the pain in his leg, he managed to stand and turn facing the direction the plane would take him to reduce the risk of more injury when he would be instantly yanked upwards at more than 100 miles an hour.

The plane hit the target perfectly, immediately closing the bars to tugged grasp the cable that was intertwined with a thick bungee cord to reduce the sudden snatch. The balloon was set free when the cable was cut by the bars and the C-130 immediately yanked Murphy upward. He blacked out. Within seconds, the plane was over the Finnish border with Murphy being towed behind them. Schaible, strapped to the loading device for his own safety, began pulling Murphy upward to the back of the plane.

It had been nearly three minutes since they began reeling him upward to the rear door. Fred Unser stood next to Schaible, anxiously waiting to help pull Shawn into the safety of the plane. Both wore safety harnesses. They watched Shawn's body moving back and forth as the Fulton Recovery winch slowly pulled him toward the plane. When his body reached the hoist they carefully pulled Murphy inside the plane and Schaible closed the large rear door. Gomula immediately increased the plane's air speed and climbed to a higher altitude.

Major Stan Brooks, an Air Force aeromedical physician assistant, immediately began checking Murphy's body for injuries as he laid on the floor unconscious. After several minutes he had revived Shawn enough so that he could talk. Fred crouched down and asked Shawn how he felt.

"How do you think I feel?" replied Shawn weakly. "Don't ever ask me to do you a favor like this again. I didn't mind all the problems with getting the papers, but the ride home was a bitch!"

They all laughed and Murphy closed his eyes again as he thought about going home. His entire body felt as if it had been beaten with baseball bats, but the alloy composite samples were now Fred Unser's problem. The information soon would be on its way to the Navy's David Taylor Research Laboratory in Bethesda, Maryland.

Brooks took off the Fulton Recovery suit then helped Shawn into a seat. First, he secured the seatbelt, then Brooks took out a knife and cut a larger slit into his pants leg. The bullet appeared to have gone through the muscle without hitting the bone or a major artery. He cleaned out the wound and wrapped his leg with a large bandage.

Shawn tried to rest, but the plane was already starting to descend. Uncharacteristically, Fred sat at the other end of the plane and showed no interest in Shawn's injury or about what had happened to John Matulewicz. Having obtained the formula and samples, Fred seemed unconcerned about anything else.

This seemed strange to Shawn. But what the hell, right now his only thought was to get to a phone and call Angela. His ordeal had so consumed him that he had hardly given a thought to Angela. She must be really worried.

The plane landed at the Helsinki airport without any problems and Fred told Shawn to meet him at the CIA office within the hour. Shawn chatted with the crew briefly, then got a taxi. Gina Helbling greeted him when he walked in the office. Wes Ryerson was on the phone, and motioned to him to come over. He handed the phone to Shawn. On the other line was Gary Circe.

"Great work, Shawn!"

"Good afternoon, Mr. Circe. At least, I think its afternoon. Hell, I really don't know what time it is, or even what day it is."

Circe chuckled. "It doesn't matter, Shawn. I'm relieved that you're okay. What you did was incredible, and we all appreciate your dedication to get the job done. Is Fred with you?"

"No. I think he's briefing the flight crew. He said he would meet me here in an hour."

"Have him call me as soon as he gets there, and let me thank you again. When will you be back in Washington?"

"I don't know. I had planned to go to Albany first to visit with my wife."

"We really need to talk to you right away to close up any loose ends. It would be best if you came here to Langley first. I'll have a private plane take you to Schenectady when we're finished."

"That sounds good. I'll have Fred call you as soon as he gets here," Shawn hung up the phone, looking at the clock on the wall. Fred should be here soon he thought.

"Is there anything we can do for you?" Gina asked.

"Yes. I've been surviving on energy bars, and haven't eaten any real food since the mission began except a couple of terrible tasting, grease-filled sandwiches."

"Is there anything special that your might want?"

"No. Just solid food."

She left and Shawn chatted with Ryerson while they waited for Fred. He told Wes about Matulewicz and the problems that he had after leaving Leningrad. Fatigue was getting to him and he sat in a chair and closed his eyes. Hunger pains and flashes of the shootout with the Soviet soldiers nagged at his busy mind. Gina returned shortly with three large sandwiches and pastries. A turkey on rye made Shawn feel much better.

Nearly an hour later and Unser still hadn't arrived. Shawn was puzzled. Perhaps, Fred had returned to his hotel room to take a nap. Gina had explained that he hadn't slept all night. Whatever the case, Shawn was exhausted, so he asked Ryerson to take him to the hotel room they had reserved for him.

When Shawn got into his hotel room, he was too tired to call Angela, and instead, crashed, sleeping until noon. When he woke up, his body ached from head to foot. Sitting on the side of the bed, he began to piece together what had happened. He showered and dressed in new cloths that someone left for him.

A quick call to Ryerson told him that Unser had never shown up. They gave Shawn the name of Fred's hotel, but when Shawn called there, he learned that Fred had checked out. How strange for Fred to just leave, he thought. Nevertheless, Shawn called Ryerson back and asked him to arrange for a flight to Washington National on the next available plane.

He wanted to get home soon. Fred really upset him by not showing up at the office. After all the risk and pain he had suffered. But instead he got the impression that Fred really didn't give a damn about him.

Langley, Virginia

The guard at the gate looked at his computer screen then told Shawn to go to Gary Circe's office. The Director was waiting for him.

"Shawn, are you feeling better?" the Director asked, rising from his seat and shaking his hand.

"Much better, sir."

They both sat down.

"And what about Fred, have you met with him yet?" Circe observed Murphy intently as he spoke.

"No. When the plane landed, he told me to meet him in an hour at Ryerson's office. I waited and he never showed. I called his hotel and they said he checked out yesterday."

"That's strange. I wonder if he's okay. I still haven't heard from him which is very odd." Circe turned away and looked at the wall, giving Shawn the impression he was deep in thought.

"What do you mean by okay?"

"This mission has been difficult on him. He was worried that something might go wrong, and he'd been having flashbacks of another mission in South America that went bad. A female agent who was close to Fred was killed, and he's never completely gotten over it."

"You know, of course, sir, that he has the only copy of the formula and the composite samples."

"Yes, I know," replied Circe.

"You don't think that perhaps the KGB kidnapped him?"

"Or, he might've contacted the KGB himself, to sell them the formula," Shawn's mind began to search for other answers.

"Fred? This is a strange business, Shawn. You never know when your friends will suddenly become your foes. Time is precious. Once we are actually finished, I'll have you flown to Schenectady. Please excuse me, I have to make a phone call right away."

Shawn shut the door and went into the next office. He couldn't understand what was happening. The jet lag was really beginning to catch up with him and all he wanted to do was flop down on a bed somewhere and go to sleep. Shawn waited patiently in the connecting office until the Director finished his phone call and called him back inside.

"Do you remember Ron Harrison?" he asked.

"Of course. I coached him on the Olympic team."

"Ron will pick you up here in thirty minutes. He's fairly certain that he can find Fred."

"Really. How?"

"This doesn't leave this office. Understood?"

"Yes."

"The FBI knows who assassinated Lester Fetor."

"You're kidding. Why didn't they arrest him?"

"What makes you think it was a man?"

"I don't know. I just assumed it was."

"You're right, but don't assume anything," the Director said as he leaned back in his chair. "They spotted the best man in the business at Logan Airport and followed his tracks to Switzerland. In their unofficial opinion, justice was done, case closed."

"Ron Harrison knows all this?"

"Affirmative. He'll brief you and then you two will make contact with the hit man who we'll hire to track down Unser. We don't want to have Fred killed. We just want to find him and get back what belongs to us. If it's not already too late. Understood?"

"Of course. Oh, my God, the FBI knew about it, but let Lester get rubbed out. Great, that's just what he deserved!" Shawn blurted out.

"That's not what I said. They simply followed the trail and learned who killed him. They didn't know of the plan in advance."

"You might be interested to know that Fetor had plans to kill you. The FBI believes he thought it was too risky and he fled the country before Robelotto could have him whacked.

"Well, you're right about justice being served. I'm glad he got a taste of his own medicine. I guess what goes around, comes around. Does Ron really think this hit man can find Fred?"

"If anyone can, he will. Call me twice a day and let me know what's going on. My secretary has an envelope for you. It has cash, credit cards and a fake ID for you. There's a private number in the envelope where you can call me. Be careful about phones you use and what you say on the line."

Shawn said good-bye. The last thing he wanted to do was get on another airplane going somewhere other than Schenectady. At least he could sleep on the way to Europe if that was where Harrison thought Fred was hiding. It took him nearly 20 minutes to reach the motel. When he arrived, Ron Harrison was waiting in the lobby, and they went to his room without talking.

"I understand that you have the best person in the world to find Fred Unser for us!" Shawn said.

"Yes, and I don't think it will take long. Why are you limping?"

"I got shot in the leg yesterday."

"Has anyone looked at it?"

"On the plane when they rescued me. There hasn't been time since. Hell, I haven't even changed the bandage they put on in the airplane. They took my shirt and pants away, then gave me a change of clothing."

"We need to take care of this before we go to the airport." Ron called a staff doctor the FBI used in emergencies. "He'll be here within the hour. How are you for clothes?"

"I've worn these for 24 hours. Hell I wore the other clothes for five days, because I didn't have anything else to wear."

"I can tell. Look, the doctor will be here shortly. I'll run out and get you some clean clothes. After the doctor leaves, try to get some sleep."

"What about the hit man?"

"What about him?"

"Don't you have to contact him?"

"Done. He gets a million if he finds Unser. The CIA has a slush account for projects like this. He'll meet us at the airport."

Ron left and Shawn went into the bathroom. After turning on the hot water, he took off his clothes and stuffed everything in the trash basket. The water felt wonderful. He closed his eyes and let the spray pepper his back. Thoughts of Angela swirled through his mind and he was tempted to call her, but he decided to spare her the grief.

The doctor arrived as he was getting out of the shower. Shawn thought he would pass out from the pain when the doctor pulled off the bandage. It had adhered to his leg and the wound began to bleed.

"You really need to come to my office where I can treat this properly."

"There's no time for that. I'm leaving for Europe in a little while."

"I know, I know. Nothing ever changes with you people. I'll give you some medicine to prevent an infection, and it will also help with the pain. You have to change this bandage twice a day, or all the medication in the world won't help you."

"Is there a drug store nearby where I can buy more dressing?"

"You don't need to. I brought enough to last you four days. Now turn over so I can give you a shot."

"Why are you giving me a shot?"

"Because, I don't have a clue to what kind of crap you have floating around your system. We can't take a blood test, so I'll give you a healthy dose of penicillin to kill anything that might be in there. That's why. Now turn over."

The doctor left Shawn with a bottle of penicillin tablets, and almost as soon as he was out the door, Shawn dozed off again. He never heard Ron come back in the room. Ron had to shake him to wake him up. The jet lag had taken a toll on his body and he didn't know if he felt better or worse. Either way, he started to feel better as he walked around. Ron handed him the new clothing and he went into the bathroom to get dressed.

"What did the doctor say?"

"He changed my dressing and gave me a shot of penicillin. I have to change the dressing twice a day and take the meds he gave me. I'll be all right."

"Good. Let's pack your stuff together and get something to eat before we catch our flight."

Pauli DeSarbo was waiting at the airport. Ron introduced him to Shawn, then picked up their tickets. A security guard escorted them to a private entrance, so they wouldn't have to pass through the metal detector. They flew to Newark then to London and Helsinki. It was anyone's guess as to where they would go next. That was DeSarbo's call.

The plane left on time, and Shawn wondered about DeSarbo, about how he found people that the FBI and CIA with all their contacts and technology couldn't. One thing was certain, they must have had a lot of confidence in him if they were willing to pay him a million dollars in cash. He drifted off to sleep thinking about DeSarbo.

CHAPTER 44

Stockholm, Sweden

THE VIEW FROM THE ROYAL HOTEL WAS spectacular. Fred Unser stood on the little veranda outside his room enjoying the city lights for nearly an hour. Finally the cold air forced him back inside. Confident that no one would think to look for him in Stockholm, he decided to stay there for a few weeks. When it was safe, he would fly to Costa Rica. There was no hurry. He had sold all his stocks, withdrawn his life savings, and had placed the funds in an international bank in Mexico. But he was still unsure about what to do with the priceless Soviet technology.

The information was worth millions and would guarantee him a much better retirement than the 300 thousand he had stashed in his suitcase. The CIA had used him for years, and now he was in a position to reward himself for all the thankless work he had given them for years.

Soft music lured him downstairs into the piano bar. Not recognizing anyone, he entered the large room filled with strangers. Just the setting he wanted. It would be easy to blend in without attracting attention. Fred ordered a glass of French wine. Three drinks relaxed him, but didn't satisfy his hunger, so he decided to go into the dining room and order dinner. The hostess sat him next to a large picture window overlooking the bay. Lights reflecting off the water created a tranquil scene with the soft music, and he realized that he hadn't enjoyed himself this much in years. Alcohol always relaxed him until he thought about the secret torment that haunted him.

He agonized over the memory of his former lover who had been killed during a mission in Colombia. In his mind he had gone over that mission a thousand times, and to this day, no one knew for sure what had gone wrong. As the months went by, it nearly drove him crazy that he had encouraged her to take the assignment to help assassinate a drug czar in Bucaramange. The assassination was successful, but she was caught, tortured and then killed before she could cross the border into Panama.

Fred ordered more wine with dinner. It was excellent and soothing. Maybe he would meet a Swedish woman in the bar. He was lonely and would enjoy chatting with someone about something other than work. But he drank too much and by 8:30 p.m. he was back in his room. This upset him because the one rule he always stressed with his agents was to never consume too much alcohol.

There was no excuse for this type of behavior and it would be the last time. Just to be safe, he would check out of the hotel in the morning, and get a room at a different one, in a different part of the city. It was foolish to drink that much wine. He undressed and fell asleep without shutting off the lights.

Helsinki, Finland

The plane moved around violently as it flew through heavy turbulence on its way to Finland. The jarring woke Shawn, and he looked at his watch realizing that he had slept for nearly six hours. He stretched his arms and looked at Ron who was reading a magazine. Pauli DeSarbo sat next to Ron, staring straight ahead as if in deep thought.

Once they landed and their passports were checked, Pauli wanted to visit the CIA office and speak with Wes Ryerson. They found Ryerson working with Gina Helbling on a report that had to be finished by morning.

"Hi, Wes," Shawn said and introduced Harrison and DeSarbo.

Shawn felt odd introducing a Mafia hit man as someone working for the CIA.

"Come on in. Gina and I were just completing some paperwork," Wes said and carefully put the report in his desk drawer. "What can I do for you?"

"We're looking for Fred Unser," DeSarbo replied. "Did he say anything or give any indication about what he planned to do with the technology after Murphy was rescued?"

"No. The last time we saw him was when we drove him to the airport. After the rescue Shawn said Fred was supposed to meet him here, and that's all we know about it."

Pauli turned to Shawn, "Okay, I have enough. Let's go to the hotel."

Shawn's phone rang at 5:30 a.m. the next morning. It was Pauli. He wanted to meet downstairs at 6:00 to eat breakfast and then leave. After a quick shower, Shawn dressed and packed his small bag, then limped into the elevator to meet Ron and Pauli.

"What's going on?" asked Shawn, as he poured a cup of coffee from the porcelain container.

"There's an 8:00 a.m. flight to Stockholm that I want to get on," Pauli said, eating as he spoke. "Unser wouldn't stay where he might be seen. My guess is that he went to Stockholm to hide out."

"What do you plan to do after we land?" asked Ron, looking at Pauli.

"I was hired to locate Unser. If I find him, that will be your problem. We can register at a hotel and you two can relax until I get done with what I have to do."

After arriving in Stockholm, they registered at the St. Wendel Hotel downtown. Pauli said he would begin his search for Unser immediately and agreed to meet them back at the hotel for lunch. Shawn went up to his room and lay on the bed. He felt guilty about not calling Angela and looked at the clock to figure out what time it was in Albany. As it was only four in the morning in Albany, he decided to wait.

Ron called at 11:30 a.m. astonishingly, he said that DeSarbo had located Unser. Shawn went to Ron's room to wait for Pauli. At 12:15 p.m., there was a knock on the door. DeSarbo stood in the doorway with a big grin.

"This was too easy." he said, then tossed a piece of paper on the stand. "Mr. Fred Unser is registered at the Storuman Hotel on Nortkoping Street. Room number 637."

"Where is he now?" asked Ron.

"Don't know. I just located where he was registered. I would suggest that we visit him at about four tomorrow morning. He won't expect us and I don't think he will be leaving before then."

"We can't take a chance," Ron said. "We need to keep watch from the lobby."

"Has he ever met you?" DeSarbo asked.

"No. I've talked with him on the phone, but I've never met him in person. You and I can take turns, but Shawn can't take a chance of even being on the street, just in case Unser might see him."

"Okay with me," Shawn said. "As long as I'm with you when you break down his door."

"You've been watching too many TV shows, Shawn," Ron laughed. "I'll get a key from the hotel desk and we'll simply open his door."

"What if there's a chain?" asked Shawn.

"Then we'll break down his door and scare the shit out of him," Pauli added, laughing. "Either way, at four in the morning, we'll surprise Mr. Unser. Let's hope he has the alloy samples you guys are looking for."

"Here's the plan," Ron said and took out some papers from his brief case. "We can't just barge into his room. The FBI will have to make arrangements with the authorities here in Stockholm and then we can arrest him. We have to do this legally or he'll get off, because we violated his rights."

"That's why there are so many criminals in the United States running around instead of going to prison," Pauli said. "It's very simple. We go in, you get the papers and I'll take care of Mr. Unser. Clean, done and no chance of the court system screwing up and letting him go."

"That's not the way it's going to be done," Ron said and walked over to Pauli who stared him in the eye. "You were hired to find him. I agree with what you said, but we have to do this legally. Is there any more discussion about how to handle this?"

No one spoke. Ron left to make arrangements with the local authorities, while Pauli went back to the hotel lobby to keep an eye on Unser. At the police station, Ron sent a telex to FBI headquarters requesting that State Department send an official request to the Swedish authorities to allow them to make the arrest.

Shawn waited until 2:30 p.m. and then called Angela at her office in Albany. As he expected, she was upset that he had returned to Europe without seeing her. He assured her that he would be home within a couple of days. She was frustrated that he couldn't tell her more, but understood that he couldn't speak freely over the phone. When he finished the call to Angela he called Gary Circe to tell him that they had located where Unser was staying, and would call back when he had more information.

It was nearly time for dinner when Ron came to Shawn's room. He explained the State Department had sent an official request and the Swedish police would accompany them when Ron made the arrest. At 3:30 a.m. the police would arrive at the hotel and they could enter the room at 4:00 a.m. as planned. Unser's hotel window opened onto a fire escape and would be guarded. DeSarbo had insisted on staying in the hotel lobby until it was time to make the arrest.

They went to dinner and talked about everything except why they were in Sweden. When they were finished they returned to their rooms to rest until it was time to leave for the Storuman Hotel.

At 3:30 a.m., Shawn and Ron walked into the lobby of the hotel and found DeSarbo sitting in an overstuffed chair, his head bobbing up and down as he tried to ward off sleep. Six detectives arrived moments later.

Pauli told the group that Fred had gone to his room at about 1:30 a.m. with a woman he had met in the bar. She had not returned downstairs, so he assumed that she was spending the night. Ron decided not to wait until 4:00 a.m. to surprise Unser. Three detectives left to cover the rear of the hotel and the fire escape. The rest of the group, without Pauli, went up to Fred's room on the sixth floor. Pauli was content to doze in the chair until they had made the arrest.

The Swedish detective had gotten an extra key from the desk clerk. He carefully inserted it into the lock then turned it, keeping pressure on the key to prevent it from making noise. Once it was unlocked, he nodded to Ron, then opened the door.

The men rushed into the room with guns pointed and turned on the light switch. The intrusion startled Unser and his companion. Before anyone could reach Fred, he removed a pistol from under his pillow and waved it at the group.

"Don't come any closer or I'll shoot," Fred said as he looked at Shawn. "I guess I underestimated you."

"How could you do this Fred?"

"The time was right to take care of Fred Unser since the CIA was never going to do it."

"You turned against your country."

"You have no idea how much this has troubled me. Let the broad leave, she has done nothing wrong."

Ron motioned for her to get out of the room. They waited until she put on her clothes and one of the detectives escorted her outside and stayed with her.

"Do you have the papers and samples?"

"They're safe. I hid them in a small leather bag inside my suitcase. It's in the closet." He sat on the bed motionless with his pistol pointing at Ron.

Shawn looked at Fred with pity. He hardly looked like the CIA Director of Operations in Europe with the confident expression normally seen on his face. Fred's behavior completely stunned Shawn and he was completely bewildered by what was happening.

"Fred, I still can't make any sense to why you did this," said Shawn. Cold chills ran down his body.

"I guess I just got tired and didn't want anyone to get the new alloy. At first my intentions were to destroy them and retire. I never intended to sell it to the Soviets or to any other country. I'm sick of this constant battle to stay one step ahead of the other guy in our ability to kill people. There's gotta be a better way."

"Sure, that may be true, but it's not for us to decide. Like it or not, we have to do what we're directed to do, or get out," Shawn said. "Fred, you used to tell us that if we ever got tired and burned out, we should get out of the business. I heard you say it many times. You reminded me several times not to let my guard down or I'd get into trouble."

"I know. Like everyone else, I didn't listen to my own advice." Fred's eyes were ice cold and stared through them.

Shawn thought about the man who he once believed was indestructible. Like Fred had said, he didn't follow his own advice and got caught.

"Please don't do anything irrational, Fred. I just want to check to be sure the alloy samples are in the closet." Shawn stared at the gun still pointed at Ron.

"Be my guest." replied Fred.

Shawn backed slowly toward the closet and turned the knob. He reached down and picked up the suitcase. The leather bag with the alloy samples was inside. This time he would not give up the information to anyone until he got to Langley.

"Put the gun down, Fred," Ron said as he moved slowly, one step toward him.

"Don't come any closer. I'm sorry it had to end this way." Tears swelled in his eyes and before anyone could move he put the gun to his head and pulled the trigger.

The sound was deafening inside the small room. Fred slumped onto the bed then his body slid to the floor. Ron moved cautiously around the bed and kicked the pistol away. He reached down and felt his neck for a pulse.

"He's dead."

Shawn sat on the chair unable to think. Such a waste, he thought. He had to get out of the room, so he picked up the leather bag and told Ron he would wait for him downstairs. Pauli was sitting up in the chair when he stepped off the elevator.

"Who got shot?" Pauli asked without any emotion.

"Nobody. Fred committed suicide. It just didn't make sense." Shawn sat down with the bag shaking his head. Nothing made sense, and he was too tired to even attempt to figure out why Fred had killed himself. Thoughts of Angela raced through his mind as he listened to police car sirens racing toward the hotel.

"I guess you'll collect a nice paycheck," Shawn said as he looked up at Pauli.

"Actually, I won't. This was a freebie."

"I thought the CIA was paying you a million bucks."

"That's what they offered. But this one's on me. I've never served in the military, or given anything to my country. This is my contribution to help keep our country safe. I realize most people don't think much of the type of work I'm engaged in, but the people I get rid of are criminals and murderers. I'm doing everyone a big favor by knocking them off."

"You should offer your services to Circe," Shawn said. "I bet the CIA would pay a fortune to have you teach their agents how to track down people like you do."

"Do you really think they could use me?"

"There's no question about it, Pauli. Just think, they could hire you to track down known terrorists and eliminate them before they do serious damage in the United States."

They spent the next morning making arrangements for Unser's body to be sent back to the states. Ron made sure that Shawn and the technology didn't get out of his sight. The group boarded an early afternoon flight to Washington. Shawn sat next to Pauli. He could see Ron across the aisle already working on paperwork. The plane was not crowded. Shawn used the flight to catch up on the sleep he had missed. It seemed that the only sound sleep he had gotten the past three days was on airplanes.

Shawn planned to meet Circe as soon as the plane landed and personally give him the priceless papers with the technology. Later, he would recommend that the Director consider hiring DeSarbo to set up a secret anti-terrorist organization within the CIA.

Exhausted, but he couldn't sleep because he still had several issues on his mind. Thankfully, the Mafia connection with the Bobsled organization had self-destructed without any help from outside. Boris came into his mind and he realized that he had to visit him and share the good news as soon as the briefing with Circe was finished. No, Boris would have to wait until after Angela, he thought.

Unable to doze off, thoughts filled his mind about the flight to Schenectady. Once he landed he would call Angela and have her meet him at the air base then they would go to the River Road House for a nice quiet dinner. She would still be aggravated that he had returned to Europe after all the problems, but once she had vented she would feel sorry for him! A smile formed on his face as he thought… *my last job with the CIA is finally over.*

THE END